Praise for *Me and Johnny Blue*

"*Me and Johnny Blue* is old-fashioned storytelling raised to the level of homegrown art, told in an American language that is almost gone."
>— Loren D. Estleman, four-time Spur Award–winning author of *White Desert*

"Wildly comic and darkly compelling."
>— Robert Olen Butler, Pulitzer Prize–winning author of *A Good Scent from a Strange Mountain*

"Real cowboys never lie . . . except sometimes, and usually only to make a good story better. This rollicking big windy has occasional grains of truth, but not enough to keep it from being very funny."
>— Elmer Kelton, six-time Spur Award–winning author of *The Good Old Boys*

"*Me and Johnny Blue* is a tragicomedy with the humor transcendent. It is an original, imaginative work. A delight. Do not miss this one."
>— Max Evans, Spur Award–winning author of *The Rounders*

"Take a pair of pugnacious cowboys who never saw trouble they didn't like, mix them with a fiendish villain and his diabolical filibusters, and the result is comic delight. Joseph West brings to this engaging novel an encyclopedic knowledge of the West. He keeps the body count sufficient to satisfy gluttons, frosts his cake with bawds, throws a few wolfers, a boxer, and a patent medicine huckster into the pot, rings in all the Western legends worth recounting, and seasons the stew with smiles."
>— Richard S. Wheeler, Spur Award–winning author of *Sierra*

JOHNNY BLUE
AND THE
HANGING JUDGE

Joseph A. West

A SIGNET BOOK

SIGNET
Published by New American Library, a division of
Penguin Putnam Inc., 375 Hudson Street,
New York, New York 10014, U.S.A.
Penguin Books Ltd, 27 Wrights Lane,
London W8 5TZ, England
Penguin Books Australia Ltd, Ringwood,
Victoria, Australia
Penguin Books Canada Ltd, 10 Alcorn Avenue,
Toronto, Ontario, Canada M4V 3B2
Penguin Books (N.Z.) Ltd, 182–190 Wairau Road,
Auckland 10, New Zealand

Penguin Books Ltd, Registered Offices:
Harmondsworth, Middlesex, England

First published by Signet, an imprint of New American Library,
a division of Penguin Putnam Inc.

First Printing, June 2001
10 9 8 7 6 5 4 3 2 1

To my wife, Emily

One

Boys, you all read my story on how me and Johnny Blue defeated Amos Pinkney and his Confederate army and a whole tribe of wild Indians and saved our republic from a second Civil War. And I want to say right off that I thank you for all your congratulations and well wishes. You boys have me so proud I'm strutting like a gobbler at layin' time.

Now I hear tell there are them among you who want to know how me and Johnny Blue, that valiant paladin of the plains, got tied up with Buffalo Bill and Red Horse, the Injun chief who massacreed the gallant Custer, and how we got hung by Judge Parker down in the territory. And you want to know how we later bravely hunted down Buck Starr and his gang of desperadoes and became the most famous fighting marshals on the frontier.

Hell, we even got our names in the newspapers and had our picture made and a tall, skinny feller who looked like he couldn't ride a charley horse wrote one of them dime novels about us called *THE MARSHALS' REVENGE, or The Authentic Tale of How the Notorious Buck Starr Met His Terrible Fate.*

The truth is, Ol' Buck—I guess he's stringing barbed wire in hell about now, and all his men with him, especially that gunslick rattlesnake Shade Hannah—caused me and Johnny Blue so much grief that the hearing of it would jerk tears from a glass eye.

But you want to know the story, "warts an' all," as they say, so I've got a stack of paper here and my stub of pencil again and I'll write it down exactly like it happened.

Let me warn you, boys, and the womenfolk that might be reading this, that it's a story long on fighting and killing and short on church-going and hymn singing and sich. But that's how it was all them long years ago when me and Johnny Blue was young and the West was still as wild as a turpentined cat.

The story begins in the spring of 1888 as me and Johnny Blue headed into the foothills of the Bitterroots, taking a wagon load of stolen gold back to the town of Alpine, Montana, where Amos Pinkney had looted it from the bank.

We expected to be hailed as heroes, but that's not how things turned out, because in the end we had to light a shuck for Utica right quick or be shot down like mad dogs in the street by that three-hundred-pound lunatic Tube Wilson.

How it come up, me and Johnny Blue had camped for the night in a stand of aspen about twenty miles south of Alpine.

As dawn broke, the peaks of the Bitterroots stood purple against a lemon-colored sky and the trees whispered softly, nodding and bowing in polite agreement with each other as they shivered slightly in the cool breeze that padded on cat feet down the timbered slopes of the mountains.

"You hear that damn owl last night?" Johnny Blue asked me as he rolled out of his soogan, jammed his hat on his head, and began to build his first smoke of the morning, a habit he'd picked up in Texas when he was just a younker. Let me tell you, boys, one thing I learned about Johnny Blue over the years, until he smoked that first cigarette he was as cranky as an old grizzly with a burr on his butt.

"Can't say as I did," I said. I was slicing bacon into the frying pan and the coffee was boiling fragrant and good on the fire.

"Whoo, whoo, all damn night," Johnny Blue said. He lit his smoke and inhaled deeply. "I don't think I got any sleep. Damn owl."

"Owls can be noisy," I allowed. "All night long they ask the same question, and never get an answer."

Johnny Blue grunted. He stood up and pulled on his pants, stomped into his boots, then buttoned up his shirt.

He walked over to the fire. "Coffee ready?"

"Soon," I said.

Johnny Blue grunted again, tossed the stub of his cigarette into the fire, then right away began to build another.

I shook the bacon in the pan so it would brown evenly all over and crisp up good.

"You know," I said, "I reckon them folks in Alpine will give us a medal after we ride into town with all that gold."

"What kind of medal?" Johnny Blue asked sourly.

"A silver medal," I said. "Maybe even gold."

Johnny Blue just grunted again, lighting his smoke with a brand from the fire.

"Yessir," I said. "A gold medal with FOR BRAVERY written right on it. And maybe with Queen Victoria's head on one side."

Johnny Blue smoked and studied on that for a spell. Then he asked: "How come Queen Victoria will be on it? She don't live in Alpine."

"Don't make no never mind," I said. "It's gonna be a dignified kind of medal, and there ain't nobody more dignified than old Queen Vic. Hell, the old lady lives in a palace an' all."

Now usually Johnny Blue would have been right pleased about the medal, but he was still fretting over that owl and was still on the prod.

"If we was to get a medal, which I doubt we will, where would we wear it so folks could see it?" he asked.

He held out his cup and I poured coffee into it. "You can't wear a medal to a roundup. Some jealous ranny would reckon you was gettin' uppity and shoot you through the lungs sure enough."

"Well," I said, "maybe folks would invite us to tea. We could wear it then."

Johnny Blue sipped his coffee and studied on what I'd said for another long spell.

"We ain't never drank tea," he said finally.

"I know we ain't, but I hear tell it's good if you drink it with cream and sugar. If we had medals, you and me, we'd get invites to tea quick enough."

Well, boys, I don't know where that conversation would have gone, because right then Johnny Blue pointed his cup in the direction of the trail and said: "Rider coming."

I looked up from the sputtering bacon and saw a tall, rangy man on a mule rein up and sit there, looking over our camp. We had the wagon loaded with gold and five horses grazing nearby, two Percherons with blond manes and tails to pull the wagon, a dun packhorse, and two big American studs we'd taken as spoils of war after our battle with Amos Pinkney.

"He don't look like an outlaw," Johnny Blue said. But he rose and walked to his bedroll, where he got his rifle and then carried it back to the fire so it was close to hand.

"Hello the camp!" the man on the mule hollered.

I set down the frying pan to the side of the fire, stood, and yelled back: "Come on in, if'n you're friendly. Stay away if'n you ain't."

"I'm friendly," the man said. "Me, I'm what you might call a servant of the Lord."

"That's all we need after that damn owl," Johnny Blue grumbled under his breath, "a sin buster."

The preacher kicked his heels into the side of his mule a few times and it finally ambled toward our camp. When he was still a good twenty yards away, he slid off the mule's back, which was easy to do on account of how he was using a piece of sacking for a saddle.

He had a Bible in his right hand that he held high up on his chest, and he came legging toward us at a good clip with that galumphing walk farmers seem to favor. You've seen 'em, boys, where they swing their right hand and right leg forward at the same time and then do the same with the left. That gospel grinder had a farmer's walk all right, not the short-coupled, rolling gait of the cowboy, which is how the good Lord intended a man should get from here to there if he can't ride his horse.

"Been smellin' your coffee for quite a spell, since daybreak as a matter of fact," the preacher said. He had a long, brown beard down to his belt buckle, and when he smiled, which he was doing now, he showed few teeth and a lot of gum.

"Seen you when you were a ways off," Johnny Blue said. "I took you fer a farmer."

The preacher nodded. "I tilled the soil once, afore I got the calling. Now I reap souls for the Lord."

"How I knowed you'd been a farmer," Johnny Blue said, "is that you got that long farmer's face on you, preacher, an' that only comes from a lifetime spent behind a plow gazin' at a mule's butt." Johnny Blue smiled for the first time that morning. "No offense."

"None taken," the preacher said cheerfully enough. He picked up my cup and I filled it with coffee for him. Then he nodded toward the bacon sputtering in the fire. "May I?"

"He'p yourself," I said.

The preacher reached into the pocket of his black coat and fished around. He pulled out a jackknife, opened the blade, then speared a strip of bacon, which vanished down his throat in an instant. He speared another, and as it dangled from his knife, he studied me and Johnny Blue right close, looking at us from out of the corner of his eye so we wouldn't notice him sizing us up. It was like he was itching to say something but couldn't think of the right words.

Once I caught his eye, but he looked away right quick, so finally I said: "You got something on your mind, preacher?"

The preacher made no reply as the second bacon strip took the same road as the last one. He was a homely cuss, that Bible thumper, and shabby dirty, like he'd been in the outhouse when lightning struck.

He speared a third strip of bacon, and me and Johnny Blue dived in and grabbed a strip each before there was none left because that ol' boy sure enough ate like a sodbuster.

Finally the preacher wiped his mouth with his beard and gulped down his coffee. When he came up for air, he looked at me and said: "Where are you boys headed? I see you got a wagon and it looks to be heavily loaded."

"Alpine," I said cautiously. "We're taking the wagon there."

The preacher nodded, like I'd just told him something he'd already guessed.

"I suppose you heard what happened in Alpine?" he said. "I mean with the Amos Pinkney gang an' all. That's why I'm headed in that direction, to give the folks in that unfortunate burg prayer and succor."

"We know what happened in Alpine," I said. "Hell, man, we was there."

Again the preacher nodded. "Figgered that," he said.

"How did you figger that?" Johnny Blue asked suspiciously. "You'd no way of knowing we was there before my pard told you so. You got to make allowances for him—he's got a big mouth."

Well, I ignored that comment and said: "So, how did you know we was in Alpine?"

The preacher looked a mite uncomfortable and his eyes took in the Winchester at Johnny Blue's side and the Colt on my hip. He swallowed hard, the big Adam's apple on his throat bobbing, and he said quietly, too quietly, so that every nerve in my body started to jangle: "Fact is, I seen a wanted dodger in Butte on two men that sounded a lot like you two rannies."

"A wanted dodger!" I almost choked on my coffee. "You got to be mistaken. There ain't nobody looking for us. We're heroes is what we are. It was us who defeated Amos Pinkney and his whole rebel army."

The preacher shrugged. "Maybe you did, maybe you didn't, but the wanted dodger describes two men who sound a whole lot like you. Said you was known footpads, bummers and dance hall loungers and that you was wanted for murder, rape, robbery, hoss stealin', disturbing the peace, and high treason."

"What else did it say?" I asked, suddenly feeling as sick as a poisoned pup.

"Oh, it didn't go into much more detail. It just said one of the wanted men was an uppity black man who don't know his place." The preacher bowed in Johnny Blue's direction. "No offense."

"None taken," Johnny Blue said cheerfully, drawing deep on his fourth smoke of the morning.

"And the other?" I asked.

"It just said t'other feller was a big red mustache with a scrawny little drover attached to it."

Now, boys, you know me for a peace-loving man, but when that preacher smiled and showed his gums when he got to the part about me being a scrawny little drover an' all, I had a notion to draw my gun and shoot him through the lungs.

Of course I didn't, because it sounded like me and Johnny Blue were in enough trouble already.

Besides, if you put a bullet in a cowboy, nobody much cares, figgering he was bound to end up shot or dangling from a rope anyhow. But you shoot a preacher or a tax-paying farmer and the law gets mighty interested. I've seen all hell break loose after a farmer got shot. His women-folk and kids weep and wail an' carry on and the law runs this way an' that, and all the time the poor waddie who put the bullet into him in the first place knows that he's gonna stretch some hemp before it's all over.

Like I said, it just isn't worth it. Shoot anybody you like, boys, but take my advice and leave them damn farm-ers alone.

The preacher picked up the fry pan and looked into it, as though more bacon might miraculously appear. But since none did, he sighed and put it down again.

"Heard another piece of information in Butte that might interest you boys," he said casually.

"Preacher, you're just a mine of good news," Johnny Blue said sourly. "So why don't you go ahead and lay it on us?"

"You ever hear tell of Tube Wilson?"

"Sure we do," I said. "He was our foreman on the old DHS over in the Judith Basin country before the blizzard of '87. Them snows came on us so fast the front half of my pony was still frothy when the back half got frozen."

"That explains a lot then," the preacher said, looking down and shuffling his feet. "I mean, him once being your foreman an' all."

"Explains what?" asked Johnny Blue.

"Explains how come he says he's gonna shoot you two rannies on sight. See, Tube is the new sheriff of Alpine."

Boys, I was so surprised, I felt like I'd thrown a bucket down the well and brought up a skunk.

"But we heard Tube was dead, shot by the law for pluggin' some drummer down in Great Falls," I said.

"That's partly true." The preacher paused. "Tube got shot all right—plumb in the belly—but somehow he pulled through and lived."

"Don't that beat all," Johnny Blue said. "I always knowed ol' Tube was tough. But I didn't reckon on him being that tough."

"It was touch and go for a while," the preacher allowed. "And on top of that, the ladies of Great Falls set store by that drummer since he traveled in corsets and bloomers and other female dainties, so they nursed their wrath all winter long, keeping it warm until Tube was well enough to get hung."

"That drummer," Johnny Blue said, sitting forward and gazing intently into the preacher's eyes, "did them ladies ever invite him to tea?"

The preacher shrugged. "I can't rightly guess, but I suppose they did. Why do you want to know?"

"Oh, no reason. I just happen to know this ranny who says he'd like to get an invite to tea sometime so he can wear his bravery medal."

I knew Johnny Blue was hunting trouble, hoping I'd say something, but even though I felt my face flush, I ignored him and asked the preacher: "How come Tube shot the drummer in the first place?"

"It was a accident. Tube and Happy Jack Jackson got into it in the saloon and then took the fight outside. Tube, he draws a bead on Happy Jack and pulls the trigger just as that scanties drummer steps out of an eating house picking his teeth and pattin' his belly. Well, Tube's bullet hits him right in the brisket and the drummer goes down a-squealin' like a baby pig caught under a gate, an' starts kickin' around in the dirt an' chewing on the boardwalk.

"Happy Jack, he takes one look at the drummer and says to Tube, 'What did you do?' and Tube says, 'It was a accident.' "

"Which it was," Johnny Blue said. "That drummer should've paid more attention to where he was walking."

"Maybe so," the preacher agreed. "Anyhoo, Happy Jack sees the writing on the wall, gets his horse, and rides west. Now Tube's bill of sale for his pony wasn't too good to the west, but it was real good to the south, so that's where he headed an' that's where the law caught up with him."

I poured the preacher the last of the coffee and asked: "If'n them ladies were so all-fired riled up, how come Tube didn't get his neck stretched?"

"The jury was all for hanging him, especially with their wives sitting in the courtroom—in their wore-out corsets let me tell you, looking as mean as cornered cottonmouths. But then Tube's lawyer happened to let slip that his client was drunk at the time of the killing. Well, everybody knows you can't hang a man for shooting a drummer while said man was under the influence of demon drink, so they found him not guilty."

"Still, it don't make any sense that Tube would end up sheriff of Alpine," I said.

"He got religion," the preacher explained. "See, Tube was still feelin' a mite poorly after the trial and was laid up for about six or seven weeks. Now them ladies couldn't get him one way, so they figgered to get him another.

"They started preachifyin' to him day and night, and pretty soon Tube is tellin' them that he has a hankering to mend his ways and forsake strong drink and wild women and tread the path of the righteous.

"Well, after that them ladies forgot that they'd ever wanted to hang him in the first place, especially when another scanties drummer showed up to replace the dead one. They cried 'Hallelujah!' and declared that they'd made Tube a model citizen. The next thing you know, he's sheriff of Alpine, has a couple of hardcase deputies, and he's vowing to shoot you two boys down like mad dogs in the street the moment he sets eyes on you."

Boys, after me and Johnny Blue heard all this from the preacher, we agreed that things had gone mighty fast from rosy to looking pretty bleak.

"We got gold in that wagon," I told the preacher, now that I didn't care if he knew or not. "It's the gold Amos Pinkney stole from the Alpine bank. We was taking it back and we figgered they'd be so grateful they'd give us a medal with Queen Victoria's head on it. Now you tell us we'll be ventilated the moment we set foot within the town limits."

The preacher sighed. "Sorry, boys, but that's the way it is." He motioned toward the wagon. "I'm a poor man, but an honest one, so if you want, I'll take the gold back to Alpine for you. I'll try to put in a good word for you with Tube, but I don't think it's gonna help much."

Me and Johnny Blue talked it over, and decided that we trusted the preacher enough to have him take the gold back to Alpine. Hell, we didn't have much choice in the matter on account of how we couldn't take it back ourselves.

"Maybe you can smooth things over right enough," Johnny Blue told him. "Them rubes is getting their gold back. That ought to mean something."

The preacher allowed that he'd do what he could, but his long face got even longer and I could see he didn't hold out much hope.

"Of course, you boys could just climb up on the wagon and drive away," he said. "There looks to be enough money in there to keep you in clover for the rest of your lives."

The preacher cocked his head to one side like a hairy ol' bird and waited on our reply.

Johnny Blue shook his head. "Preacher," he said, "I've never wanted anything bad enough in my whole life that I had to steal it, and I don't aim to start now. That money ain't ours; it belongs to them sodbusters in Alpine, and it wouldn't set right with me to ride away with it. Besides, it's cursed. Too many men died over it."

"Johnny Blue Dupree," I said, "you're a saint. A living saint. I used to think that if I melted you down I couldn't pour you into a church pew, but I guess I was wrong."

"Does that mean you plan to steal the money?" demanded that righteous rider.

"Just twenty dollars of it," I said. "But it ain't stealing. Call it traveling expenses."

I went to the wagon and got a handful of silver dollars from a sack and put them in my pocket; then me and Johnny Blue saddled our big American horses and got ready to ride.

Just then the preacher called us over. "Boys," he said, "I'll do what I can for you in Alpine and try to turn aside the wrath of the law. But before you leave, an' I won't ask you where you're going, let us pray together that the Lord will keep you safe from harm and not let you stray once again from the straight and narrow to the path of wickedness."

Well, me and Johnny Blue figgered that was a crackerjack idea, so we stood beside the preacher and bowed our heads and he said: "Hats, boys."

We took off our hats and the preacher clutched his Bible to his chest, turned his eyes to the sky, and in a loud, booming voice that sent a flock of jays scattering from the aspens, hollered:

"Dear Lord, I don't know if these two rannies here are guilty or not of the terrible charges laid against them, but

I'm saying this prayer for them anyhow. Lord, I understand that you're too busy with other things to go worrying yourself about footpads, dance hall loungers, and lowly persons such as these, especially since you know in your infinite wisdom that these boys are doomed to someday dangle from the end of a rope. Yea, verily, an eye for an eye and a tooth for a tooth. But Lord, let them not stray too far from the path of righteousness until that terrible day of reckoning arrives. And when at last the dreadful trap falls and their necks get broke, send angels to bear them up on the railroad to heaven and bring them unto your side in paradise. For thine is the power and the glory for ever and ever. Amen."

After the preacher had finished that prayer, I felt a hot stinging in my eyes and I regretted that I'd ever thought of shooting him through the lungs. I looked at Johnny Blue and that caring cavalier was so choked up, he looked like he was about to cry enough tears to float an anvil.

I walked over to the preacher and hugged him, and Johnny Blue came over and we hugged him together.

"That's the best prayer anyone ever said for us, preacher," I said. "In fact, it's the only prayer anyone's ever said for us."

"I do what I can," the preacher said modestly. "And, God knows, it's little enough in the face of the iniquity I see all around me."

So, emboldened by the preacher's prayer, me and Johnny Blue mounted our horses and headed them east, resolutely preparing ourselves for whatever trouble was to come.

We had decided out of earshot of the preacher to head back to Utica, where we had friends and where we might be able to find work until this whole wanted thing blew over.

I was also hatching a plan.

I figgered Johnny Blue should give himself up to the

law and plead guilty to everything, the rape and murder and high treason and the rest of the stuff and say I'd noth-ing a-tall to do with it. That way I'd be free to get busy and find him a good lawyer and maybe save him from hanging. The more I thought about it, the more I figgered it was a good plan, or at least a tolerable one for our pres-ent needs. But Johnny Blue was so surly that morning about the owl and not getting a gold medal and invites to tea an' sich, I decided to wait until later to lay it on him.

Besides, you boys remember Johnny Blue Dupree, and you'll recollect how self-centered and plumb selfish he could be by times. It would be just like him to say no to the plan and declare it as unwanted as a wart on a dance hall gal's ass.

My scheme would need time to sink into his stubborn skull, so I'd have to feed it to him a little bit at a time. Boys, my mama didn't raise a pretty boy, but she didn't raise a dumb one either, so in the end I reckoned I'd con-vince him to see the light.

As we rode away, I looked back and saw the farmer sit-ting on the wagon looking after us. I lifted my hat and gave him a hearty Huzzah! But he didn't make a move. He just sat there looking at us with them red-shot eyes of his that could stare holes in an oak tree.

As I recollect it today, I reckon that preacher had the gift of second sight, and he saw something I didn't. Maybe he knew me and Johnny Blue was riding into a heap of trouble—shooting trouble—and that before long we'd be facing the greased-lightning Colts of the deadliest gunman who ever stalked the West.

I'm speaking of that man of evil, that killer of pretty Chinese women, that low-down skunk who'd steal a widow woman's only milk cow. I'm speaking of a demon in human form—that rattlesnake who went by the name of Shade Hannah.

Two

On account of how we were now wanted men, me and Johnny Blue stayed away from the main trails and wagon roads as we rode east, taking to game paths through the foothills above the open meadows and their red, yellow, and white carpet of spring wildflowers. For four weeks our only companions were bear, deer, elk, moose, and the sage grouse that flew back and forth from the hills to the grasslands to feed.

Our bacon ran out, then our coffee, and when we rode into Utica around suppertime, huddled into slickers and hunched against a lashing rain driven by a rising wind, we were missing our last six meals.

Me and Johnny Blue rode our horses to the livery stable, rubbed them down good with a dry sack we found hanging over the side of a stall, and saw to it that the old timer in charge gave them each a bucket of oats with their hay.

The old man took the dollar we gave him, and he kept looking at us out of the corner of his eye, the same way as the preacher did.

"You got something on your mind, pops?" Johnny Blue asked him.

The oldster, who was wearing a red flannel undershirt that was black around the collar and cuffs with ancient dirt, and a battered plug hat, forked hay for my horse, then said with a curious light in his eyes: "You boys be right careful. There's been a feller hanging around town for a couple of weeks. Says he's on the dodge, but he's been asking a lot of questions about an uppity black drover and his sidekick, a scrawny little ranny with a big red mustache."

The oldster laid the pitchfork against the wall of the barn. "He's been over to Jim Shelton's saloon asking if them two might be headed this way anytime soon. Of course Jim didn't tell him nothing, but if I was a certain black drover and a little ranny with a big mustache, I'd be almighty careful how I stepped out that barn door, if you catch my drift."

Johnny Blue was standing under a leak in the roof and the water dripped with a soft dub . . . dub . . . dub on the crown of his hat. "This feller, is he the law?" he asked.

The oldster shook his head. "Bounty hunter more like. Big feller, with a scar down here"—the old man traced a line down his right cheek with his finger—"an' he carries a Sharps big fifty and a Remington .44 on his hip and he looks like he knows how to use both of them. He's gunslick all right, that one."

I looked at Johnny Blue and suddenly I was chewing on a mouthful of my own heart. "That wanted poster the preacher was talking about," I said. "You don't suppose it was carrying a reward?"

The oldster cackled, phlegm rattling in his throat. "Why, you dang fools, they're offering a thousand dollars for you, dead or alive, an' it seems to me that bounty hunter means to be the one to snag that money. I'd say he don't plan to take you alive but a-hanging over the saddles of them big American studs of yours."

Johnny Blue looked at me from under the brim of his hat. "This was your bright idea. We got friends in Utica, you said. Well that hombre waiting outside with a Sharps big fifty don't sound too friendly."

"It's pouring rain." I shrugged. "Even a bounty hunter ain't gonna be out in this weather. Trust me on that. Hell, I'm so sure of what I'm saying, I ain't even gonna take my rifle." I shoved my Winchester back into the saddle boot. "See, that's how sure I am. Me an' you, we'll come back here all safe and sound and bed down right after we get something to eat over at Shelton's."

Johnny Blue groaned like he does when I say something he doesn't agree with, but he followed me outside and I quietly closed the door behind us.

The rain was heavier than ever, a steady downpour that hissed like a cow pissing on a flat rock, and it ran off our hats in silvery sheets.

I turned from the door and caught the quick glisten of reflected light from the window of a shack across the road. It looked to me like the rain-wet shoulder of a yellow slicker like the one I was wearing had picked up the glare of an oil lamp inside. Then it was gone.

"What do you see?" Johnny Blue asked anxiously.

"Unbutton your slicker and shuck your iron," I said urgently. "I think there's somebody over there watching us."

Suddenly the shadows were washed away as a lightning bolt forked from the sky and I heard the loud bang of a rifle. Instantly the wood on the barn door about an inch away from my head splintered, and I brought my Colt up to eye level and fired at where I'd seen the patch of yellow slicker.

The blue-and-white flash from my gun blinded me, and after firing just one shot, I was out of the fight. All I could see was blackness shot through with streaking blue-and-orange lights.

Beside me I heard Johnny Blue's gun roar once.

Then there was a commotion from the direction of Jim Shelton's saloon, and I heard a man holler: "Here, that won't do! What's going on out there?"

A moment later I heard the pounding of hooves, and after that all was darkness and silence with only the sound of the falling rain and the distant grumbling of the thunder.

Suddenly a storm lantern was thrust in my face and I heard Jim Shelton's voice say: "Oh, it's you. I heard you'd been hung already."

Then he swung the lantern in Johnny Blue's direction. "And you ain't been shot yet either? I don't know what the world's coming to."

Jim was wearing a slicker, a fisherman's oilskin hat, and a sour expression. He held a Greener sawed-off shotgun in his right hand, cocked and ready for business.

"Somebody took a shot at us, Jim," I explained. "We reckon it was a bounty hunter, but we scared him off."

Jim's laugh was harsh and unpleasant. "Hell, you boys didn't scare off anybody. That man was a professional and his kind don't scare easy. A bounty hunter is a surefire killer with no need to prove what a brave hombre he is. He just didn't like the odds tonight because of the dark and the rain, but he'll be back to try again."

Jim swung the lantern toward me again and studied my face. "I seen your shot kick up the mud about ten feet from where you was standing. And you"—he swung the lantern toward Johnny Blue—"I didn't even see where your bullet went. Up toward the moon someplace maybe." Jim lowered the lantern and added frankly: "You boys take my advice an' stay away from the gunfighting business. You ain't cut out for it."

"We didn't have our rifles, Jim," I said defensively. "Me and Johnny Blue, we're dab hands with rifle guns. If I'd had my Winchester, I'd have nailed that drygulcher for sure. We been down that road a fair piece afore an' in all kinds of weather."

As the lightning flared again, I saw Jim shake his head.

"Talking to you boys is about as useless as teats on a boar hog. An' unlike you two, I got enough sense to get in out of the rain."

Without another word, he turned on his heel, muttering and stomping through ankle-deep mud back toward his saloon.

Me and Johnny Blue, being wet, tired, cold, and hungry and not wishing to tangle with the bounty hunter again, followed so close behind him—looking over our shoulders all the while—we must have raised blisters on his butt.

The saloon was empty, which suited us just fine. It was warm and dry and kind of homey. Several oil lamps cast pools of yellow light on the worn wooden floor and reflected off the dark mahogany of the bar. Blue triangles of shadow stood like sentinels in the corners.

My worn-out boots squelched water as I walked with Johnny Blue to the bar. I ordered two beers and rang another of our dwindling supply of silver dollars onto the counter.

Jim pulled the beers and placed them in front of us. He ignored the money on the bar.

"There was a U.S. Marshal here before the bounty hunter showed up. He asked a heap of questions about you two boys."

I nodded. "I guess it was about that business in Alpine."

"That," Jim allowed, "and other things."

"We had nothing to do with hoorawing that town," I said. "A feller named Amos Pinkney did that. He was in cahoots with the devil until me and Johnny Blue done for him in the end."

"We sent coal oil down the chimbley and roasted him good," Johnny Blue commented.

"Then I shot him," I said flatly.

Jim nodded, his face thoughtful. "Be that as it may, but

there's a thousand dollars on your heads. That's a lot of money in these parts, or any other parts come to that."

Johnny Blue's face was grim. "Would you turn us in, Jim?"

Jim Shelton looked like Johnny Blue had just slapped him. "You don't know me a-tall, do you?" he demanded. "I'm no Judas to sell my fellow man for thirty pieces of silver. That's blood money and it's cursed. Still, there are others around here who ain't quite so particular."

Johnny Blue lowered his head and rainwater poured off the brim of his hat, splashing onto the bar. "Sorry, Jim. I guess I spoke out of turn."

"No need to apologize. A wanted man's got a right to look out for his own self." He wiped up the water on the bar and asked: "You boys hungry?"

"We're missing our last six meals, Jim," I answered.

"I got some sonofabitch stew simmering back in the kitchen if you want a bowl. I got plenty of sweetbreads in there, an' a set of brains, a calf's heart an' liver, and about five pounds of prime beef."

I felt my mouth water and I looked at Johnny Blue and that ravenous rider was licking his lips. I hardly dared ask, beggars not being choosers, but I went right ahead anyway. "You manage to find some marrow gut?"

"Of course!" Jim exclaimed. "If it ain't got marrow gut, it ain't stew."

I don't know if you boys recollect after all these years, but marrow gut was the half-digested grass from a cow's stomach, and in them days it gave sonofabitch stew its mighty fine flavor and made it a cowboy favorite.

"Set at a table and I'll feed you," Jim said. "Then take my advice and light a shuck out of here."

"In this storm?" I asked. "We're soaked through already."

"Better wet than dead," Jim said.

He followed my eyes to the painting by Charlie Russell that hung behind the bar. It was the last roundup at Utica before the big blizzards hit and Charlie had got it just right. We was all there, Jim sitting in the doorway of his saloon, me on a gray pony, and Johnny Blue off in the distance chasing a yearling steer with Tube Wilson.

"They're mostly all gone now, all those hands," Jim said quietly. "Some were shot, some hung, some are up there in the mountains sleeping the seasons away in caves or hollow logs. Others, well, they just shucked their spurs an' curled up next to ol' she bears, waiting for better times."

"The good times will be back," Johnny Blue said. "First the cows, then the good times. That's how it always was, and that's how it will always be."

Jim shook his head. "Cowboy, you're dreaming. When the blizzard of '87 destroyed the herds, it ended everything." He waved a hand toward the painting. "All that, the drovers and the cows, is ancient history."

Now this was pretty depressing talk from Jim, and me and Johnny Blue was as quiet as snowflakes on a feather when we walked to a table and sat down.

What with us tangling with that bounty hunter an' all, I figgered now was as good a time as any to lay my plan on Johnny Blue. While he sat there, his face making all kinds of changing expressions from surprise to disbelief to plumb ornery, I laid out my scheme as simple as I knew how.

"An' that's how you can make the supreme sacrifice," I finished, "and be forever known as Johnny Blue, the noble soul who laid down his own life for his pardner." I bowed my head. "Amen and amen."

For a spell Johnny Blue just sat there looking at me with a stunned expression on his face. Then he choked: "You're nuts! Do you know that? You're plumb loco. You're certifiably insane an' should be locked up to protect innocent, God-fearin' folks. You're . . . you're"—that rattled rider threw a loop over his fevered brain and finally dabbed a thought—"you're right out of your tiny, ever-lovin' mind."

Meeting Johnny Blue's sharp glance, I said: "Then you mistrust me, me who was going to snag you the best lawyer money could buy. An' this is all the thanks I get for it."

I lowered my head and shook it sadly, but glanced from under my hat brim to see what effect all this was having on Johnny Blue. "I always reckoned you had selfish ways about you," I said, "an' this just confirms my suspicions. You're surely a sore disappointment to me."

"I'd get hung!" Johnny Blue exclaimed. "I'd be dangling from the end of rope and you'd ride away nice as you please."

Again I shook my head. "Selfish, selfish, selfish."

"Well, selfish or not I ain't doin' it," Johnny Blue said. "I ain't gonna put my head in a noose for anybody."

I sighed and said: "Then that time when we was riding for the Matador in Texas in '81 didn't mean a thing to you."

"What time?" Johnny Blue asked suspiciously.

"Oh, that time when you roped a big brindle longhorn an' your saddle girth broke an' you was being dragged through the cactus an' junipers an' you was squealin' like a pig, hollerin' that you was gonna die, if'n you recollect."

"I don't recollect nothin' about that."

"I rode in after you an' cut the rope that was wrapped around your wrist and saved the life of my pardner. 'Course, I got tore up something terrible by them cactus." I winced and rubbed my left shoulder. "I was just a younker then, but them awful wounds still pain me tolerably in this rainy weather."

"I don't recollect nothin' about that," Johnny Blue repeated stubbornly.

I nodded. "Sometimes a man don't like to recall that he

owes his life to another man, especially when it comes to payback time. At least, that's been my sad experience."

"Well, I'll pay you back some other time," Johnny Blue said. "I ain't gonna stick my head in a noose an' you can't make me."

Boys, my plan had come to naught because of my pard's selfishness, an' I was back at square one, trying to figger a way out of the mess we was in. I got to tell you, right then, things didn't look too rosy.

Jim walked over to the table, a letter in his hand. "I almost forgot," he said to Johnny Blue, "this came for you about a month ago. I guess whoever wrote it reckoned you boys would head back here."

Johnny Blue opened the envelope and squinted at the letter inside. He rose and took a lamp from the bar and set it on the table. "It's from Doc Fortune," he said. "Why would that old crook be writing to me?"

"I dunno," I replied. "But read it out loud. It could be important."

You boys will recollect Doc Fortune, the snake-oil salesman and all-round con artist who helped us in our fight with Amos Pinkney. Doc's sidekick was the Mauler, a bare knuckle prizefighter fallen on hard times, and his lady love was that famous woman of color and cathouse madam Miss Georgia Morgan.

Johnny Blue, who wasn't much of a hand with reading to begin with, studied on the letter for a spell because Doc liked them big words that ran two dollars to the pound. But Johnny Blue finally got a handle on the gist of it, because he began to read:

Houston, Texas. April 3rd, 1888
My Dear Friend,
    The die is cast and I am undone. Let the wretched outcast who now addresses you say only that Miss Georgia is

well and is with child. Cottontail, who recently jumped over the broom with my adopted son, the Mauler, is also well, and is also with child. Thus my family grows as my woes, pecuniary and otherwise, increase apace.

Despite my lowly condition, made worse by rheumatisms contracted during our flight from Amos Pinkney amid the cruel Montana snows, I have news to impart, viz: Your little sister, so cruelly snatched from the bosom of her family by the bloodthirsty Geronimo and his wild Apache band, is not in Florida with the savages as you once supposed. I received intelligence from a gambling gentleman of my acquaintance that a woman of color named Mattie Dupree is working in a cantina on the Rio Grande near Brownsville in the great state of Texas. If you wish to find her, I suggest you begin your noble quest there.

Alas, I can write no more. A dark shadow is fast being cast over the cheerless dungeon of my existence. The Mauler has just informed me that a mob of rubes is gathering outside making ominous noises about tar and feathers. It seems my Elixir of Life, far from curing their ills, made most of them sicker, caused perhaps by my injudicious overuse of plug tobacco, rattlesnake heads, and cayenne pepper.

Alack, there is no time to waste. Like a thief in the night or, in my case like the great Napoleon himself, the victor of Marengo and a host of other epic battles, fleeing the confines of that barren isle of Elba, I must now seek the untrodden path where the night owl hoots and decent men durst not travel. In short: It's time to skedaddle.

Written in haste,

By that miserable and poor, hunted creature,

Silas T. Fortune IV, M.D. Ph.D. M.A.

"Well, that pretty much settles things," Johnny Blue said. "I got to head for Texas an' find my sister."

"Now hold on a second there, Johnny Blue," I said. "We're blood brothers, me and you, so she's my little sister too. But we can't go lightin' a shuck for Texas until we fatten up some and get a few dollars in our jeans. Right now, we're both so underfed an' skinny we could crawl through the pipe on a depot stove and not get soot on a white shirt."

Johnny Blue nodded. "Maybe so, but we can't just sit around here a-doin' nothing."

"Something will turn up," I said, with more certainty than I felt. "Trust me on that."

Johnny Blue groaned and shook his head. "How come that don't plumb fill me with hope?"

Boys, you might recollect that Johnny Blue's daddy was a field hand and his momma was a cook on a plantation in Davidson County, Tennessee. His momma died, then his daddy, an' his little sister was sold down the river a few months before the War Between the States ended. Johnny Blue was raised by Nat Love, known to most folks as Deadwood Dick, an' it was Nat who taught him everything he knows about cattle and horses and cowboying.

But Johnny Blue's sister wasn't so lucky. She was captured by Geronimo down in the Arizona Territory, and later took up with one of the chief's young bucks. She had been at Skeleton Canyon when the Apaches surrendered to General Miles.

"Maybe it's a different Mattie Dupree," I said. "There could be a lot of women by that name." Johnny Blue shook his head. "It's her all right, an' I aim to find her."

Outside, thunder roared like the clouds were lying right on the roof, and every now and then the saloon lit up in a white glare as lightning flashed. The rain hissed like an angry rattlesnake on the muddy street outside, and I felt a cold hollowness in me that didn't come from hunger alone.

Jim brought the stew, along with some pan bread and

two cups of strong, hot coffee, He sat at the table for a while and silently watched us eat. Then he said: "You boys just don't know what you've done, do you?"

I swallowed a mouthful of stew, which was rich and good, and said: "Jim, I told you we had nothing to do with what happened in that town."

Jim shook his head. "I'm not talking about that. I'm talking about you." He nodded in my direction. "What age was you when you first came up the trail?"

"Fourteen, I guess. Maybe thirteen. I came up the Western Trail from San Antone to Dodge. Had us three thousand head. You know, a few years later, in 1883 I think it was, I oncet stood on a hill near the North Platte and seen the dust of twenty-eight herds all moving north. That was a sight to see."

"And you?" This to Johnny Blue.

That dusky drover shrugged. "I came to cowboyin' late. I'd just turned fourteen when I signed up with Tom Snyder in the spring of '79 to take a herd of twenty-five hundred from the Green Ranch north of Corpus Christi to Dodge. It was a ten-man outfit, not counting the trail boss, an' I rode drag all the way. Mister, I ate my fill of dust that trip."

Jim shook his head sadly. "An' you boys still don't know what you done?"

"Sorry, Jim," I said, "but we just ain't catching your drift here."

"Why, you dang fools, you wrote a page of history!" Jim exploded. "You wrote it with the cattle barons like Jesse Chisholm and Shanghai Pierce and Granville Stuart. You wrote it with every cow you drove to Dodge and Abilene and Hays. You wrote it with Earp and Masterson and Hickok, and you wrote it with the buffalo and the Sioux and the Comanche and the Arapaho.

"You rode across one-third of the United States to deliver beef to the starving masses back East, and in doing all that you endured heat and cold and exhaustion for a lousy thirty dollars a month. You and your kind fought Indians and outlaws, rode half-broke mustangs that killed you or crippled you for life, and you ate spoiled bacon and beans until your insides rotted.

"But your page has been written, it's done, and you're either too dumb or too stubborn to recognize the fact. Now you got to draw a line across the last paragraph and hand the pen to others, to the farmer and the miner and the logger and the merchant and the schoolteacher, civilized folk who're impatient to begin writing their own page."

Jim leaned his elbows on the table. "It's over, boys. The last words were written by the snow and the dying cattle. Now there are fences going up everywhere and the prairie is being turned over by the plow and there's nowhere left for fellers like you to go. Hell, boys, nobody wants you no more."

He sighed and shook his head sadly. "Your time is past," he said, an odd little catch in his voice, "and the sooner you realize it, the better."

Boys, just about then I felt so down in the mouth I could have eaten oats out of a churn. I glanced at Johnny Blue and he had a stunned, disbelieving look on his face.

You know what comes to mind when I recollect that night with the thunder and lightning raging outside and the sonofabitch stew lying like lead in my belly?

I remember that preacher with the long white beard and the bad piles that come up to the old DHS one time and got all the hands together and told us the end was nigh and the world was about to end. Said we was all heading for hellfire within the next couple of weeks unless we changed our ways and forsook whiskey and wild women and went up into the mountains to pray and wait for the fire an' brimstone.

Well, a lot us figgered that preacher knew what he was talkin' about and we was so depressed we didn't touch a drop or get laid for weeks after that. Even Tube Wilson swore off rye for a couple of days and drank beer.

Of course, we started to doubt that preacher some when he went up into the mountains his own self to wait for the angel trumpets and got et by a cougar.

But, still, it made a man think, and that's what I was doing right now as Jim finished his speech.

"That's mighty hard talk, Jim," I said finally. "And it makes us feel useless an' low down."

Jim shrugged and got up from his chair. "I tell it like I see it."

He stood there, studying me and Johnny Blue for a long spell with genuine sympathy in his eyes. Then he said: "That marshal I was telling you about was a talkative feller, and he happened to let drop that Buffalo Bill will be in the Indian Territory near Fort Smith next month, recruiting rough riders for his Wild West Show. It seems Bill is taking the show to England in the summer and needs more folks.

"That might be a job for you boys, and it will get you out of the country away from the law and the bounty hunters." He smiled faintly. "That's what you and others like you who don't know their time is past have become— freaks in a circus show."

Just then the door of the saloon burst open and who walked in, scattering rain everywhere, but Charlie Russell. You boys will recollect Charlie when he was working on the OH Ranch near Utica. Charlie was never much of a hand, but he could draw and paint like everything on the paper was real. He was already making his mark as an artist that spring of '88, and before long he'd cut a mighty wide path and become famous all over the world.

Charlie looked well fed and prosperous and his hands

were smooth and it was plain to see he hadn't touched a rope or a branding iron in a long time.

I recognized the woman who was with him even though she was wrapped to the eyes in a red cloak. It was Sweet Dora Darling, the Drovers' Friend, one of the finest whores who ever laid her back on a bed.

Charlie, who was never one to stand on ceremony, stamped over to our table, the jinglebobs on his spurs ringing like bells. "Do you boys know you're wanted by the law?" he asked.

"We've heard nothing else for weeks, Charlie," Johnny Blue said.

"Well," said Charlie, "you got nothing to fear from me. You're my own kind an' I wouldn't turn you in if my life depended on it."

He dropped into a chair beside us, and Dora found her own chair and sat.

"Before Charlie gets to talking," she said, "I want you boys to know right off that I'm out of the whorin' business."

"How come?" I asked, feeling disappointment tug at me, not for the first time that evening. "You was always a right good lay, Dora, and gave a feller his money's worth, honest and true."

Dora shook her damp curls. "Since the ranches closed down and the drovers left, business has been real bad. So I said to myself about a month ago: 'Dora, I figger now is a right good time for you to make the break and leave behind the whorin' and become respectable.'"

"I get it," I said. "You're Charlie's woman."

Dora shook her head at me again. She had aged some since I last saw her, and there were fine lines around her eyes and mouth and her face had thinned down and hardened. "I'm nobody's woman. Charlie here reckons I've the makings of a fine actress and he says he'll teach me how it's done."

"I met Lily Langtry one time when I made a trip back East to Chicago," Charlie explained. "She told me a lot about the acting profession and I believe I can pass that knowledge on to Dora." He studied that retired whore closely. "This little lady has the look and manner of a thespian and she'll make her mark behind the footlights one day."

I allowed as that was an excellent choice of career, and Johnny Blue said it sure was and Dora looked mighty pleased with herself.

Jim brought us drinks, and Charlie began: "Me and Dora is headin' up to the Blackfoot reservation because I—"

"Wait, Charlie," I interrupted, "you should know there's a thousand-dollar reward out for me and Johnny Blue. Dead or alive. I just wanted to get that out of the way."

Charlie took off his hat and smiled. He'd let his hair grow long and he had it pulled together in the back in one of them ponytails, as the ladies call them. "Boys, I won't sell out my fellow man for thirty pieces of silver," he said, echoing what Jim Shelton had told us earlier. "Besides, I don't want to see you rannies get hung, at least not anytime soon."

I glanced over at Dora to see if what Charlie was saying set right with her, and when she saw me look at her, she nodded her agreement. But there was a mighty cold, calculating look in her eye I didn't like, and I reckoned me and Johnny Blue would have to tread carefully if she ever found herself around the law.

"How did you know we was gonna be in Utica, Charlie?" Johnny Blue asked, suspicion edging his voice.

"I didn't know you boys were in town until the geezer at the livery stable told me what all the shooting was about," Charlie replied. "Dora and me, we was sitting in her shack drinking coffee when we heard the guns go off over to the barn."

Johnny Blue, who had been slumped in his chair showing little interest in the conversation, suddenly sat upright. "Dora," he said, "you ever serve tea?"

She shook her blond curls. "Never tried it. Why do you ask?"

Johnny Blue shrugged and settled back in his seat again. "Nothing, just wondered is all."

I was getting as exasperated with Johnny Blue as a snake without a pit to hiss in, so I said testily: "You really got a hang-up about this tea thing, don't you?"

"Nah, I'm not hung up on it," quoth that rueful rider. "I was jest a-settin' here woolgathering, reminiscing about tea an' gold medals and sich."

Johnny Blue reached under his slicker and brought out his tally book and a stub of pencil, and right off I knew what he was doing. "You're gonna set there while Charlie is visitin' an' make a list of my faults again, ain't you?"

"Lemme see here," Johnny Blue said quietly. "Well, doesn't that beat all, I still only got but one."

"Which of his faults is that?" Dora asked sweetly. And I shot her a look.

"Stupidity," Johnny Blue replied. "Trouble is, it seems to cover all the rest."

Dora sat there for a spell, and I could see she was thinking hard. "Have you tried giggling?" she asked. "He always giggled when he was drinking and he was horny."

Johnny Blue dabbed the lead of the pencil on his tongue. "He's got faults a heap worse than that, but I reckon I'll write it down anyhow. Let's see . . . g-i-g-l-i-n-g. Yeah, that's a pretty good fault."

"Let me think, there's a lot more—" Dora began.

But I cut her off right quick. "Listen, a man doesn't like

to be told he giggles and is low down and have all his
faults put in a tally book."

I was about to say more, but then I had a flash of in-
spiration, one of my truly great ideas, an idea that involved
Charlie and that could provide me and Johnny Blue with
a grubstake.

"Look," I said, "I've suddenly got a great plan that could
be profitable for all of us."

Johnny Blue sighed, put the tally book away, and said:
"Fire away. We're listening."

"Good," I said. "Now, here's what's happening. Charlie's leaving . . . when?"

"Tomorrow," said that good-natured artist. "I'm leaving
tomorrow morning and heading north into Blackfoot territory to paint the Indians while they're still wild and their
way of life is more or less still intact."

"I thought you done that already," Johnny Blue said.

"I did. Last spring. But I'm going back because there's
still a lot I want to put down on canvas before the Blackfoot's time runs out. Right now they're still warriors, but
they won't be that way for much longer."

"And that's exactly where me and Johnny Blue come
in," I said.

"We ain't artists," Johnny Blue pointed out, building a
cigarette.

"I know that. But Charlie don't need another artist. He
needs people who can do other things like tend the horses,
cook the meals, wash out his brushes, and see to the can-
vases and sich. That way, he can devote all his time to
doing the one thing he can do pretty well—paint. Charlie
knows time is runnin' out for the Blackfoot, and because
of that, it's running out for his own self."

"Well, I don't—" Charlie began, but I cut him off and
said: "What do you think, Johnny Blue?"

Johnny Blue thumbed a match into flame and lighted

his smoke, and I knew he was thinking of the money we'd need to reach Brownsville, Texas. "How much would you pay us, Charlie?"

"Well, I mean, I don't know that I want—"

"We'll be gone a month or so," I said quickly. "So I reckon Charlie could pay us each twenty dollars and all our meals. That ain't good money, but it's enough for a couple of out-of-work hands riding the grub line. Besides, it will put us well out of the reach of the law for a spell."

I glanced at Dora, and again I saw that strange gleam in her eye. That young lady would bear watching! Believe me, boys, I'd just begun to realize that there was at least one soiled dove who didn't have a heart of gold.

At first I thought she might be opposed to my plan, and want Charlie all to herself, but she surprised me when she said: "That might be a good idea, Charlie. If you had a couple of menials to do all the dirty work, you'd have more time to paint and teach me how to act."

Charlie sat there thinking over my offer, and I could see he wasn't too thrilled with the idea, but me and Johnny Blue, we needed that job bad.

We had three good horses and Colt guns and Winchester rifles that we'd taken from Amos Pinkney's gang, but other than that we was so poor as to be almost destitute. The soles of my boots were so thin, I never struck a match on them for fear I'd set my socks on fire, and Johnny Blue's were even worse.

We had patches on the patches that covered our britches and but one shirt each, the ones we was wearing, and those had been washed so many times, they looked like lace curtains.

Add to all that the fact that we hadn't been eating good lately and I reckon you'll know why I wanted Charlie to accept my proposition.

"Well, how about it, Charlie?" I asked after giving him

time to think it over. "Do you want to give us a job? Artist's assistants is what we'd be."

At that Johnny Blue sat up, a glow of interest in his brown eyes. "I've never been an artist's assistant before. It could be a whole new career."

Charlie nodded. "It's an ancient and honorable profession."

That artist's assistant title swung Charlie in my direction, playing as it did to his considerable vanity, though he still wasn't exactly as happy as a pig in a peach orchard about the plan.

"Okay," he finally said, "you've got a job. But I've got to tell you boys that you've got a reputation as real troublemakers and you're known outlaws and desperate men. I must admit it troubles me some." He studied my face intently, then added in a worried tone: "I hope you won't step out of line or do anything low down. I've got my reputation to think of, and you boys ain't exactly respectable folks and you ain't near civilized yet."

"Trust me, Charlie," I said, "we'll make this trip go as smooth as silk. You'll never know we're around and you'll never regret talking us into becoming your assistants an' hiring us."

"I think perhaps," quoth that dithering dauber, "that I've already begun to regret it."

Suddenly Shelton's saloon shook as thunder boomed right above the roof and Dora let out a little squeal of fright, either real or pretend, and grabbed on to Charlie's arm.

Boys, thinking back on it, I didn't take that thunderclap and Dora's squeal as ill omens—but I've spent all the intervening years of my life wishing to hell I had.

Me and Johnny Blue spent the night in the barn, a comfortable enough place once the storm had passed, and come

morning Charlie showed up with Dora. Gone were her red
cloak and low-cut dress and in their place a man's blue
shirt tucked into a riding skirt of brown canvas. She wore
fancy-stitched boots and on her head was a Montana peak
hat. She looked as pretty as a picture that morning.

"Hell, Charlie, she ain't really coming with us, is she?"
I yelled. "All a woman will do is slow us down."

Dora stepped toward me and got right into my face.
"Listen, buster," she said, "my pony's nose will be in your
hoss's ass all the way to the Canadian border, so don't you
worry about me none."

Johnny Blue, who was building his first smoke of the
morning, laughed. As did Charlie.

"She's got you buffaloed for sure," Charlie said, slapping his thigh.

Well, I knew I was in a no-win situation, and I saved
as much face as I could when I allowed that maybe a
woman would be good for cooking and washing dishes and
sich. Dora gave me a hard look but didn't say nothing.

We stopped over to Shelton's saloon and ate a good
breakfast of steak, eggs, and fried potatoes, and as we sat
with our coffee, Jim came over to the table, his face looking old and tired in the harsh morning light.

"I don't want to see you boys back here," he said to me
and Johnny Blue. "There's nothing for you here in Utica
anymore, unless it's a violent death. My advice is to do
this job for Charlie, then head south for the territory and
hitch up with Bill Cody. Maybe you could even stay in
England after his show heads for home. The Montana law
can't touch you there."

I told Jim that I'd study on his advice, but I didn't want
to believe I'd never see Utica again, and it was Johnny
Blue who voiced my thoughts: "We'll be back when the
herds come back, Jim," he said.

And Jim Shelton, that warmhearted, kindly man who

had fallen on hard times like the rest of us, didn't say a word. He just shook his head sadly and walked away.

Thus it was that after breakfast me and Johnny Blue, along with Charlie and Dora, resolutely headed our horses north toward the land of the wild Blackfoot and its attendant perils.

As we rode away, I looked back and saw Jim standing outside his saloon watching us leave. I waved my hat and yelled Huzzah! But Jim just stood there, unmoving, like a man made of stone. The rain started again, a steady, hissing downpour, and soon Jim Shelton was lost behind a falling gray curtain, fading slowly away before my eyes as though he, and Utica, had never been.

Three

The rain stayed with us off and on for the next couple of days.

We rode north, and to our left the high peaks of the Rockies were lost in cloud, their slopes green with Ponderosa pine and fir, spruce covering the gently rolling foothills. We kept to the valleys, our horses walking knee-deep in a sea of wildflowers and buffalo grass, and we saw plenty of elk and moose, and once a grizzly stood up on his hind legs to watch us curiously as we rode by.

On our third night out from Utica, we camped by a small mountain stream under the welcome canopy of a spreading cottonwood because it was still raining pretty hard.

Charlie was fussing with his paints and brushes and Johnny Blue had just returned with an armful of firewood when Dora, who'd been kneeling by the fire laying slices of beef into the frying pan, stood and brushed grass off her skirt.

"Wagon coming," she said. "And riders."

I followed her pointing finger and saw a small blue-painted wagon come toward our camp across the meadow.

"That's an Army wagon," Charlie said.

As the wagon got closer, I saw a young feller in a plug hat in the driver's seat, holding the lines of the two-horse team. Beside him sat a gray-haired man with an officer's shoulder straps and two mounted troopers acted as out-riders on each side of the wagon.

When they were about fifty yards off, the officer stood
and hollered: "Haloo the camp!"

Charlie laid aside his artist paraphernalia and rose to his
feet. "Come on in," he yelled.

The officer was a small, elderly major with a round pink
face and quick, birdlike eyes. He wore a huge set of muttonchop whiskers that must have stood out four inches on each
side of his jaw and a trimmed military mustache.

"Donnelly's the name," he said, "Major Mark Donnelly,
United States Army paymaster." He waved a hand toward
the men with him. "The young lad in the stingy brim hat
there is my civilian clerk, Walter Schmidt, and those other
two are troopers Yates and Smith of the First Cavalry out
of Fort Custer." He gave a little bow toward Dora. "At
your service, ma'am."

For her part, Dora blushed and smiled shyly, and looked
for all the world like she'd never been in the whorin' trade
or ever set foot in a bawdy house. "Charmed, I'm sure,
Major," she said.

I learned a couple of things that day, boys, that would
later cost me dear. I learned that Dora was an actress who
would've given Lily Langtry a run for her money and I
learned she could make herself look as innocent as Little
Red Riding Hood when she had a mind to.

Getting back to that paymaster, he told us he was taking soldier wages to Fort Shaw and the other Army posts
in the territory.

"The troops should get paid twice a month," he said,
"but they're already running a month behind. I've got sixty
thousand dollars in gold and silver coin in that wagon, and
the boys will surely be glad to see it."

"Major, that's a powerful lot of money to be carrying
with such a small escort," Charlie pointed out.

The major smiled. "The Army is so understrength out
here"—he nodded toward the young troopers who were

gazing at Dora in openmouthed admiration—"I considered myself lucky to get these two."

The major looked tough and competent and wore his Colt like he was born to it, but the troopers were just half-grown boys and I doubt either of them had seen his eighteenth birthday.

I guess those soldiers had been living on Army bacon and hardtack, because when it came to eating time, all of them, the major included, made short work of the beef and beans we fed them.

When me and Johnny Blue were working on the old DHS and making thirty dollars a month steady, we used to look down on thirteen-dollars-a-month soldiers. They could only afford the cheapest whiskey and the ugliest, worn-out whores, soldiers' women we called them then. But now, being just as poor as they was, we didn't mind them soldier boys one bit. Poverty has a way of changing a man's attitudes right quick.

Major Donnelly was a real nice feller, and he told us this would be his last trip as paymaster before he retired in a couple of weeks.

"My little lady is waiting for me in Great Falls," he said, "and we plan to head back East to Philadelphia where her folks live. I'm thinking of entering the hardware business, though I've been in the Army since I was about the age of those youngsters there"—he nodded toward his troopers again—"and I know nothing else but soldiering." The little major sighed. "A fine career, soldiering on the frontier, but it's cost me much over the years."

Major Donnelly raised his arm to about waist level. "I can't lift it any higher. I took a bullet in the shoulder fighting Victorio down in the Arizona Territory in '78, and I still have a Kiowa arrowhead buried in my thigh I got with Colonel Carson when we whipped Little Mountain and his band along the Canadian in '64."

The major flushed and looked across the fire at Dora. "Begging your pardon, ma'am, I shouldn't be speaking of . . . er . . . thighs in a respectable lady's company."

Dora smiled as though butter wouldn't melt in her mouth. "Think nothing of it, Major; I was so enthralled by your tales of derring-do that your little breach of etiquette passed quite unnoticed."

"Thank you for your forbearance, ma'am," Major Donnelly bowed. "I am very much sensitive on the point since Miss Libby, the lady wife of our late and gallant Custer, once took me to task at Fort Riley, Kansas, for commenting on the fine needlework of the hand-crocheted bloomers that, for modesty's sake, covered the legs of her piano. Unfortunately, in praising her handiwork, I was perforce obliged to use the word 'legs' and instantly met with that dear lady's disapproval.

" 'Lieutenant Donnelly,' quoth the consort of our valiant and much lamented hero—a beautiful young creature in pink—'you're new to this post and perhaps do not understand our little ways.

" 'But, and I have the general's complete agreement on this point, we do not mention the private parts of the anatomy at a social gathering where there are ladies present. Perhaps in the future you might confine yourself to referring to the supports of the piano.'

"Thus chastened, I kept all comments to myself for the rest of the evening and durst not venture, for fear of reproach, another single word."

The major inclined his head toward Dora and sighed. "So you can see, ma'am, why I am somewhat sensitive on the subject of . . . er . . . limbs."

Dora's smile was as sweet as a grandmother's kiss. She reached over and touched the soldier lightly on the wrist. "Dear Major Donnelly, I'm sure you intended no impropriety, nor was I in the least offended. I do declare, if the arrowhead is in your thigh, then it's in your thigh, and there's an end to it!"

That Dora, when she was active in the whorin' trade, I reckon she'd done a lot more than lie on her back and study the cracks in the ceiling. She'd listened to the way her customers talked—not us cowboys, for we were rough of speech and short on book learning in them days—but to all them lawyers and judges and politicians who'd been her customers from time to time. Dora had learned how to speechify like a real lady when she put her mind to it, and for some reason, don't ask me why, it made me feel a mite uneasy right then.

Johnny Blue glared at the coffee grounds in his cup then threw them moodily on the fire. "Major," he said, "that Miss Custer, did she ever serve tea?"

"Oh indeed, she often did," Donnelly replied. "She'd serve afternoon tea to the officers' ladies with little cakes one of the post cooks baked especially for her. They had a dollop of cream on top and little wings of pastry sticking out from the cream. Miss Libby—she had the most agreeable of faces, not absolutely beautiful but extraordinarily pleasant—called them in her own sweet way 'fairy cakes.' "

"Did she ever invite fellers to tea?"

"Certainly. Now and again she'd invite the officers with their ladies."

Johnny Blue nodded as though Donnelly had confirmed something he already guessed at.

"Them officers, if they had a gold medal for bravery, would they wear it to tea?"

Donnelly nodded. "Dear me, yes. Why Captain Tom Custer, the valiant general's equally valiant brother, often showed up wearing both his Congressional Medals of Honor to Miss Libby's little soirees." The Captain paused, his face puzzled. "Why do you ask?"

Johnny Blue shrugged. "Oh, no reason, 'cept this feller
I know wants to go to tea sometime wearin' his gold medal
with old Queen Vic's head on it."

Donnelly nodded. "He must be brave indeed if he has
a gold medal bearing a likeness of Her Britannic Majesty."

Johnny Blue stretched and said through a yawn, "This
feller ain't brave, Major. And he ain't any too bright either."

Now no man likes a feller to say to his face that he's
yellow and dumb and low down. I was about to tell Johnny
Blue angrily that if he ever fought me, he'd think he was
tied in a sack with a bobcat. But Dora, who had caught
Johnny Blue's yawnitis, stood and announced that she was
turning in, and Major Donnelly and his men instantly rose
to their feet and the moment passed.

As I lay in my blanket that night and studied the stars
overhead, I figgered that Johnny Blue had this tea thing
lodged in his brain and nothing short of dynamite was
going to blast it out of there. When he had something stuck
in his craw, that ruminating rider worried it to death.

Before Major Donnelly and his men pulled out next
morning, he told us he planned to first visit Fort Shaw,
where there were 4 companies of the 25th Infantry, 17 officers, and 230 men, and then on to Fort Benton.

"The twenty-fifth are Buffalo Soldiers," he said, "and
good troops. But they're infantry and can't be everywhere
keeping the peace."

Then he warned us to be on our guard because the territory was full of the vilest desperadoes and wanted outlaws, which was something of a sore spot with me and
Johnny Blue. For a spell I couldn't look the major in the
eye so I glanced down at the toe of my boot as I kicked
the dirt at my feet.

Charlie, who was gettin' plumb nervous about them desperadoes, was all for heading part of the way north with

the payroll wagon, saying there was safety in numbers and that few outlaws would dare try to rob the U.S. Army.

But I told the little officer we were a well-armed and well-mounted party, gallant and determined enough to deter any attack from bandits and that we didn't need their help.

The truth was them Army boys was pretty much the only law in the northern territory and it made me uneasy to think that they might come in contact with one of them wanted posters.

"We can handle anything that might come our way," I assured the major again, talking over Charlie's stammered objections as I tried my best to wave him into silence.

"That may be so," Donnelly allowed, "but there desperate men around these parts, especially wolfers who have been collecting bounties for lobo scalps since the big snows of the Hard Winter." As he climbed into the seat of the wagon, he added: "From what I've been told, they're not adverse to slitting throats if there's a profit to be had from it."

I said we'd keep our eyes skinned and look both to our right and left, since we had no wish to fall prey to drygulchers who were both dangerous and low down. As the soldiers left, we all gave voice to several cheerful Huzzahs! and Charlie took off his hat and waved it and hollered: "God bless the U.S. Army!"

Major Donnelly looked back, smiled, and tipped his forage cap, and Charlie, watching him, said: "That's a right nice officer. I still think we should've gone with him."

"Trust me, Charlie," I said. "We're in no danger. I told you this trip would go smooth as silk, and I meant it."

Of course we'd no way of knowing it then, but we would meet the little major, again—only next time it would be to the drumbeat thunder of rifles and the lethal whine of flying lead.

Four

We had broken camp and had spent less than an hour on the trail north when disaster struck. They came at us out of the aspens that grew down to the green meadows, fanning out as they approached our gallant little party at a fast gallop.

There were a dozen of them, big men riding small ponies still shaggy with their winter coats, and each rider carried a rifle. They came on us like wild Indians, whooping and hollering, and we had no time to react before they had us surrounded.

My hand strayed down to the walnut butt of my Colt, not because I'd any intention of drawing it, but because of the small measure of comfort it brought me.

One of the riders, a huge man wearing the skull and scalp of a wolf on his head, saw what I was doing and shoved the muzzle of his Winchester into my face.

This ranny had a mass of dirty yellow hair growing down to his waist and a beard that spread out across his chest. He looked as mean as eight acres of snakes, and right then and there I made up my mind that I wanted no part of him.

"See the end o' this rifle, sonny?" he asked.

I allowed that I did and added that I couldn't take my eyes off it.

"Good boy," he said, the smile on his face revealing

white teeth that had been filed to sharp points like a cougar's. "Now make like it's your momma's teat."

Behind me I heard Charlie yell: "Now see here, you barbarian, this is an outrage!"

There was a dull clunk! as one of the riders bent his rifle barrel over ol' Charlie's head and I heard that pathetic painter fall to the ground with a horrible cry.

"Now do as I say, boy," the big man snarled at me.

I opened my mouth and he shoved the muzzle of the rifle into it, jamming it hard against the back of my throat.

"You got the look of the Texas gunslick about you, boy," the big man said, "an I'm a nat'rally cautious man. So if your hand moves another hair's breadth toward that iron, I'm gonna blow your tonsils clean out the back of your head."

He studied my face quizzically for a spell, then said: "Do I make myself clear?"

I couldn't talk with that rifle barrel in my mouth, and I was so nervous my belly felt like it was full of bedsprings, so I just nodded my head, real slow.

The big man's head moved up and down in time with mine, smiling like a possum eating persimmons. "Much obliged," he said, yanking the rifle muzzle out of my mouth. "Now, slow as a hound dog in August, shuck that gun belt. An' you too"—this to Johnny Blue, who looked about as scared as a rabbit in a coyote's back pocket—"an' don't even think about makin' fancy moves."

Far from making fancy moves, me and Johnny Blue quickly did as we were told, unbuckling our belts and letting them fall to the ground.

Most of the hardcases surrounding us wore gray lobo pelts on their heads, and I knew they were the wolfers Major Donnelly had warned us about.

Since the Hard Winter of '87 when there had finally been a disastrous collision of terrible weather and worse

management in the ranching industry, men such as these
had infested the open range from the Montana border to
the Yellowstone, trapping wolves to collect the government
bounty. The wolves were gorging on the carcasses of tens
of thousands of dead cows, and they were fat and slow
and plentiful.

As the cowboys and ranchers had starved, the wolfers
had prospered.

Boys, in them days they were a mean, treacherous, and
dangerous breed, and right then and there I reckoned me
and Johnny Blue was fast running out of room on the dance
floor.

A tall, skinny ranny with a knife scar down one cheek
kneed his pony alongside the giant who had shoved his
rifle in my mouth. "He giving you trouble, Boone?" he
asked.

"Some," Boone allowed. "He was goin' for his iron till
I showed him the error of his ways."

The skinny man laughed. "That little runt? Why, if'n he
was a fish, you'd have to throw him back."

The big wolfer nodded. "That's right, Sierra. Why, he
ain't much bigger than Shade Hannah back at the camp.
Maybe you'd like to go tell Shade he's a runt who ought
to be tossed back in the river."

"You go to hell," Sierra said, and he wheeled his pony
away and rode back toward the packhorses.

I glanced behind me and saw Dora help Charlie to his
feet. For a spell he just stood there rubbing the egg on his
noggin; then he stomped toward the wolfer named Boone.

"Now see here, Mister . . . whatever your name is . . ."

"Boone," the big man said. "Curtis Boone."

"Well, Mr. Boone," Charlie snapped, an angry expression on his pale face. "My name is Charles M. Russell,
and I'm a well-known and respected artist and I will not
be handled this way. These people"—he waved a hand to-

ward me and Johnny Blue—"are my assistants and as such must be treated with respect. I warn you, I have powerful friends looking out for my welfare, and if anything should happen to me or my assistants, they will send out a party of marshals, all well-armed and determined men, to ascertain my whereabouts and bring our assailants to justice." Charlie stretched to his full height. "Now, step aside and let us pass or suffer the consequences." A small man with yellow eyes and teeth dismounted then sidled up to Boone and grinned evilly: "Do you want I should hang 'em now, Boone, huh?"

Curtis Boone studied on that for a spell; then he shook his head. "I don't think so, Andy."

The small man reached into a sack that hung from his saddle and brought out a noose. "Boone, I got a rope."

"Nothing doing, Andy," Boone said. "I've heard of this feller. The Indians call him a magician or sorcerer or something because his pictures are so dang real they reckon he captures the souls of the people he puts on the canvas. I got an idea the boss might be interested in this ranny."

"What about the woman?" Andy whined. "Can I at least hang the woman?"

"Maybe later," Boone allowed. "After the boys have had their fun with her."

Andy didn't try to hide his disappointment. "Aw, Boone, you ain't let me hang anybody since I strung up that preacher an' his wife what brung us religion that time."

"You done bad, Andy," Boone said mildly. "The boss said you wasn't to hang them preachers."

The little man cackled. "I done it anyhow. The boss can't get out of bed with them bum legs o' his, so what did he know? Hee, hee, hee, they done a jig to ol' Andy's tune, all right. I made 'em dance for nigh on twenty minutes afore they choked to death, their tongues stickin' out of their heads an' all. Hee, hee, hee."

Johnny Blue looked at the little man and said: "Mister, I guess you don't know it, but a long time ago you snapped a link in your trace chain."

"Are you callin' me, crazy?" Andy yelled, leveling his Henry at that reckless rider.

Boone, as fast as a rattlesnake, pushed the rifle aside and said: "Why are you so sore, Andy? You know you're crazy. Every hangman is crazy."

Andy slapped his thigh and cackled. "Ain't that the goddamn truth. They say ol' George Maledon, Judge Parker's hangman down in the Territory, is even crazier than I am."

"All right, enough of this palaver," Boone said. He pointed at Charlie. "You, get up on your horse and we'll go talk to the boss."

"I refuse," declared that defiant depicter. "I will not be handled in this way for I have powerful friends. I am a famous paint—"

There was a dull clunk! as a second rifle barrel got bent over ol' Charlie's head and with another horrible cry he again fell to the ground.

He rode into the wolfers' camp draped over his saddle, two eggs on his poor tortured head, cussin' so bad he singed all the grass within ten yards of his horse.

The wolfers' camp was an abandoned farm surrounded on three sides by thick groves of aspen, birch, and fir trees. There was a clapboard barn, much neglected and falling apart; a couple of corrals, one of them containing eight good-looking paint ponies; and, beyond the corrals, a main cabin.

The cabin was made of logs chinked with mud and it had a sod roof, sagging in the middle and much overgrown with buffalo grass and wildflowers. Wolf pelts were nailed to the outside walls and on the door, and its two windows were covered with sacking. A thin trail of woodsmoke rose from the chimney, tying knots in the still air, and the whole place had a depressing feel like someone had just died and was lying in the parlor stiff and cold in his go-to-prayer-meeting suit.

I could see no children or womenfolk, just a few thin, mangy dogs that sniffed around the corners of the cabin or lay in the sun, their long, pink tongues lolling out of their mouths. Our sorry cavalcade stopped outside the cabin; then Boone ordered us to dismount.

"Keep an eye on them pilgrims," he told Andy and the others. "Especially the runt with the big mustache. He's gunslick an' he's capable of making fancy moves."

Andy cackled and swung his Henry on me. "Don't make me use this, sonny," he said. "I'd rather hang ye than plug ye."

Boys, that ranny had loco camped out in his eyeballs, and with his rifle steady on my belly, I didn't even want to blink for fear he'd cut loose with that .44.40.

Charlie was still draped over his horse, hollerin' to be untied as Boone walked up to the cabin, opened the door, and went inside.

Johnny Blue walked over and stood beside me, the wolfers warily covering him with their guns. "Don't reckon he'll serve tea, do you?"

"Who?" I asked.

"That boss wolfer feller."

"I doubt it. These hombres don't look the tea type."

"Pity." Johnny Blue looked up at the hazy blue sky. "You could've worn your medal."

"You ain't gonna let that go," I said testily. "Forever and ever."

Johnny Blue nodded, smiling. "That's right. Never."

Boys, scared as I was, I decided to end that tea business right there and then by telling Johnny Blue a few home truths.

"Do you recollect the time you said Tube Wilson was just a big, fat tub of guts who'd have to study up to be a half-wit an' some skunk told him what you said?"

"Yup, an' I recollect you was the skunk who told him," Johnny Blue said.

"Well, he was real mad and he made me do it," I said hastily. "Anyhoo, that's beside the point. The thing is, Tube got his Colt's gun an' came lookin' for you meaning to call you out an' shoot you through the lungs and you hid in the smokehouse and smelled like a side of bacon for a month after that."

"I do recollect," Johnny Blue said, testy as you please, and I could see he didn't want to be reminded of what had happened in the smokehouse an' all, so I knew I had him good.

"Well," I persisted, "after Granville Stuart got Tube calmed down and the big feller said he didn't plan on shooting you no more, did I bring it up all the time? I mean did I keep saying, 'I wonder if there's bacon for supper?' or 'Gee, I smell bacon frying,' or 'Smoky in here, ain't it?'"

"You tell me, did I keep it up like some people do, banging away at it like an outhouse door with a broken latch? Did I do that?"

Johnny Blue shook his head. "No, you sure didn't. You didn't even mention it, that is, once Tube put his gun away, an' you stopped tryin' to get on his good side."

"Well, that's just fine," I said. "So now you're gonna pay me back, tit fer tat, and you'll never mention that tea business again, will you?"

"Sure won't," Johnny Blue allowed.

"Good, then it's settled."

Johnny Blue nodded. "Settled, fair and square."

He glanced up at the sky again. He studied on that sky for a long time, then he said: "I wonder if the wolfer boss will serve them fairy cakes with the cream on top when he has us to tea."

Boys, I was thinking up something real nasty to say to Johnny Blue and was about to jump on him like a hawk on a prairie dog when the cabin door opened and Curtis Boone stepped outside.

"Bring the prisoners!" he yelled.

A wolfer cut Charlie loose from the saddle, but being a man big in the chest and shoulders, he slid forward, banging his battered head on the ground, immediately bringing forth another horrible cry followed by a string of cusses.

Our heavily armed escort pushed and prodded us to the door of the cabin and Boone motioned us inside.

The cabin was dark, and it took a while for my eyes to get accustomed to the dim light from the miserable log burning bleakly in the fireplace. The first thing that assailed my senses was the stench. The cabin smelled like a manure wagon in July, and flies, huge and bloated, buzzed around my head.

I looked around at my companions. Johnny Blue was struggling to breathe, like he was trying to catch air through his ears, and Dora had a lace handkerchief to her nose.

Charlie was leaning forward from the waist, trying to peer through the gloom, when I heard a man's voice say: "Boone, light a lamp so I can see the prisoners."

"Sure, boss," Boone replied.

There was the scratch of a match; then an oil lamp blossomed into flame and then I could pretty much see all around the cabin because it was only one room and fairly small.

The sight that immediately attracted my eye was a man lying on a bunk in the corner. He was huge, with a mass of red hair hanging over huge, bare shoulders. He wore a red beard, uncombed and shaggy, and a thick mat of red fur covered his wide and powerful chest.

Even lying down I could see he was a giant, and I estimated he'd be almost seven foot tall when he stood. But he wasn't about to stand anytime soon, because both his tree-trunk legs were encased in rough splints of pine branches, bound with strips of foul rags.

He lay on his bunk like a hog in a sty, wallowing in his own filth, the floor around him covered in empty whiskey bottles and dirty tin plates crawling with flies.

Now that I could see pretty good, I noticed a thick blue chalk line, about waist high to a tall man, ran around every wall of the cabin and even crossed the door.

I reckoned that chalk line was strange—but then everything about this place seemed as strange as a sidesaddle on a sow.

It seemed ol' Charlie had also located the man on the bed, because he strode forward and stood beside him, his hands on his hips.

"Now see here, my good man," Charlie began, glancing nervously over his shoulder for rifle barrels. Satisfied that none were present, he continued: "My name is Charles M. Russell, an artist of no small reputation with many powerful and influential friends, and I demand that you release me and my assistants immediately!"

For a spell the man in the bed said nothing. Then he let out a terrible scream, clutched his great head, and hollered: "I am in hell!"

Even Charlie was taken aback by that terrible cry and hastily moved away from the bunk a few steps, but he recovered quickly and persisted: "Ahem, that may be so, but since you are apparently the chief of these ruffians, I demand—"

"My beloved!" the man on the bed bellered. He grabbed hunks of his hair in both hands and began to yank at them. "Come to me, oh my beloved. Come to me! I am in despaaaair!"

The big man's voice tailed off into a dreadful groan, and, boys, I was beginning to think that every one of them wolfers was half a bubble out of plumb, the boss man being even crazier than the rest.

Curtis Boone pushed through us and roughly grabbed Charlie by the arm. "Here now, don't you go upsettin' him like that." He pushed a protesting Charlie toward the bed. "Boss, remember what I tole you. This ranny is the artist the Indians call a magician. They say he's a great sorcerer because his pictures is so real. Boss, clear your mind of that woman and try to recollect the plan we made just five minutes ago."

"My beloved!" the man on the bed wailed. "My dearly beloved!" He raised himself up in the bed, his face wincing with pain. "Yes, now I recollect the plan. Tell them Boone. Tell them the whole . . . tragic . . . story . . ."

"Okay," Boone said, "you rannies, listen up. See, we was buying supplies at the Buffalo settlement near Fort McKinney when Jeb—the boss's name is Jebedaiah Anthony—met this here Indian."

"A chief," Jeb wailed. "White Quiver, a great war chief of the Blackfoot nation."

"Yeah, whatever," Boone said. "Anyhow, this here chief promises the boss his eldest daughter in marriage, and the asking price is eight ponies."

"Them must be the paints we saw outside in the corral," I interrupted.

"My, you're as smart as a bunkhouse rat, ain't you, boy?" Boone said irritably.

I bit my tongue and he went on: "We was heading north to the Blackfoot village about a month ago when the boss's horse shied at a 'coon and fell on him. Busted both his legs, so we found this place and have been holed up here ever since."

"Tell them the rest, Boone," Jeb groaned. "Recount it all. Spare nothing. Oh, my lost beloved!"

"Well, a couple of days ago an Indian rider comes in and tells us that if the boss don't show up with the ponies pretty damn quick, the deal is off. It seems the Army plans on herding the chief and his people back to the reservation, so he's thinking about giving his daughter to someone else. I hear tell he's dickering with a Canadian mountain man who has a new Winchester rifle to trade."

"Pig in a poke, Boone," Jeb groaned. "Tell them about the pig . . . in . . . a . . . poke . . ."

"See, the boss don't want to buy no pig in a poke. The chief says his daughter is—"

"A vision of loveliness," Jeb finished for him. "Oh my beloved! My irreclaimable bride!"

"But the boss don't want to take his word for it. He wants to see his new bride-to-be for his own self afore he turns over them ponies and that"—he poked his finger into Charlie's chest—"is where you come in, artist."

"Why don't you just have the chief bring his daughter here?" I asked.

"Because White Quiver don't trust us, that's why," Boone replied. "He figures we'll just grab the woman an' keep the ponies."

"Tell them I can't ride, Boone," Jeb said. "Tell them that."

"Boss," replied that wily wolfer, "I think they got that all figgered out already."

"What do you want from us?" Charlie demanded. "Speak plain and be damned to you."

"Simple," Boone replied, completely unfazed by ol' Charlie's outburst. "You will go to the Blackfoot village, paint a picture of the Indian princess, and bring it back here. That way the boss can see it and decide if'n she's really worth eight ponies."

"She is, Boone," Jeb hollered. "Oh, indeed I know deep in my broken heart that she is."

"Well, we'll see," Boone answered. "Once the magician here paints her picture."

"I'll be damned if I will," Charlie exploded. "I'm a famous artist not a . . . a damn pimp!"

Boone shrugged. "He won't do it, boss."

The big man on the bed let out a shuddering sigh. "Then all is lost. My beloved is gone."

Boone waved a hand in our direction. "What do you want me to do with them?"

Jeb sighed again, even sadder than the first time. "Hang 'em if you must," he said. "I don't care. Don't you see, it's all over for me?"

The big wolfer turned his face to the wall and his great shoulders heaved as he was racked with sobs.

"Now see here, you," Charlie protested to the weeping man. "I realize you're upset, but I am a famous artist with powerful friends and I will not be handled in this way. I insist that you—"

Poor Charlie forgot to look over his shoulder and didn't even see it coming. Boone drew his Colt and there was a dull clunk! as he bent the barrel over that demanding dauber's head. Charlie fell to the ground with a horrible cry and lay still.

But big as Charlie was, Boone picked him up and threw him over his shoulder. With a vile curse he prodded us out the door with his .44 and then stood there, Charlie's butt hanging in front of him for all to see. Boone raised his arms over his head and hollered:

"Listen up, everybody." He waited a long time to let the drama build, then hollered: "Necktie party!"

Immediately a man to our left struck up a lively tune on a fiddle, and from out of the woods dozens of women-folk and kids appeared as if by magic. The women were

Indians, Flatheads mostly, judging by their braids, and they were carrying woven baskets full of berries and herbs. The women immediately started singing and laughing, throwing chunks of meat into stewpots that hung over open fires.

As the jugs began to get passed around, wild-eyed wolfers grabbed their women and started dancing as the fiddler's foot-stompin' music filled the whole clearing. Boys, there was one hell of a fandango in the making, and me and the others was the guests of honor.

Boone was joined by Andy and his Henry and they shoved us into the empty corral and closed the screeching gate. Poor Charlie, they just threw him over the rails and that pathetic painter fell to the earth and lay still.

Andy climbed up on the gate, his noose in his hands.

"Like the music?" he asked. Then he showed his gums and cackled like a man in cahoots with the devil as he screeched: "I'll soon have ye dancing to a different tune. All four of ye, by God!" Boys, right then my heart was skipping beats like a drummer with the hiccups and I was more scared than I'd ever been in my whole life.

Five

Johnny Blue walked over to the unconscious Charlie and cradled his head in his arms. He slapped the groaning man's cheeks, but Charlie's eyes remained shut because he was out like a dead cat.

I watched as four grinning men strolled up to the corral, passing a jug between them. These weren't wolfers, but were dressed in range clothes, and they had the look of Texans with their high-crowned hats and Mexican spurs, jinglebobs chinking at every step.

All wore guns on their hips, except for the man who walked in front, a small, narrow-shouldered hombre who wore two ivory-stocked Colts in crossed gun belts.

Boys, if you can imagine a rat with a sparse fuzz of blond hair covering its upper lip, then you got a good idea of what that little ranny looked like. His mouth was small and crowded with long yellow teeth, and his ears stuck out on each side of his head like wings. He had the coldest eyes I've ever seen in a man, so pale blue they looked white, completely without lashes, and even though he was smiling, his smile didn't reach any higher than his top lip.

The little man's hands where they rested on the brass buckles of his gun belts looked to be soft and smooth and thin in the fingers, and I reckoned it had been a long time since this ranny and the others with him had dabbed a loop over a cow.

He had the arrogant, confident look of the slick gun-man, and no one had to tell me that this feller was pure poison, kin to a rattler on his daddy's side and a black widow on his ma's.

The little gunman strolled up to the corral and I said "Howdy" as nice as you please.

Right then I was trying to figger out what these boys were doing here. They didn't seem the type who cared for hard work, and running down and killing lobos in the hills wasn't easy, to say nothing of skinning them out and lug-ging their hides back to camp.

No, it seemed to me those boys were bent on some other kind of mischief, though what it could be in this wilder-ness I could not guess.

"Nice day, ain't it?" I said.

"Nice enough," the little gunman replied.

"Look, boys," I said, "I'll lay it out for you. We've fallen into the hands of these wolfers and they're about to hang us. You look like cattlemen, so how about bustin' us out of here? Call it professional courtesy from one waddy to another."

The gunman nodded. "Why sure, cowboy." He turned to Andy, who was still settin' on the fence like the angel of death. "Hey, Andy," he said, "turn 'em loose."

"Thank you, mister," I said. "Let me tell you I surely do . . ." I heard Andy's cackle and glanced over to see him slapping his thigh like a demented ghoul and my voice faded away to a choked whisper. ". . . appreciate it."

"Good one, Shade," Andy giggled. "That's a good one."

Shade smiled at me. "Sorry, boy. It seems Andy here is all contrary this afternoon and don't want to let you go."

"That's right, Shade," Andy hollered. "I gotta make 'em dance. We're having us a necktie party!"

"Not the woman," Shade said with a thin smile. "Me and the boys want some fun first. Then you can hang her."

"No," Andy wailed. "I want to hang the woman first. I like hanging women the best. Takes 'em a long time to choke an' they dance light as a feather."

As quick as a cat, Shade moved to face Andy. His hands dropped from the buckles of his gun belts and hovered above his holstered Colts. "Maybe you don't hear too good, old man," he said softly. "I said, not the woman."

Andy's face turned ashen and his Adam's apple bobbed as he swallowed hard. "Why sure, Shade. You can all have a taste of the woman; then I'll hang her. First or last, it don't matter—as long as we see her dance."

"You foul fiend! I've heard of you."

Charlie was lying on the ground, his head in Johnny Blue's lap, and he was pointing a trembling finger at the little gunman named Shade.

"What have you heard?" Shade asked.

"That your name is Shade Hannah and that you're a snake and low down an' that you've killed a dozen men."

"That few?" Hannah shrugged. "I reckoned the score was more than that."

He talked over his shoulder to the men arranged behind him. "Get a rope an' cut out that mare. We'll take her into the woods an' see how she bucks."

Now Dora had been with lots of men in her whorin' days, but this was different. I guess she knew she'd never come out of those trees alive because she was trembling like a willow in the wind and her face was as white as a bleached bone.

"Charlie," she whispered. "Do something, Charlie."

Johnny Blue raised Charlie to a sitting position and said: "Charlie, you was always a fair hand and a good companion when you was sober, but you're a bull-headed cuss. Right now would be a really, really good time to forget all about being stubborn an' tell that wolfer ranny you'll paint his damn picture."

"This is an outrage—" Charlie began, but Johnny Blue winced and interrupted: "Don't say that! Every time you say that, somebody lays a gun barrel over your thick head."

Johnny Blue grabbed Charlie by the front of his shirt and hauled him to his feet. "Call over Boone an' tell him you've changed your mind, Charlie, or I swear, if by some miracle we get out of this alive, I'm gonna hunt you down an' shoot you through the lungs."

I don't know if it was Johnny Blue's threat or Dora's screams as a rope was thrown around her waist and she was dragged to the rails of the corral, but Charlie nodded his head vigorously. "Okay, I'll do it."

I hollered for Boone and that wayward wolfer strolled over to the corral, a couple of his men at his heels. "What the hell do you want?" he asked. "For rannies that are gonna be hung soon, shouldn't you be on your knees prayin' or something?"

Dora screamed frantically, and Boone looked beyond me. "Looks like the boys are startin' their fun early," he laughed.

I glanced over at Dora. Shade and the others had hauled her out of the corral and they were already tearing at her clothes. I ran over there, stepped up on the first rail, and swung a roundhouse right that connected with Shade's big left ear.

After that things happened mighty sudden.

Shade yelped and clapped a hand to an ear that was already turning a bright red. At the same time he drew his right-hand gun so fast it was like the snap of a bullwhip and fired. The bullet hit the top rail and threw splinters into my face and I fell backward into the dirt.

Shade screamed and fired again and again, but I was rolling and he missed both times.

Then Andy leapt in front of me and hollered: "No, Shade! I want to hang him!"

Shade thumbed back the hammer of his Colt and would have drilled Andy dead center, but Boone ran around the corral and grabbed the little gunman around the chest, pinning his arms to his sides. "No, goddammit, Shade!" he yelled. "You'll spoil the hanging!"

Shade screamed like a man possessed and kicked his legs in the air. "Let me go! I'll kill that little runt. I'm gonna kill him!"

Shade's men had so far taken no part in the brawl, but now they angrily moved in to free their boss.

But Andy had drawn his gun and his insane cackle stopped them cold. "I'll shoot the next man that moves," he grinned. "I'll plug him right through the belly then get a jug an' watch him screech and holler and grind his heels in the dirt for hours. I done it afore an' it's a whole lot of fun. Better than any woman, I can tell ye."

The three hardcases stopped, looking at each other uncertainly. They knew Andy had a reputation of being good with a gun and was kill-crazy. Right then they were bucking a stacked deck, and they knew it.

Boone leaned down and whispered in Shade's throbbing ear. "You can help Andy hang the runt an' see him dance, Shade. So why don't you just calm down and take the woman an' you an' the boys can work your spurs on her?"

Shade took a deep breath. "Okay, let me go."

Boone released him, and Shade slowly turned to face him. "Don't ever touch me again, Boone," he said. "You do and I'll kill you, make no mistake."

Now, boys, Curtis Boone was a tough hombre who had killed his share of men, but he looked kinda green around the gills as he gazed into Shade Hannah's white cobra eyes that day and saw nothing but death. "No offense, Shade," he said huskily. "Didn't want the hanging spoiled is all."

Like the practiced gunman he was, Shade punched the

three empty shells out of his Colt and reloaded from the rounds in his belt.

He smiled, sly as a ten-year-old pickpocket. "Just remember what I told you, Boone." He spoke over his shoulder to his men. "Okay, boys, bring along that mare."

"No!" Charlie stood at the rail of the corral. "Boone," he said, "I've changed my mind. I'll paint your boss's damn picture."

Curtis Boone looked stricken.

"What?"

"You heard me, you oaf," Charlie returned. "I said I'll paint the picture of your boss's bride."

Boone shook his head incredulously. "You mean you're gonna spoil this party?"

"That's exactly what I mean," Charlie retorted. "But the woman must be unharmed or the deal is off."

Now Boone's mind wasn't real quick, and for a long while he stood studying on this new problem. Even Shade and his hardcases stood around as Dora tried, more or less successfully, to cover her nakedness.

Boys, the fate of all of us hung in the balance as Boone was torn between loyalty to his stricken boss and his desire for a necktie shindig, but in the end loyalty won out, because he said: "I'll go tell Jeb."

But before he left, Boone motioned to Dora. "Sorry, Shade, I can't give you the woman. At least, not right now."

A couple of slow seconds passed, and I thought Shade—who was seething with anger—was going to draw on Boone. But the gunman, who didn't seem to think Dora was worth a close-range gunfight with two dozen wolfers where he might take a couple of hits his own self, finally shrugged and said: "Ah, the hell with it. She's probably a lousy lay anyhow."

Dora's professional pride was stung, and she snapped: "How would you know? The next time you get laid will be your first."

Shade turned and backslapped Dora viciously, jerking her head back with the force of his cowardly blow. "Bitch, you keep a civil tongue in your head around me," he snarled.

I took a step forward because I thought about leaning over the corral rail and punching Shade's other ear, even though I knew he'd kill me for sure. But Johnny Blue grabbed my shirt and yanked me back.

"You got this habit of making few friends and mighty powerful enemies," he whispered. "One more step and that gunny will plug you through the brisket."

"Boone, this won't do," Charlie yelled. "I told you—no woman, no deal."

Boone groaned his frustration, walked over to Dora, and grabbed her by the arm. "You, come with me," he said. He marched over to where the Indian women were cooking and shoved her toward them. "Here," he said, "put her to work."

Then he turned on his heel and stomped into the cabin.

Shade Hannah walked over to the corral, looked at me, and said: "This ain't over between us. The next time I see you, I'm gonna kill you. I won't call you out, an' I won't give you an even break. I'm just gonna shuck my iron an' shoot you dead. Is that clear enough?"

I allowed that it was and behind me I heard Johnny Blue wondering aloud how an insignificant little feller like me who don't drive the train or blow the whistle could get so many folks riled up enough to shoot me.

Boys, that's long been a mystery to me too, but it seems like it happens all the time.

The cabin door squeaked open and Boone reappeared. He stepped over to the fiddler and kicked his butt, and the tune he was playing stopped in midnote.

"The party's off," Boone told him sourly.

He walked over to the corral and opened the gate. "Out, all of you out!"

"What did your boss say?" Charlie asked.

"You go paint his beloved," Boone said. "Leave now."

"I'll need my assistants."

"Take these two," pointing at me and Johnny Blue. "The woman stays."

"This is an out—" Charlie began, but remembering those gun barrels, he hastily corrected himself. "I mean, this isn't fair. I need all of my assistants."

"You got ten days," Boone said. "It's a four-day ride to the Blackfoot village, so you got plenty of time. But if you ain't back in ten days, the woman hangs."

Andy, who'd been lurking in the background, shook his noose at Boone and whined: "You tole me I could hang the woman. I wanted to see her dance at the end of a rope."

"If these rannies ain't back in ten days, you can have her," Boone said.

Andy shot us a look of pure, malevolent hatred before he stomped away toward the cooking pots, muttering to himself.

I looked around. "Where's Shade Hannah and his bunch?"

Boone shrugged. "They just pulled out. Shade's got business elsewhere and he was plumb disappointed when the necktie party done got canceled."

I thought I detected a note of relief in Boone's voice, because having a trigger-happy gunman like Shade Hannah around was kin to bedding down next to a scorpion with its tail up. Shade didn't cut those notches on his gun for whittling practice, and Boone knew it.

Again I wondered what those outlaws were doing in this neck of the woods. It just didn't make sense. There were no settlements close by, no banks to rob, nothing—just hills, trees, and buffalo grass.

What was Shade and his gang planning, and why around here? No matter which way I tackled the problem, I kept coming back to the same conclusion: It just didn't add up.

"If'n I was you fellers, I'd get moving," Boone interrupted my thoughts. "You ain't got a whole lot of time. Just head due north and you'll find the chief's village on the Judith."

As me and Johnny Blue and Charlie saddled up, Dora walked over. Blood had dried on her chin and she had a split at the side of her mouth that would leave a scar.

"You boys are coming back, ain't you?" she asked.

At that moment I felt right sorry for her and said: "We'll be back, Dora. You can count on us."

Dora ignored me and said to Charlie: "You'll be back, won't you, Charlie?"

Charlie nodded. "Never fear. I wouldn't dream of leaving you to this bunch of savages, especially that crazy old coot with the rope."

Dora laid her fingers lightly on that gallant's shoulder. "I trust you, Charlie."

Just then one of the Flathead women stomped over and hit Dora on the butt with a horn spoon, yelling at her to get back to work. With one lingering look at Charlie, Dora turned and went back to the cooking pots.

"That's a right nice lady," Charlie said.

I nodded, but I was thinking though Dora had said she had faith in Charlie, I didn't trust her as far as I could throw a stubborn mule.

We loaded up a packhorse with supplies and Boone brought us our Winchesters and gun belts.

"Ten days," he repeated. "And remember, Andy's crazy an' he wants to hang that woman real bad."

I mounted my big American horse an' once settled in the saddle, said to Boone: "Something been botherin' me, Boone. Why did ol' Jeb draw that blue chalk line around the walls of the cabin?"

Boone shook his head. "You're a right curious little feller, ain't you?"

"Well, it ain't normal," I replied. "The chalk line, I mean."

"I don't know why he draws that line," Boone said. "He carries a piece of chalk with him an' every time he's in a room, he goes ahead and draws a line around it. He even done it when we was staying in one of them fancy hotels in Austin, Texas, and the manager got all riled up about it an' was gonna throw us out until Jeb stuck a gun in his face and read to him from the Book. As to why he does it, I don't know an' I've never been inclined to ask."

"Well," I said, "it's right strange anyhow."

Johnny Blue kneed his horse over against mine. "You just love stickin' your nose in other people's business, don't you?" he said, rolling a smoke.

"No, I don't," I said. "I just get plumb curious when strange things happen."

Johnny Blue sighed. "You remember that young widder woman that cooked on the ol' DHS for a spell, and she said she was feelin' right poorly by times an' you kept after her, asking her what was wrong?"

"I recollect that," I said, not liking where this was going.

"Well, one day she told you, and for a week you went around sayin' you wished to hell she hadn't. Do you recollect that?"

"She was right poorly, that widder women," I said defensively. "She had female troubles."

"An' she told you exactly what they was, didn't she?"

"Well, she did," I said. "But some things a Christian man ain't supposed to hear."

"Just my point," Johnny Blue said, thumbing a match into flame and lighting his cigarette. "You're always a-pryin' into other folks' business an' it's gonna get you kilt one day."

"Curiosity," Charlie said, "killed the cat. Now let's get moving."

Six

Our first couple of days on the trail passed without incident, yet I had the eerie feeling we were being followed. I felt the skin of my back crawl like a goose was flying over my grave, and once when I looked over my shoulder, I was sure I saw dust rise about a mile behind us.

I didn't say anything to Charlie and Johnny Blue for fear those haughty horsemen would tell me I was seeing things and that I was plumb loco. But when we made camp on our third night in a thick stand of birch and cottonwoods beside a small mountain stream, I went into the trees to answer a call of nature and saw the brief flare of a match in the distance.

The pinpoint of light lasted only an instant before it was extinguished, but it was enough to convince me that someone was tracking us—someone who had good reason to make a cold camp and keep himself hidden from sight.

As casual as I could, I buttoned up my pants and strolled back to the fire.

"I don't want to alarm you gents," I said, "but we got some ranny on our back trail."

Charlie got out his pipe and tamped it full. "How do you know?"

I told him about the flare from the match and the uneasy feeling I'd had since we left the wolfer camp.

"There's someone out there all right," I said. "And I think he means us harm."

Charlie lit his pipe and Johnny Blue, his appetite whetted by the fragrance of the tobacco, began to build a cigarette.

"Could it be Shade Hannah and his bunch?" he asked no one in particular.

Charlie answered. "Nah, Shade isn't afraid of us. He wouldn't keep a cold camp."

"Maybe it's that bounty hunter," I said. "He already tried to kill us once. Maybe he's fixing to try again."

"Could be," Charlie allowed. "As a precaution we should sleep in turns from now on and keep one man on guard."

Johnny Blue fired his cigarette and nodded. "Sounds like a good idea." He nodded in my direction. "Dan'l Boone there should keep the first watch since he's the one that's seein' things."

I allowed that this was a crackerjack plan since I was the smartest one present and that only my constant vigilance had thus far saved us from disaster. I would have gone on about it further, but then we saw the lights.

They came toward us through the trees bordering the stream: round, bobbing globes that splashed the trunks of the birch and their dark canopies with a shifting blue, red, and yellow glow. The globes looked to be about eight feet off the ground and they were coming right at us, illuminating the gloom with dazzling bright color, like a rainbow had overstayed its welcome and fallen to earth in the dark.

Boys, you know me, I've ridden in some wild and lonely places and I'm not one to be scared of ha'nts and sich, but them lights was real high on the pucker scale and I felt my knees start to knock.

"Goblins!" Charlie cried, drawing his Colt.

Johnny Blue picked up his rifle and cranked a round into the chamber. Me, I just stared at those lights like a man mesmerized, thinking my time had come and those goblins were going to do for me at last.

Cowboys were a superstitious bunch in them days, and you boys probably recollect the story of ol' Lonesome Lon Sinclair who rode for Captain King down on the Santa Gertrudis. Lon was a fair hand and a nice enough feller when he was sober, until the fall of '82 when he got struck by lightning on the trail into the ranch—him and his pony being the tallest objects in sight and soaked through with rain an' all.

Well, they brung Lon's body back in a buckboard to the Santa Gertrudis, but his hat lay right there on the trail where it had been blowed off his head and there it sits to this day. A cowboy will ride a half a mile out of his way to avoid that hat, and nobody's ever going to pick it up, so I guess it will lie there forever. Even the captain himself, afore he died a few years back, used to tip his battered old Stetson to Lon's hat every time he passed, and ol' Captain King was scared of nothing, man or beast or booger.

Of course, the captain never faced a bunch of goblins coming out of the mountains looking to make mining slaves of decent Christian folk.

"Declare yourself," Charlie yelled in an unsteady voice. "Or by God we will open fire."

The lights stopped right where they were.

They just hung there in the darkness, bathing the trees around them in that unnatural glow, and I imagined that's what the gates of hell must look like to some poor, sinful pilgrim bound for damnation.

There were a few minutes of deathly silence when everything in the woods—men, trees, and critters—seemed to hold their breath, waiting to see what would happen next.

Then a man's voice in a strange, foreign accent cried out: "Haloo the camp!"

"Damn," Charlie whispered, "I told you they was goblins."

"Sure enough," Johnny Blue whispered back out of the

corner of his mouth. "Come out of the mountains lookin' for slaves."

Charlie cupped a hand to his mouth and yelled: "Go away. We'll have no truck with goblins and booger men here."

"Friend!" the strange voice said. "No booger man. Friend."

Johnny Blue turned his head to Charlie. "You're the boss," he said under his breath. "Should I cut loose with this here Winchester?"

Charlie studied on that for a spell, then replied in a husky whisper: "Nah, I don't hold with shooting at somebody without warning, even goblins." He cupped a hand to his mouth again and hollered: "You out there!"

"Friend!"

"Yeah, whatever. Come in real slow and your hands better be empty as an old maid's girdle on a clothesline."

"Friend," came the voice from the darkness. "Friend of all, enemy of none."

"Dammit," I found my voice at last, "that's goblin talk for sure."

The lights came bobbing toward us again, and Johnny Blue tightened his grip on his Winchester. "I hope you know what you're doing, Charlie," he said. "Goblins ain't to be trusted."

Ol' Charlie, he just bit his lip and said nothing, and my mouth was so dry, I couldn't add a single word to the conversation.

Let me tell you, boys, seeing those lights bobbing through those trees wasn't a fit sight for a Christian, especially when the woods were as dark as the inside of a coffin and full of critters that scuttled and squeaked in the underbrush.

Slowly the lights emerged from the woods into the clearing where our camp lay. Pretty soon I saw that the lights were round lanterns that looked to be made of paper attached to the corners of a wagon. The wagon was attached to a broken-down horse, and above the horse, attached to the seat, was a Chinaman!

"Haloo the camp!" declared that heathen, pulling his horse to a stop. "Sorry to drop in at such inopportune time."

"Dammit," Charlie said, irritated now his fear was leaving him, "we took you fer a goblin and was likely to dust them woods with a .44.40."

"So sorry," the Chinaman said. "I am no booger man but a poor peddler and healer. My name is Dr. Chang."

Johnny Blue scowled. "We"—he nodded in my direction—"him and me, we knew a ranny afore who called hisself a doctor, an' he was no great shakes. Maybe I should've cut loose with my rifle after all."

Dr. Chang smiled, unfazed by the surly greeting from this tall and hostile horseman. "I think if you ever put me to the test, you'll find that I excel in the healing arts."

Johnny Blue just shook his head then muttered something under his breath about there being too many damn pill rollers an' quacks in the Territory if you asked him, and maybe it was time he started to shoot a few through the lungs with his Winchester gun because folks would live longer and be a sight healthier without them.

Boys, I don't have to tell you all he said because you recollect how Johnny Blue was in them days. When something scared him, he got real grumpy before he got over it. It was just one of his many character flaws that I'll write down for you someday and you can read them when you've a month or two to spare.

"You say you're a peddler," Charlie addressed Dr. Chang brusquely. "What exactly do you peddle?"

The Chinaman nodded. "Ah yes, always the peddler first, the healer second." He waved a hand at the wagon behind him. "Pins, needles, pots and pans, cloth, buttons, yarn, soap, ribbons, rock candy, mustache wax, shoelaces, salt, pepper, blue-speckled tin plates and cups, and cheap tin trays from Sheffield, England, spices and herbs from the furthest lands of the Orient . . . in other words, everything the settler might need to make his life on this harsh frontier a little easier."

Charlie snorted. "Well, we don't need any of that stuff here, Doc, but you're welcome to camp by our fire tonight and have some coffee."

That Chinaman was small and thin, dressed in a black, high-button suit and a freshly boiled white shirt with a celluloid collar. He had a plug hat on his head and polished ankle boots on his feet. A tiny pair of round eyeglasses perched on the end of his nose, attached to his vest with a black string. He was very neat and clean, and shiny as a new mirror.

"I'm very much obliged to you," Dr. Chang said to Charlie, smiling with a grin that stretched from one of his ears to the other. "But I should tell you that I'm not alone. In addition to my goods, I carry great treasures."

"Treasures!" I exclaimed. "Doc, you're in the wrong neck of the woods to be carrying treasure. If'n you've got gold or silver, there are more than enough outlaws around who'd be glad to take it off your hands."

The little man climbed down from the wagon. "These treasures are more valuable than gold or silver coin," he said. Then he clapped his hands together once.

And boys, that's when Johnny Blue met the only woman he was destined ever to love.

They come from out of the back of the wagon, three tiny young women in long dresses, one wearing blue, the other red, and the other green. The garments came halfway up their slender necks and fit snug around their tiny waists and hips before falling without a pleat to the ground. Charlie later told me the dresses were made of watered silk, and I'd never in my whole life seen anything so delicate and so lovely as those gowns and those women.

"My treasures," Dr. Chang was smiling broadly. "More precious than silver or gold, my daughters Lo May, Lo Kim, and Lo Sue." His smile got even wider and he held up three fingers. "Triplets," he said, "all born same day."

The three girls stood there looking at us, their eyes bold and unafraid, and suddenly I felt all hands and feet and elbows and I took off my hat and ran my fingers through my hair so that it stood bolt upright, then put the hat on again, then took it off again and tried to talk and couldn't and felt like a complete idiot.

Charlie, being more worldly and better with womenfolk than me and Johnny Blue, swept off his hat and bowed. "Ladies, welcome to our camp." Then he straightened up and declared: "Treasures indeed, Dr. Chang."

Two of the women giggled and covered their mouths with their hands. But the third, wearing a blue gown with a bright scarlet, long-legged bird on the front, its wings seeming to encircle her shoulders, just stood there, her beautiful dark eyes fixed on Johnny Blue.

For his part, that lanky rider returned her gaze and then some. He stood there by the fire, openmouthed, and I realized his world had suddenly narrowed to just one person. I wasn't there, nor was Charlie nor Dr. Chang or the other sisters. For Johnny Blue there was only Lo May, and from the very instant when he first set eyes on her, he was her captive and her slave.

There was no pausing to look down into the abyss, no backward glance, no hesitant step to the ledge, wondering. Johnny Blue plunged right in. He had fallen in love with this woman before he'd even said a single word to her, and I believed she felt the same way about him.

Standing there, they were two people alone, and for

them, there was now no one else in the whole world, nor could there ever be.

I felt a sudden sense of loss.

Boys, I realized then that the man I'd ridden many a trail with since we were both fifteen years old was about to choose a path that would take him to places where I couldn't follow. I'd always known this day would come, but the knowing of it didn't make it any easier.

Charlie's voice ended my gloomy trail of thought.

"Sit ye down by the fire, Doctor," he said cheerfully. "And the young ladies."

Dr. Chang sat and the rest of us followed. I don't know if anyone else but me noticed, but even as she and Johnny Blue sat, they didn't take their eyes off each other.

Charlie poured coffee into Dr. Chang's cup and said: "Your wife doesn't travel with you?"

"My wife is dead these ten years," replied that poignant peddler. "She passed on when my daughters were eight years old. That was back in the old country. Her disease was a mouth with fangs that ate her breasts and in the end she was glad to seek relief in death."

"Sorry to hear that," Charlie said softly. "Losing a wife like that makes it rough on a man."

Dr. Chang shrugged. "I was a famous physician in China, but even all my skills could not save her. But what is death, Mr. Russell, but going from one room to another, ultimately the most beautiful room?"

Charlie allowed that this was a beautiful way of putting things, and for a while we all sat in silence as the conversation dried up, and each of us were busy with our own thoughts. I glanced across at Johnny Blue and he still hadn't taken his eyes off Lo May nor she off of him, and I wondered if Dr. Chang would approve of his daughter taking up with a penniless cowboy.

"The coffee's not to your liking?" Charlie asked Dr. Chang at last.

"It's not my usual drink, I must confess." He abruptly turned to Lo May—so he had noticed!—and said: "Bring the pot and cups, daughter." She hesitated a second or two, like she was unwilling to tear her eyes from Johnny Blue, and Dr. Chang added with a hard edge to his voice: "Now!"

Lo May nodded, then quickly walked with tiny steps to the wagon and returned with a blackened kettle and some little blue cups. She went to the stream, Johnny Blue's eyes following her every move, and filled the kettle. Then she returned and placed it on the fire.

When the kettle boiled, Dr. Chang threw some black leaves into the water and let it sit for a few minutes while he and Charlie talked of San Francisco and New Orleans and other places they both knew.

Finally Dr. Chang lifted the kettle, looked right at Johnny Blue, and said: "Tea?"

"Tea!" exclaimed that startled rider. He eagerly took one of the little cups from Lo May and extended it to the waiting Dr. Chang.

Boys, what happened next may have been a accident. But maybe it wasn't. Just maybe it was a warning.

As the peddler poured the tea into Johnny Blue's cup, his hand suddenly jerked and the boiling hot liquid splashed over Johnny Blue's wrist. That roasted rider let out with a yelp of pain and surprise and dropped his cup.

"Sorry," Dr. Chang said, his voice flat. "That was very clumsy of me."

"No harm done," Johnny Blue said, sucking his wrist. "I've been burned afore."

"I have a salve I can put on it for you if it hurts too bad," Dr. Chang said, his eyes glittering. Johnny Blue shook his head. "I'm fine."

Lo May walked around the fire and sat by Johnny Blue's

side. She took his wrist in her little hands and studied it closely. Then she kissed it.

"Daughter!" Dr. Chang said harshly, pointing at the ground beside him. "Here."

With one last, lingering look into Johnny Blue's eyes, Lo May rose and sat down beside her father, her head lowered.

"Ah yes, ahem," began Charlie, realizing something was going on that could get rapidly out of control, "an unfortunate accident to be sure." He picked up Johnny Blue's cup and said: "Allow me, Mr. Dupree."

"I believe I'll have a cup too, Doc," I said. I held out one of those little porcelain cups and he filled mine and the one Charlie held for Johnny Blue and I said, "Thankee," just as polite as though nothing had happened.

Johnny Blue sipped his tea and his whole face lit up. "This is good," he said. "I mean, this is really good."

"I'm glad it's to your liking," Dr. Chang returned. "It is national drink of China. My wife made it very well, and so do my daughters. They will make their . . . ah . . . Chinese husbands very happy someday."

Doc Chang's emphasis on the world "Chinese" didn't go unnoticed by anybody, including Johnny Blue, so I said hastily: "I don't suppose your daughters' talents stretch to fairy cakes, Dr. Chang."

He shook his head and replied: "Unfortunately, I have none of those. However . . ." He turned and whispered something into Lo Sue's ear and she giggled and legged it to the wagon, using those little mincing steps calculated to drive a man wild.

When Lo Sue returned, she had a tin plate heaped with small, round cookies that were a pale brown in color.

Dr. Chang offered them to me first, declaring: "These are rice cakes. I hope they meet with your approval."

Well, boys, I tried one and it was sweet and just kinda

melted in my mouth. It was all right, I guess, but nothing to compare to a good buttermilk biscuit covered in honey.

Johnny Blue tried a rice cake, and his eyes opened in astonishment. "Good," he said as he chewed. "Very good."

Then I heard Lo May's voice for the first time that night: "I baked them," she whispered, her eyes downcast, drawing a hard look from her pa.

Johnny Blue, he swallowed that cake and took another one, and seemed to enjoy it all the more after what Lo May had told him.

"These are powerful good," he said, looking right at Lo May. "Even better'n the ol' DHS buttermilk biscuits an' honey."

Which they wasn't, not by a longshot, but I guess love improves the taste of everything.

Well, for the next hour we sat and drank tea and ate cookies and Charlie and Dr. Chang talked about art and artists, mostly a bunch of pictures done by dead foreigners. They wound up discussing a young feller named Frederic Remington who'd been in the Montana Territory off and on since '81 painting soldiers and Indians just like Charlie.

"He's good," Charlie said. "An excellent draftsman and colorist."

That started them jawing about a feller named Degas, who Charlie called an impressionist, and I was about bored out of my mind, especially since Johnny Blue and Lo May just sat there in silence, looking across the fire at each other.

Boys, the sparks from the fire wasn't the only sparks flying that night, and I heard this little voice deep inside me say over and over again, trouble . . . trouble . . . trouble . . .

Finally Dr. Chang yawned and stretched and said it was time for bed and he rounded up his girls and herded them into the back of the wagon, How those three ladies managed to cram into there I don't know, except that they were real small and slim and didn't take up hardly any space. Lo May hesitated a little before she went inside, looking back at Johnny Blue, and Dr. Chang gave her a none-too-gentle push and Johnny Blue waved a hand at her and then she was gone. Before the peddler spread his blankets next to the wagon, Charlie told him about the feller on our back trail, and Dr. Chang said to depend not on fortune, but on conduct, and that he'd sleep as close to his Greener shotgun that night as though it was a new bride.

Johnny Blue and Charlie bedded down beside the fire, and as we had agreed upon earlier, I took my rifle and headed into the trees.

It was quiet and still out there away from the crackling fire and I was really spooked, jumping at every little sound. After a little spell I went and got Johnny Blue's Winchester and added it to my own, deciding that to be well armed was to be forewarned.

Seven

The moon was almost full, playing peekaboo behind dark, silver-edged clouds that moved slowly across the night sky. I smelled the fragrance of pine and the wildflowers that grew among the buffalo grass. The night was alive with the sound of chirping insects and far off an owl questioned the night, receiving no reply but the sigh of the wind as it rustled through the aspen trees.

I leaned my back against the trunk of a juniper and thought of the good times when the range was full of cows and me and Johnny Blue were rich, drawing thirty dollars in silver coin every month. Sure we had some hard times, like when rustlers would cut out whole herds and drive them into the Missouri Breaks and we'd have to go out after them, both of us scarcely nineteen years old and some we rode with even younger.

Them rustlers were no-accounts anyhow, unemployed whiskey traders, wolfers, woodchoppers, and trappers, and the like, and they'd never stand and fight but scatter like scared rabbits, One time they did decide to shoot it out. That was the July of '84, when a bunch of reprobates led by a hardcase named Stringer Jack made a stand at Bates Point on the Missouri.

Ol' Granville Stuart of the DHS led us that day and we killed a passel of them rustlers in the gun battle that followed, then hanged the rest. And Granville Stuart said desperate times call for desperate measures, and hard though it was to a hang a man—even though it was done not in anger, but with a sense of justice and with the blessing of God—those desperadoes would kill and steal no more.

In later days, we'd be known as Stuart's Stranglers, and be called vigilantes and a lot worse, but a rustler is a low person and a thief and a plague on any range.

Like I said, we was all young fellers then, and I guess we looked kinda green around the gills what with the hangings an' all because Granville Stuart said maybe someone would like to volunteer to say a prayer for the dead rustlers and that's when Shorty Stevens stepped forward.

Boys, do you recollect Shorty? He was a fair hand and a good enough hombre when he was sober—until he froze to death a-sitting his horse in the Hard Winter, grinnin' like a puppy with a thigh bone.

Well, Shorty was a good singer and he had a way of wailing the words through his nose that was right pretty to hear. An' he could make up a song about anything. If some ranny's favorite pony died, Shorty would make up a song about it. If you lost your best gal to another man, Shorty would sing a song for you an' make you feel even sadder. He could make up a song about anything that ever happened, and things a-plenty happened on the range in them olden days, both good and bad.

Anyhoo, Shorty goes to the packhorse and gets his banjo and he stands right among all them swaying boots at the bottom of the tree and he makes up a song right there called "I'm Hanging Around Jest A-waitin' for Jesus"— and boys, it was the prettiest and the saddest thing you ever did hear.

Us cowboys, we was clapping our hands and stomping our feet as Shorty wailed and yodeled that baleful ballad, pickin' and grinnin' fit to bust as he broke our poor, sentimental hearts for about five verses afore it was all over.

When the tune finally came to end, we was all swallowing hard and was scared to look at each other for fear the other feller would notice the salt tears on our cheeks. Even Granville Stuart, a hard man who could tie a bow knot in a horseshoe, wiped his eyes with his handkerchief and said to Shorty:

"That was right nice, and, Shorty, you sung it right pretty. Fact is, it was a better send-off than these rannies deserved after all them cows they stole."

Then we saddled up and rode home, leaving them rustlers to hang in the wind.

Well, boys, that's all ancient history because now all the cows were gone and me and Johnny Blue were poor, hunted men ourselves with little prospects of any kind of future.

Jim Shelton told me and Johnny Blue that we was just a pair of uncivilized drovers and nobody wanted us anymore. He said the West was changing and there was no longer room in it for the likes of us—and maybe he was right.

It seemed to me that Johnny Blue had taken what Jim had said to heart. He'd met the love of his life in that little Chinee girl and his fussin', fightin', and feudin' days could be coming to an end and with them the only life me and him had ever known.

As I sat at the base of the juniper and looked up at the moon that evening, I had an overdose of woe that felt like it would never leave me.

As the warm, drowsy night wore on, I got to thinking about Jeb Anthony's wolfers and how close we'd come to being hung. And that snake Shade Hannah taking a shot at me and—That was it!

I jumped to my feet and ran through the trees toward my slumbering companions, hollering: "Shade Hannah! I know why he's here!"

Suddenly there was an uproar by the fire.

Johnny Blue sat up, jammed on his hat, leaped to his feet, then ran around like a chicken with its head cut off in his long-handled underwear yelling: "My rifle! My rifle! Where's my goddamned rifle?"

Charlie tried to rise but he got all tangled up in his saddle and fell flat on his face, cussing enough to melt the ears off a Baptist preacher. He struggled to his feet and grabbed his Winchester. "Who is it?" he yelled. "Is it the bounty hunter?"

Being an artist an' all, Charlie was a little on the temperamental side and a tad nervous by times. He didn't wait for my reply but cranked his rifle and began to dust the bushes around the camp, the racketing row of his rifle shattering the silence of the night, echoes clamoring around the surrounding hills and bouncing like giant rocks off the walls of the coulees.

Johnny Blue saw me carrying the two Winchesters and yelled: "Throw me my goddamned rifle!" I tossed the rifle to that overwrought rider and the roar of his Winchester soon joined that of Charlie's.

Dr. Chang rose from his blankets and screamed something in Chinese, and in English added: "Bandits! To arms!" Then he cut loose with the Greener, blasting the trees near the fire. A huge branch took a load of double-aught buckshot and crashed just behind Johnny Blue, and that excitable rifleman jumped about three feet in the air then turned quick as a roadrunner on a rattler and pumped two shots into it, killing it dead sure enough.

Me, I stood there and waited until their guns ran dry and the ringing in my ears subsided and then I said: "When you three are quite finished."

"Did we git him?" Charlie hollered.

"No, you didn't git him," I replied. "There was nobody to git. It was only me. I was just trying to tell you rannies why Shade Hannah and his boys are in this neck of the woods."

Johnny Blue's jaw dropped. "You mean you just came a-hootin' an' a-hollerin like a scalp-huntin' wild Indian into a camp of sleeping men just to tell us that?"

"I was excited is all," I said defensively.

"I swear," Johnny Blue said, "I should take this here rifle and shoot you through the lungs. I would, too, if'n I didn't know you was sore tetched in the head."

At this dreadful threat, Charlie said now, now, and he added that Johnny Blue should calm down because no harm had been done and Dr. Chang pursued the subject, adding that it's not what we say that hurts, but how we say it and that Johnny Blue's voice had held no real malice.

As for that disgusted drover, he walked over to his shirt and got the makings from the pocket and tried to build a smoke. But he was shaking so much he was having a hard time of it. "Look at my hands, Charlie," he said. "Look how plumb riled this loony has made me."

Lo May, who had left the wagon after the shooting stopped, stepped up beside Johnny Blue, and as women do, rubbed the small of his neck as she would comfort a small child and cooed: "Poor Shonee Blue."

Then she took the makings from his trembling hands and deftly rolled the cigarette, her little pink tongue licking the gummed paper before she sealed it shut.

Johnny Blue, he accepted that smoke like it was something sacred and thumbed a match into flame, lighting the end like he was having a peace pipe with Big Chief Sitting Bull himself.

"Much obliged," he said to Lo May, and that little gal smiled and batted her eyelashes and went right on rubbing his neck. "You so welcome, Shonee Blue," she said, and Johnny Blue kicked the dirt at his feet and looked about as embarrassed as an old maid babysitting a pirate's parrot.

Charlie shook his head at Johnny Blue. "I agree that all this was very tiresome," he said, "and your opinion on the state of your fellow assistant's mental health was most clearly put, yet"—Charlie turned to me—"I believe he really has some intelligence to impart to us."

"You bet your life I do," I said. And never being one to plow around a stump, I added quickly: "I know why Shade Hannah is here—he plans to rob the Army payroll."

Charlie studied on that for a spell, then nodded. "Makes sense. But where do we come in?"

"We have to warn the major," I said, surprised that he would need to ask.

Charlie studied on that for another spell, and I fully expected him to say it was none of our affair, but what he said next really surprised me.

"I liked that major," he said, "and I was roughly handled by those wolfers and I haven't forgotten that Hannah struck Dora. Yes, yes, the more I think about it, the more I believe a warning to the major to beware might be in order."

Dr. Chang, who had corralled Lo May and had her by the wrist, shrugged his thin shoulders: "I'm sorry I can't join you gentlemen in your noble quest, but I am heading for the Indian Territory where both my goods"—he waved a hand toward his wagon—"and my healing arts are so badly needed. It is said that he who has health has hope, and he who has hope has everything, and that that is what the settlers in this wild land need most—hope."

"Think nothing of it, Doc," Charlie said. "This is not your quarrel."

But Johnny Blue looked like he'd been slapped.

He'd found true love real sudden after a lifetime on the

fast-and-loose, but now it seemed like he was about to lose it again just as quickly.

Johnny Blue had smoked his cigarette and he was building another with steadier hands. "The major had tea with Libby Custer," he said. "I can't see letting a man who drinks tea an' eats fairy cakes get shot by Shade and his low-down bunch. But I dunno, I think maybe now I got other things to do, other places to go. Charlie, I think maybe I got to ride."

I walked up to him: "Johnny Blue," I said, "a word. In private."

Boys, he didn't want to listen to what I had to say, I could see that, but I took him aside and put it to him straight. "There was three of us left that wolfer camp, an' they're gonna want three of us to ride back, otherwise it could go real hard with Dora, to say nothing of me and Charlie." Johnny Blue started to protest, but I held up my hand and silenced him. "Besides, what do you have to offer a woman? You got a horse and a saddle and your rifle, and that ain't much to start a life with."

Johnny Blue's face took on a pained look, and I bored right ahead. "After this is over, we'll head down to the Territory ourselves an' look up Buffalo Bill. I hear he's paying rough riders a hundred and twenty dollars a month an' three squares a day. Look at it, Johnny Blue, with that kind of wampum you'd be somebody. You could marry that little Chinee gal and have enough money to start your own spread. Hell, I'd come work as your foreman an' you'd only have to pay me thirt . . . forty dollars a month.

"Listen to what I'm saying, because it makes a lot of sense. You can't go chasin' that little gal down to the Territory an' you so raggedy-assed the bank won't even let you draw breath. I don't think her daddy is gonna let any penniless saddle bum come a-callin' on his precious daughter. Do you?"

Boys, I'm sure you recollect that Johnny Blue was as stubborn as a government mule in them days, but even he could see the sense of what I was saying.

"After this thing with Dora and the wolfers is over, I'm headin' for the territory an' Lo May," he said. "An' that's a fact."

"I wouldn't have it any other way," I said. "Hell, Buffalo Bill is gonna make us rich. We'll have a pile of money so high, we could burn a wet elephant. An' remember, we'll have to leave the ranch for a spell to find our sister, an' that will take money."

"No tricks," Johnny Blue said.

"Trust me," I told him.

That crestfallen cavalier made no reply, except for a long, drawn-out groan.

We walked back to the fire and I told Charlie that we was all in favor of warning the major about Shade Hannah, and that Johnny Blue was as keen to go as a frisky fiddler.

"Then it's settled," Charlie said. "The only question is: How do we find him?"

"There's another question maybe you didn't think about, Charlie," I said. "Do we have the time?"

"We must make time," replied that stalwart. "The lives of four men are at stake, to say nothing of the taxpayers' money. Don't worry. When we finally get to the Blackfoot village, I'll paint fast."

We boiled up some coffee and sat around the fire for a powwow. None of us had forgotten the mysterious hombre who was dogging our back trail, so we kept our guns close to hand as we talked.

We argued it around and decided that Major Donnelly and his men would probably still be at Fort Shaw, but must soon leave to take the wagon road to Fort Benton.

"He isn't moving fast with that wagon," Charlie said.

He consulted his pocket watch. "It's just after midnight. I believe if we leave now, we can intercept him at the post sometime tomorrow morning. My hunch is that Hannah and his gang have already set up an ambush on the road somewhere, so it's imperative that we get to the major before they do."

This decided, we unloaded the packhorse and let him loose. That swaybacked old nag was so tame you could have staked him to a toothpick, so we figured he wouldn't stray far from this spot where there was plenty of good grass and fresh water.

Dr. Chang said he was staying put until first light and not to worry about him because he'd keep his Greener loaded and handy.

He'd put Lo May back in the wagon, but Johnny Blue walked over there, and Dr. Chang watched him go but didn't say anything. Maybe he saw how determined Johnny Blue was to talk to Lo May, and decided not to start any trouble.

Just to make sure, I strolled over there myself, determined to head off any unpleasantness at the pass.

Johnny Blue called out for Lo May and she came to the door of the wagon and he told her that after this was all over, he was riding down to the Territory to look for her.

"An' when I find you, we're gonna get married," he said. "An' we're gonna have a ranch an' raise some Hereford cows an' a passel of kids."

There were tears in Lo May's eyes as she replied: "Shonee Blue, don't leave me."

But that stalwart shook his head. "I got things to do, places to go, Lo May. But when it's done, I'll find you. I promise."

"Don't leave me, Shonee Blue," Lo May said again. And she handed him one of the little pink wildflowers that were growing everywhere among the buffalo grass.

Boys, I could see that my pardner was weakening fast, so I said right quick: "We got to go, Johnny Blue. It's time to throw the coffee on the fire an' saddle up."

Dr. Chang, carrying his Greener, walked over to the wagon and at a glance took in what was happening. He made an annoyed face at Johnny Blue and said: "It's time you were riding, young man."

Johnny Blue ignored the Chinaman and whispered to Lo May: "Don't worry, I'll find you." He took out his tally book where he kept a list of my faults and pressed that little flower between two of the pages. Then he turned on his heel and walked away as Lo May wailed and started to caterwaul and her daddy told her to shut up an' get back inside the wagon as she called out: "Shonee Blue!"

But Johnny Blue, his face set and grim, didn't look back. We mounted up, three well-armed and determined gallants bent on saving the United States Army from disaster. As we rode away, Johnny Blue never once looked back to where the campfire burned cheerfully in the clearing and his lady love was crying her beautiful eyes out.

We pushed our horses hard through the bright, moonlit night, and our big, Montana-bred studs, with their distance-eating stride, made short work of the rough terrain and the miles. We thought Charlie, who forked a little Texas cow pony that couldn't have weighed more than eight hundred pounds, would fall far behind, but that mean-eyed, shaggy little bronc not only kept up with us but insisted on being out in front.

When we hit the Mullan Road, made to handle wagon traffic to and from the settlements and forts in the area, we increased our pace, spurring the horses to a steady lope under a full bright moon that silvered the aspens and made the grass look like we was riding through a rippling lake.

Tired as I was, I glanced at my valiant companions and

was gladdened to see that they sat tall in the saddle, the moonlight casting their faces in a heroic mold, their manly chins jutting determinedly as they rode through the darkest hours of the night in their quest to save the army of our young Republic.

Boys, three braver men never set forth on such an expedition as me and Johnny Blue and Charlie Russell, and that's a natural fact.

Night was shading into dawn as we reached Fort Shaw, and the lemon-colored sky above the distant mountains was streaked with splashes of bright crimson. The peaks themselves were still dark because daylight had yet to wash the shadows out of the crags and fissures of the rock and waken the pines that covered the foothills.

Charlie had once spent a couple of weeks painting the soldiers and trappers who wintered at the post, and he knew the area well. "It was one helluva ride, boys, but we made it," he said.

Slowing our lathered horses to a walk, I heard the distant ring of a bugle as Old Glory rose above the parade ground, fluttering in the cool morning breeze. "Now that's a right pretty sight," Johnny Blue said, reining in his horse.

But Charlie urged us onward. "Hurry," he said anxiously, "for there is but little time to waste."

Boys, in them days Fort Shaw was called the Queen of Montana Forts because it was even more impressive than Fort Assinniboine out there on the northwestern slope of the Bearpaw Mountains that was made of brick and cost the government a million dollars to build back in '79. Fort Shaw was a sprawling collection of barracks, officer rows, and sutler stores, and was bigger than most Western towns. The streets were wide and lined with shade trees, and the houses for the officers and their families were painted white, sitting pretty as you please behind picket fences and clipped lawns.

As I told you boys earlier, I was filled with the heroic spirit of our brave quest, and though tired from our long ride, as we rode into the fort I burst into a rousing song for the benefit of our gallant lads in blue. And very soon Charlie and Johnny Blue joined their voices to mine:

When Johnny comes marching home again, Huzzah! Huzzah!
We'll give him a hearty welcome then,
Huzzah! Huzzah!
The men will cheer,
The boys will shout,
The ladies they will all turn out,
And we'll all feel gay when Johnny comes marching home.

A young lieutenant who stood outside the headquarters building waited patiently while we finished our triumphant song, and he allowed that it was right pretty and nicely sung. Then he told Charlie he remembered him from his last stay there in '85 and asked what he could do for him. "The troops are all out," the lieutenant cautioned. "There's no one around to pose for you, Mr. Russell."

But Charlie swiftly explained our urgent, life-saving mission and told of the terrible threat to the paymaster that was lurking somewhere on the road to Fort Benton.

"Major Donnelly's gone," the young lieutenant said. "He pulled out just before sunup."

"Then we must warn your commanding officer at once," Charlie said urgently. "He must send a galloper after the paymaster. The life of that brave officer is in terrible danger."

Charlie's name meant something in the West, even in them early days, so the lieutenant led us past a couple of smartly turned out Buffalo Soldier sentries and into the commanding officer's office where a stern, scholarly-looking lieutenant colonel sat behind a cluttered desk.

The officer seemed tired, with lines of exhaustion etching his face and black circles under his eyes. He was a fine-looking, middle-aged man with iron-gray hair and a full, sweeping cavalry mustache like my own, that being the fashion of the times.

Without even a howdy-do, he started right in, his clipped, military voice very loud in that small room: "What can I do for you gentlemen?"

Charlie, who could talk water into a boil at twenty paces, began to explain about how he'd been kidnapped by wolfers and hit over the head all the time. Then he talked about the dastardly Shade Hannah who had killed a dozen men and how he had slapped Dora and was planning to rob the paymaster, and I could see the colonel was getting more and more agitated. Finally that short-fused soldier slammed his hand on his desk and hollered: "Enough!"

The colonel stood and walked to a map of the Montana Territory hanging on the wall. He slapped the map with the back of his hand. "I've got four companies of the twenty-fifth in the field right now, fifteen officers and two hundred and twenty men, almost my entire command. Two companies are herding Indians back to the reservations after the usual drift south for the spring hunting and the other two"—he paused briefly—"are rounding up deserters from the other forts in the territory. Toward spring"—the colonel shrugged—"the men desert. It's a vernal right."

"But surely," Charlie suggested mildly, "one man on a fast horse?"

"No," the colonel said. "Major Donnelly is a fine officer with a well-trained escort adequate for any eventuality. I'm not going to deplete my strength further by sending even one man on a wild-goose chase just because you three believe this . . . this . . ."

"Shade Hannah," I offered.

"Thank you," the colonel said. "This Shade Hannah—

a man you admit you met but once and dislike intensely—plans to rob the paymaster. There has never been a robbery of a payroll in United States Army history and I don't believe we're about to see one now."

"Colonel," Charlie said patiently, "think about it. Why else would Shade Hannah and his bunch be in this neck of the woods?"

The colonel shook his head. "I don't know. Maybe he's hunting. And by the way, I know most of the bad men in this territory by name if not by sight, and I've never heard of this Hannah."

"He's a Texican," I said.

"Well, by this time he's probably headed right back to Texas."

Boys, it was dawning on all of us that you can get nowhere arguing with a soldier, especially an officer as bullheaded as this one. It was true that the fort was almost empty of soldiers, but when a man puts a limit on what he'll do, he can become as stubborn as a balking mule.

I looked at Charlie and saw his shoulders slump in defeat, and I guess the colonel saw it too, because he said: "You boys should go to the mess hall and get the cook to rustle you up something to eat. I assure you the paymaster is quite safe."

The colonel smiled. "Major Donnelly is an excellent officer and not the kind of man to ride into an ambush, I guarantee that. It's true that his career was somewhat slowed by an act of impropriety while in the company of the gallant Custer's lady wife." He waved a hand. "Some indelicate matter concerning a piano of all things. But he's still a first-class soldier, wounded twice in the field, and well able to take care of himself."

That stern warrior walked to the door and opened it. "You'll find we have excellent facilities for your horses and you can bunk here at Fort Shaw tonight if you wish," he said. "Now run along and get some breakfast, there's good fellows."

We found ourselves back in the street, bewildered and smarting from the colonel's high-handed behavior.

But then that young lieutenant feller stepped forth and saved the day.

"Do you really think the paymaster is in danger?" he asked Charlie as he fell in step with us as we walked our exhausted horses toward the livery barn.

Charlie nodded. "Lieutenant, I believe he may be under accurate and deadly fire from Shade Hannah and his nefarious band even as we speak."

"Look, I believe you boys and I've got a proposition for you." The lieutenant glanced over his shoulder. "The colonel is right; we're stretched to the limit and the fort is seriously undermanned. But I can lend you fresh horses and you can go warn the major yourselves."

Charlie stopped walking and studied on that for a spell. "What you suggest has merit, Lieutenant," he said finally. He waved a hand toward me and Johnny Blue. "But despite their rough and ready appearance, these men are artist's assistants and I do not wish to place them in danger."

"Don't you worry none about me, Charlie," Johnny Blue said. "I don't like that Shade Hannah any more'n you do. I'll take my chances. The quicker we get this over with, the quicker I can get back to Lo May."

"Does that go for you too?" the lieutenant asked me.

"Count me in," I said by way of reply.

"Then it's settled," Charlie said with gusto. "Lead us to those fresh horses, Lieutenant."

The officer rounded up a couple of his Buffalo Soldiers and they helped us switch our saddles to Army mounts, huge brutes with iron mouths and dispositions two shades meaner than the devil himself.

As we saddled up, I heard one of the soldiers whisper to Charlie: "Hey, artist, how did you get tangled up with these two?"

Charlie laughed. "Hell, I don't know. It just sort of happened."

The soldier whispered: "The tall lanky one is a brother, but he looks kinda green, and the little one seems plumb sneaky, so you step careful out there, you heah?"

With another laugh Charlie allowed that he would, then we mounted and headed out of the barn. Before we left, the young lieutenant said: "If the colonel finds out about this, I'm going to be in a world of trouble, so you boys hurry back here as quick as you can. Just warn the major and let him take it from there. Remember, that's all you have to do. Don't even think of playing hero."

"Depend on it," Charlie said cheerfully. "We'll be back long before sundown."

Alas, boys, as we cantered out of the post, little did we know that we were heading into terrible danger and ere the afternoon shaded to evening, dead men would be sprawled amid the spring wildflowers, with the smell of blood and gun smoke fouling the pine-scented spring air.

Eight

We pushed those big Army horses hard all morning, but although Charlie had said the major's progress would be slow, we seemed no closer to overtaking him. As the sun hung straight above us in the sky, Charlie, consulting his watch as he rode, announced it had gone noon.

We were heading east on the Mullan Road and to our left rose the foothills of the Rockies, the rises and gullies covered in thick groves of aspen and spruce. To our right in the distance lay the majestic, glittering sweep of the Sun River, now empty of the beautiful riverboats that once plied these waters, since the coming of the railroad in 1883 had put them out of business.

I kneed my horse beside Charlie's mustang and said: "Maybe we was wrong, Charlie. Maybe ol' Shade had something else in mind besides the payroll."

"Could be," Charlie nodded. "We'll soon have to stop and let these horses rest. If we don't come upon the major before then, we'll head back to the fort."

Johnny Blue turned in the saddle. "I don't know if you two realize it, but we got a rider on our back trail. I've been catching his dust since sunup."

Those were the first words Johnny Blue had said since we left the fort. He'd been quiet as a deaf-mute's shadow, except for now and again when he'd take out the little pink flower that Lo May had given him from his tally book and look at it and sigh. That little gal had her brand on his heart all right, and before long if'n he wasn't careful, he'd be broke for domestic work.

I looked behind me and saw the rider in the distance. He didn't seem to be in any hurry to overtake us, but hung about a mile behind, matching his speed to our own.

"That's the ranny who's been trailing us," I said. "It's him for sure."

"Who is he?" Charlie asked uneasily.

"Hell if I know," I replied. "But I got the feeling he means us harm."

"I don't like that ranny behind us when we're worrying about Shade ahead of us," Charlie said. He nodded in my direction. "Rein up and pop a few shots at him with your rifle and see if it scares him off."

I pulled up the big bay I was riding and yanked my Winchester from its scabbard. The mysterious rider was still coming after us, so I cranked off three shots, dusting the trail around him pretty good.

The man jerked his horse to a stop so sudden its rump hit the grass; then he turned and loped into the shelter of the trees beside the trail. I levered another couple of .44s in his general direction then galloped after Charlie and Johnny Blue.

"Did you scare him?" Charlie asked.

"Yeah," I replied, "but I got the feelin' he ain't gonna stay scared for too long."

"Goddamn," Johnny Blue swore. "That rider worries me."

"He's giving me the willies too," Charlie began. "I'm getting plumb—"

The racket of a distant scattering of shots stopped him in midsentence.

To a man, we all exclaimed at the same time: "The major!"

Without another word Charlie spurred his mount in the direction of the gunfire and me and Johnny Blue followed. Ahead of us the wagon road followed a slight rise, and when we reached this crest, we pulled our horses to a skidding halt because before us lay a horrible sight.

The payroll wagon was stopped on the trail, the civilian driver sprawled in the driver's seat. In his death throes the poor man had pulled the wagon around so that it was pointed back down the trail toward Fort Shaw. But it was going nowhere because both horses lay dead in their traces, shot many times.

Beside the horses lay the still body of one of the young cavalry troopers and we could make out the major and his remaining guard under the wagon, firing now and again at the trees to the left of the trail.

But Shade's battle was almost won, because a tremendous volume of accurate and rapid fire from him and his four hardcases ripped into the wagon, kicking up little plumes of dust around the gallant little officer and his blue-clad companion.

"We're too late," I said. "It's all over for the major."

"Never!" Charlie exclaimed. He was the most mild-mannered of men when he was sober, but right then I guess he was still smarting over how Shade and his boys had treated Dora because he said: "Gentlemen, we have begun the play; now we must see it through to the last act."

That pugnacious painter pulled his Winchester from the scabbard and set spurs to his horse, uttering a fearful war cry as he charged.

Johnny Blue glanced over at me, swept off his hat, and pointed it in the direction of Shade and his men. "After you."

I set spurs to my mount, yanking out my Winchester as I rode, and behind me I heard the thundering hooves of Johnny Blue's horse.

Like Charlie, I too uttered a furious cry as I rode at a fast gallop toward the sound of battle. Boys, we was so lucky that day I declare we'd have gotten American change if we'd spent a Confederate dollar.

It seemed to be Charlie's intention to charge straight toward the trees where Shade and his men were in hiding. But that reckless rider—and me and Johnny Blue with him—would've been shot all to pieces before we'd even covered half the distance—had Shade not chosen that exact moment to mount his troops and charge the wagon.

They didn't know we were there, so we took them completely by surprise when we slammed into their flank.

I saw an outlaw go down under Charlie's rifle; then Johnny Blue shot another from the saddle. I took aim at one ranny who was yanking his horse around to face our onslaught and fired, but I missed him clean. A split second later he gurgled horribly, clutching at his scarlet-splashed chest, and I looked and saw that the major, who'd come running out from under the wagon, had nailed him with his Colt.

Charlie and Johnny Blue reined up their horses and kept up a steady fire at the remaining outlaws. Between shots, Charlie yelled at them to surrender or die like dogs.

Shade Hannah and the one man left to him frantically spurred their horses, charging headlong in my direction. Shade came galloping on toward where I sat my bay, spurts of dust kicking up from under his horse's hooves. But his companion suddenly thought better of it and turned toward the trees, bent low over his pony's neck. I cranked the lever on my rifle and fired at Shade, then at the fleeing outlaw. Missing both times, I levered the rifle and fired again, and this time the escaping desperado threw his arms in the air and toppled from his horse.

Shade was now almost right on top of me.

He screamed, an inhuman cry of hate and fury, as he

charged his mount broadside into me. Big as he was, my horse crashed to the ground under the impact and I lay on the ground stunned, the huge Army horse pinning my right leg to the ground. I glanced up and looked into Shade's soulless white eyes.

He leveled his Colt at my head and shrieked: "Die, goddamn you! Die!"

I closed my eyes and heard a dull click.

Shade screamed and pulled the trigger again. Click! And again. Click!

Each time the hammer of his deadly revolver fell on a spent cartridge.

Seeing what was happening, Charlie and Johnny Blue rode at a fast lope toward Shade, their rifles leveled, and with a terrible oath that raging gunman swung his horse around and raked his sharp-roweled spurs along its flanks, drawing blood. His horse bounded away like a jackrabbit and Shade galloped as far as the rise where we'd first caught sight of the battle. He reined up and sat his prancing mount, looking down at me. He didn't yell out, but just raised his arm, his finger pointing straight at my head.

Even when Charlie and Johnny Blue rode to my side, Shade just sat there like the shadow of death, his unwavering finger still pointing and his strange and terrible eyes white as bone in the distance.

Then, as Johnny Blue raised his rifle, the vicious little gunman turned his horse and was gone.

"I believe," Charlie whispered, adding after a lengthy silence, "that we have made a terrifying and vengeful enemy this day."

Boys, if I'd had a crystal ball and been able to foresee the dreadful tragedy and heartbreak Shade Hannah was to visit on me and Johnny Blue, I'd have taken out after him. I'd have followed him to the ends of the earth and then some—and I'd have killed him for sure or died in the attempt. But I didn't know any of those things then, so at the time I was just happy to see him go.

We rode back to the wagon, and except for a bullet burn across his right shoulder, the major was unhurt.

Needless to say he was overjoyed at his deliverance and praised our gallantry to the skies, and even the surviving trooper gave out with a weak Huzzah! before he doubled over and started to puke, being a high-strung young soldier an' all.

Three of Shade's gunmen were dead, including the one I missed but the major hadn't, his chest burst asunder by the impact of the officers unerring ball.

The ranny I'd shot while he was trying to get away was wounded in the hip, and he was cussing so much it made the air around him sulfurous with profanity.

Johnny Blue helped the major and Charlie hog-tie the bleeding prisoner and they threw that outraged outlaw into the back of the wagon. Then Johnny Blue, tall and skinny as a lizard-eating cat, walked with that long stride of his to my side, his frowning face contorted into a question mark.

"What?" I asked.

"Is this something new?" he inquired in turn.

"Is what something new?" I replied, wondering what that lanky rider had up his sleeve this time.

But in that irritating way of his that always chaps my butt, he answered my question with yet another of his own.

"Do you recollect that time you took a notion to shoot everybody's hoss an' leave the whole Montana Territory afoot?"

I still didn't see what he was driving at, but because the major was listening closely to our conversation, I said defensively: "I only shot but two hosses and both times it was a accident. My Colt's gun went off right unexpected an' I plugged 'em."

Johnny Blue, who'd been listening attentively, nodded. "So, after you shot everybody's pony out from under him and we was all walkin', you kinda dropped the idea. But now I reckon you're fixin' to try something new."

"And that might be?" I asked testily.

"Shootin' folks up the ass," Johnny Blue replied.

"You mean the outlaw I plugged?"

"The very same."

"He was bent over the saddle horn at the time. Where else was I gonna shoot him?"

Johnny Blue studied on that for a spell, then he said: "Y'know, you plug some feller through the lungs an' he don't much care, except maybe he reckons that next time he'll need to work on shuckin' his iron faster. But you shoot a feller up the ass an' he'll get mad enough to kick a hog barefoot an' come right after you. One thing Christian folks won't stand for is being plugged in the patoot, an' that's a true fact."

"Hell, that outlaw hombre was bent over the horn so far, all I could aim at was his butt."

Johnny Blue nodded again. "Could be. But if'n I was you, which thank God I ain't, but if'n I was, I'd clean fergit about pluggin' folks up the ass." Johnny Blue shook his head. "If you keep this up, someday you're gonna shoot the wrong feller in the butt an' that'll be the end of you."

Boys, little did that prophetic puncher know just how soon his warning would become a ghastly reality—for my next ass-shooting almost became my last.

As it was, I'll never know if Johnny Blue intended to worry the thing to death, because the major interrupted us. "Boys," he said, "we've got some burying to do."

Well, using a shovel we found in the payroll wagon, we laid them outlaws to rest real nice and Major Donnelly said some fine words over them from the Good Book.

Even though these were outlaws and killers and low

down, me and Johnny Blue were much affected by the major's words and I ended up with a lump in my throat that took me an hour to swallow.

Charlie, being an artistic and thoughtful feller, told us we should weep for men when they're born, not when they die, and that cast a gloom over the funeral for a spell. But we soon cheered up when the major led us in singing that grand old hymn "Shall We Gather at the River" and by the time the burying was over, we were in good spirits again.

We laid the civilian clerk in the wagon with the dead young trooper—who would be buried at the fort in his soldier suit—and Shade's gunman raised a fuss about being in the wagon with two dead men. But we paid him no mind.

The outlaw horses were hitched to the wagon and the remaining trooper took the reins. Then we all mounted up and prepared to return to Fort Shaw in triumph.

But just then a strange thing happened.

A paint pony, saddled and bridled, walked out of an aspen grove about a hundred yards to the west of where Shade and his boys had laid their ambush and began to crop the grass at its feet. Me and Johnny Blue and Charlie rode over to the trees and pretty soon we heard a low moan of a man in pain coming from the underbrush.

We dismounted and followed the sound—and found Andy lying on his back, the front of his shirt scarlet with his own gore.

When that poisonous little killer saw us coming, he tried to draw his gun, but Johnny Blue quickly reached down and took it from his weakening fingers.

"Damn ye all to hell and perdition," Andy groaned. "I was watching the fight when I took a stray round an' it's done for me at last."

"You was following us, Andy," I said. "It was you who was dogging our trail."

The old man cackled, his gray-stubbled cheeks crinkling. "Damn right I was. I was gonna kill all of ye when the time was right. Kill all of ye; then I'd have the woman to myself. I'd hang her. Make her dance a right purty jig jest for ol' Andy."

Charlie shook his head. "Andy, you ain't nothing but a filthy old sinner and you're low down to boot, but your time is close. Better make your peace with God."

The major rode up, dismounted, and stood beside us in time to hear Andy snarl: "Damn God and damn each and every mother son of ye to hell. Ye swindled me, cheated me of my woman. Damn—"

He made a horrible gurgle in his throat; then his eyes opened wide as though he saw something that made him mortally afraid and then he died.

The major ordered us to take the dead man's guns and horse. When I asked him if we should bury Andy where he lay, he shook his head. "This is hallowed ground," he said. "The outlaws we buried were no-accounts, but they were brave enough lads and I'll not lay a man in the same earth who died cursing God and his fellow men. Just leave him where he lies and let nature take its course."

Thus we rode away from that place, leaving Andy, a man who hated God because he so much hated himself, unburied and unmourned.

As we topped the rise above the bloody field that will forever be known as the spot where me and Johnny Blue saved the United States Army from destruction, I once again allowed myself to think of a medal and communicated this intelligence to Charlie.

Charlie was silent for a while. "It's possible," he said at length, nodding sagely. "Men of my acquaintance have received medals for very much less."

Johnny Blue was scowling, looking at me suspiciously as he tried to make out what me and Charlie were talking about. But I knew better than mention a medal to him a second time, so I kept my mouth shut and didn't open it again until we rode triumphantly into Fort Shaw in the gathering darkness, heroes all.

"Arrest those men!"

The colonel stood in the street outside his office, surrounded by a group of burly Buffalo Soldiers. A huge sergeant reached up and yanked me from my horse, and I could see the same thing was happening to Johnny Blue and Charlie.

Charlie struggled violently with the two soldiers who held him and yelled at the colonel as he swung his fists at his captors: "This is an outrage!"

"Here it comes," Johnny Blue whispered under his breath.

There was a dreadful thud as one of the soldiers bent his rifle barrel over Charlie's head and that pathetic painter pitched to the ground with a horrible cry.

"Why are you arresting us, Colonel?" I asked, trying not to hear the hideous moans issuing from Charlie's open and drooling mouth. "Major Donnelly can explain everything."

"Bring those men to my office," the colonel ordered, ignoring me. "I'll deal with them there."

But then Major Donnelly rushed to the colonel's side, and those two officers had a heated and agitated discussion, with much finger pointing in our direction.

Finally the colonel waved a hand toward his men. "Bring them," he said.

The colonel's office was a large, well-furnished room with a carpet on the floor and an oil lamp burning brightly above his mahogany desk.

But what immediately took my eye was the huge woman who stood beside the desk, her hands on her hips, scowling at us as we were pushed inside. Boys, if that lady had been able to fit into a pair of pants, I swear her butt would have stretched two ax handles wide from hip pocket to hip pocket.

Her face was set in an angry, self-righteous grimace like she'd been raised on nothing but prunes and prophecy, and the colonel, when he saw me looking at her, introduced her as "my lady wife."

"It was my intention," he said, "to turn you boys over to the civil authorities charged with horse thievery, a crime that calls for hanging in this territory. However"—he waved a hand toward Major Donnelly—"the major here has told me what happened on the road and that makes me inclined toward leniency."

The colonel's lady harrumphed and declared: "Ha, here's leniency indeed. Better to send them to the gallows, Matthew, I say."

"Hush, my dear," the colonel said mildly. "This is an Army matter."

That dear lady fell into a vexed silence, though she continued to look daggers at me and Johnny Blue.

Charlie, who had somewhat recovered from his latest brush with a gun barrel, said groggily: "Then we are free to go."

The colonel nodded. "Not only free, but with my advice to get as far and as fast from Fort Shaw as you can before I change my mind." The colonel reached into a desk drawer and brought out a long, slim cigar. He stood and lighted it from the oil lamp. When he regained his seat, he said: "I must admit, Mr. Russell, that I'm somewhat surprised to see an artist of your burgeoning reputation in the company of these two"—he nodded toward me and Johnny Blue—"scalawags."

"Scalawags indeed," echoed the lady wife. "There's an apt name for such as them." She surveyed me and Johnny

Blue with ferocious contempt. "Born to end up on the gallows, I say."

Charlie pulled himself up to his full impressive height and drew his much-tattered dignity around himself like a cloak. "Madam," he said, "these boys are artist's assistants. And though I agree that they're not much to look upon, they are engaged in an ancient and honorable profession and deserve a degree of respect."

"La," said the lady wife, "respect indeed!" She turned to her husband, her several chins wobbling. "Matthew, let them get their comeuppance and be done with it, I say."

Now while all this was going on, Johnny Blue was studying that fat lady closely, and I had a horrible feeling he was fixing to say something that would send her into a fit.

He didn't disappoint me.

"Excuse me, ma'am," quoth that reckless cavalier, "before we leave, do you think we could have some tea?" He smiled, those big white teeth of his shiny as an open mussel shell in the light of the colonel's oil lamp. "An' maybe some of them Army fairy cakes."

The lady wife looked like she'd been slapped. Boys, she must have gone three hundred pounds on the hoof, but she staggered back a few steps, her eyes fixed on Johnny Blue in mute astonishment like he'd just crawled out from under a rock.

"Mat-thew," she gasped, "he just invited himself to tea. And"—that large lady swayed like a ponderosa pine in the wind—"he's a *black man*!"

"She's going down!" Charlie cried in alarm.

The colonel rushed to his wife's side, yelling for an orderly. He put his arm around her huge waist.

"Are you ill, my precious?" he inquired.

"Faint," replied the lady. "Very faint. Tea! Matthew, he asked for tea!"

"I know, I know, my love," the Colonel soothed. "Pay him no mind."

The orderly rushed into the office and took in the situation at a glance. He ran to the fat lady's side and she in turn glanced behind her and saw that the colonel's overstuffed leather couch had been moved some distance against the far wall.

She now staggered rearward in that direction, pulling the colonel and his orderly with her. When she figured it was safe, she put the back of her right wrist against her forehead and swooned onto the couch with a jangling crash that rattled the rafters, the sweating soldiers landing in an untidy heap on top of her.

The orderly sprang to his feet, yelping like he'd been stung, and the colonel rolled off his lady and kneeled by her side, taking a hand the size of a ham hock into his own. He proceeded to rub her wrist frantically as he urgently inquired as to her state of consciousness.

"If that fat lady had gone down," Johnny Blue observed quietly, "it would've been like trying to lift an elephant tusk with the elephant still attached."

I don't know if she heard, but the lady in question opened one eye, glared at Johnny Blue from a single hazel eyeball, then called out for whiskey and our immediate execution.

The colonel sprang to his feet, obeying one order but ignoring the other.

He returned to his wife's side with four fingers of bourbon in a glass, which she drained with gusto. "Thank you, Matthew," she said after a few moments of deep meditation, "I believe I'm feeling very much recovered." She opened both eyes and glared at me and Johnny Blue. "Now shoot them, Matthew." Adding with stern emphasis, "Gun them down like the mangy curs they are."

The colonel turned to us and roared: "Out! Out, all three

of you—and don't let me see your faces in Fort Shaw
again!"

"Shoot them, Matthew," pleaded the lady wife in a qua-
vering voice.

But the colonel murmured: "There, there, my dear,
you're overwrought. Just relax. I know you've been through
a great deal."

"More whiskey, Matthew," whispered the fat lady. "I
confess I'm quite undone."

Once outside, we found our horses saddled and waiting,
the young lieutenant and Major Donnelly standing beside
them.

The major extended his hand to Charlie, which he shook,
and then to me and Johnny Blue. "I want to thank you
boys again," he said. "You saved my life out there, to say
nothing of the Army payroll. If I'm ever in a position to
do you a favor, all you have to do is ask."

Charlie said thankee most kindly and it were a pleasure
and we'd do it all again if'n we had to and that the major
was a right nice feller and anyhow we was only doing our
duty as responsible citizens.

"And I hope," said that patriotic painter to the lieutenant,
"that our little adventure won't get you in too much trouble."

That officer smiled and said he wasn't concerned because he'd put in for a transfer to the Arizona Territory
anyhow. And if that didn't pan out, he was thinking of
going into his uncle's hardware business in Missouri, nails
and pots and buckets being just the ticket for a bright young
feller to get ahead.

Thus assured, we three mounted and rode out of Fort
Shaw under a bright canopy of stars just as taps played,
the haunting notes of the bugle echoing in the crystal darkness like silver chimes in a prairie wind.

Nine

We planned to get well away from Fort Shaw and the colonel and his bloodthirsty wife before making camp for the night. Then we'd pick up our packhorse and swing north into Blackfoot country.

As we rode, Charlie told us that, in 1873, President Grant had signed an executive order that set aside for the Blackfoot, Gros Ventre, Assiniboine, and Sioux all of northern Montana from the Continental Divide to the Dakota line, with the southern boundary of the huge reservation running along the Missouri and Sun Rivers.

But a year later, in 1874, the government moved the southern boundary of the Blackfoot Territory northward from the Sun to the Marias River, depriving the tribe of most of their best hunting grounds.

By the mid-1870s, the Blackfoot and Gros Ventre had been pushed north of the Missouri. This arrangement pleased Montana whites, for it opened the lush grasslands of the Judith Basin to ranchers like Granville Stuart of the old DHS.

For the Indians, it meant a narrowing of horizons and a deepening dependence on the federal government. But an indifferent Congress and an Indian Bureau riddled with corruption often failed to provide the food and annuities promised by treaty.

"Today the Blackfoot face a hard and depressing future," Charlie said as we made camp and put coffee on to boil, using a rusty battered pot, a gift from the U.S. Army. "In fact they don't have any future at all. That's why I want to put their way of life on canvas before they go the way of the buffalo and the whole Indian country is plowed under and occupied by chicken chasers."

Boys, it was a depressing thought, and as we picked up the packhorse then rode north to meet up with White Quiver and his band on the Judith, I kept thinking that the cowboy's days were numbered just like the Indian's, and that we were a bunch of uncivilized, freedom-loving rannies who'd simply outlived our time.

As for Johnny Blue, I don't think he thought of anything at all but Lo May. He kept taking out that little flower, withered now, and he'd moon over it and press it to his lips. Boys, he even stood around the place where Lo May's wagon had sat, turning his head this way and that like he half expected her to suddenly run laughing out of the trees and into his arms. That pining puncher was a sick man with a bad case of calico fever.

We rode due north for three days after leaving our old camp, and as it happened, we didn't find White Quiver—he found us.

A dozen or so armed and mounted Blackfoot, all of them wearing braids and naked except for breechclouts and moccasins, surrounded our little party and with much hallooing and downright aggressive jostling, they herded us toward their village.

Them Indians was all young, little more than half-grown boys, the older warriors having long since left their bones on battlefields all over the northwest, especially on the Marias River in '70. As Charlie told it as we rode, hemmed in by those whooping Indian boys, General Philip H. Sheridan, who'd made a name for himself during the War Between the States, took a notion to declare "total war" against the Blackfoot.

"Sheridan ordered Major Eugene M. Baker at Fort Ellis to move out against the Indian villages," Charlie continued. "He telegraphed Baker to 'strike 'em hard,' and that's exactly what that soldier did. In bitter, subzero cold, he led four companies of the Second Cavalry and two infantry companies from Fort Shaw to an unsuspecting Blackfoot camp on the Marias.

"Baker, who was as drunk as a pig, attacked at dawn on the terribly cold morning of January 23. In the massacre that followed, a hundred and seventy-three unarmed Indians, including fifty-three women and children, were shot and sabered to death. There were others, because when Baker discovered that some of the captive women and children had smallpox, he turned them out into the snow to die."

Charlie shook his head sadly, "I knew one of them dead Indians, a chief called Heavy Runner. When Baker attacked, the old man rushed out of his teepee brandishing a government paper that testified to his good character. They shot him down like a dog in the snow and shoved the paper down his throat."

Waving a hand toward the Indians surrounding us, Charlie added: "So if these boys don't look too friendly, now you know one of the many reasons why."

"What happened to that Baker ranny?" I asked. "He was woman killer an' low down."

"Oh, he was hailed as a conquering hero and they give him a gold bravery medal," Charlie said.

"Wonder if he wore it to tea?" observed Johnny Blue, looking hard at me.

And I resolved right there and then never to mention bravery medals again.

Boys, when we rode into the Indian village in the spring

of '88, the old, glory days of the Red Man were long gone. Where once stood tall lodges covered in painted buffalo hide and vast pony herds, now there were sway-backed, Army-issue canvas tents, broken-down buckboards, and a few scrawny mustangs grazing here and there on the spring grass.

There were no barking dogs to greet us because they'd all been eaten during the winter, but dozens of children came out of the tents to stare solemnly at us with huge dark eyes as we rode past.

The village, maybe home to around two hundred people, lay on the south side of the Judith, where the river made a sharp bend around a high clay bank. About a hundred yards to the north rose a sheer bluff, its top crowned with a stand of mixed fir and aspen. To the west lay another bend of the river, shaded here and there by well-grown cottonwoods, and to the east the village was open to a vast plain of buffalo grass and wildflowers that stretched as far as the eye could see.

It was a pleasant enough place for a camp, though we'd seen no game for days and I reckoned you could bet the farm that those Indians weren't eating too good.

The Indian boys crowded us toward a large, conical Sibley tent with a smoking stovepipe sticking out the top, and here we halted.

"This is White Quiver's lodge," Charlie said. "Now we got to do some palavering."

Boys, you remember how Indians always cottoned to me—mostly because I could talk their lingo real good—so when we walked into the smoky gloom of the tent and beheld a figure wrapped in an Army blanket sitting near the stove, I didn't waste any time in getting down to the brass tacks. Before Charlie could say a word, I addressed that robed figure in the ringing tones much admired by the wild Indian. "Hail, great chief of the Blackfoot nation," quoth

I. "Howdy-do an' well met." White Quiver didn't look up, but muttered wearily: "Yeah, yeah, right back at ya."

But then he stirred, turning his head as his eyes tried to penetrate the fog of wood smoke. "That voice," he said in a low, tremulous whisper, "I recollect that voice."

He turned to face me and in that instant we recognized each other—White Quiver was the chief who'd given us a little help in our final battle against Amos Pinkney and his gang!

I grinned at him like a possum eating persimmons, about to give another cheerful howdy as old friends do, but that sentimental savage buried his face in his hands and groaned: "Oh God, it's you!"

That chief, he was always funnin' so I knew that deep down he was really happy to see me again.

"All hail, great chief," I began again, but Charlie cut me off right quick.

"I'll take it from here, if you don't mind," he said.

He sat cross-legged on the floor and me and Johnny Blue joined him.

Charlie quickly outlined the purpose of our expedition, his hands busily waving in the air. He put great emphasis on the fact that Jeb Anthony had a herd of eight prime ponies he was ready and willing to exchange for the hand of White Quiver's daughter—just as soon as he gave the okay to her picture and determined that he and the chief were dancin' to the same fiddler.

White Quiver heard all this in perfect silence, and when Charlie was finished speechifying, he said: "Russell, Wapiti Fawn is a good cook and she keeps a clean lodge. But she sure as hell ain't no oil painting."

Boys, that chief could speak American nearly as good as me. Once when we was hunting Amos Pinkney, I asked him how come, and as near as I can recollect he said: "Custer and Crook and Bearcoat Miles an' the rest, they

taught Indians how to speak American pretty damn quick."
An' he was talking good American right now as he told
Charlie that his daughter had another suitor who was right
anxious to have her share his blanket.

"He's a mountain man," White Quiver said. "Short feller.
Horny little cuss. Goes by the name of Paul le Homme.
Me and him is dickering for his brand new Winchester gun
and sixty rounds of ammunition."

The chief shrugged. "But given my druthers, I'd rather
have the ponies." He waved a hand and added with a dis-
mal groan: "As you can see, the Blackfoot are no longer
rich in horses."

Just then a homely looking young squaw walked into
the tent bearing a smoking cooking pot and some wooden
bowls.

"Eat," the chief said. "Then we'll talk some more."

Indians are naturally a hospitable folk, and even though
those Blackfoot were mighty hungry after the long winter,
the woman filled our bowls with what looked like government salt pork cooked with wild onions.

The food was good, even though the pork had a green-
ish tinge and didn't smell real good if you brought it too
close to your nose.

While we were eating, the chief kept looking closely at
me, until finally he said: "I couldn't recollect if I'd shot
you or not. I guess I didn't."

I laughed. "You're funnin' me, chief. You was a real
good help to us in that fight against Amos Pinkney, playing your part honest an' true. I don't think we could've
done nearly as good without you and your boys."

The chief grunted in reply and turned to Johnny Blue.
"And what about you, buffalo man—did the scars on your
back heal?"

"Some did, some didn't," Johnny Blue answered. "A
man doesn't forget a whipping real easy."

The chief nodded, motioning with his bowl toward me. "You ride with low companions. It seems to me that is the beginning and will be the end of your troubles."

Johnny Blue allowed that the chief was right and that low companions were a trial and an affliction to a man. "Although," he added thoughtfully, "I had a good mother."

Charlie placed his bowl at his feet and said with an air of finality: "Now, White Quiver, if it's all the same to you, I'll get my gear and start painting Wapiti Fawn. If Jeb Anthony likes what he sees, I reckon we can be back with the ponies in three or four days." Charlie rubbed his hands together. "Now, can I meet the young lady?"

White Quiver looked at Charlie as though he pitied his ignorance. "Meet her? You've already met her. Russell, it was my daughter who served the food."

Johnny Blue looked at me in alarm. "I don't reckon that little gal's gonna set too good with ol' Jeb Anthony," he whispered. "She's downright homely."

"Maybe so," I replied.

"Maybe so! If I woke with her asleep on my arm, I'd chew it off rather than wake her up."

I didn't let Johnny Blue see how worried I was right then. If the big wolfer chief didn't like the picture of Wapiti Fawn, he was liable to get mad and hang Dora—and us with her.

Glancing over at Charlie, I saw that he looked like he didn't have a care in the world. "She's a charming young lady, White Quiver," he beamed. "And a credit to you."

The chief, that melancholy prince of the plains, merely shrugged. "Like I already told you, she's no oil painting."

Charlie sprang to his feet. "Well, it's settled then. I'll get started right away."

White Quiver made no move except to raise his red-rimmed eyes and look at Charlie. "Haven't you forgotten something?"

Charlie denied any amnesia on his part, replying that he was well supplied with paints, brushes, and canvas and was right anxious to get busy.

The chief shook his head sadly. "How far must the Blackfoot have fallen when an old friend no longer thinks it necessary to bring presents."

At this sober intelligence, Charlie snapped his fingers and said: "White Quiver, how remiss of me. Of course I bear presents. It . . . just somehow slipped my mind."

He turned and stomped out of the tent, and through the open flap I saw him walk to the packhorse. He rummaged around for a few minutes then returned with a bowie knife and one of them forged iron tomahawk pipes the Indians set such great store by in them olden days.

The chief grunted as he accepted these gifts, then held them near to the stove, closely examining the blade of the knife where it joined the staghorn handle.

"Both were made in Sheffield," Charlie said.

"Sheff-ield," White Quiver nodded as he read the name on the blade. He then looked at the tomahawk and smiled. "Good, Russell. Sheffield."

"The chief will have no truck with American blades," Charlie whispered. "He knows the best steel in the world is made in Sheffield, England." To the chief he said: "I'm glad the gifts meet with White Quiver's approval. Carry them in good health."

"They're little enough," the chief muttered. He waved a hand at Charlie. "Now go do what you have to do and"— he chopped the air with the tomahawk in the direction of me and Johnny Blue—"take these two galoots with you."

Well, boys, we hung around that Indian village for the rest of that day and most of the next while Charlie was busy painting that Indian maiden. White Quiver came out of his lodge a couple of times to see how the work was going, and each time he'd walk away shaking his head in disbelief.

The chief was well aware that his daughter had a face that would wilt knee-high cotton, and maybe he realized he'd a mighty slim chance of ever seeing them eight paint ponies.

Charlie wouldn't let me and Johnny Blue see the painting until it was done, saying he never let critics look at a work in progress—unless it was White Quiver who had vested interest in the proceedings and who tended to be one mean Indian if he was crossed.

Then on the early evening of the second day Charlie carried the finished picture from the village to the bend in the riverbank where we'd made our camp.

"Well, boys, what do you think?" he asked proudly, holding up the canvas for our inspection. Me and Johnny Blue just stood there and gawped.

It was Wapiti Fawn all right, but it wasn't her, if you know what I mean.

Charlie had pulled her dress off her left shoulder so it was naked, and she was looking over that shapely expanse of pink skin with a shy smile on her face, a fan of eagle feathers held coyly to her half-exposed breast.

"Damn," Johnny Blue swore, "but if that ain't as pretty as a speckled pup under a wagon."

"But . . . but . . ." I spluttered, "but Charlie, it ain't her. You've taken a little gal who has to slap her legs to get them to go to bed with her an' turned her into a . . . a . . ." I was trying desperately to find the right word and finally came up with: "An angel!"

Charlie, his professional pride stung, said: "Well, that's how I see her. She's got a lot of inner beauty, that little darlin', and if you look at her close enough, it shines through like the gleam of a new-minted penny."

"But Jeb Anthony said he didn't want to buy a pig in

a poke," I protested. "What's this, if'n it ain't promising a lot more than we can deliver?"

Charlie shook his head. "That oaf wanted a picture of his beloved, and that's what I've done. This is how I see her and he'll have to be content with that."

I stood there, my jaw on my chest, and right then I knew we were in a heap of trouble.

The Indians called Charlie a great magician because of what he could do with paint, and this picture proved it. He wasn't an artist—he was a damned sorcerer.

"If we let Jeb Anthony see this beautiful painting and then present him with the real, homely Wapiti Fawn, he'll be so mad he'll hang us all," I said. "Charlie, believe me, this ain't gonna fly."

Charlie carefully laid the painting down beside his blankets. "We've done what he asked," he said. "He won't fault us for that."

Then he lay down and within minutes he was in a deep and untroubled sleep.

I looked at Johnny Blue. "We're done for," I said, letting my voice sink to a confidential whisper. "An' that's the truth."

That mooning rider rolled his eyes, fished in his shirt pocket, and took the little withered flower from his tally book. He looked at it tenderly and shook his head, a great shuddering moan escaping his lips.

And I figured he reckoned on never seeing Lo May again.

Ten

When we rode into the wolfer camp, nothing had changed, except Dora looked dirty and unkempt, her dress stained with grease from the hard work them Flathead women had forced on her at the cooking pots.

As we rode past, she pushed a strand of hair from her forehead and stood there watching us, her blue eyes hard as chunks of quartz.

"How are you faring, Dora?" Charlie asked.

"Just get me the hell out of here," replied that surly soiled dove.

"Soon," Charlie said, "real soon."

"It can't be soon enough for me," Dora snapped. "Being a slave to these . . . these animals is doing nothing for my acting career."

"Be patient, Dora," Charlie said. "Your captivity is close to an end."

Curtis Boone stood outside the cabin, watching us come, a couple of wolfers carrying rifles alert and ready on each side of him.

When we dismounted, he asked: "Did any of you rannies see Andy? He took off out of here just after you did."

Charlie told Boone about our fight with Shade Hannah and how Andy had taken a stray bullet, dying like a mad dog in the buffalo grass.

Boone, having no love for Shade, shrugged. "A man

takes the outlaw path, he lives with the consequences. As for Andy, he was crazy as a loon and no good. He hung people just to see them kick, and I reckon the world is better off without him."

"It is," Charlie said earnestly. "There's no doubt about that."

Changing the subject, Andy totally forgotten now that he was dead, Boone asked: "Did you make the picture?"

"I have it right here," Charlie replied, tapping his fingers on the front of his shirt. "Safe and sound." Boone told us to wait and he disappeared into the cabin. He came to the door a few seconds later and beckoned us inside.

If anything, the place stank worse than it did when we left. Jeb Anthony still lay in his filthy bed, his red hair and beard matted with bits of stale food and spilled whiskey. There were great black circles under his eyes and his face was gaunt with pain. Every time the giant moved, he groaned as his busted legs punished him something terrible.

The cabin reeked like a buzzard's breath. Roaches scuttled across the floor and I heard the squeak of a rat from one of the dark corners.

"Did you make the picture?" he asked Charlie in a weak, broken voice.

Charlie made no reply. He opened the top button of his shirt and pulled out the canvas, gingerly passing it to the wolfer chief.

Jeb called for a light and Boone brought a smoking oil lamp closer to the bed.

The big wolfer studied the painting for a long spell, then looked up at Charlie, his eyes alight.

"She is even more than I expected, more beautiful than the dawn." He studied the painting again. "Oh my beloved, my dear, my dearly beloved."

Boone asked to see the picture, but Jeb waved him away.

"Begone, wretch," he exclaimed. "This is not for a lustful hog like you to drool over. You'll see my princess soon enough."

Boone looked hurt. "Hell, boss," he said, "I only wanted to look at her, not fu—"

"Desist!" Jeb yelled. "Don't dare to say that awful word in the presence of my angel."

He looked hard at Boone until that tough wolfer shuffled his feet and seemed downright uneasy, especially since Jeb had a holstered Colt on the floor near his bunk, half a dozen notches cut into the walnut handle that he didn't put there for whittling practice.

"Boone," he said. "Come here." Jeb struggled to sit up in his bed and grabbed his second in command by the front of his buckskin shirt. "Boone, there is love like a small lamp that goes out when the oil is consumed. Or like a stream that dries up when it doesn't rain. But there is a love like a mighty spring gushing up out of the earth—it keeps flowing forever and is inexhaustible. That"—he jammed a thick forefinger into Boone's chest—"is the love I feel for this woman. Now, do you understand?"

"Sure do," replied that wary wolfer. "No offense, Jeb."

Jebedaiah Anthony sighed. "None taken. Now, Boone, tell these rannies to hasten back to the Blackfoot village and return with my snookums."

"You heard the boss," Boone said. "It's time to ride."

Charlie harrumphed and addressed Jeb in these exasperated terms: "Now look here, mister . . . mister whatever-you-call-yourself, we've lived up to our part of the bargain. Now all you have to do is release Dora and dispatch one of your own men for your new bride."

Jeb was aghast. "You want me to send one of my rabble to fetch this"—he waved the canvas—"this beautiful creature? I'd rather trust a ravening wolf!"

The stricken chieftain cut loose with a terrible oath and

dropped his eyes once again to the painting, his finger tracing the outline of Wapiti Fawn's naked shoulder and the shapely in-curve of her lower back.

"You," he said to Charlie finally, "I trust you, but only because I hold your own woman hostage." He waved a dismissive hand. "Now go—bring me my love."

We were walking toward the door, Charlie's face bright red with anger, when Jeb called us back. "Wait," he said, "I almost forgot. I've written an ode to my sweetheart"— he reached under his stained pillow—"read this to her and tell her it comes straight from my impatient heart."

Jeb handed a grubby sheet of notepaper with some pencil scribblings on it to Charlie; then he said—and I swear that hardcase blushed—"You can read it if you like."

Charlie scanned the paper and after a few moments' pause he exclaimed rapturously: "Art. This is pure art."

"You really think so?" inquired Jeb.

"Think so and indeed say so," retorted Charlie. He passed the poem to me. "Read this."

I've read some poetry in my life, especially up in the ol' DHS line shacks in the winter when there was nothing to read but that big fat book *The World's Greatest Poems for Young Readers*. It seems every cattle ranch between the Canadian border and the Brazos bought that book in carload lots.

But, boys, I'd never read poetry as beautiful as the one written by Jeb Anthony. As I recollect, it looked and went something like this:

> Haste to my side my beloved,
> Tho' the way be long and rugged.
> I'd love to come to you my dear,
> But both my legs is buggered.
>
> I yearn to see yore lovely face,

And feel yore warm, sweet embrace.
It's oft I think of you my dear,
You Member of the Blackfoot race.

I plan to make you My Queen
Even tho' I'm buying you sight unseen.
Still, I'm very sure my dear,
You'll be my Bonny Jean.

Touched to the quick, I dashed away a tear and handed
the poem to Johnny Blue. That sentimental rider read it,
his lips moving, and when he finished, his voice was unsteady: "That poetry beats all I ever knew or ever heard
tell of," he said. "Jeb, you're a word wrangler. No doubt
about that."

"I do what I can," replied that winsome wolfer. "Now
beat it."

Boys, I'm not going to weary you with the details of
our journey back to the Blackfoot village, herding them
unbroke, ornery ponies. Suffice to say a frog in a skillet
would have had more fun than we did, what with them
nags constantly breaking away from the herd and trying
their best to kick and bite us right into a funeral home.

But the chief was right glad to see us again and he sure
set store by them ponies, sending that horny Canadian
mountain man and his Winchester gun sulking back into
the woods.

As we rode out of the Indian village with Wapiti Fawn,
I kept everybody's spirits up by singing "Oh Dem Golden
Slippers," which was a right popular song in them days.

And when I turned in the saddle—grinning as friendly
as you please—to see how White Quiver was enjoying the
tune, that sentimental paladin of the prairie had his hands
to his ears, maybe to hear me better. Then he picked up

his rifle right smartly, pretending to aim it at my head. He was always funnin', that chief, and I wish him well, wherever he is. He really cottoned to me a lot.

That Blackfoot gal was just as homely as when we'd left her. And she could talk the ears off a cigar store Indian, babbling away from can't see to can't see in her native language that only Charlie seemed to understand.

"She's a talker all right," Charlie said. "But mainly she's telling me that you two smell like hogs and have the table manners of pigs. Stuff like that."

Well, a man doesn't like to be told he smells like the business end of a polecat, but it was only when we were two days out of the Indian village and making good time south that things really got out of hand.

And Johnny Blue got the worst of it.

We were camped by a small mountain creek in a stand of cottonwoods and Johnny Blue was slicing bacon into the frying pan nice and thin when that little gal took out after him, screeching a blue streak. She had a switch that she'd cut from a tree and she was hollering at him something fierce, laying the switch across his back, raising puffs of dust off his shirt at every whack,

"Woman, have you gone nuts?" Johnny Blue bellered, jumping away from that switch right smartly. He turned to Charlie and yelled desperately: "What's gotten into this crazy Injun?" Charlie laughed and slapped his thigh. "She says you smell worse than a wet buffalo and she ain't going to eat anything you cook because you're so dirty. She wants you to take a bath in the creek right now."

"The hell I will!" Johnny Blue yelled, dodging that switch. "This is only spring and I ain't scheduled for an all-over bath till July."

Boys, it was a real funny sight to see that little Indian gal chasing Johnny Blue, swiping at him with her switch.

But then she came right at me, and I hid behind Charlie's big shoulders. "She's crazy," I told him as she tried her best to reach around Charlie and whack me. "She's gone plumb loco in the head."

Charlie laughed all the louder, wiping tears from his eyes. "If'n if I was you boys," he gasped, "I'd do as she says. She ain't going to stop with that switch until you're both so clean your own mothers wouldn't know you by sight or smell."

But at that moment Wapiti Fawn sighed loudly and dropped her switch, and for a spell I thought we'd escaped with nothing worse than a good scare.

But the situation suddenly took a turn for the worse.

Johnny Blue's rifle had been lying by the fire and she dived on it and picked it up, cranking a round into the chamber.

Charlie's laugh was a real belly shaker. "Hell, boys, now she really means business," he roared. The Indian gal yelled something that sounded mean and Charlie laughed even harder. "She says if'n you boys don't strip off and bathe, she's gonna burn some powder an' pump you full of lead."

"She wouldn't do that," I told Charlie. And I hollered over at Johnny Blue: "She wouldn't do that. Trust me."

BLAM! BLAM! BLAM!

The crazy little gal smoked Johnny Blue's boots and that startled rider began to dance like a bobber on a fishing line, shucking off his clothes as he went.

"She's loco!" he yelled. "Goddammit, better do as she says or she'll plug you fer sure!"

"The hell I will!" I yelled.

BLAM! BLAM! BLAM!

Them big .44.40 bullets kicked up plumes of dust just inches from my toes and the next thing I knew, me and

Johnny Blue is dancing to the same crazy fiddler, shirts and pants and long johns flying through the air.

Charlie was hoorawing like a double-jawed hyena—until Wapiti Fawn turned the rifle on him and ordered him to shuck.

"Wait," Charlie yelled, waving his hands in front of him, "I don't need a bath, dear lady. See, I had—"

BLAM! BLAM! BLAM!

Charlie's duds were soon following ours, and he ran to the creek as nekkid as a jaybird and jumped in, gasping in numb shock as the cold water hit him. Keeping a wary eye on that Indian gal and her Winchester, me and Johnny Blue joined him right quick.

The water, coming off a snow melt high in the mountains, was cold as an outhouse seat in January, but all three of us sat in it, our private parts immediately shriveling up like shelled walnuts in a general store barrel.

Wapiti Fawn went to the packhorse and got a bar of lye soap, which she threw to us. Then she gathered up our clothes, got them good and wet, and began to pound them on a flat rock sticking out of the creek bed.

We was just sitting there watching her, but that homely little gal did a mime, lifting her arm and pretending to wash under it with the soap. When we didn't make a move, she stomped toward that Winchester again and we began to lather up right quick.

Later, shivering in blankets by the fire as our clothes dried, the three of us ate bacon and beans and glared at that Indian gal, each of us thinking up at least a dozen agonizing ways to punch her ticket to the hereafter.

But Wapiti Fawn just sat there, combing her long black hair, singing some heathen Indian song as though she hadn't tried to murder us all just an hour before.

Boys, that little woman was so cold-blooded, just one drop from her veins would've frozen a frog.

"Well," Charlie said thoughtfully, chewing on a mouthful of beans as he studied that nonchalant maiden, "the way I see it, at least we're nice and clean."

And Johnny Blue replied simply: "Fuck you, Charlie."

Eleven

Boys, as we rode into the wolfer camp, the moment I'd dreaded for so long was finally here. When Jebedaiah Anthony saw his real-life bride, all hell was gonna break loose and it would take a miracle for us to escape the rope.

If I'd had my druthers, I'd have lit a shuck away from there, especially since I didn't like Dora that much anyhow. But Charlie had that sense of honor artists catch like a cold, and even Johnny Blue had no such thoughts. He rode in front of me and tugged at the seat of his pants as he grumbled: "Dammit, my duds don't fit me any longer."

"That's because they're clean," Charlie said. "Give them another three or four months and they'll fit just fine."

Wapiti Fawn rode between me and Charlie, her eyes modestly downcast as befits a new bride, and before long we had a whole procession of people following us, including Dora, who looked grubbier and meaner than ever, wolfers, their Flathead women, and a passel of noisy younkers. Curtis Boone waited for us outside the cabin, beaming a smile that stretched from ear to ear. He walked up to our little party and gallantly helped Wapiti Fawn from her broken-down mustang. Still beaming, he put his hand under her chin and lifted up her head—and his smile turned into a grimace of horror.

He looked up at Charlie, who was still sitting his horse and gasped: "Wha . . . wha . . . ?"

"Allow me to introduce Wapiti Fawn," Charlie said pompously. "A princess by blood of the Blackfoot nation."

"Wha . . . wha . . . ?" Boone gasped, grabbing at his chest as he staggered a few steps backward.

"She's come a long way, and I'm sure she's anxious to meet her groom," said Charlie, laying down the obvious.

It seemed Boone couldn't tear his horrified gaze from the Indian gal's homely features. His eyes bugging, he again gasped: "Wha . . . wha . . . ?"

"If that's all you have to say, Boone," Charlie said, "I reckon we'll be standing here all night."

The big wolfer shook his head, trying to recover his composure. "You boys . . . you boys are so deep in the shit. Oh, I can't even begin to tell you how deep in the shit you are."

Johnny Blue looked at me out of the corner of his eye. "That's always good to hear," he whispered.

As for me, I was filled with a sense of foreboding as I dismounted and joined the others at the door of the cabin.

Boone made it clear that he wasn't going in by himself because he might get himself shot just as soon as Jeb laid an eye on his bride.

"With you all in there, he'll have more targets," he explained gloomily. "Spread them bullets around."

Boys, it was all over pretty sudden.

Jeb Anthony, lying like a hog in a wallow, kept looking from Charlie's canvas to the real thing standing right there in front of him, his bearded jaw dropped to his chest.

"Wha . . . wha . . . ?" he gasped.

"Allow me to present Wapiti Fawn," said Charlie proudly. "Your princess bride. And"—he added majestically—"she loved your poem."

"Wha . . . wha . . . ?" Jeb slumped back in his bunk, a stricken look on his face. He turned to Boone and muttered in a broken voice: "I pray you, Boone. Whiskey!"

That obedient desperado hurried to a shelf on the wall and picked up a jug, hurrying back to Jeb's bedside. The wolfer chief pulled the cork and glugged down a mighty draught. Then he wiped his mouth with the back of his hand and looked at Charlie, his eyes murderous. "This was ill done," he snarled, adding a terrible oath.

Charlie drew himself up to his full height and snorted in indignation.

"Listen, mister whatever-your-name-is, let me tell you something about beauty," he said. "The bottom line of true beauty is that it increases upon examination. If it is false, it lessens. Now, look again upon this maiden and tell me that she is not beautiful."

Now two things happened right then that kinda dropped the bottom out of Charlie's little speech. First, Jeb looked at the picture again then back to his bride and at the picture again and back to his bride, took another pull at the jug, and roared: "You showed me the picture of an angel, then, God damn your eyes, brung me a two sacker! I'm personally going to string up all of you for this."

Boys, in them days a two sacker was what was said about a right ugly woman. It meant if you put a sack over her head, you ought to put on two—just in case one of them fell off.

"He's right, you know," Johnny Blue whispered. "That little gal is a two sacker if ever I seen one." I was about to say something right sharp to Johnny Blue, but then the second thing happened, worse than the first.

Wapiti Fawn began to scream at Jeb. She grabbed the jug from his trembling hands, threw it in a corner, then stood there with her hands on her hips, blattin' like a momma blue jay protecting her nest.

Charlie, who was already bristling with anger, said to Jeb: "She's says you're a filthy pig and you smell like a bouquet of stinkweed and you're low down and she's sorry she ever took you for a husband."

"I know what she's saying," Jeb replied angrily. "I can talk Blackfoot."

Then things got rapidly out of hand.

That little Indian gal's fangs were flashing and her nails were twitchin'. She ran over to the filthy wood stove and grabbed a horn ladle. Then she stomped back to Jeb's bed and began to belabor him around the shoulders, screaming all the while in her heathen native tongue.

"Get this rabble out of here, Boone!" he yelled, trying to dodge the blows raining on him. "I'll attend to their hanging personally." He swung open-handed at Wapiti Fawn, but that nimble creature sidestepped his blow easily. "I'll deal with this woman myself."

"Now see here," said Charlie. "Leave that little gal alone, you lout. This is an outrage."

"Oh God," Johnny Blue whispered. "Not again."

Boone bent the barrel of his Colt over Charlie's head and that palavering painter dashed to the ground with a horrible cry.

The big wolfer slung Charlie over his shoulder and prodded the rest of us out of the cabin at gunpoint. He stood at the doorway, Charlie drooling at the mouth and babbling nonsense, and yelled to all and sundry: "Necktie party!"

Once again the fiddler struck up a lively tune and the Flathead women threw meat in the cooking pots as jugs passed around the grinning wolfers and we were again bundled into the empty horse corral—pathetic prisoners once again.

From the cabin there came a series of terrible crashes and bangs, and above it all the angry roar of Jeb Anthony and the terrible screeching of Wapiti Fawn.

"Oh my God, he's killing her in there," I said.

"Or she's killing him," Johnny Blue suggested.

Charlie was sitting on the ground, his battered head cocked to one side. "Listen to the little birds, Momma," he said. "Listen how the little birds sing tweet-tweet. Can I go out and draw them with my crayons, Momma? Can I, huh? Can I? I'm a good little boy."

Shaking his head sadly, Johnny Blue said: "Crazy as a loco'd calf. He's had one too many bumps on the noggin if'n you ask me."

"Well," I said, "it's all his fault we're in this mess. He shouldn't have made ol' Jeb's painting look so nice he'd fall in love with Wapiti Fawn."

"He didn't fall in love with that Indian girl, you idiots," Dora said angrily. "He fell in love with the soul of the artist. He fell in love with Charles M. Russell."

Me and Johnny Blue studied on that for a spell, and allowed that Dora was probably right.

"Of course I'm right, you churnheads," quoth that frail sister. She glanced toward the cabin as something that sounded suspiciously like a whiskey jug shattered against a wall, followed by an outraged roar. "Right after that door opens over there, we'll all be hung," she said. "I warned Charlie you two were nothing but trouble, but he wouldn't listen." She sighed. "Now look at us—doomed to dangle at the end of a rope in a wolfer camp as far away from the footlights as it's humanly possible to be."

Dora burst into tears and me and Johnny Blue shuffled our feet uncomfortably. Then Johnny Blue walked over to Dora and took her in his arms as she laid her head on his manly chest.

"I don't want to hang, Johnny Blue," she sobbed. "Don't let them hang me."

And Johnny Blue looked at the cabin door and his dark eyes were deeply troubled.

*   *   *

Well, boys, the door didn't open for the rest of that day or the whole of the second, though the crashing and screeching and roaring continued from inside without cease.

On the third day around suppertime—which came and went for us without a morsel of food—Wapiti Fawn threw open the cabin door and my heart stopped, figuring we were finally about to meet our maker.

But that Indian gal, her face like thunder, ignored us and stomped over to them idle Flathead women and thumped them over their slender backs with that horn ladle of hers, screaming cusses in Blackfoot.

The next thing I knew, those Flatheads, shooting furious glances at Wapiti Fawn, were hurrying into the cabin carrying buckets of hot water, followed about a minute later by a roar of affronted anger from Jeb Anthony.

Wapiti Fawn next grabbed Curtis Boone by his ear and pulled that wincing wolfer to the timber line near the camp. She shrieked at him in Blackfoot and he shucked his bowie knife and cut down two young spruce trees, shaving off the branches until he had a couple of stout poles about chest height to a tall man.

The little Indian gal took the poles, swiped at Boone with her ladle, then stomped back into the cabin.

Boone, rubbing his smarting ear, strolled over to the corral.

"What was all that about?" he asked me.

I shrugged. "Dunno."

"Well," returned Boone, "the chief better get to the hanging pretty damn quick. The boys"—he waved toward the wolfer encampment—"is getting downright surly."

It rained that night, and the four of us huddled wet, hungry, and miserable into a muddy corner of the corral under a canvas tarp that Boone had thrown to us. We couldn't see our guards, but I knew they'd be under shelter somewhere, watching us.

The cabin was still, ominously quiet, and the only sound was the hiss of the rain and the occasional male grunt and frenzied female cry from the darkened tents.

Dawn broke wet and sullen, the clouds so low they hung like gray ghosts among the tops of the pine trees. I was stiff an' sore all over and rose to my feet, trying to get the kinks out of my spine. Dora slept on Charlie's shoulder and Johnny Blue was bent over, still dozing, rain running off his hat, muddying the ground at his feet.

I'd been right about the guards, because a rifleman wearing a yellow slicker stepped out from the side of the cabin and stood there watching me. I waved at him, but he didn't wave back.

One by one my slumbering companions woke and stretched. Charlie, who was finally back to normal, gently shook Dora awake and she rose to her feet.

"Where's that oaf Boone?" Charlie asked. "I demand that we get something to eat."

"Or at least some coffee," Dora said, shivering.

But Boone didn't appear until the morning had brightened into afternoon. He walked over to the corral around noon as the rain stopped and the clouds parted, revealing a warm sun.

"Sure been quiet in there," he observed, nodding toward the cabin.

Charlie ignored that comment and said: "Now listen here, you lout. I demand you feed us, or would you rather starve us to death?"

"It's bad enough we've got to think about the rope," Dora added piteously.

"Then don't think about it, ma'am." Boone sneered.

But then he smiled and continued: "You're right. I'd rather see you hang than starve to death. I'll have one of the women bring you some food." He began to walk away, then stopped and looked back at us. "Where is Andy when you need him, eh?" he asked cheerfully, followed by a loud guffaw.

"God," said Charlie. "I hate that man."

However, Boone, low down as he was, kept his word, and after a few minutes one of the Flathead women brought us hot coffee in a sooty, battered pot, along with four tin cups and some cornbread and cold bacon.

The coffee was strong and bitter, but it was good. We shared our meager vittles then stood around with nothing to do but watch the sunny afternoon shade into evening.

The moon rose above the pine trees, silvering the branches and casting long blue shadows across the wolfer camp. Each tent glowed with a faint orange light.

Wapiti Fawn slipped out of the door of the cabin like a wraith and lit the oil lamps she'd hung on each side of the door and they immediately threw a pool of honey yellow on the porch and splashed the walls with the same color. Then she slipped noiselessly inside again.

It was a homey, comforting scene, though I drew little solace from it. I knew the next time I saw that door open it could be one of the last things I'd ever see in this life.

It happened an hour later.

Twelve

The door didn't just open, it crashed loudly on its rawhide hinges against the wall. And there, outlined against the glow from inside, stood Jebedaiah Anthony, tall and terrible, a crutch under each arm.

Dora let out a little squeal of fear and I suddenly caught a mouthful of my own heart. Beside me I saw the eyes of Johnny Blue and Charlie glued to the dreadful apparition in the doorway; then I heard Charlie whisper hoarsely: "Then it's come at last."

Curtis Boone appeared out of nowhere. He took one look at his boss, threw his arms in the air, and yelled: "Necktie—" But then he stopped as he saw Wapiti Fawn sidle up to Jeb's side, the big wolfer circling her waist with his massive right arm.

"Come!" Jeb roared from the doorway. "Come one, come all, join me and my bride." He laughed and hugged Wapiti Fawn closer. "Tonight we celebrate our betrothal."

Boone, his face perplexed, yelled: "Boss, what the hell is goin' on? Ain't we gonna hang these here rannies?"

Shaking his massive head, Jeb replied joyfully: "No, Boone, no hanging. Tonight we kick up our heels—and glorify a miracle!"

Boone thought that over for a few moments; then he snarled: "You heard the boss. You're gonna celebrate a god-damned miracle."

"What miracle?" asked Johnny Blue.

Boone shook his head. "Hell if I know. I think maybe that Indian woman slipped something into ol' Jeb's whiskey and he's gone plumb loco."

As we walked toward the cabin, Charlie whispered to me urgently: "Listen, if I make any attempt to say the"—he glanced uneasily over his shoulder—"the o-u-t-r-a-g-e word, shove your fist down my throat."

"Sure will, Charlie, " I replied. "But what does o-t-u . . . o-u-r . . . what does it spell?"

"Outrage, you idiot!" Dora snapped.

And Charlie winced.

Boys, when we walked into that cabin, I knew I was seeing a miracle all right.

The place smelled of sweet herbs and something delicious bubbled on the glowing stove. The floor was scrubbed clean, as were the walls, and Jeb's filthy crib was gone, replaced by white blankets spread across the pine boards as though for a pair of lovers.

Jeb himself was shiny as a new pin, his hair and beard trimmed and his buckskins free of grease and stains. He stood upright on the crutches Wapiti Fawn had made for him from the spruce trees, and I had to admit—now that he was cleaned up—he cut a fine figure of a man. Even the mysterious blue chalk line around the walls had been renewed and it seemed to glow in the light of the oil lamps as Jeb roared: "Where is he? Where is the magician?"

Johnny Blue shoved Charlie forward, and that bashful dauber allowed that he was present.

"You knew this would happen, didn't you?" Jeb roared. He slapped Charlie on the back, a blow that staggered him, then passed him a jug, which the artist gratefully applied to his mouth with an unsteady hand. When he had drunk, Charlie said, a bit doubtfully if you ask me: "Ah . . . yes . . . I knew it would happen."

"Damn right you did!" Jeb roared again.

He turned to Boone. "You were right, Boone, when you told me the Indians call this man a great sorcerer. Now I've experienced his magical arts firsthand."

Jeb stepped closer to Charlie, using his crutches skill-fully, and dug him with his elbow. "You knew the picture would change her, didn't you, you crafty devil? You used your powerful sorcery to transform her into the woman you painted."

"Oh yes," Charlie said, emboldened by the whiskey. "I knew that for sure."

Glancing at Boone, Jeb shook his head then hobbled his way to a shelf and got Charlie's canvas. He held it up and said to the big wolfer: "Look, Boone, you doubting Thomas. Look how my beloved has grown to look just like her pic-ture. Don't you see? A blind man could see it." Boys, the truth is, that little gal was still as homely as a buck-toothed buzzard, but neither Boone, nor nobody else, was about to say so.

"She sure has, boss," Boone nodded. "I'd never have believed it if'n I hadn't seen it with my own two eyes."

"And no wonder," Jeb roared. "It's magic, goddammit!"

Jeb spread his arms wide, Wapiti Fawn at his side help-ing his balance. "Now, everybody, let's get started on this here fandango and our wedding feast!"

Boys, them wolfers knew how to party. The shebang went on all night and there was plenty of whiskey and broiled beef and dancing. Jeb even made a canvas sign that he wrote himself with his blue chalk and hung around Char-lie's neck that said:

GrATe MaGiKiaN

Later one of them comely Flathead women took a shine to me in the wee hours as the fiesta got into full swing, and we vanished together into the woods for quite a spell. Boys, I ain't going to tell you what we done because you've all gone into the woods with a woman at one time or another. Let me just say that by the time she smoothed her dress over her pretty knees and we returned to the party, "a good time was had by all."

One by one, them wolfers and their womenfolk staggered off to bed, and by the time dawn broke over the mountains and began to wash out the night shadows, only the four of us and Jeb and Wapiti Fawn were still standing.

Not wishing to wear out our welcome, and right anxious to put some distance between ourselves and that dangerous wolfer band, we saddled our horses and prepared to leave.

"Wait," Jeb ordered, "I want to present you with rich gifts for what you have done for me and my bride."

"There's no need—" Charlie began.

"Oh yes, there is," Jeb interrupted.

As Wapiti Fawn beamed at us and batted her eyelashes, Jeb hobbled over to where Boone lay on the ground, open-mouthed and snoring, an empty jug lying beside him.

Skillfully balancing on his crutches, Jeb kicked Boone hard in the ribs, and the wolfer groaned, "What the hell?" then looked up and saw his boss.

"On your feet, Boone," Jeb said. "I've got work for you to do."

Boone, his eyes bloodshot, grabbed at his pounding head and groaned again: "Geez, boss, can't you let a man die in peace?"

Jeb's reply was yet another kick, and Boone rose woozily to his feet. Jeb grabbed the man by the back of the neck and leaned down and whispered in his ear. The scowling Boone left, looking back at us and cursing.

Now we were alone again, I said: "Beggin' your pardon, Jeb, but I got to ask you a question."

"Ask away," replied that cheerful bandit, holding his little Blackfoot gal close to his side.

"That line of blue chalk around the cabin," I said, "it's been buggin' the hell out of me because I can't figure why you put it there."

Jeb smiled, showing big white teeth. "In my younger days I was a simple sailorman—"

Wapiti Fawn said something in Blackfoot, and Jeb shrugged. "As always, my little darlin' is right. Nay, lad, I was no simple sailorman, but a black-hearted pirate rogue, the scourge of the South China Seas. I sent many a fine ship and many a poor sailorman to Davy Jones's locker, heathen and Christian alike, and laughed as I done it."

He shook his head, a gesture that conveyed both wonder and sadness. "Lord above, I was a bloodthirsty buccaneer."

He hugged his bride closer. "Well, those sinful days are all behind me, and now I'm a respectable married man and I'm making my way in the world through the wolfer's profession."

"And that chalk line?" I prompted, catching an alarmed glance from Johnny Blue, who seemed to think I was prying into something that could get us killed.

But Jeb merely smiled. "Oh that. Well, it's been ten years since I stood on the deck of a ship, but even now, when I find myself closed in by four walls, I still need a sight o' the sea. And that's why I draw that blue chalk line." Jeb studied me closely. "It's my horizon, cowboy. Does that answer your question?"

"It does," Johnny Blue interjected, looking hard at me. "An' he ain't gonna ask you any others."

Just then Boone returned carrying a small sack that he gave to Charlie.

"Rich gifts," Jeb beamed. "Rich gifts for all."

Later when we looked at those gifts on the trail, they

consisted of a side of bacon, some coffee, a dollar and sixty cents in small change, and a sack of tobacco.

But we were so glad to leave that wolfer camp and mad Jebedaiah Anthony and his homely bride behind us, it didn't bother us none. Anyhow, the bacon was welcome and Johnny Blue snagged that Bull Durham right quick.

"Ol' Jeb sure took a shine to that little gal," I said as we rode north toward Blackfoot country. "I guess that was lucky for us."

"He's in love," Dora said.

"Yeah," I agreed, not wanting her to call me an idiot again. "With Charlie."

"No, you idiot," Dora snapped. "With Wapiti Fawn."

Right there I gave up trying to figure it out.

Boys, we were two days out of the wolfer camp when I had one of them brilliant ideas that made my name famous throughout the West. In later years, folks used to say I was smarter than a tree full of owls, and I was about to prove it.

"The way I figger it," I told my three companions as we made camp that night, "me and Johnny Blue is going to be lookin' for work just as soon as our artist assistant job with Charlie here is over."

"That's a fact," said Charlie, looking pensive.

"Right," I said, "so me and Johnny Blue is gonna head down to the Indian Territory and hook up with Buffalo Bill on account of all our wild Injun and outlaw fighting experience."

"Now hold on right there," Johnny Blue said, rolling a smoke. "I got to head for Texas an' find my little lost sister."

"And what are you gonna use for money?"

Johnny Blue shook his head, lighting his cigarette with

a twig from the fire. "Dunno. I haven't thought that through yet."

"That's why we're gonna throw in with Buffalo Bill," I said. "Right now we're so broke we ain't got a tailfeather between us, but if we become riders for Bill, an' maybe even go to England with him, we'll be settin' pretty and have enough money to light a shuck for Texas."

"Well . . . I dunno . . ." Johnny Blue began uncertainly.

That's when I threw in the clincher.

"Of course," I said, "you know we'll have tea an' cakes with old Queen Vic."

"Don't piss on my boots an' tell me it's rainin'," Johnny Blue retorted. "That ain't gonna happen."

But I could see he was mighty interested because he was leaning forward and his cigarette was burning away between his fingers, forgotten.

"That's a natural fact," I said. "Ask Charlie."

I really didn't expect Charlie to agree, but he jumped right in and said: "I hear tell the old lady is right anxious to have tea with Bill an' his cowboys and wild Indians."

"You don't say," said Johnny Blue. "How come you know that, Charlie?"

Without a moment's hesitation Charlie replied: "The way I heard it from this politician feller in Great Falls who heard it from this English feller, old Queen Vic says to her prime minister: 'Mister Gladstone, I do hope them Injuns of Bill's ain't too wild when we're having tea and fairy cakes. If they was, and they waved around them awful tommyhawks, I swear I'd pee me royal knickers.'

"And Mister Gladstone, he says, 'Now don't you worry none about that, mum. I'll have our Inniskillen Fusiliers standing right close by to make sure things don't get out of hand.' And then he says to Queen Vic: 'Bless your kind old heart, mum, your knickers is as safe an' dry as the inside of the snuff box in your apron.' That's what Mister Gladstone said."

"Is that a fact?" asked Johnny Blue.

And Charlie replied: "It's a natural fact, true as I'm set- tin' here. You can hang your hat on that."

"I'd like to have tea and fairy cakes with the Queen," Johnny Blue observed thoughtfully, building another smoke. "I hear tell she's a right nice old lady."

"She is," Charlie said, "an' she'll make you right wel- come at Buckingham Palace."

Boys, that Charlie was a treasure, pure gold dust. I knew he was right sorry that we'd be leaving him soon, but he was such a straight arrow, he put me and Johnny Blue's welfare before his own. Even as I sit here an' write this, the memory of it brings a tear to my eye.

Then Charlie proved again how unselfish he was when he said: "If I was you boys, I'd leave tomorrow at first light and get down to Fort Smith right quick. That way you'd be among the first to volunteer for Bill's show and get your pick of the jobs. Why," Charlie added decisively, "you'd be top hands, is what you'd be."

"And that brings me to the brilliant idea I had," I said.

Johnny Blue groaned. "Now why do I feel right uneasy every time you say that?"

"No, let's hear him out," Charlie said eagerly. "Speak your piece and tell us your idea." And he added brightly: "You know Buffalo Bill is eager to leave for England and he won't linger in the territory for long."

"It's," I began, looking at the faces of my companions in turn, letting the suspense build, "it's . . . a Buffalo Bill Bear."

"A what?" Dora exclaimed.

"A bear. A big ol' Buffalo Bill Bear."

"I don't catch your drift," Johnny Blue said uneasily.

"Listen," I said, "a few years back I was talkin' to a

mountain man over to the Judith Basin country, an' he tole
me how Davy Crockett and Dan'l Boone and them used
to grin a grizz, an' make that big ol' bear just as tame as
a puppy dog.

"Now I guess that mountain man noticed I was payin'
partic'lar attention because he tole me about this feller
named Don Jose Joaquin Estudillo of the ol' Mission Santa
Clara ranch in California, who took his vaqueros out into
the woods one night in the 1830s an' roped forty big grizzlies by the light of the moon."

"You still got me buffaloed," said Johnny Blue.

"And me," echoed Charlie.

"It's simple," I continued. "With all the ranches closed
down because of the Hard Winter, there's gonna be all
kinds of rannies who've been ridin' the grub line askin'
Bill for a job." I poured some coffee into my cup. "See,
we need an advantage because we'll be up agin a stacked
deck gettin' in line behind all them out-of-work hands."

"And that advantage will be—" began Charlie.

"The Buffalo Bill Bear," I finished it for him. "Can you
imagine how Bill will feel when we present him with a
big ol' tame grizzly for his show? Why, he'll welcome us
with open arms and—just as you said, Charlie—make us
top hands sure enough."

"I dunno," said Johnny Blue, "a grizz is a mean b'ar. I
seen one kill a full-grown longhorn one time, an' that steer
stood six feet at the shoulder and his horns must've
stretched eight feet across if'n they was an inch."

"Well," said I, "that ol' bear must've been starving."

"It was in the winter," Johnny Blue allowed, nodding.

"That's what I mean. In the spring, like it is now, all
them grizzlies care to eat is honey. Big ol' lazy honey bears
is what they are."

"So how did that mountain man tell you to do it?" Charlie asked. "Grinnin' a grizz, I mean."

"Well," I replied, "a couple of fellers do the grinnin', tipping the bear a nod now and then, an' another feller stands by with his rope, ready to dab a loop on him the second he becomes tame enough. Then you slap a brand on him and you got yourself a puppy-dog grizz."

"You know, I reckon you boys are on to something there," Charlie said shrewdly. "If I were you two, I'd find me a real nice grizzly and get to work on the grinnin' right away."

"Count me out," said Dora. "I don't know if I'm with a bunch of ten-year-old boys or a passel of idiots. Either way, I'm heading south at first light." She laid the tips of her fingers on the back of Charlie's wrist. "Sorry to leave you, Charlie, but I need to be where there are people so I can advance my acting career. I think I'll head down to Fort Smith way my own self."

I glanced at Dora and her eyes in the firelight had a hard glitter, and for some reason I suddenly felt like a crippled fly in a spider's web. That little gal would take some watching.

"I'll be right sorry to lose you, Dora," said Charlie. "But I guess come sunup I'll head up to the Blackfoot country and get to work before all them wild Indians are gone forever." Charlie nodded, smiling. "Well, I guess that's that."

I coughed. "Sorry, Charlie, but it don't work that way. The mountain man said two rannies a-grinnin' an' one with the rope. That makes three, and without you, we'd only have two."

"I don't think I—"

"You already done said it was a good idea, Charlie," I interrupted. "You said that your own self."

"Yeah, I know, but—"

"Listen, Charlie," Johnny Blue said, "it's not often I agree with my compadre here, mainly because he's a loon, but for once what he says makes sense. A tame ba'r would sure put us in good with Bill."

"You know," said Charlie, shaking his head, "since I've been around you boys, I've had nothing but grief. I sure as hell don't want to end up as dinner for a grizzly."

I sighed, disappointed with Charlie's spoilsport attitude. "Well, my plan won't work with just one grinner," I said, shrugging. Then I slapped that gloomy Gus on the shoulder. "Oh hell, Charlie, since your confidence in my idea is so frail, we'll just tag along with you an' brace them Blackfoot. Quien sabe, by and by, I might come up with another idea just as good."

Charlie, that sensitive soul, must've thought I was mad at him because he looked like I'd just slugged him in the stomach.

"Come first light," he said, his voice breaking, "we'll go find ourselves a grizzly."

Thirteen

Next morning Dora pulled out right after breakfast. But before she left, she said to me and Johnny Blue: "I hope I'll see you boys in Forth Smith."

Her eyes still held that hard glitter that made me feel uneasy, and I was glad to see the back of her.

That reformed whore was trouble with a capital T, and there would come a time when she'd cause me and Johnny Blue nothing but a washtub full of misery.

But such thoughts were far from my mind as we rode out of camp in search of a suitable bear. Boys, I've had some brilliant ideas in my life, but to date, the Buffalo Bill Bear was the best one I ever had.

Of course, finding one, even among the foothills of the Rockies and after their long winter sleep, wasn't easy. Even in them days, the big bears were becoming mighty scarce because they'd been hunted by both Indians and mountain men for a long time.

On our second day out we did sight one a long way off as he loped along the timberline of a mountain slope. By the time we rode to where we'd seen him, he was long gone and we'd nothing to show for that day's work but some paw prints among the aspens.

That night as we lingered late over our coffee in camp, Charlie asked me how I was planning on branding the bear once we tamed him.

I fished around in my pocket and pulled out an old saddle ring. "With this," I said.

Using a red hot saddle ring to alter the brand on a cow was an old rustler trick and I told Charlie I figgered on making an O with it, then putting another on top and joining them with a straight line so I got a B.

"Bill's gonna like that, his own brand on the b'ar," said Johnny Blue.

"Sure enough," I allowed. "Ain't no way we're not gonna become top hands."

As for Charlie, he just sat there worried and glum. I think the thought of the bear scared him because that ol' boy was big and strong but he could be a real sissy by times.

We found our grizz the very next morning.

Truth to tell, it was the horses that found him.

As we headed up a slope toward a stand of aspen that looked like bear country, the horses started to shy and tried to turn back the way we'd come.

Charlie had a hard time staying with his mustang because it had been born wild and knew plenty about bears and didn't want any part of them.

"Maybe it's only a cougar," Johnny Blue suggested nervously.

"Could be," I replied, "but we got to go an' take a look-see."

We rode back down to the base of the hill and ground-tied the horses among the pines, and I took my rope from the saddle, shaking out a loop.

"Remember," I warned my companions, "nice friendly grins an' don't fergit to tip him a nod now and again. A grizz likes that."

Charlie pulled his Winchester, but I told him to leave it where it was in the rifle boot, "We're tamin' this bear, Charlie," I said. "We ain't pluggin' him."

Charlie shook his head doubtfully, "The closer I get to a grizzly, the less I like your plan," he said.

We walked up the hill, Charlie lagging behind a few steps, and right off I spotted the grizz feeding on an early crop of blackberries growing on a bush between a pair of tall aspens.

I stopped when I was about thirty feet from the bear to let Johnny Blue and Charlie catch up.

When they were alongside me, I whispered: "We got to get a mite closer."

"How close?" Charlie asked, his eyes wide, fixed on that grizzly.

"Oh, maybe six feet," I said.

Boys, I may have been mistaken, but I thought I heard Charlie whimper. In them olden days he sure didn't cotton to bears much.

"How we gonna play this?" Johnny Blue asked.

"You an' Charlie just walk toward him real slow and easy like, grinnin' an' tippin', then squat on your heels when you're about six feet away. As soon as I see that he's good an' tame, I'll dab a loop on him."

Boys, you'll be interested in this: I planned on using the hoolihan catch, which as you recollect is a nice gentle throw because the cowboy swings the loop in the air for only one revolution before tossing it. It's a fast loop, designed for a head catch, and it was used all over the West in them days to snag horses in a corral. The hoolihan is a quick throw and very quiet and is downright tailor-made for bears.

"My," said Charlie, studying the grizz, "that's a big bear."

"Sure is," I said. "He'll go maybe eight feet tall when he stands on his hind legs, and I reckon he weighs in at around five hunnerd pounds."

"God," said Charlie, never once taking his eyes off that silverback, "that's a huge bear."

"Bill's gonna love him," I said. "We got it made, trust me."

The bear turned and saw us. But he just studied on us for a spell then shook his huge head back and forth a few times, grunting deep in his throat, and went back to gorging on them blackberries.

"What did I tell you boys?" I said. "He's nothing but a big ol' neighborly honey bear."

I told Johnny Blue and Charlie to start walking real slow toward him. "An' grin all the time," I said. "Right now, I'd say the grin is more important than the tip."

I stood to the side and watched Charlie and Johnny Blue walk toward the bear, the two of them taking little baby steps and grinnin' like crazed possums.

"Tip him a nod," I whispered. "Tip him a nod now."

Charlie grinned, and tipped the bear a nod, as did Johnny Blue, but the big grizzly just ignored them, stuffing berries into his huge mouth.

I was walking close behind Charlie and I whispered: "This is going great. Even better than I expected. It's so easy, like playin' poker with somebody else's chips."

When we got to within half a dozen feet of the grizz, we all sat on our heels and the three of us began grinnin' and tippin' and the bear kept on ignoring us.

"Hell, boys, this is larrupin' good—we got him near tamed already," I whispered.

Maybe it was the sound of my voice so close, but the bear rose on his hind legs—and I swear the sky only came up to his collarbones—and growled at us, and Charlie was so surprised he fell backward on his butt.

"Jesus God," exclaimed that distraught dauber, "we're done for."

"Nah, Charlie," I said, helping him back on to his heels again. "That ol' honey bear, he don't want to make it look too easy, is all. Bears always do that, trying to make easy things look real difficult. That's what they call the 'bear way,' them as knows about the critters."

And I was right, because the grizz settled down again and went right back to chewin' on them blackberries.

As Charlie and Johnny Blue kept up their grinnin', I rose slowly to my feet and shook out my loop after it got tangled up in a thorn bush. Then I walked a few steps toward the bear and got ready to make my hoolihan.

That's when the grizz rose to its feet and let out with a roar that shook the trees and sent a flock of jays fluttering and flapping out of the branches in a panic.

"I don't," gritted Johnny Blue through his grin, "think . . . this . . . is . . . working."

"We're dead," Charlie wailed. "We're all dead."

"Keep grinnin'," I whispered, "an' tip that bear a nod now and then. Dammit, Charlie, I swear you're a sissy britches an' you're letting everybody down."

The bear took a step toward us and roared again, and poor Charlie gasped: "I think . . . I think I just peed myself."

"Keep grinnin', Charlie," I said. "Or I'll tell everybody you're a scaredy cat."

Charlie grinned and tipped the bear a slow nod, and the great creature roared even louder than before, the long, curved claws on his paws slashing at the air in front of him.

"Right," I said aloud. "Now it's time to dab the loop on him. I reckon he's tame enough."

Well, boys, it had been a long time since I'd dabbed a loop on a horse, or a cow for that matter, and I missed with the hoolihan. The rope flew threw the air true enough, but the honda ran down the tallowed Manila hemp fast as the snap of a bullwhip, taking too much slack out of the loop, and the rope hit that grizzly smack on the snout.

Then all hell broke loose.

That closed loop with its metal honda must've stung because the honey bear roared in a kind of outraged voice and came right for us.

"Oh my God!" Charlie shrieked. "We're buzzard bait!"

He turned on his heels and ran. Johnny Blue jumped to his feet, his eyes wild, and lit a shuck close behind him.

"Wait!" I yelled. "I'll toss a loop again. Come back, you two, and get to grinnin' an' tippin'!"

The bear was almost right on top of me. He roared and took a tremendous swipe at my head that missed, and I decided enough was enough and took off after my running companions.

Boys, you let everybody know that Charlie and Johnny Blue let me down that day because they never had enough faith in my plan to begin with, and that's why it didn't pan out. It sure wasn't my fault.

Hightailing it like a six-legged bobcat, I passed Charlie right quick and closed in on Johnny Blue.

"God help us all!" Charlie yelled as he ran. "I guess I'll never hold a paintbrush again."

I glanced over my shoulder and saw the bear was galloping within snappin' distance behind us.

"Keep your breath for runnin', Charlie," I hollered. "He's right on your heels."

Charlie squawked like a frightened hen and the bear roared and Charlie shrieked: "I'm dead! He's gonna kill me!"

"You're a lunatic!" Johnny Blue hollered at me as I tried to pass him. "You're a goddamned natural-born lunatic!"

"The horses!" I yelled, ignoring that hurtful remark as Johnny Blue pounded farther ahead of me with them big strides of his. "Get to the horses."

But the horses saw us coming with the bear close behind us, an' boys, I swear their manes stood on end. They stampeded out of there fast as settin' hens on a June bug and we fogged it after them ponies and the bear fogged it after us, especially Charlie, who was squealin' and squeakin' like a mashed cat and attracting more than his fair share of attention from that pesky bruin.

I've no way of knowing how long the chase would have lasted, had not the grizz finally caught up with Charlie. I can't say it was his fault because he was showing a real nice turn of speed for a portly feller, all things considered.

"This," Charlie panted as he ran, "is an outrage!"

I glanced behind me just as the bear took a mighty swipe at Charlie's head and that pathetic painter fell to the ground with a horrible cry. Then there was silence.

"What happened to Charlie?" Johnny Blue threw over his shoulder as he continued to run, his knees coming up to his chest at every stride.

"The Buffalo Bill Bear's eatin' him," I gasped.

"Too bad," Johnny Blue panted. "He was a good hand and a nice feller when he was sober."

Well, boys, we kept on runnin' until we were well shot of that bear; then we stopped and recovered our breaths. Then we looked for the horses.

It took us till nightfall to round up them ponies, they was so spooked, and it was a real sad thing to see Johnny Blue lead Charlie's mean-eyed mustang with nothing on its back but an empty saddle.

"Et," Johnny Blue whispered thoughtfully as he chewed on a bacon and sourdough bread sandwich by the campfire. "Et by a bear. Poor Charlie sure bought the farm in a hurry."

"That's a natural fact," I replied. "An' I don't reckon we'll find enough left of him to bury."

Johnny Blue studied on that for a spell and then he said finally: "We could shoot the bear and plant it with Charlie still inside. It would just be like layin' that good ol' painter boy to rest in a coffin, a hairy coffin I gotta admit, but better than nothing."

Well, I chewed on that idea for a moment or two then said: "That's a tolerably good plan. I say that come mornin' we plug the Buffalo Bill Bear and give Charlie eternal rest, snug as a bug inside him forever and ever, Amen."

"That's a right nice thing you just said," Johnny Blue allowed, nodding. "It will be like they was both hibernatin' eternity away, except poor ol' Charlie will do it in little bite-sized pieces."

Now this was such a sad thought that as soon as me and Johnny Blue finished our supper, we sang "Railroad to Heaven" in Charlie's memory, or as much of it as we could remember, and that grand old hymn cheered us up considerable.

After we was finished with the singing, I poured us both coffee and Johnny Blue began to build a smoke.

"Y'know," he said, lighting his cigarette with a brand from the fire. "It was as hard to do as scratching a porcupine's back, but I think we was just beginning to help poor Charlie mature as an artist before the grizz et him."

"That's a fact," I agreed. "We was learnin' him real good an' he never once regretted making us his assistants, and that's to his credit."

Johnny Blue nodded and was about to speak again when we heard a commotion in the woods in the darkness beyond the glow of our fire.

Johnny Blue grabbed his Winchester and stood and I shucked my Colt and we was both standing there ready for anything, which was how it was back in them olden days.

"Who's out there?" I hollered into the darkness.

No answer.

Johnny Blue cranked a round into the chamber and yelled: "Come in real slow or I'll cut loose with this here .44.40."

There was a sight of crashing and thrashing in the underbrush and a thud as a body hit the dirt followed by a string of cusses.

"Ain't only one man I know can cuss in American and Blackfoot both," Johnny Blue whispered tensely, all the slack in him twisted into a tight knot. "It's ol' Charlie's ghost come back to ha'nt us."

"Stay away, Charlie," said I. "You was et by the Buffalo Bill Bear an' shouldn't be wandering the night a-hauntin' decent Christian folks."

But Charlie's ghost kept on a-coming until it appeared in the orange glow where the firelight faded into the darkness of the woods. For a few moments it just stood there, tall and terrible and spooky, its bloody head hanging on its chest.

"Should I smoke a couple of rounds into it an' see what happens?" Johnny Blue whispered.

I was about to allow it seemed like a good idea, when the ghost wailed: "Don't shoot! It's me, you idiots."

"We know it's you, Charlie," I said. "But you ain't supposed to be walkin' around. Don't you recollect, you was et whilst you was grinnin' a big ol' grizzly bear?" I shook my head. "That was a bad idea of your'n, Charlie."

Charlie took a step toward us and I saw Johnny Blue take a tighter grip on his rifle.

"I'm not dead," Charlie said, exhaustion making his voice ragged. "Goddammit, I'm only half dead."

"You mean you wasn't et?" Johnny Blue asked uncertainly.

"No, I wasn't et," Charlie replied, walking up to the fire. "That damn bear sniffed around me for a while, swatted me a few times an' then left me for dead. I reckon he was anxious to go back to them blackberries. Next thing I know, I blacked out, and when I come to, both you rannies was long gone." Charlie looked at me across the fire.

"Remind me to shoot you just as soon as I've got strength enough to shuck a gun."

I was about to tell Charlie that it was his own self's weakness in the grinnin' and tippin' department that done for him, but right then that pitiful painter swayed on his feet and I rushed to his side and helped him to a seat by the fire.

"Here, take this," I said, handing him a cup of coffee, "while I take a look at your head."

The bear's claws had broken the scalp in three or four places and Charlie had lost a lot of blood.

But the wounds didn't look too serious, though they'd have to be bandaged.

I walked to Charlie's saddlebags and found a folded white shirt and yanked it out of there.

"No," Charlie yelled, "that's my only spare sh—"

But he was too late. I'd already ripped the garment in half, planning to use one half for bathing his cuts, the other to wrap his poor mangled head.

As I bathed Charlie's wounds, he kept nodding off into unconsciousness, and Johnny Blue said all an exhausted man needed was a good night's sleep and he'd be as right as rain in the morning.

"Yeah," I agreed. "That bear took a lot out of him."

"I'm not talkin' about him," Johnny Blue said, drawing his blanket over him. "I'm talkin' about me."

But after I laid Charlie by the fire and he was sleeping soundly, I shook Johnny Blue awake, and surly as he was about being roused, me and him had a long powwow.

"This is gonna hurt poor Charlie's feelings real bad," I said finally as I rolled myself in my own blanket, "but it's got to be done."

"It's for his own good," Johnny Blue agreed.

"And ours," I added.

I lay there for a while, thinking about the bear and our

narrow escape from death, and was slowly drifting off to sleep when I was suddenly jolted wide awake by a noise in the woods where we'd first seen poor Charlie's ghost.

Reaching out, I shook Johnny Blue awake and that surly hand growled: "Wha . . ."

"Shh." I put my forefinger to my lips and whispered. "Listen."

From the underbrush there came a crash followed by a snuffling sound and a low growl.

"What the hell is that?" Johnny Blue asked.

"I know what it is," I exclaimed. "It's the Buffalo Bill Bear! We did tame him! He's lonely an' follerin' after us like a big ol' puppy dog, just like the mountain man said he would."

I grabbed my hat, which was the first item of clothing a cowboy reached for in them days, meaning to get up and finally dab a hoolihan on that ol' honey bear.

"Don't take one step toward that grizz, or by God, I swear I'll shoot you through the lungs."

Turning, I saw Johnny Blue sitting up, his Colt in his hand. Boys, I never in all my born days knew he could shuck an iron that fast.

"And that goes double with me."

Charlie had raised himself on one elbow, weak as a day-old kittlin', but the gun in his hand was pointed right at my brisket.

Well, boys, there was only one thing I could do, faced as I was by the ornery pair, so I eased back on my blanket real slow.

Them two rannies kept their guns on me for a long spell while the Buffalo Bill Bear snuffed and huffed in the woods, but I didn't so much as twitch a muscle.

I didn't know if Charlie would've shot me—but Johnny Blue would, sure enough.

*   *   *

Come sunup, Charlie seemed a lot stronger, and after breakfast I changed the bandage on his head; then we saddled up. And that's when I told him what me and Johnny Blue had decided.

"Charlie," I said, "you're a fair hand an' a dandy painter an' as neighborly as a pup in a box when you're sober, but you got a serious problem."

"And what might that be?" Charlie asked in an offended tone, his hat balancing on top of the fat bandage around his mashed head.

"See, Charlie," Johnny Blue said, "you jest nat'rally attract trouble. Since we signed up as your assistants, we've been nearly hung by wolfers, had lead thrown at us by outlaws, got our toes shot off by a wild Indian gal, run out of the Territory by the Army, and chased by wild bears."

"An' that's just for starters, Charlie," I said, as kindly as I could. "It ain't your fault, it's just that you're an unlucky cuss. I think if you bought a graveyard, people would stop dyin'. That's how unlucky you are."

Boys, poor Charlie grinned from ear to ear, trying his best to hide the hurt I know he was feeling inside. "Are you boys telling me you're quitting?" he asked.

"Well, it's nothin' personal, Charlie," I said. "It's just that we want to be rough riders for Buffalo Bill or, if that don't pan out, maybe join up with the Texas Rangers an' find our little sister."

"See, what we need is a safer line of work, Charlie," Johnny Blue added. "The artist assistant profession is too plumb dangerous."

Charlie didn't say a word. He just walked to his horse and opened his saddlebags. His back was turned to us, but I could see his shoulders shaking and I knew he was sobbing his poor broken heart out.

I guess he knew we was watching him, because he tried

to cover up his grief by slapping his thigh and yelling, "Hee . . . haw!"

When he came back, his face was real flushed and he was grinning fit to bust an' I wished he'd done it that good when we'd been trying to catch the Buffalo Bill Bear.

"I got a double eagle for each of you boys," he said, thumbing the coins into each of our palms.

"That's a month's wages and more. I reckon it will be enough to take you to Fort Smith or anywhere else you care to go."

"You're gold dust, Charlie," I told him. "And we're right sorry to be leavin' you."

"Think nothing of it," replied that noble soul. "I don't want to hold you boys back when you could be top hands with Bill and maybe meet old Queen Vic."

Charlie broke into another grin and I could see he was overwhelmed with emotion at the thought of us cutting out on him.

He turned on his heel and stepped into the saddle, gathering the packhorse's lead rope.

Right then I felt so sorry for him, I said: "Wait, Charlie," meaning to tell him maybe we was too hasty and should go into the Blackfoot country with him after all.

But Charlie set spurs to his mustang and headed for a break in the trees; then he swung north as soon as he'd cleared the timber. He kept on riding at a fast gallop, kicking hard at the mustang's ribs, the old packhorse scrambling to keep up.

Charlie startled a jackrabbit, then a small herd of antelope, and kept on going, glancing over his shoulder at us now and again. I knew he hoped me and Johnny Blue would follow after him, but we just stood there and waved our hats and hollered, "Huzzah! Huzzah!" until he disappeared over a rise and was lost from sight.

"Well," Johnny Blue said after a spell, settling his hat

back on his head, "all things considered, I think we done right by ol' Charlie."

"Sure enough," I allowed, "but it was no easy thing, for he's a man born to trouble—an' that's a true fact."

Boys, in later years when Charlie settled down and learned enough hoss sense to spit downwind, he done all right. They say nowadays a cowboy would have to blow a year's wages to buy one of his pictures, an' a little bitty plain one without any color in it at that.

You boys go right ahead and talk it out among yourselves, but I guess you'll wind up agreeing that it was me and Johnny Blue that helped him become the famous man he is today. An' if he has no more harebrained ideas like the one he had about grinnin' a grizz, he'll go right on making his mark in the world.

But as they say, life goes on, so me and Johnny Blue put poor brokenhearted Charlie out of our minds as we mounted up and pointed our horses south toward Buffalo Bill's Wild West Show and our destiny.

"Damn," said Johnny Blue as we rode out of the trees onto the buffalo grass, "that damn chicken rustler took the coffeepot."

Fourteen

The arrival of the railroads in western Montana during the early 1880s was welcomed with open arms by cattlemen like Granville Stuart of the old DHS Ranch, but the rails gave the biggest push to the silver industry. By 1883 the Territory ranked as the nation's second largest supplier of silver, and it kept that position until the mid-1890s, except for 1887—the year of the Hard Winter—when it ranked number one, and it was all due to the coming of the iron road.

Me and Johnny Blue figgered if we headed southeast we could pick up the Great Northern somewhere south of Great Falls and that way stay clear of the city where there was law, on account of how we was both wanted and desperate men with a price on our heads—dead or alive.

Saddle worn and hungry from missing our last six meals, we put the timbered foothills of the mountains behind us and rode toward a single ribbon of track cutting across the buffalo grass prairie like a slim knife blade.

It was hot enough to hard-boil an egg in a stock tank and even the birds were silent, having sought shade against the burning sun. We followed the shimmering rails south until we came to a small station with a water tower and a signal pole. The station house was a converted boxcar set beside a sidetrack alongside the main line.

Two roughly constructed windows cut into the front of

the car stared blankly across the prairie and the door between them stood open, sagging on its rawhide hinges.

There was a horse trough to the left of the door and our ponies gratefully dipped their noses into the water as a big, red-faced man with muttonchop whiskers and a few wisps of hair on the top of his head came to the door, picking his teeth with a straw as he studied us closely.

He was wearing a pair of them round, dark glasses that were becoming popular on the frontier as a protection against the glare of the sun.

"Howdy," I said. "Hot, ain't it?"

The big man ignored my greeting and said: "You boys is kinda early for the train, ain't you?" He took one of them big silver railroad watches from his vest pocket and glanced at it. "It won't be through here until midnight, maybe even later."

"We can wait," Johnny Blue said. "Me and him, we're headed south into the Indian Territory."

"Gonna jine up with Buffalo Bill and his Wild West Show in Fort Smith," I said by way of explanation.

"Could be," the big man nodded. "Could be."

Behind him, a telegraph key chattered noisily into life, and he turned and went inside. That's when I saw that he'd been hiding a Sharps big fifty behind his right leg, and he struck me as being a mighty careful feller.

What the telegraph was telling him I didn't know, but the man tapped out a reply then came back to the doorway. This time he left his rifle behind.

"That was Great Falls," he said. "They say the train is on schedule: an express car, a passenger car, five empty boxcars, and a caboose. Plenty of room for men and horses, I reckon."

The railroad man stood there looking at us, and I felt the hot sun burn my shoulders, sweat trickling down my brow from under my hat. I couldn't see that ranny's eyes behind his dark glasses, and when you can't see a man's eyes, you might as well be looking at a brick wall.

"You two fellers climb down," he said finally. He nodded toward a cottonwood that spread its branches over a shallow pond a few yards back from the sidetrack. "You can picket your horses over there in the shade."

There was a good patch of grass under the tree with water close by and we unsaddled the horses and let them graze and walked back to the boxcar.

"Are ye sharp set?" the big man asked.

"I can't remember when I last ate," Johnny Blue allowed. "It's been that long."

"Then come inside," the man said. He turned to walk into the boxcar but stopped and said: "Name is McDermott, Shamus McDermott. I've worked for the railroad, man and boy, this last twenty-five year."

I gave him my name and Johnny Blue offered his, and McDermott shrugged and replied: "Names is names and yours don't mean a thing to me." He looked at Johnny Blue. "You ain't Irish, that's for sure. Unless of course you're one of them black Irish."

This amused the railroader so much he was still laughing at his own wit as he slapped half a dozen slices of fried bacon and a thick wedge of cornbread onto each of our plates and shoved them toward us across his rough, pineboard table.

As he poured coffee, he said: "You boys can ride this train all the way to Wickes, that's a mining camp just south of Helena. You hop a freight there headed south and catch up with the Union Pacific in Wyoming. You can ride the Pacific all the way into Fort Smith. Take you maybe, oh, five, six days."

He studied us closely from behind those shades as we ate. "You'll be changing trains aplenty afore you get where you're going, and that's why you ain't gonna make it to Fort Smith in no hurry."

McDermott tagged at his right sidewhisker. "How much money are you boys holdin'?"

I didn't see any point in lying, so I said: "Forty dollars and change between us."

The big man nodded. "It will take all of that, and maybe more to get you where you want to go. My best advice is to dicker with the conductors. They'll set the fares and maybe feed you—if you're lucky."

He settled back in his chair and smiled. "In the meantime, that will be fifty cents for the grub. Each."

Boys, it took me and Johnny Blue ten miserable days, riding them rails day and night, to get to Fort Smith.

We changed trains a dozen times, kicking our heels in deserted stations along the route for hours at a time. Then we'd mostly bed down in a boxcar with the horses, and the Union Pacific conductors were right careful to take us for every penny we had. A big chunk of the money went on fares, the rest on oats and hay for them big American studs of ours, and as I recollect, very little by way of grub went down our own throats.

The conductor on the last train was an old feller with white hair and a bad case of piles that kept him standing the whole trip. He stopped the train for us a mile north of Fort Smith and we unloaded the horses as the heavens opened and a cloudburst made us hurry into our slickers. The old railroader pointed to a sidetrack angling into the rain-shrouded distance off the main line.

"Bill's got a private car on that there track," he hollered above the hiss of the downpour as the engine began to chug forward. "Jest foller the rails a couple of miles until you see a water tower an' you'll ride right into him."

"Much obliged," I yelled as me and Johnny Blue mounted our horses.

The old conductor waved, then shook his head before slamming shut the door of his caboose.

We sat our mounts and watched the train until it curved around a steep bluff covered in stunted pine and was lost to sight; then Johnny Blue reached inside his slicker and produced a thick biscuit that he carefully broke in two, handing half to me.

"Where did you get this?" I asked as I bit into the biscuit, the first solid food I'd tasted in two days. Johnny Blue nodded toward the curve where the train had disappeared. "From the old geezer's lunch pail."

"You mean you stole it?"

Johnny Blue shrugged. "I took it. An' I got this as well." He reached under his slicker again and this time he produced a fried chicken leg.

"How we gonna share that?" I asked.

"You take a bite; then I take a bite, an' we keep on doing that until it's gone."

"Johnny Blue Dupree," I smiled at him, reaching for the chicken. "You surely are a one."

Buffalo Bill's private railroad car was right where the old conductor said it would be, sitting on the track beside a ramshackle, green-stained water tower.

Although this was just a recruiting drive, being the showman he was and ever eager to impress the rubes, Bill had brought most of his show with him. There were dozens of tents, large and small, set up on each side of the track, and a couple of them were being used as temporary barns because they were crowded with horses, including dozens of the paint ponies that were much prized by Indians in them days.

The rain had stopped and there were scores of people

walking around, cowhands in wide-brimmed hats and high-
heeled boots, grizzled trappers in greasy buckskins, blanket-
wrapped Indians with drooping feathers in their hair, and
gawping townsfolk from Fort Smith who bothered the cowboys with fool questions or stood around the railroad car
hoping to catch a glimpse of Bill. Me and Johnny Blue
stowed our slickers and dismounted, leading our horses toward Bill's car. A young woman in a long black skirt and
a black-and-white-striped shirt watched us from the platform outside the car door, then raised one eyebrow in a
question as we stopped and looked up at her.

Her glossy brown hair was piled high on her head, topped
by one of them little straw boaters with a pink ribbon
around it, and she looked as pretty as a picture.

"Ma'am," I said, removing my hat and giving a little
bow, "me and him"—nodding toward Johnny Blue—"has
come to jine up with ol' Bill."

"See, we're aiming to have tea an' cakes with Queen
Vic," Johnny Blue said. "That's why we're here."

"An' we're top hands," I added, trying to impress the
girl. "Been at it man and boy"—I borrowed the railroader's
expression—"for nigh on ten year."

The girl studied us for a spell, and I could see by the
expression on her face that we didn't impress her as top
hands or any kind of hands come to that. "Mister Cody is
busy right now," she said. "Judge Parker and the mayor of
Fort Smith and their ladies are with him." She smiled
vaguely at us. "Perhaps if you'd care to wait . . ."

"We can wait," I said.

The woman nodded, still smiling. "Oh good. Maybe you
can go talk with the cowboys or something."

"Lady, I been speakin' with cowboys all my life," Johnny
Blue said. "They got nothin' to say I want to hear."

"Oh good," the girl said brightly. "You just go ahead
and do that."

She abruptly turned on her heel, her skirt swishing, and disappeared inside the car, and I heard a burst of laughter and the clink of glasses as she opened and closed the door.

I looked away from the car and caught sight of a small man in a brown suit with a ratlike face above a tight celluloid collar studying me and Johnny Blue intently. When he saw me look at him, he took to his heels and stampeded in a panic in the direction of Fort Smith.

I didn't pay much attention to the little man at the time, but given what happened later, I should have.

"You boys lookin' for work?"

A trapper in buckskins stood a few feet away, giving us the once-over. He had a brass-framed Henry rifle in the crook of his arm and a fur hat decorated with an eagle feather on his head.

"We're studyin' on it," I said.

The trapper nodded. "You could do worse. Beef an' beans three times a day an' forty a month. Not too shabby."

The biscuit and bite or two of chicken had done nothing to appease my hunger, and stomach growling, I allowed that it seemed like a fair proposition.

I looked around and saw that Bill had set up a couple of tall posts on each side of the cinder path leading into his compound with a banner stretched across saying, BUFFALO BILL'S WILD WEST SHOW. And beside one of the posts stood an Indian in full regalia, flanked by two tough-looking huskies in plug hats and lace-up boots, each holding a hickory ax handle.

Every time one of them rubes from town passed, the Indian bowed and said: "God bless Queen Victoria."

"Who's the Injun?" I asked the trapper, watching a matronly woman in a blue dress give that Indian a wide berth, her eyes popping out of her head like she was sure he was about to scalp her. "Is he Sitting Bull?"

"Nah," the man answered. "That's Red Horse; he's an Oglala Sioux."

"What's with the guards?" Johnny Blue asked.

"Sonny," the trapper said, "that there's a wild, dog-eatin', fightin' Indian right off the plains. He ain't even green broke yet, so Bill hired them two big Paddies to keep tight rein on him."

"Is Bill taking him to England?" I asked.

"That's the word goin' around. Bill reckons them Englishmen will pay plenty to see a brave that was in the Custer fight."

"Are you sure?" I asked. "I mean about Red Horse an' the gallant Custer?"

The trapper spat a stream of brown tobacco juice. "Just as sure as I'm standing here."

Boys, about then I was starting to get an idea, and it involved my poor Aunt Prudence and her eldest son, Billy Bob. I don't know if you recollect Aunt Prudence; she was a tall, skinny ol' gal with a face built for a hackamore and she never went anywhere without the Good Book under her arm. She baked a mean huckleberry pie, though, and had a right nice voice for hymn singing and she was always eating them stewed prunes. Claimed they kept her reg'lar as clockwork.

"That Injun," I said to the trapper, "does he speak American?"

The man spat again. "Good as you an' me, sonny. What you got in mind?"

"I was thinkin' about asking him a question," I said. "It's about General Custer an' my cousin Billy Bob an' all."

The trapper shrugged. "Then ask away, but recollect that there's no reservation Injun, so don't go getting him upset. Bill would sure hate to see him runnin' loose in the streets a-choppin' Christian folks with his tommyhawk."

"That ain't likely," I said. "Indians cotton to me on account of how I speak their lingo."

"Injuns cotton to you because they know you're a lunatic," Johnny Blue said. "Maybe you should jest leave that brave alone. You heard what the man said, he's wild an' Bill ain't even got him green broke yet."

I shook my head at him. "This won't take but a minute. There's something I got to ask him for my Aunt Prudence's sake."

"You mean her that ate the prunes all the time an' had the simple son?" Johnny Blue asked.

"The very same."

Leading my horse, I walked over to the Indian, Johnny Blue trailing behind me. Them two big Paddies tightened the grip on their ax handles and looked at me suspiciously, but I didn't pay them no mind.

"All hail, great chief," I cried, raising my right hand in a salute.

Red Horse slowly looked me up and down, fingering the steel blade of the tomahawk at his belt, then replied: "Right back at ya, cowboy."

"This is going good," I whispered to Johnny Blue. "This Injun's took a fancy to me sure enough."

"I hear tell you was in the Custer fight back in the olden days," I said to Red Horse, smiling so he knew I didn't hold it against him.

"What's it to ya?" demanded that resolute redskin.

"Well, see, " I began, "my cousin Billy Bob was in that battle. He was like me, a stingy-sized, good-lookin' feller, an' he was always right partial to mules. Trouble was, he was right partial to other folk's mules."

"You don't say," declared Red Horse. "Partial to mules? Well, I can't say as I take to them much myself, though the Apaches reckon they're good eatin', even better than buffalo."

"Well, Billy Bob was a mite simple by times," I allowed, "an' it was on account of a pair of Missouri mules that he had to light a shuck out of Texas with a sheriff's posse takin' potshots at him all the way to the Louisiana border."

"Here, you," said one of the Paddies, taking a step toward me as he slapped his ax handle into the palm of one huge hand. " 'Tis not a good idea to be talkin' about shootin' an' killin' an' be gettin' this Hindoo upset."

"He ain't upset," I replied. "Anyhoo, I'm just gettin' to the point of my story."

"Well, make it quick an' be damned to ye," the Paddy growled.

"Anyhoo, Red Horse," I continued, "the next thing Aunt Prudence knows is that cousin Billy Bob's gone for a sod'ger and jined the cal'vry. He sent her a letter sayin' he was just a private but they was plannin' on makin' him a general right quick.

"But he never got to be a general because then she gets a letter from the Army sayin' Billy Bob was kilt stone dead with the gallant Custer on the little Big Horn."

"Sorry to hear that," said Red Horse, all the time studying my hair where it showed under my hat.

"You got nice hair," observed that sentimental savage. "I never seen hair as red as that in all my born days."

"Well, thankee," said I, "but to get back to the point. See, ever afterward Aunt Prudence would sit with her Bible on her lap, eating a dish of prunes, and say, 'Y'know, I hope poor Billy Bob was fetched with a Christian bullet an' not one of them heathen tommyhawks. I'd sleep better o' nights if I knew it was a grand old American ball that done for him.' "

"I love your hair," said Red Horse by way of acknowledgment as he reached out and felt it between his fingers.

Trying to keep that Injun on the point, I pushed his hand away and said: "What I was wonderin' was, did you by any chance see cousin Billy Bob get fetched? I know you was real busy what with the massacree an' the scalpin' an' sich, but you couldn't miss him. He had a big mustache like mine and yeller hair an' he t-t-talked l-l-like th-th-this."

Red Horse sighed, dropping his eyes from my hair. "I don't rightly recollect," he said, "but I'll study on it an' by and by it might come back to me. Yeller hair, you say?"

"Like a Palomino," I replied, "an' he had a big mustache an he c-c-couldn't s-s-say h-h-his w-w-words r-r-real g-g-good."

"Maybe I seen a ranny like that," the Sioux nodded, rubbing his chin. "I seem to recollect a young sod'ger with yeller hair an' a big mustache yellin', 'I s-s-surrender.' But like I said, I'll study on it some and let you know."

Then Red Horse stepped toward me until his mouth was close to my ear, them two big Paddies got up on their tippy-toes, following his every move. "Listen, cowboy," he whispered, "cousin Billy Bob aside, I got a feeling you ain't long for this world on account of how somebody's gonna put a bullet in you for askin' too many questions of folks."

I made to interrupt, but he held up his hand.

"Now listen good, I want to be around when you get plugged because I never took me no red scalp afore an' I can't do it for my own self because nowadays the law would string me up right quick. So I plan on following you real close until the day you're fetched." He stepped back and smiled. "No offense."

"None taken," I replied brightly, but boys, I got to admit that the thought of that wild Sioux dogging my footsteps, waiting to take my hair, bothered me a whole barrelful.

Next thing I knew, that wild Injun started to sing this heathen chant, and the two Paddies hollered, "Back! Back!" and prodded him in the chest with their ax handles.

The trapper in the fur hat strolled over to my side and said: "Well, I'll be damned. That's a Sioux scalp song. I ain't danced to one o' them in ten years, maybe longer."

Well, boys, that trapper commenced to singing and dancing, him an' that Sioux harmonizing on the tune, and the bigger of the two Paddies turned to me and yelled: "Get out of here, you. You've got this bloody Mohammedan on the warpath, you have!"

I decided I should get well shot of that Indian, so I led my horse away as Johnny Blue looked at me and growled: "You're a complete lunatic, you know. You're sore tetched in the head an' someday it's gonna be the death of you."

I was about to make a right sharp reply when the pretty gal in the straw boater walked up to us and said: "Oh, there you are. I've been looking all over for you." She smiled sweetly, her hifalutin glance taking in me and Johnny Blue; the dancing, hollering Indian; the dancing, hollering trapper; and the two cursing, panicked Paddies, and she added calmly: "Mister Cody will see you now."

Leaving that riot behind, we got to Bill's car just in time to see two men and two women leave and climb into a waiting carriage. One of the men, a tall, thin ranny wearing a black broadcloth suit and a thick chin beard, took the reins and clucked the matched pair of sorrels into motion.

Following my eyes, the pretty gal said: "That's the distinguished jurist, Judge Parker."

"You mean Hanging Judge Parker?" Johnny Blue asked.

The little gal sniffed. "Some people call him that." She gave Johnny Blue a hard look. "The low, criminal element mostly."

"Well," observed that canny rider, "I hope I never have the pleasure of making his acquaintance."

Boys, let me tell you, that railroad car of Bill's was a rolling palace. It was all done out in red velvet plush and brass, lit by sparkling crystal chandeliers that hung from the ceiling.

But what you noticed when you first walked in was the great frontiersman himself.

He was wearing white buckskins decorated with elaborate Cheyenne beadwork, and I reckon some little Indian gal wore down three pairs of teeth chewing on that buckskin to get it as soft as it was.

Bill's hair was scented with some kind of fancy perfume and it hung over his shoulders in loose ringlets. He wore a mustache and goatee and his eyes were bright blue against his brown skin. When the little straw boater gal led us in, Bill sprang to his feet from behind his desk and hollered in a loud, booming voice: "Well, well, I've heard a lot about you two rannies. Welcome, welcome." I'd no idea how Bill could have heard anything about me and Johnny Blue, but I let that pass and said: "Bill, we've come to jine up with your Wild West Show. Me and him"—I nodded toward Johnny Blue—"is top hands and famous Injun fighters."

"See, we want to go to England and have tea with ol' Queen Vic," Johnny Blue added.

"Is that a fact?" said Bill. "Well, you boys have come to the right place."

He stepped back to his desk, where there was a bottle of Old Anderson's Little Brown Jug sour mash Kentucky bourbon that cost a dollar a shot in some of the higher-class saloons.

"You boys look like you could use a drink," he said.

"Sure could, Bill," I replied. "We've been riding the boxcars for nigh on two weeks an' we're thirsty enough to spit cotton."

"Well, once again, you've come to the right place," Bill smiled.

But he corked the jug of Anderson's and reached into

his desk, producing a green bottle without a label. There were glasses on the desktop that had been used by the previous guests and he shoved two of these in front of us then filled them with a colorless liquid from the bottle.

"Drink hearty, boys," quoth that chivalrous showman. "You're among friends here."

He sat in the ornate red-velvet chair behind his desk and took a long, thin cigar from a cedar box, which he proceeded to light, filling the car with fragrant smoke.

As we sipped his cheap who-hit-John, Bill studied us closely and I could tell he didn't seem too impressed. As you boys will recollect, me and Johnny Blue was so poor we didn't have a nickel between us. We were down-at-heel and ragged, too poor to paint and too proud to whitewash, as they say.

"So you've done some Indian fighting?" Bill asked finally.

"Sure have," I said. "Blackfoot mostly, but we've had a run-in or two with Flatheads."

"An' we've fit outlaws," Johnny Blue added.

"Mmm," Bill said, nodding. "And you were top hands. Where was that?"

"Up on the old DHS," I replied. "We worked for Granville Stuart."

Bill fell silent, then seemed to make his mind up about something.

He stood and said: "You boys watch this."

He got his big white sombrero from the desk, settled it on his head, then thrust his left leg in front of his right, clenched his fists, bending them upward at the wrist by his sides, and raised his eyes to heaven like he was seeing a holy vision.

Bill was standing at such rigid attention, he found it hard to talk, but he gritted between clenched teeth: "What . . . do . . . you . . . boys . . . see?"

"You're a fine figure of a man, Bill," allowed Johnny Blue.

"Hell, I know that," Bill replied, relaxing. "What else did you see?"

I guess me and Johnny Blue was looking at him blankly, because he said in an exasperated tone: "All right, listen to this and maybe you'll get the idea."

He adopted his previous pose, though this time not so rigid, and in a voice loud enough to rattle the rafters, hollered: "Fear not, fair maiden, for I, Buffalo Bill, am at hand to save you from the vile lust of the bloodthirsty savage, and I am willing to lay down my life, if need be, to preserve the innocent flower of American womanhood."

Boys, this was such a powerful performance that me and Johnny Blue burst into applause and gave Bill many a hearty Huzzah! and begged him for more.

But that humble hero merely bowed and shook his head, saying: "Thank you, thank you, but no more for today. I must save my voice."

Then he looked first at Johnny Blue, then at me, and asked: "Well, did you see it?"

I shrugged. "You looked like a real hero, Bill, but I still don't catch your drift."

"It's presence. Stage presence," Bill said. "Hickok had it; so did Sitting Bull." He shook his head sadly. "But I could see right off that you hombres don't have it."

Bill sat behind his desk again and refilled our glasses— at three dollars a gallon I guess he could afford to be generous with the stuff—and said: "The question is, what do I do with you boys?"

"Give us a job as rough riders anyhoo," I suggested mildly. "Stage presence or no."

Bill shook his curls again. "Never let it be said that Buffalo Bill Cody turned away any man in need of honest employment. I have a situation in mind for you boys that will pay a dollar a day and three squares for as long as I'm here in Fort Smith."

"We'll take it," I said eagerly.

"You two are tailor-made for it," Bill said. "And it's honest work."

Fifteen

I sank my shovel into a huge, steaming pile of horse manure and tossed it into the back of the wagon where a farmer stood slouched against a wheel, puffing on his pipe as he watched me and Johnny Blue work.

"If'n you boys don't shovel that stuff a mite faster, we're fixin' to be here all day," the sodbuster said conversationally.

Johnny Blue leaned on his shovel and wiped sweat from his brow with his bandana, "Maybe if you helped, it would go faster."

"Maybe," the farmer allowed. "But I ain't gonna. You boys is the ones being paid for it."

That chicken chaser wore canvas pants and a straw hat, and he was sporting one of them farmer beards that fell all the way from his cheeks to his belt buckle.

Johnny Blue threw a shovel of manure into the wagon, then turned to me and said. "This was a great idea you had. Let's go join up with Buffalo Bill, you said, he'll make us top hands and take us to England an' we'll have tea with the Queen. Well, how come we're standing here shoveling shit?"

I couldn't answer that question right off, so I swatted at the cloud of flies buzzing around my head and said finally: "It's on account of how we didn't snag the Buffalo

Bill Bear. If'n we did, you and me would be top hands right now, livin' high on the hog an' no mistake."

Johnny Blue growled under his breath about Charlie Russell being a born troublemaker and no hand with either cows or bears, and he took the tally book out of his shirt pocket where he kept the little flower Lo May had given him. He looked at it for a long while, then sighed: "I'm glad my little gal doesn't know how low I've sunk. This ain't no work for a man."

"Ahem," the farmer said, "if'n you two don't mind, I got to get this stuff spread on my cornfield afore dark."

Johnny Blue turned to that pumpkin roller and was about to say something right sharp when a voice behind us, low and as cold as ice, said: "You boys stay right where you are. You're under arrest."

I stood stock still as did Johnny Blue, but craned my neck around until I made out a tall man in a black shirt and pants standing a few feet away, a Winchester in his hands.

"That's right, boys," the man said. "Take it real easy."

He walked around until he was facing us and I saw the lawman's star on his shirt. Another lawman stood beside him, a huge red mustache covering his top lip.

"Don't make no fancy moofs, by Gott," this man said. "Or I'll choot you down, by Gott."

"Mister," Johnny Blue said, "you got a Winchester gun an' I got a shovel o' shit. Do you really think I'm gonna make any fancy moves?"

"Watch the little one, Chris," the first lawman said. "He's sneaky and he's gunslick."

"I watch him right close, Heck," Chris said. "He make one fancy moof an' I choot him tru der belly."

"By way of introduction," the man named Heck said pleasantly, "I'm Heck Thomas and this here German feller is Chris Madsen and we're marshals for Judge Isaac C.

Parker and the United States Court for the Western District of Arkansas, having jurisdiction over the Indian Territory." He kept his cold blue eyes on me the whole time he spoke. "Now both of you shuck those gun belts real easy like and take two steps away from them."

He turned his rifle on Johnny Blue. "Mister, I don't have a prejudiced bone in my body. I'm tellin' you that so you know ahead of time that I shoot black men as quick as white ones."

Me and Johnny Blue did as we were ordered and dropped our gun belts.

"What's the charge against us, Heck?" I asked. "If'n you don't mind me callin' you Heck."

"Rape, murder, high treason, horse theft, disturbing the peace . . . you name it. The said offenses occurring in the town of Alpine, in the Idaho Territory, while you rannies was members of the Amos Pinkney gang. And yeah, I do mind you calling me Heck."

"What are you planning to do with us?" Johnny Blue asked.

"You will be escorted to Fort Smith, where you will receive a fair trial and then be hanged at Judge Parker's convenience." Heck turned to Chris Madsen. "Chris, bring up the wagon."

"Who turned us in?" I asked as Chris reappeared driving a cage on wheels drawn by a rangy gray mule. "Was it Bill?"

"Nah," Heck replied, "it was some little rat of a feller in a celluloid collar and a plug hat. He's claiming the reward for you two, and he's liable to get it too, from what I hear." Heck motioned with his rifle. "Now step up to that wagon so we can get the chains on you."

Boys, as long as I live, I'll never forget my first glimpse of Judge Parker's Hotel.

The Fort Smith jail was located beneath the judge's courtroom and it consisted of two low-ceilinged basement rooms. The floor and walls were made of stone, and into these dank and dark caves were jammed about one hundred and fifty prisoners, professional desperadoes and murderers mostly, with a sprinkling of rustlers, moonshiners, and the assorted riffraff of the Indian Territory.

Heck shoved us into a cell that was already crowded with another sixty or seventy men. It had a sawn-off barrel to serve the prisoner's bodily needs and had but one washbasin.

The place reeked of rotten pork, sweat, urine, tobacco juice, and fear, and the sick slept on the bare floor with the well, coughing and groaning under the pale yellow light cast by a few oil lamps that did little to penetrate the gloom.

As he slammed the door shut on us—Chris Madsen standing alertly to his left, a Greener scattergun in his hands—Heck said: "I got good news for you boys. One, you won't be here long because the judge likes to try capital crimes first, and two, you're just in time for dinner."

Boys, in them days the judge was allowed fifty cents a day to feed each prisoner, but somebody was skimping on the grub because dinner was a small wooden bowl half-filled with watery beans, a few pieces of green pork floating on top, and a square of Army hardtack that probably dated from the Civil War.

As he chewed on his hardtack, Johnny Blue held the withered little flower Lo May had given him and started into sighing. "I'll never see my little gal again," he said, crumbs falling over his bottom lip. "I'm gonna be hung for sure."

I was about to tell him that there was no evidence against us and what we needed was a right smart lawyer, when there was a commotion at the cell door and Heck stood there turning the key in the lock. Four marshals were with him, all heavily armed and determined-looking men, along with a preacher in a white beard who took a swig from a silver hip flask and began to read from the Bible.

His Colt in his hand, Heck walked into the cell and hollered: "Martin Joseph. It's your time." A small, thin man, barefoot and in a ragged shirt and pants, rose from the floor in a corner of the cell and walked toward Heck. The little feller had a swagger about him, but his face was as white as bleached bones, and when he pushed a strand of hair away from his eyes, his hand was trembling.

"It's almost dusk, Marty," Heck said. "Time to pay for your many crimes, including rape and murder committed in the Cherokee Nation on or around last February 12 in the year of Our Lord 1888. You were duly found guilty by a jury of your peers and the sentence of Judge Isaac C. Parker was that on this day, April 8, you be taken from this room by armed marshals to a convenient place and there be hung by the neck until you're one dead little son of a bitch."

Marty padded over to Heck on his bare feet and said: "Heck, you shot my pa through the belly and blowed my brother's head clean off with a Greener, but you give us an even break and always treated me square. I got nothing agin you." Marty looked up at Heck towering above him and added: "I just wanted you to know that."

Heck just stood there for a few moments, looking unbelievingly at the condemned man. Then he reached up a big hand and dashed a tear from his eye. "Marty," he said, "that's one of the nicest things anyone's ever said to me, an' I'm right sorry I done for your brother and pappy because it would've been crackerjack for you to be hung as a family." Then he hugged the little man close and choked: "Now make me proud, you little skunk. Go out there an' die game."

Boys, we was all so struck by Heck's kindness and re-

gard for his fellow man that the whole cell broke into loud
Huzzahs! and I could feel tears start in my own eyes.

As Marty was being led away, Heck waved his Colt like
the conductor of a band, and sang in a fine baritone voice:

> In the sweet by and by
> We shall meet on that beautiful shore . . .

Looking around him, Heck hollered: "C'mon boys, all
together now." And as one man we raised our voices in
that grand old hymn.

> In the sweet by and by
> We shall meet on that beautiful shore.
>
> There's a land that is fairer than day,
> And by faith we can see it afar,
> For the Father waits over the way,
> To prepare us a dwelling place there.

As we sang, Marty waved and yelled: "See you in hell,
boys!"

The preacher gulped, took another swig from his flask
and let Marty have a belt, and prayed harder than ever before.

Boys, right about then I could feel the hemp around my
own neck, and so did Johnny Blue because he put Lo May's
flower away and groaned: "We gotta get ourselves a good
lawyer."

Well, after about an hour Heck came back and stood
outside our cell and hollered: "Listen up, everybody. I just
want you low-lifers to know that Marty died game as a
bigamist, and the little son of a bitch didn't kick for no
more'n two minutes afore he was gone."

Again, a heartfelt Huzzah! leapt to the throat of every

prisoner and Heck took off his hat and waved it around his head and led three more cheers; then he walked away and left us to the gathering dark and our own misery and growing fear.

Well, boys, we didn't get a good lawyer. Instead we got Silas T. Bramwell III.

On the morning after Marty's hanging, a couple of marshals put chains on me and Johnny Blue and took us out of the cell. We were prodded by rifle muzzles up the stairs to the courthouse level and then pushed toward the open door of a small room adjoining the court.

We smelled Silas Bramwell before we saw him.

He arrived in a cloud of rye whiskey fumes, a man of medium height who must have gone three hunnerd pounds if he was an ounce. He had a huge red nose with two bleary blue eyes set close together and he wore one of them lawyer beards on his chin, squared off where it met the greasy top of his collarless shirt. Two splendid burnsides adorned his cheeks and a gold watch chain crossed the enormous belly that hung in front of him like a sack of grain.

"I am Silas T. Bramwell the Third," he told us by way of introduction as we stood outside the door of the room. "I am your attorney, duly appointed by Judge Parker's court." And he gave us a stiff little bow.

Boys, you know I've never set great store by lawyers. It ain't the world's oldest profession, but the results to the client are just the same.

"Pleased to make your acquaintance," I said, but Silas Bramwell ignored me, turning to one of the marshals. "Snakes, if you please, Marshal."

The man, a tall, skinny galoot wearing a Colt in a cross-draw holster, sighed and said: "Silas, there ain't no snakes in there."

"Snakes," the lawyer insisted. "If you please, Marshal."

The lawman sighed again and walked into the room. He stomped around in there for a minute or two and came back out. "No snakes."

Silas shuddered, looking from me to Johnny Blue. "I hate snakes, and I see them all the time." He glanced over his shoulder like a man walking in a dark alley. "They lie in wait for me, the slithering, wriggling demons, peeking out from behind my desk, in my drawers—the kind I wear and the kind I put stuff in—and grinning at me with their little beady eyes from the top of the picture of my sainted mother."

"Well, there ain't no goddamned snakes in there," the marshal said unpleasantly.

Silas pulled a pint of rye from the inside pocket of his frock coat and took a long, gulping swig.

Then he rounded on the marshal. "You think me a weak creature, do you not?"

The lawman stood there stone-faced, but his mustache bristled. "You see snakes, you see snakes, Silas," he said. "That's your problem, ain't it?"

"We're all weak creatures," Silas said, ignoring the man's question. "These two rannies, here"—nodding toward me and Johnny Blue—"are weak creatures born to be hanged. As for me, I drink, which will one day be my folly."

Silas sighed, took another swig from his bottle, and shoved it back in his pocket, slapping the bulge in his coat to reassure himself that it hadn't mysteriously vanished.

"The whole world is populated by weak creatures and that"—he tapped the side of his bulbous nose with a shaking forefinger—"is what keeps us lawyers . . ." He searched for the right word. ". . . bustling."

"Whatever you say, Silas," the marshal sighed. "Whatever you say."

By this time the lawman must have been in a fair-tomiddling bad mood, because he shoved me and Johnny Blue roughly into the room, our chains clanking, and when Silas hesitated at the door to study the floor and ceiling, he shoved him inside as well.

"Ten minutes," the marshal growled. "That's what the judge said."

Silas T. Bramwell III looked like a man walking on eggs. He tippy-toed across the floor to a desk shoved into a corner of the room, his head swiveling on his neck as he studied every nook and cranny. "Damn snakes," he muttered.

"I didn't take you for a lawyer, Silas," Johnny Blue said.

"Oh, how come?"

"Because you'd your hands in your own pockets."

At that moment I happened to glance outside the room's sole window and beheld a sight that chilled my blood.

Down below in the busy courtyard in front of the courthouse stood a tall man, his arm wrapped around the waist of a woman who was gazing up at him adoringly.

The man sported a mustache as fine as mine, and he had a marshal's star pinned to his shirt.

There was no mistaking that lanky, muscular frame—he was Frank Canton, one of the most vicious members of the Amos Pinkney gang. The man who'd vowed to shoot me down like a dog on sight—and the woman in his arms was Dora!

When Canton turned to say something to Dora, I saw the half-moon nick in his ear where I'd shot him in the desperate gun battle that made my reputation as one of the West's top gunslicks, and I felt sudden fear clutch at my belly.

Boys, fate is a strange thing, because Canton and Dora chose that moment to glance up at the window where I stood, and they saw me looking at them.

Canton mouthed words I couldn't hear, but there was no mistaking the message in what he did next. He tapped the holstered gun at his waist with the middle finger of his right hand and grinned.

Then Dora said something to him and they both laughed.

Right then, for the first time since I'd been a guest at the Parker Hotel, I felt the first stirrings of doubt—and began to think that me and Johnny Blue would never leave this place alive.

As Silas settled himself behind the desk, and was busy checking under it, gingerly pulling out each drawer, I motioned to Johnny Blue to come to the window. He took in the scene outside in a glance, especially when Canton made a gun with his forefinger and pointed it right at us, dropping his thumb like the hammer of a Colt, his lips framing the word "Pow!"

"That's it," Johnny Blue said, turning away from the window, "we're dead as hell in a parson's parlor."

Silas overheard him, because he said brightly: "Not if I can help it. You boys can't be hung here in the Arkansas Territory. You must be sent back to Idaho to be tried fair and square and then hung. It's all a matter of"—shuddering, Silas checked under the desk again—"what we lawyers call jurisdiction." He shoved his head close to the top desk drawer. "You boys hear something?" he asked.

I shook my head at him.

"I could've sworn I heard a rattle," Silas said.

"That's just my breathing," Johnny Blue said, looking at our lawyer like he'd just crawled out from under a rock. "It's my death rattle."

Silas was about to speak again, but I interrupted him. "Walk over to the window here, I want to show you something," I said.

The lawyer grunted and groaned his way out of the chair, then waddled over to the window.

"See that tall ranny down there with the woman on his arm?" I asked.

"Indeed," quoth Silas. "And a lovely young couple they make, too. I hear—though I haven't confirmed it as yet—there's been talk of wedding bells and a reception with cake and ice cream."

"That," I said, "is Frank Canton, one of the worst members of the Pinkney gang. And that gal with him is a Montana whore who used to call herself Sweet Dora Darling, the Drovers' Friend."

Silas looked like I'd just slapped him. He stood there studying me for a few moments then snapped: "You are a weak, forlorn creature." He waved his hand toward the courtyard below. "Frank Canton is a fine young man, one of the judge's best and most loyal deputies. The young lady is a veritable princess"—he put his dukes up and balanced on his toes like a prize-fighter, pumping his fists up and down in an alarming manner—"and I will fight any man who speaks evil of her. She is a famous actress lately arrived in Fort Smith to practice her art and entertain the citizenry."

"But I—" I began.

"Say no more," Silas said, dropping his fists. "Do not try to thrust blame on the innocent and thus escape the consequences of your own iniquities. Victory does not lie in that direction. We will, and I say we will, sir, fight this case on jurisdiction alone. And by God sir, we . . . will . . . prevail."

Silas ended his little speech in a triumphant shout, and this heartened me and Johnny Blue considerably because right about then we were both scared stiff as a new rawhide rope. We gave Silas a rousing Huzzah! and that lamentable lawyer merely bowed and took out his bottle, tipped it in our direction, and said: "Your health, gentlemen."

Silas chugged the rye, his Adam's apple bobbing, then wiped his mouth with the back of his hand.

"I believe," he said, "our business here is concluded."

He reached out and put his hand on my shoulder. "Put your trust in me, boy. Never let it be said that Silas T. Bramwell failed in his duty, to his client or his country."

Then he turned and waddled to the door. "Guard!" he yelled.

As we were being led away, Silas said: "By the way, boys, your case will be heard at ten o'clock tomorrow morning."

"That quick?" I asked, stunned.

"Yours is a capital crime," Silas replied. "The Judge likes to hear those without delay so if there's a hanging involved . . . well, it gets the whole thing over in a hurry." He bowed again in our direction. "I'll see you 'pokes again in the morning before court."

The marshal prodded us out the door with his shotgun, but Johnny Blue turned and yelled: "Behind you, Silas! Snake!"

The fat man screamed and with amazing nimbleness leaped on the desk, pulling up the legs of his pants as he did a dance that would make any saloon girl proud.

"Oh, sorry," Johnny Blue said, after observing this performance with the shocked lawman for a few moments. "I guess I was mistaken."

After we were shoved back into our cell, standing amid all that filth and human misery, I said to Johnny Blue right sharply: "You had no call to scare poor Silas that way."

But that reckless rider just shrugged and said: "Hell, I don't like lawyers, especially my own."

Silas seemed to have forgiven Johnny Blue—or maybe the whiskey had made him forget—because when he showed up at our cell early the next morning, trailed by a sleepy and irritable marshal, he was beaming from ear to ear.

"This is your big day, boys, and I've got something here

to make you took more presentable in court." With a flourish Silas produced a bottle that he proceeded to pass through the bars to me. But the marshal grabbed his arm and asked harshly: "Here, you, what's that? It ain't poison, is it?"

Silas shook his head and held up the bottle so the lawman could read the label. "It's Prince Albert's Hair and Mustache Pomade for Ladies and Gentlemen," quoth our assured attorney. "I want to clean the accused up a little bit before they appear in court."

Well, boys, the marshal didn't like this one bit, because he growled: "A damned noose don't much care what they look like."

But Silas insisted: "Nevertheless, I want them to look their best when they come before the Judge."

"Well, go ahead, damn your eyes," the marshal said, "but it's a waste of time and effort if you ask me."

As Silas passed me the bottle, the marshal, a tough-looking ranny with a knife scar running down his right cheek, muttered that in the good old days he just strung up outlaws and low persons right off, and that all this fair trial stuff was just a load of hooey, if'n you asked him.

But I ignored the man and poured Prince Albert's pomade into the palm of my hand. The stuff was thick and black and smelled like lavender, and Johnny Blue refused to have anything to do with it, saying if they stretched his neck on the gallows, he didn't want to go to hell smelling like a pansy.

Boys, you'll recollect that in them days my hair was bright red and stuck up in spikes all over my head and nary a comb could get through it. But I used a lot of that pomade and parted my hair in the middle, slapping it down on each side of my head until it lay flat and shiny as a new-minted penny.

Then I put a big dollop on my mustache, twirling the

ends into handsome points that stuck out a good three inches on each side of my face.

You boys will agree that I made a fine appearance as me and Johnny Blue entered court that morning to face the Hanging Judge Isaac C. Parker—a man I knew to be strict but scrupulously fair.

Sixteen

"Oh yes, yes, they look like men. But are they human? Nay, I say. They are creatures of blood, wild animals of the plains. Before you today are not men, but brutes and demons, the sorry refuse of humanity with a tigerish appetite for blood."

Thus I heard Judge Parker describe me and Johnny Blue to the jury before the trial had even begun, and beside me Johnny Blue groaned, "We're dead," his chains clanking as he held his head in his hands.

But he looked up when a woman's voice, harsh and shrill, cut across the silence of the court: "Well, thou old Nero, is this two more for your butcher's block?"

"That's Belle Starr," Silas whispered. "She sits in the Judge's court almost every day."

The reason Belle was there was that in them olden days, the most popular heroes of the West weren't gunfighters or peace officers, they were lawyers. Men and women would ride for miles to hear a well-known lawyer plead a case, especially prosecutors like William Henry Harrison Clayton, who was sitting at a table opposite our own, glaring at Belle Starr.

Lawyers like Clayton knew folks came for the show, and they usually put on a good performance. A courtroom was a theater of the West, usually long before towns like Fort Smith had a theater. Nobody had to ask if Judge

Parker's court was in session, you only had to look at the number of rigs and horses tied to the hitching rails and the folks all decked out in their Sunday best. People came from miles out in the Territory and they brought picnic lunches to enjoy while they watched the fun.

So, as always, the courtroom was packed to overflowing as Judge Parker leaned forward over his bench and pointed a finger at Belle Starr, a scrawny, horse-faced woman sitting in the front row of chairs.

"Nero, madam? Nero, is it? Well, you won't find me fiddling while Rome burns, I can assure you of that."

The Judge beamed and, nodding his head sagely, looked round the courtroom, opening the door to the laughter that soon followed.

As the merriment subsided, Silas slowly got to his feet in a cloud of whiskey fumes and roared: "I demand, Judge Parker, that you adjourn these proceedings immediately. As God is my witness, there will be no trial here today."

"Holla," the Judge declared angrily. "Here's an impertinence for you. On what grounds, sir, do you make this demand?"

Silas tried to draw himself up to his full height but succeeded only in staggering against the table where me and Johnny Blue sat. Recovering his balance, he mustered as much of his tattered dignity as he could and said: "Because, sir, you are out of your jurisdiction. The alleged offenses were committed in the Idaho Territory and that is where these men should be returned for trial."

The Judge sat for a spell, studying on that bold statement, and then said words that I made particular note of, even asking Silas to write them down for me later.

"*Jurisdictio mea est ubi dico meam jurisdictionem esse,*" Judge Parker intoned solemnly.

"What the hell does that mean?" Johnny Blue whispered.

Looking down at him, Silas said: "It's Latin, and it means, My jurisdiction is where I say my jurisdiction is."

"And what the hell does that mean?" Johnny Blue asked again.

"It means," Silas sighed, "that we're royally screwed."

Just then Belle Starr left her seat and walked over to our table.

That was one homely ol' gal, and no mistake. She was wearing a wrinkled black dress and an old hat with a white feather drooping off the brim, and in her hands she carried wooden knitting needles and a ball of red yarn. Belle Starr looked like something the cat drug in and the dog won't eat, and she smelled like she'd a goat under each armpit and a dead fish in her back pocket.

But her smile was wide and friendly as she looked at me and Johnny Blue and said: "Boys, after the hangin' I'll see you buried real nice with a preacher and a proper marker an' all." She reached out and patted Johnny Blue's cheek and that reckless rider was so startled that his chains clanked as he jerked away from her.

"I like the shy ones," Belle told him. "Too bad we'll never get together."

Dora was the first witness for the prosecution.

And that little gal was a first-rate actress all right.

She told William Clayton that she'd been in Alpine— "singing the lead role in Mr. Gilbert and Mr. Sullivan's *H.M.S. Pinafore*"—when the town was attacked by Amos Pinkney and his evil band as a prelude to their planned overthrow of the United States government.

Holding a little lace handkerchief in her hand that she used to dab her eyes with now and then, Dora described how she'd been dragged from the stage by two men and then "savagely assaulted."

"Do you see those two men in this court today?" Clayton asked.

Dora pointed at me and Johnny Blue and sobbed: "Yes I do. It was those two."

"She's lying," I whispered to Silas. "That never happened."

"Shhh," said our lawyer. "We must step carefully. Ah, she's so innocent. So pretty. So vulnerable."

"Now," Clayton said, "think back to that day, Miss Darling. Was the nature of this terrible assault sexual?"

"Yes," Dora sobbed in a tiny voice. "They both done me good."

"You mean, and I know how distressing this must be for you to recall, that you were dragged from the stage where you were innocently practicing your art only to have full penile penetration thrust upon you—not once, but twice?" Clayton turned dramatically to the jury. "What am I talking here, gentlemen? By God sirs, I'm talking rape!"

"Oh, yes indeed," Dora replied, dabbing her eyes. "They both done me, and him"—pointing at me—"he slapped me here"—her fingers brushed the scar on her lip where Shade Hannah had struck her—"and he giggled the whole time he was at me with his . . . thingy."

"Oh, the inhumanity!"

Judge Parker was slumped back in his chair, his eyes raised to heaven as he clutched at his head.

"Oh, the inhumanity!" he wailed again. "Must I hear more? Can I take any more? Yet I must, for it is my duty. Proceed, Mr. Clayton."

"And you, sir," Clayton rounded on Silas, who at that moment was hiding behind a sheaf of papers, trying to take a sip from a silver hip flask, "you who sit there, fangs bared, determined to destroy the reputation of this unfortunate lady, what of you?"

"Eh?" Silas replied, startled, so taken aback by this attack that he spilled whiskey down his shirtfront.

"Yes sir! You sir! My God, why don't you reach your

calloused hand into that fair and tender bosom and rip out her very heart!"

Cries of Shame! Shame! went up from the spectators, and Dora screeched piteously: "Oh, I am undone. What decent man will want me now, poor despoiled creature?"

One bald ranny in a darned coat six inches too short for him in the arms and tight across the chest legged it toward the witness box yelling: "I'll take you, Dora! I don't care how many done you!"

Judge Parker ordered the marshals to remove the man and he was quickly thrown into the street, still protesting his undying love and devotion.

"My God," Clayton yelled at Silas after order was restored, "why do you seek to torment this lady further? Must she suffer even more? Is there a shred of decency left in you? Come, sir, is there no end to your malice? Must you cross-examine?"

"But . . . but . . ." Silas stammered.

"Look at her," Clayton roared. "Where the white lily of purity once glittered on her girlish brow, burning shame has now set its seal forever," Clayton walked over to Silas and threw his arms wide. "In the name of God, man, let her go in peace."

Again cries of Shame! rose from every throat in the courtroom, and more than one voice was heard to declare that Silas better start packing iron because from this day forth he was a marked man and low down.

"I do not wish to cross-examine this witness," choked that shocked shyster, seeing the writing on the wall plain as the ears on a Missouri mule.

The Judge looked at him sternly. "Indeed I should hope not. For shame, Mr. Bramwell. For shame."

"Silas," I whispered urgently, "you can't let Dora get away with this. She's lying, telling a real big windy. I used to do her all right, but only on payday because it cost me a dollar every time, an' sometimes two if business was brisk."

That spineless lawyer shoved his papers in front of his face again and took a pull from his flask; then he burped and said: "No, no, not the young lady. That way lies disaster because she has the sympathy of the jury. But fear not, I have a plan that can't fail. Trust me."

"Where have I heard that before?" Johnny Blue asked, and he buried his face in his hands and groaned.

Boys, the second witness was Frank Canton, looking handsome and heroic with his fine cavalry mustache and a red bandana carelessly knotted around his neck. A marshal's star glittered on the front of his dark blue shirt and he wore tooled Texas boots with heels a good two inches high.

"May I compliment you on the fine appearance you present in court, Marshal Canton," Judge Parker said. "You do me credit, sir."

There was a round of applause for Frank and a few Huzzahs! and that heartless hardcase nodded and smiled and waved his hand at the spectators and then the jury.

Then Clayton got down to business.

The story he got from Frank was simple—and a pack of lies.

He said he saw Dora being attacked by two outlaws—pointing out me and Johnny Blue—and heedless of his own safety, he'd rushed to her defense. But the little one, he said, pointing at me, was a skilled and desperate gunman who had killed at least a dozen men in Texas and Montana, and Frank allowed as how he hadn't stood much of a chance.

"As quick as lightning he drew his murderous revolver and discharged several balls in my direction," he said. "One took a nick out of my ear"—he touched the half-moon

where I'd shot him after my gun went off by accident—
"but the second and third struck me in the body."

Frank buried his face in his hands and began to sob, his
big shoulders shaking.

"Please continue, Marshal," Clayton urged gently. "I
know the recollection of the events of that terrible day in
Alpine must be an ordeal for any decent man. But you
must go on, sir. You must go on."

Frank—the low-down skunk who'd actually led the attack on Alpine with Amos Pinkney—sat upright in his chair
and, wet-eyed, said: "I was shot through and through and
fell to the floor with a cry of utter despair. Then the little
one sitting there laughed as he had his way with Miss Darling while I watched in horror. Then the black man had his
way with her as she looked at me and wailed in the most
piteous fashion, 'I am undone . . . oh, kind sir, I am undone.' "

Frank buried his face in his hands and was again racked
by sobs.

The court fell silent but for the soft tick-tock of the
clock on the wall and the muffled gasps coming from behind Frank's hands. That ranny was proving to be an even
better thespian than Dora, and that's saying something.

As it happened, it was Belle Starr who broke the silence.

She jumped to her feet, turned in our direction, and
hollered: "What I said to you boys don't go no more. I'll
have no truck with violators of women, so you can find
somebody else to bury you decent."

Then she plopped back down on her seat to resounding
cheers and Judge Parker yelled above the noise: "Well said,
madam. Yes, very well said."

Boys, things looked bleak for me and Johnny Blue right
about then, especially when Silas refused to cross-examine
Frank Canton, saying the man was a bona fide hero and

one of the Judge's best fighting marshals and it would reflect badly on our case if we tried to question his honor and integrity.

"Then who the hell are you gonna cross-examine, Silas?" asked Johnny Blue testily.

But the lawyer put his finger to his lips and replied: "Hush now. I have a plan."

The judge was about to say something to the jury when there was a commotion at the back of the court. People were jumping off their chairs and stampeding toward the door and a woman screamed.

"What's going on there?" the Judge demanded.

"Snake!" somebody yelled.

"Snake!" Silas shrieked, and wild-eyed he prepared to scramble on to the table.

Johnny Blue looked at our lawyer, shook his head, and drawled: "Relax, Silas, it's a real one."

The bailiff got a stick kept in the courtroom for just such an occasion and scooped up the offending reptile and threw it outside. When he returned to his post beside the bench, he said to the Judge: "Big ol' bull snake, your honor."

Judge Parker nodded. "Then go back outside and retrieve it and place it in a box for two weeks for contempt. I'll have no disturbances in my court from either man or beast."

As the bailiff did as he was told and the court settled down again, there were excited whispers of "Bill," "It's Bill," and "Bill's coming."

Then the doors burst open and Buffalo Bill appeared in all his glory, resplendent in his white buckskins and flowing locks.

The crowd roared and even Judge Parker stood and applauded the famous frontiersman. As for Bill, he waved his hat around his head and laughed and hollered: "Hee . . . haw!"

And the wild-eyed spectators yelled back: "Hee . . . haw!"

And the Judge beamed and clapped his hands even louder.

"Let me just say what an honor this is, sir," said the Judge as Bill took his seat in the witness box.

"I know," allowed Bill modestly.

And once again the court broke into loud Huzzahs, me and Johnny Blue among them.

Clayton started in on Bill right away, and that shameless showman was happy to oblige the court.

"These two rannies came to me looking for work, saying they had to leave for England in a right hurry," he said. "But I could tell they was up to no good, especially the little one. He had the look of the revolver slick about him, kinda shifty-eyed and twitchy, so I told them both to skedaddle or I'd get me my rifle and put an end to their outlaw careers for good right there and then."

The spectators cheered and Bill smiled and waved his hat and Judge Parker said: "Oh, well done."

"Now, Mr. Cody," Clayton said, "shortly afterward the accused had a bloodcurdling meeting with an Indian, did they not?"

"Indeed," replied Bill. "The little ranny there, he talked to Red Horse, a wild Sioux war chief who massacred the gallant Custer and his brave band of heroes."

"And what did the accused ask him?" Clayton prompted. "Come now, Mr. Cody, the whole truth. Hold nothing back, no matter how horrible."

"Oh," said Bill, "he wanted to talk about cutting and scalping, and he asked Red Horse to learn him how to do it, stuff like that."

"And then what happened? Please tell the court."

"Well, my Injun got so scared, he ran away. Stole a Winchester and a horse and took off for the Nations."

"You mean," gasped Judge Parker, "that even as we speak there's a wild Indian with a repeating rifle loose among Christian white folk?"

"Sure is, your honor. And he's a wild one all right. Red Horse ain't even green broke yet. And he's running scared, and all on account of that little ranny sitting right there looking as guilty as a hound dog stealing eggs. Red Horse was my best Indian too, and I learned him to say, 'God Bless Queen Victoria' real good."

"All in all," said the Judge, "this is an appalling turn of events."

Bill nodded. "Red Horse is one mean Indian, an' no mistake."

Silas finally found the sand to jump to his feet and declare: "Your honor, I object, this testimony has no bearing on the case before this court."

"You think not?" Judge Parker boomed. "I think it carries a great deal of significance since it establishes the bloodthirsty and tigerish inclinations of the accused." He slapped his hand on the bench. "Objection overruled."

When Silas sat down, I whispered in his ear: "I ain't trying to rush you or nothin', but it seems to me this is a really, really good time to come up with that plan of your'n."

At this prompting, the lawyer nodded. Then he jumped to his feet and hollered. "Your honor, my clients plead guilty and throw themselves on the mercy of the court."

"Oh great," Johnny Blue said. "That was a crackerjack plan, Silas."

As the hubbub in the court over our guilty plea subsided, Silas said: "Mercy, your honor. We humbly beg for mercy."

The judge nodded, then said sternly: "Yes, mercy. There is always mercy in this court—but mercy tempered with justice."

He turned and dismissed Bill with many warm thanks, and that hero yelled, "Hee . . . haw," and waved his hat in the air as he left the courtroom to echoing cheers.

Boys, I'm not saying Bill lied on the witness stand. He just didn't tell the truth, and that's because telling false-hoods is easy and telling the truth is mighty difficult.

Well, after that, Silas informed the court that we were guilty as sin, and it was all over pretty quickly. After reel-ing off the charges against us, including, as I recollect, high treason, rape, murder, horse theft, and disturbing the peace, Judge Parker said he'd known all along we were guilty.

"You," he said to me, "tried to pass yourself off as an honest cowboy, yet one look at that slicked-down hair and much-twirled mustache—cultivated to cut a dash among ladies of the lower sort, no doubt—convinced me that you are a gunman, a desperado, and a lothario of the basest de-gree.

"And you"—this to Johnny Blue—"are a man of color whom I suspect happened into bad company, led astray by low companions and the twin demons of whiskey and wild women.

"When you men return to the solitude of your prison cell, bring to your recollection the mortal struggles and dying groans of your murdered victims. And when, by such reflections as these, your heart shall become softened, lis-ten awhile to the piteous cries of the innocent women you have outraged in your inhuman lust.

"Consider too, your treason against these United States, the land that gave you birth then nurtured you to manhood. How Liberty must be weeping today!

"I urge you to at once fly for mercy to the cross of the Savior and endeavor to seize upon His salvation."

Judge Parker leaned across his bench, his cold blue eyes darting back and forth from me to Johnny Blue like a rapier blade. "Listen now to the dreadful sentence of the law and then farewell forever until the court and you and all here today shall meet together in the general resurrection.

"Three days hence, not at dawn or dusk, but in the full light of day, you both shall be taken by Marshal Heck Thomas to a convenient place and then hanged by the neck until you are dead.

"May God have mercy on your souls."

The Judge then turned to the armed marshals sitting behind our table.

"Marshals," he said, "take them down."

Me and Johnny Blue didn't have much of an appetite for the beans and salt pork they served us for dinner that night, and every time I looked at him, I could read my own fear in my compadre's eyes.

Silas Bramwell came by the cell and said he was appealing our case to the Supreme Court.

"Though," he added, "since they agree to hear only one case in every hundred, it's a long shot. And given the terrible crimes you boys have admitted to, it's unlikely they'll reverse the Judge's sentence on grounds of jurisdiction alone." He shrugged. "Sorry."

That loathsome lawyer took a pull from his whiskey flask then added: "Now for some good news. I'll be at the hanging, just to make sure George Maledon does it right and you don't suffer none."

"Mister," Johnny Blue growled, "you better hope he does it right, because if he don't, I'm gonna come after you and shoot you through the lungs."

Later Heck Thomas came by and told us to die game and to not make things hard for him because it was an upsetting thing to drag rannies screaming to the gallows. Then he gave us each a little piece of rock candy and said not to tell the other prisoners on account of how that was all he had.

Lying on the cold stone floor trying to sleep amid the groans and shrieks of my fellow prisoners, I nudged Johnny Blue and said: "We ain't gonna hang, you know. Innocent men don't get executed in this country. It's never happened afore and it never will."

"You reckon?" asked that rueful rider hopefully, raising himself on one elbow.

"Sure," I replied. "Something will happen, Somebody will step forward an' prove our innocence, just you wait and see. We ain't gonna stand on no gallows with ropes around our necks."

"You mean that?"

"Of course I mean it," I said. "Trust me."

Seventeen

The rough hemp of the noose tapped against my cheek blown by a soft, pine-scented spring breeze. Around my waist was a heavy leather belt with a dozen bags of lead shot suspended from it, since I was so small and light there was some doubt that the fall through the gallows trap-door would break my neck.

Beside me, his hands tied behind his back like mine, Johnny Blue spat and said: "When will I ever learn not to trust you when you say 'trust me'?"

"Johnny Blue," I said, ignoring that comment, "I just want you to know that you were a good friend when you was sober an' a top hand, an' it's been an honor to ride with you all these years since we both come up the trail as younkers." I turned my head so I could look him in the eyes. "I just wanted you to know that, compadre."

Johnny Blue spat again. "You was all right," he allowed. "Most of the time."

The gallows was about one hundred yards from Judge Parker's court and jail, and there was plenty of breathing room since the platform had been built for size, being about fourteen by fifteen feet.

The nooses dangling by our heads were tied to a great crossbeam of seasoned oak that could handle a dozen condemned men at a time, and the gallows was located out in the open, providing a good view for the hundreds of spectators who'd been gathering since the early morning.

It was to be a well-reported hanging, Heck Thomas told us proudly, and all the local reporters were present as well as others from Little Rock, St. Louis, and even a few bigtime correspondents from New York and Boston.

There were whites, blacks, and Indians in the crowd and every mixture of the three.

I saw farmers in long beards and suspenders and their gaunt wives, well-dressed city folk in their Sunday best, scores of yelling kids, and rough-clad frontiersmen, many of them in buckskins.

But I didn't see any sign of Silas Bramwell, which was no surprise since Heck told us the lawyer was on a drunk with a whiskey drummer and hadn't bothered to make an appeal to the Supreme Court since it was a losing proposition anyhow.

Johnny Blue turned to me, then pointed with his chin. "Lookit, over there," he said.

I looked out and saw Dora and Frank Canton in the crowd.

Frank had his arm around her slim waist and she was gazing up at him adoringly. As for Frank, he was looking right at me, grinning like a persimmon-eating possum. He reached above his head like he was pulling upward on a rope, then tilted his neck over to one side and stuck out his tongue horribly as if he was being choked to death.

Dora saw this and laughed, slapping him lightly on the arm, and I distinctly heard her say: "Oh, you!"

Boys, I can't tell you how much I hated those two. They were bad people and low down. The crowd had been noisy at the start but they settled into an expectant hush when Heck led out me and Johnny Blue, preceded by the prison chaplain and George Maledon, the Judge's hangman.

Maledon was a stooped, slouchy little man with a gray beard and black piercing eyes.

As he walked though the crowd, I heard a plump matron whisper to her equally rounded companion: "That's Maledon. They say he won't drop the trap on a Freemason or a boy who wore the blue."

"He's said to be right careful," another woman said. "Look how he's giving them ropes a final check. They say he doesn't want anything to happen like it did in Mississippi last month."

"What was that?" the plump matron asked, gnawing on a fried chicken leg.

"Why, they nearly tore the boy's head clean off his shoulders, but he was still alive. Then they had to haul him up and hang him a second time, and all the time he's screaming, 'Don't choke me,' and 'Jesus save me.' "

The plump matron studied the chicken bone closely and from every angle, decided she'd picked it clean, and threw it over her shoulder. "Lord, what a rum do," she said, wiping grease from her chin with the back of her hand. "I hope nothing like that happens here."

But judging by the joyful gleam in her eye when she looked up at me, I'm sure that's exactly what she was hoping would happen.

As Heck, Chris Madsen, and half a dozen well-armed marshals stood around the gallows, the crowd hushed in tense expectation.

The chaplain asked me and Johnny Blue if we'd any special request for the hymn. Johnny Blue shook his head and told the preacher to go to hell, but I allowed how I'd always been right partial to "Railroad to Heaven" and had sung it at many a funeral.

The chaplain nodded and, in a trembling little tenor, led the crowd in singing that grand old hymn. To hear all those voices uplifted, mixed with the chants of the Indians, was an experience that felt as fine as a dollar shirt. Boys, I felt a rush of tears to my eyes as the folks sang, and if'n it hadn't been me that was getting hung, I'd have enjoyed the hell out of the whole thing.

After the hymn was over, Maledon came over to us and asked Johnny Blue if, being a black man who fell in with low companions, he cared to address the crowd.

"Go to hell," replied that sulky rider.

"Dang," Maledon yelped in disappointment. "You're plumb determined to spoil this hanging."

He looked at me. "How about you, boy?" He leaned over and whispered confidentially in my ear: "You can give 'em the one about whiskey and wild women. The wives really cotton to that one." I studied on that for a few moments, then figgered I'd nothing to lose, so I said: "Sure. I don't mind."

Maledon smiled happily. "Good lad! You got ten minutes afore the drop."

Well, I took a deep breath and began: "Whiskey and wild women brought me to this pass, though I had a good mother . . ."

Belle Starr, who had elbowed her way to the front of the crowd, looked over her shoulder and addressed all present in a loud, nasal voice: "He says he had a good mother."

"A saint," said the plump matron, squinting at another chicken leg she held at arm's length the better to judge its quality and meaty roundness. "An' she raised him by hand an' gave him a proper eddication, I'll be bound."

"And she raised me by hand an' gave me a proper eddication," I said.

"Told you so," said the matron, dabbing at her eyes with the corner of her apron. "Bless her."

"But," said I, "there was a wildness in me, and at an early age I ran away from home and pursued the cowboy profession, falling in with bad companions."

"He had bad companions," Belle Starr echoed loudly. "Low persons and no-accounts."

"For shame," cried the matron.

Despite the melancholy circumstances, I was beginning to enjoy myself as I went on: "These low companions led me astray, introducing me to strong drink and lewd women . . ."

"Lord," said the fat matron, covering her face with her apron, "here's shame for you."

But she could see well enough to dig her husband hard in the ribs. He was a small, mousy-looking man who looked so henpecked the roosters must have chased him every time he passed a chicken coop.

"Hey," he yelped. "What's that for?"

"Lewd women," the matron replied, and the crowd cheered lustily.

"Ah yes," said I, growing poetic, "many a bawd I've tumbled, many a cot I've rumpled."

"He's rumpled many a bawd," echoed Belle Starr, and again the crowd cheered.

"Tell us more about the bawds," one ranny yelled. "How many have ye done?"

"Too many," I hollered, "and that's why I stand before you now facing the drop."

This went down well with the crowd, and figgering to quit while we was ahead, Maledon walked over to me and said: "That's enough, boy. You done good and got them all worked up." He raised his eyes to heaven. "Now your time is short, and you must make your peace with God." Maledon studied both me and Johnny Blue for a spell then asked: "Do you have any last requests?"

"Yeah," Johnny Blue said, "don't put no black hood over my head. I want to see the sky as I go."

"Same for me," I said.

"So be it," said Maledon. And that humane hangman added: "No hoods."

He took a big silver watch from his vest pocket and thumbed open the cover. "Five minutes until two o'clock," he said. "That's all the time you boys has got left to you in this world."

Maledon put the noose around Johnny Blue's neck and then mine, adjusting the loop so the knot lay snug against my left ear. "Comfy?" he asked, and I allowed how it was.

I turned to Johnny Blue. "So long, compadre," I said. "I guess we'll meet again on that big open range in the sky."

"Don't count on it," said that rattled rider, and I guess he was still smarting over the fact I said he wasn't gonna get hung and now he was.

Boys, there was just no pleasing Johnny Blue in them days, especially when he was about to get his neck stretched.

"Studying on it some, there's only one thing I regret," Johnny Blue said after he'd been quiet for a spell.

"What's that, Johnny Blue?" I asked.

"That I never did get invited to tea and fairy cakes."

I was about to tell Johnny Blue that there was plenty of fairy cakes in heaven, when there was a commotion at the outer edge of the crowd and a wagon drawn by a hammer-headed buckskin barreled toward the gallows, scattering spectators as the cursing driver lashed the horse into a flat-out gallop.

"What the hell!" Heck Thomas yelled, taking a step forward as he tightened the grip on his Winchester.

And beside him Chris Madsen shucked his Colt and hollered: "Stop! You in the vagon, stop! Or by Gott I'll choot!"

The wagon driver hauled the buckskin to a skidding

stop, and for a moment or two both horse and wagon were obscured by a choking cloud of dust.

But even through that yellowish gray fog, there was no mistaking the driver or the woman sitting beside him.

It was my old ally in the desperate fight against Amos Pinkney, Doc Fortune and his paramour and now wife, the large—and grown even larger as she was now with child—woman of color Miss Georgia Morgan.

Doc leaped from the wagon and threw up his arms, legging it toward the gallows.

"Stop the hanging!" yelled that charging charlatan. "I demand that these dreadful and doleful proceedings are brought to an immediate halt."

"Here," said Heck, swinging his rifle muzzle in line with Doc's belly, "who the hell are you?"

"Me," replied Doc, "I am a man with vital evidence that will prove the innocence of the two rannies you're about to hang. In addition"—here he made a small bow—"I am a doctor of medicine, a doctor of philosophy, a lecturer (at university level) in English and history, and above all, sir, above all, I am an honest and concerned citizen of this fair republic who will not, and cannot, stand idly by while innocent wretches hang."

"Well, you're too late," said Heck. "These men were found guilty by a court of law and will take the drop in a few minutes." Heck gestured with the muzzle of his rifle in a threatening manner. "Now, be off with you."

"That, sir, I will not do," declared Doc, defiantly standing his ground.

The Mauler, Doc's adopted son, his battered pugilist's face grinning from ear to ear, stepped out of the wagon and strode as close to the gallows as the marshals allowed. He looked up at me and Johnny Blue. "How have you boys been?" he asked cheerfully.

Out of the corner of my eye I saw Maledon, his hand

around the lever of the trapdoor, glance impatiently at his watch.

"Oh, fair to middlin', Mauler," I said. "It's been a right nice spring."

"It's been all of that," agreed the Mauler. "Unseasonably hot, though. Hey, did you boys hear tell me and Cottontail tied the knot?"

"So I heard," I said, trying to crane my neck to see the Mauler, but because of the noose all I could make out was the top of his shaved head. "An' I also heard tell there's gonna be a happy event soon."

"Right again," quoth the Mauler. "In fact I got my little pregnant darlin' right here beside me."

"How are you boys doing?" asked Cottontail. "It's been a long time."

Being small as she was, I couldn't see that young lady at all, but I allowed as it had been a fair spell an' then some.

"Pleasant as this conversation may be, it's time for action, not talk," said Doc. "Mauler, do what you have to, but get those boys down from that lofty and sinister platform."

Immediately there was a scuffle and muffled curses as the Mauler pushed marshals aside as he battled to mount the gallows steps. The crowd, enjoying the show, cheered as Heck and the others pounded on the big man with their rifle stocks and soon Doc and Georgia joined in the fray.

Maledon, humming tunelessly between clenched teeth, kept his eye on his watch, and I saw his knuckles whiten as his hand closed around the lever.

"Onward, Mauler, onward!" Doc yelled. "Onward to victory!"

They were so close to the gallows I couldn't see a thing, but I heard the meaty SOCK! of a fist meeting a chin and

I heard Doc yell: "A mighty blow, Mauler! Oh, prettily done."

Heck Thomas laid off pounding on the Mauler, who could take that kind of punishment all day, and retreated to the gallows where he leaped up the steps two at a time. When he reached the top, he levered his Winchester and fired into the air, then fired again.

The commotion below ceased immediately and the overly excited crowd fell silent.

"Goddammit," Heck roared, "I swear I'll plug the next man that moves."

He was very close to me, his smoking rifle in his hands. "That's better," he said. "Now, let's get on with this here hanging, and, marshals, arrest those two men and their . . . ladies."

I knew the drop was very close, so I yelled out: "Doc, thanks anyway!"

But right then a familiar voice demanded to know what was going on and what all the shooting was about.

It was Judge Parker himself.

Boys, me and Johnny Blue made history that day, because that was the first and only time in his twenty years on the bench that the Judge ever came near the gallows when there was a hanging, and it was also the only time a marshal ever had to use a gun to foil a rescue attempt.

"Well met, thou Solomon of the plains," Doc said quickly. "Alas, under the present circumstances I have not the time to discourse upon your fame, which has spread far and near across our great republic, from the hoary walls of Washington D.C. to the verdant shores of California and yes—I do not try to deceive you—even unto the barren badlands of Texas.

"It is my belief, thou jurist wise beyond his years, that—"

"Mister Maledon," the Judge said, ignoring Doc, "is all in order?"

"Aye, your honor. We're ready to go."

"How long?"

"Less than two minutes."

"Then, sir, we must proceed apace."

"No, we mustn't," Doc wailed. "These men are not guilty of any crime—at least the ones you're hanging them for. And there are four voices here who will rise in a shout of INNOCENT! louder than those brassy trumpets of yore that tumbled the lofty and mighty walls of Jericho. These boys, and yes, they are mere boys, cowboys if you will, foiled the nefarious schemes of that repulsive bandit chieftain Amos Pinkney and saved our republic from the horrors of yet another War Between the States, a war that would have pit brother against brother, father against son, North against South—"

"How long, Mr. Maledon?"

"Less than a minute, your honor."

"Hurry it up, Doc!" I yelled.

And Johnny Blue growled: "Doc, I swear you're the talkingest man I ever had the misfortune to meet."

"In short," quoth Doc, seeing the writing on the wall, "these two rannies are as innocent as Little Red Riding Hood a-goin' to visit grandma."

"You have evidence, I suppose?" inquired the Judge, apparently without much interest.

"Evidence aplenty," replied Doc, though I was sure he had none. "Evidence that will turn your court on its head, stun your eloquent tongue into silence, and sound the clarion call of justice all the way to the Supreme Court. In short, sir, I have evidence that, if ignored, will make you a pariah to all honest men and will condemn you to live the rest of your life in shame, a homeless wanderer with every man's door closed and shuttered unto you."

There was a long silence and Maledon's eyes were glued to his watch. He kept his right hand on the lever, and his other arm pumped up and down like a steam piston.

"Ten . . ." he hollered, and the crowd took up the cry, roaring out the numbers at every pump of the hangman's skinny arm.

"Nine . . ."

"I am in hell!" the Judge screamed suddenly, drawing a gasp of startled surprise from the crowd.

"Eight . . ."

"New evidence, you say?" cried the Judge.

"Indeed, thou bearded Solomon come to judgment," wheedled Doc.

"Seven . . ."

"This is unprecedented," wailed the Judge.

"Six . . ."

"Halt these proceedings," implored Doc, grabbing the lapels of the Judge's coat.

"Five . . ."

"Oh, I am in anguish," jabbered the jostled jurist.

"Four . . ."

"Save those boys!" Doc hollered.

"Three . . ."

"Christ above, give me guidance!" the Judge screeched.

"Two . . ."

"Now!" yelped Doc. "Now, damn you!"

"One . . ."

"STOP THE HANGING!" yelled the Judge.

"Noooo!" came a voice from the crowd that even now I cannot recall without a shudder.

I looked in the direction of the cry and saw Frank Canton level his murderous revolver at my chest and pull the trigger, intending to burst my breast asunder.

But Maledon, who had run forward to remonstrate with

the Judge, crossed in front of me and took the ball full in his left shoulder.

That hard-hearted hangman let out a strangled yelp of pain as he was spun around under the impact of the big .45, and to save himself from falling, he grabbed on to my shoulders. Weighted down as I was by lead shot and the body of the executioner, the noose around my neck tightened. I kicked and struggled to get Maledon off me, but that ranny, gasping and groaning and foaming at the mouth, clung to me like a leech.

The crowd roared its disappointment at being robbed of the hanging, yelling "Booo!" and "Shame!" and "Here, this won't do!" Meanwhile the noose closed even tighter and I could no longer breathe. I heard a commotion on the platform and heard Johnny Blue yell, as though from the end of a long tunnel, "He's done for!"

Then I plunged into blackness.

Eighteen

I woke slowly, and as my eyes focused, I beheld the dark and shining face of Georgia Morgan bending over me.

"He's coming round," said that large and comely lady.

"Am . . . am I in heaven?" I inquired softly.

Another face, round and concerned, hove into my view. "Nah," said Doc, "you're in the prison infirmary, an' that's just this side of hell."

I reached up a hand to my neck, feeling the hot burn scar of the rope. "What happened?" I asked.

"They nearly done fer ye, boy," said Doc. "You was half-hanged."

As my brain cleared, I recollected Maledon holding on to me and the noose tightening around my neck. "The hangman, is he—"

"Nah," replied Doc. "He'll recover. It will take more than a pistol ball to kill that scrawny old buzzard."

I looked around and saw Johnny Blue standing in chains, a shotgun-toting marshal at his elbow. Cottontail, who'd given up the whorin' profession sometime back, looked even prettier now that she was pregnant and going straight, and beside her stood the Mauler, his eyes wet with tears.

"I thought you was a goner fer sure," said that pained pugilist. "I had me such an overdose of woe, I was gonna make an itty-bitty little coffin for you with my own two hands."

"I appreciate that, Mauler," I said, hot tears rushing into my own eyes. "You was always a good friend."

"The Mauler saved your life," Johnny Blue said. "He lifted up you and Maledon to get the weight off the noose and held you there until Heck cut you down with his bowie."

"And Frank Canton. Where is—"

"Gone," Johnny Blue said. "He took off on a fast hoss after he shot Maledon instead of you, and Dora's lit a shuck as well."

The infirmary was a small room off the main cells lit by a small, barred window. I lay on an iron cot and there was another empty one beside me and nothing else. The Judge didn't believe in mollycoddling prisoners, so you had to be real sick or half-hung like me to get in here.

"Doc," I said, "you've got to stick around. It seems you always bring me and Johnny Blue good luck."

"Alas," said that solemn snake-oil salesman, "that I cannot do, my boy."

"How come?" I asked, trying to hide my disappointment.

Doc rubbed a hand over his shiny bald dome and replied: "We four are poor, hunted creatures, beggared outcasts with every man's hand against us."

"But why?" I asked. "I thought you was all going straight."

Doc, who was sitting on the edge of my cot, turned and looked suspiciously at the marshal. But that bored lawman sat on the other bed building a smoke, his shotgun lying beside him and a newspaper spread across his knees.

"We were treading, though somewhat warily I admit, on the right side of the law, but we were undone by human ingratitude, false witness, violence, and downright contrariness," said Doc, resuming his former position. "Let me warn you, my young friend, I have a tale to tell so terrible it will turn your carroty hair white and curdle your very blood. Oh, it is a dreadful tale."

Doc paused and made a horrible show of putting an imaginary razor to his throat, sawing it back and forth in an alarming manner, his pale blue eyes wild. "Sometimes I think this is the only course left to me!" he wailed. "Poor, hunted man that I am, the only peace I may ever find is through that dark and dreaded portal from which there is no return."

"No, my love!" exclaimed Georgia. "Not that. I couldn't bear it, my dear one."

"My angel," said Doc tearfully. "Remember that the gods conceal from men the happiness of death only that they may endure life."

Doc and Georgia fell into each other's arms, weeping copiously, and me and Johnny Blue and all others present, including the hard-eyed marshal, joined in the lamentation.

But happily Doc recovered sufficiently in a moment to inquire of his weeping wife if she had enough money in her purse—which he had been testing as to weight even as his tears flowed—for steaks and potatoes and rum punches all round.

Assured that she had the wherewithal, Doc composed himself and continued:

"Now, my young friends, did you receive my letter informing you of the hayseeds who planned to set about us with tar and feathers?"

I nodded an affirmative.

"Well, I'm happy to say we escaped that melancholy fate by the skin of our teeth and the Mauler's pugilistic abilities, only, alas, to fall into an even greater peril.

"We were traveling through the Texas wilderness in the Matagorda County country—"

"That's where the Rancho Grande spread's located," I said.

"Ah yes," said Doc ominously, "I know. But more of that later. Anyhoo, as we crossed that mossy plain, I beheld a sight that made the blood quicken in my veins. Alone in a pasture, prey to any passing thief, footpad, bummer, low person, wolf, coyote, or cougar, grazed a magnificent equine. It was indeed a thoroughbred sorrel horse of unsurpassed grace and beauty.

" 'Behold Bartholomew,' said I to my adopted son the Mauler, 'some cruel person has abandoned this fine animal to its fate.' And that soft-hearted creature replied, 'We must intercede at once, *mon père*, and save the poor beast from a terrible fate.'

"No sooner said than done! We lured the steed to the fence with a generous display of green apples, and I gazed on that magnificent stud for the first time as the Mighty Alexander must have looked upon Bucephalus as that prancer grazed on the verdant Macedonian plain, or as the valorous Wellington first beheld his charger Copenhagen on the bloody field of Waterloo, or as Robert E. Lee, the South's hero among heroes, made his first acquaintance with his warhorse Traveler, the dainty destrier that was to carry him in many a desperate encounter in that terrible conflict of brother against brother.

"In short—I decided to snag him."

Doc shook his head sadly. "But you know me, I am as honest as the day is long." He held up a hand. "Now, Mrs. F., do not remonstrate with me for revealing this facet of my character. I will not be denied in this. My young and half-hanged friend here must know the truth of my honest intent or else nothing wonderful can come of my sadly tragic tale."

Georgia, who was startled by Doc's sudden attention and looked to me like she didn't have the slightest intention of attesting to her consort's honesty, merely said "Hmph," and let it go at that.

"Now bear in mind that we had laid hands and a rope on this high-strung animal, and thus, not wishing to alarm the brute, I cried out as softly as I could, a trembling hand cupped to my mouth, 'Halloo. Will the owner of this fine horse please step forward?'

"There was no reply.

"Again I called, 'Halloo . . . halloo . . . I've found your horse.'

"But again there was no reply. A third and a fourth time I called, and finally a fifth, but no one stepped forward to claim the orphaned beast.

"Thus it was we adopted the horse and made him one of the family, tying him to the back of the wagon as we prepared to skedaddle out of the Matagorda country with all due haste.

"Alas, fate—in the shape of a pale and light-fingered gentlemen in a frock coat—intervened and changed all our plans.

"This reeling refugee galloped up to our wagon on a foundering nag and informed us that he had to flap his chaps and leave Texas in an almighty hurry. A discussion of a trifling nature followed, some distressing little matter about his shooting a rube through the lungs after a discussion around the gambling table that centered on the fact that there are only four aces in a pack of cards, not five as my gambling friend so vehemently averred.

"Anyhoo, to make a long story short, a sum of two hunnerd dollars at once changed hands, me getting the cash, him getting the horse."

Again Doc held up his hand. "I know, I know, Mrs. F, it was a small enough sum and I admit I am generous to a fault. But there is no need to say it in public, my love." He put a finger to his lips. "Best to keep such matters to ourselves."

Again Georgia merely replied, "Hmph," then laid her hand on my forehead. "No fever," she said. "That's good."

"So then what happened, Doc?" asked Johnny Blue.

"Then I learned from a passing clodhopper on a mule who the actual owner of the horse was—a mean, vengeful, and violent cattle baron named Shanghai Pierce."

I sat bolt upright in bed. "You mean, you sto . . . you adopted Shanghai's horse?"

"Indeed I did," replied Doc. "And not any horse, my boy, but a valuable racehorse and a quite famous one at that."

"Geez, Doc," I said, "Shanghai is hell on hoss thieves and rustlers. He's strung up dozens of them in his time."

"I know that only too well," replied that contrite con man. "Even as we speak, the vengeful Shanghai is in hot pursuit of me and mine with a dozen cowboys, all hard-cases well mounted and heavily armed."

"How long have you got?" I asked.

"He's a day behind," Doc said, "maybe less. See, we lost time coming to your aid, hearing on the trail that a couple of rannies—one an uppity black feller, the other a big red mustache with a little drover attached to it—was about to get hung in Fort Smith. Given that description and your propensity for trouble, I knew it could only be you two boys."

Doc paused dramatically and then made the horrible razor gesture at his throat again. "So you can see why the best friend I have in the world," he said darkly, "is my shaving tackle."

"Oh, I can't bear it," swooned Georgia.

And Cottontail screamed.

The marshal jumped up from the bed and rubbed the back of Georgia's hand, while that large lady moaned: "Oh, I am undone . . . my love . . . my love."

Doc leaped up and gathered Georgia in his arms, raising her more-or-less to an upright position.

"We must away, my angel," he cried. "This is no time to tarry."

"Where will you go, Doc?" I asked.

"The far north!" replied Doc, pointing dramatically to what I was pretty sure was the east. "We are but poor outcasts, condemned to dwell forever among the wild Canadians."

Then, with many a hug and tearful kiss, Doc, Georgia, Cottontail, and the Mauler began to take their leave of us.

"I would we had more time to sit and chat, dear boy," Doc said, "but with a vile and remorseless man dogging our trail there is not another moment to be lost. Though"—he consulted his watch—"I do believe there is time for steak and potatoes and a few rounds of rum punch."

"And a nice kidney pudding, if such a thing can be found in this benighted burgh," added Georgia.

"Indeed, my love, indeed," said Doc. Then he turned to me and said: "One thing you can be assured of—you and Johnny Blue will soon be released. We gave Judge Parker written statements, and let me tell you he was singularly impressed with us, that will clear your name and restore your reputation in the eyes of men everywhere."

He gave a little bow. "Until we meet again in happier circumstances, farewell, my young friends, and farewell."

Doc winked. "And remember, you're free as birds."

Nineteen

"Don't think for one minute you're going to walk out of here as free as birds," said Judge Isaac C. Parker as me and Johnny Blue stood before the desk in his office in our chains. Heck Thomas stood close by cradling his shotgun.

The clock on the Judge's wall showed it was a couple of minutes after six, and outside dawn had begun to feel its way across the dusky sky with long scarlet fingers.

"I can keep you locked in my cells for years if need be while I gather enough evidence to either retry you or, a very unlikely event I must admit, let you go free," Judge Parker continued.

"But Judge," I protested, "Doc Fortune told you—"

"A scoundrel and low person, destined for the rope himself. Did you know that Shanghai Pierce the Texas cattleman was here in Fort Smith looking for your friend and his companions? Something to do with the theft of a racehorse?"

"Doc explained that to us, Judge," I said. "It was all a little misunderstanding."

"There will be no misunderstanding when Pierce stretches his neck," the Judge said grimly. "And just as well too. Saves the time and expense of my court."

The Judge studied me and Johnny Blue for a few moments, then shook his head: "Marshal Frank Canton is still on the run, as is his sweetheart. He was one of my best men, yet I very much fear he may have committed perjury."

"To say nothing of taking a shot at me," I reminded him.

"Yes," the Judge said, shrugging, "there is always that."

He sighed deeply and reached into his vest pocket. He took out a little silver snuffbox, put a pinch in each nostril, sneezed heartily, then continued: "I've dispatched Marshal J. H. Mershon to Alpine, a first-rate officer and my best detective, in order to gather evidence to be used in a new trial. He may be gone a month, perhaps two, perhaps longer."

My heart sank. Two months in the Parker Hotel was a death sentence, just as surely as if we'd been hung.

"However," the judge said, "since there is some small doubt as to your guilt or innocence, you have a choice."

"Choice!" I exclaimed, jumping on that word like a bull out of a chute. "Me and him"—nodding toward Johnny Blue—"will take the choice."

"Perhaps you won't be so eager to take it once I tell you what it is," the Judge smiled coldly. He leaned his elbows on the desk and steepled his fingers. "I am mounting a major expedition into the Indian Territory to seek out and arrest a notorious bandit named Buck Starr and his gang of cutthroats. The force will be under the command of Marshal Thomas here, who will bring Starr back alive so that he can be given a fair trial and then be hanged at my convenience.

"Starr has already robbed, raped, and murdered many settlers," the Judge continued, "and part of Marshal Thomas's orders are to evacuate the more isolated farms and ranches and bring the families here to Fort Smith, where I will place them under my personal protection until the territory is safe from Starr and his depredations."

"Beggin' your pardon, Judge, but where do we come in?" asked Johnny Blue. "I mean with the choice you mentioned an' all."

"I'm getting to that, young man," the Judge replied impatiently. "Since Marshal Canton was to be part of this expedition and is no longer with us, I'm offering you two the opportunity to take his place. You will only be acting marshals, and still prisoners of this court, and it will be your responsibility to escort the settlers back to Fort Smith. You will take no part in the hunt for Buck Starr and his men. Is that clear?"

"Clear as mother's milk, Judge," said I.

Heck Thomas slapped the stock of his Greener and told his honor that he had a barrel for each of us and he'd see to it that there was no hanky-panky, by God, and that we stayed on the square and followed orders.

"Yes, thankee Marshal," the Judge said, "I know you will."

"Judge Parker, you got yourself two new lawmen," Johnny Blue said quickly, and I knew he was thinking about Lo May being out there in the territory with the Starr gang on the rampage.

Boys, sixty-five deputies were killed in the line of duty during the Judge's twenty years in Fort Smith, and about two hundred were badly wounded, some of them maimed for life, so in them days he'd pin a badge on just about anybody who could use a gun and showed some sand.

But I guess he figgered he was really scraping the bottom of the barrel with me and Johnny Blue.

"You will be paid the usual rates, six cents a mile going out from Fort Smith, ten cents for the return trip with the settlers," the Judge said, his distaste for us clear in his voice. "If you make an arrest, which is unlikely under the circumstances, you will be paid two dollars plus expenses not to exceed a dollar a day for time spent chasing the criminal." The Judge sat back in his chair. "Are there any questions?"

Me and Johnny Blue allowed that we had none, so the Judge said to Heck: "Remove their chains, Marshal."

As the big lawman clanked his keys into the steel locks, the Judge reached into his desk and pulled out me and Johnny Blue's gun belts, placing a silver star on each.

His nose wrinkling, he said: "Marshal Thomas, these men have the stink of the jail about them. Please see that they take a bath."

"Another one?" Johnny Blue said incredulously. "Man, we're gonna be the cleanest deputies in the territory. That's two in less than a month."

The Judge reached into a pocket and produced a little steel purse that opened with a creak like a rusty bear trap. He studied the contents for a few moments, let out a shuddering little sigh, and brought out four silver dollars, counting them out on the top of his desk.

"These are expenses on account," he said. "Marshal Thomas, take these men down to O'Reilly's general store and see to it that they buy new shirts and pants and underwear. Don't let them spend the money on drink and loose women."

It felt good to buckle on my gun again, since only slaves and oppressed men are denied weapons, and proudly I pinned the Judge's star on to the front of my shirt.

Heck Thomas told us to pick up our chains then shook his head and groaned under his breath: "I don't know what this court is coming to. We got more drygulchers, hoss thieves, and long riders wearing stars than we got honest lawmen."

"I heard that, Marshal," the Judge said. "But remember, we are at war, and I, the author of that war, must use men like these and know that in doing so, I'm letting loose the whole contagion of hell." Judge Parker buried his face in his hands and whispered: "That is my right and my burden and it is mine alone. Now, get them out of my sight."

Boys, a couple of hours later, dressed in new shirts and pants, me and Johnny Blue were once again mounted on our big American studs, waiting outside the courthouse while Judge Parker stood beside Heck's horse giving him last-minute instructions.

"The last reports of Starr's whereabouts say that he's still operating east of the Cimarron," the Judge said. "You will proceed as far as the river and send any settlers you come across back here until you apprehend him."

Heck touched the brim of his hat. "You got it, Judge."

Judge Parker reached up and grabbed the marshal's arm. "Listen, Heck, it's bad, real bad. I'm hearing reports from Cherokee lawmen out in the Strip that Starr and his outlaws are raping and murdering whites and Indians alike. If he's not stopped and stopped soon, the whole Territory could go up in flames."

"We'll bring him in, Judge," Heck said grimly. "If he's still east of the Cimarron like you say, we'll run him down in four, maybe five days."

As I sat my horse, I looked around at the rest of our force.

Chris Madsen, huge and ferociously mustached, straddled a zebra-striped dun. He'd been in the Danish and German armies at various times of his life and had spent four years in the French Foreign Legion. He'd also seen service in the 5th Cavalry, and had been at War Bonnet Creek when Bill Cody done for Chief Yellow Hand.

Chris had killed three or four outlaws in the line of duty and was considered a dangerous and determined man.

Beside him, Mournful Murdo McKenzie sat on a rangy steeldust. He was a long-faced Scotsman who had been in the British Army and had fought Zulus for old Queen Vic.

Well, I didn't know nothing about Zulus and foreign countries in them days, knowing only those places I could get to on a horse. But closer to home, Murdo had ram-rodded a Texas outfit along the Brazos for a few years, and just a month before in a Guthrie saloon had gunned a wanna-be bad man named Shafter who'd been real quick with his mouth but real slow with the iron.

The others marshals were a couple of Texas hardcases who called themselves John Smith the Elder and John Smith the Younger.

Heck said each had a string of killings to their credit. The Elder had ridden with Frank and Jesse back in the old days, and the Younger with Billy the Kid and Henry Brown and that wild bunch in the Lincoln County War down in New Mexico.

All in all, I figgered, we were a fine body of fighting men, well able to take on Buck Starr and his gang and emerge victorious.

"We're a' doooomed," wailed Murdo McKenzie, knee-ing his horse alongside Chris Madsen's dun. "Chris, we're riding with murderers, bank robbers, footpads, dance hall loungers, and low persons. We're doomed, I tell ye. We're a' doooomed."

"Mournful," quoth Chris, "ve must do our best vit vot ve haff. It is not for us to question the visdom off der Chudge, by Gott."

Johnny Blue had been studying Murdo's horse intently for some time. "Excuse me," he said to that sad Scotsman. "What's that you got tied on the back of your saddle?"

Mournful studied Johnny Blue with evident distaste. "It's ma' pipes, ye damned Hindoo."

"Oh," said Johnny Blue, shrugging. "I figgered you'd shot some kind of animal."

"They're both troublemakers," the Judge whispered to Heck, but loud enough so that I could hear, "especially the little one. He's got the look of the Texas gunslick about him and he'll make fancy moves and he'll be almighty sudden."

But Heck just smiled and tapped the holstered Colt at his waist and said the Judge wasn't to worry about that none because he had the cure for fancy moves right here, and besides, he could be almighty sudden his own self.

"Still," Judge Parker said, "keep an eye on him. He's said to be pure poison with a sixgun."

After the Judge left, Heck stood in his stirrups and hollered: "Move out!" and we fell in line behind him.

But just then I heard my name being called and I saw a younker running toward us, waving what looked to be an envelope.

""Over here, son," I called out to the boy, a straw-haired lad about ten years old.

"Yup, it's for you, all right," the boy said, revealing a cheeky, gap-toothed smile. "The man who give me this letter said to hand it to no one else but a scrawny little squirt with a big red mustache who could take a bath in three fingers of creek water."

"Give me that damned letter, boy, or I'll punch your head," I growled.

"Big man picking on a little kid," the boy said.

"That's right," I said, "a little kid who's gonna get the toe of my boot up his ass if'n he don't give me that letter right quick."

The boy handed me the envelope, blew me a long, wet raspberry, then took to his heels.

"Who's it from?" Johnny Blue asked, reining up alongside me.

I shrugged. "Dunno. Maybe it's from a female admirer." I sniffed the envelope. "Don't smell no perfume, though."

"One way to find out," Johnny Blue said. "Open it."

Well, boys, I opened that letter and wished to hell I

hadn't. It was short, not very sweet, and very much to the point:

SKUM,

I AIN'T FERGOT WHAT YOU DONE TO MY EAR AND THINGS AIN'T OVER ATWEEN US. I'M CUMMIN AFTER YOU AND I'M A-CUMMIN SHOOTING. I'M GONNA SHOOT YOU THROUGH THE BELLY AN WATCH YOU DIE SCREEMING.
CAPT. FRANK CANTON

Heck Thomas drifted back to see why we were lagging behind. I handed him the letter and he read it slowly, seeming to hesitate over each word, his lips moving the whole time.

Finally he looked up and said: "You've crossed a mighty dangerous man. Frank Canton is not a ranny to be trifled with, and best left alone. If'n I was you, I'd ride with eyes in the back of my head from now on."

Heck gave me back the letter. "Now, rejoin the column."

Johnny Blue shook his head. "You're a man born to trouble, and no mistake. I don't reckon you're gonna live long enough to scratch a gray head."

But I ignored that comment and resolutely put all thoughts of Frank Canton out of my head.

Me and Johnny Blue and the other marshals were now embarked on a dangerous adventure that would bring us into a clash of arms with the most evil and bloodthirsty gang of outlaws in the history of the West.

Ahead of us, though we didn't know it then, lay much sorrow and much violence, and we'd burn more than our share of powder and shed many a salt tear before it was all over.

Yet we were destined to perform great deeds of valor

that would carve our name with pride on the annals of the frontier, exploits that are still spoken of today around the campfire wherever men with bark on them gather to remember the good old days.

Thus it was, as we rode into the Indian Territory, I glanced at Johnny Blue and noted the stouthearted jut of that black knight's manly chin as he galloped forth to save the woman he loved—and I knew in that splendid moment that many mighty feats of gallantry lay ahead of us.

Twenty

"Travelin' kinda light, ain't we, Heck?" I asked as we rode northwest, the lowering sun already shadowing the draws and gulches of the Boston Mountains to our north, shading the aspen- and pine-covered slopes into a dark mass of green. The sky was ice blue, shot with fingers of red as we rode across a lush carpet of buffalo grass mixed with bluestem. Here and there dogwood and redbud flowers shyly peeked out their heads as we passed. The Arkansas River lay behind us and before us was the broad sweep of the prairie with its rich ranch and farmland stretching all the way to the Cimarron. We passed jutted outcrops of tumbled rock, usually crested by a stand of stunted pine or oak, where nearby small herds of antelope grazed, watching us warily as we passed.

"What did you say?" Heck asked. He looked like he'd been dozing in the saddle under the waning spring sun.

"I said we're travelin' light."

I nodded my head toward the packhorse that was being led by John Smith the Elder. "He's carrying a coffeepot and not much else."

"We always pick up supplies on the trail," Heck explained. "It's a lot cheaper than buying them in Fort Smith."

"Oh, you mean the farmers sell you stuff," I said.

"Something like that," Heck said, and behind me I heard John Smith the Younger snigger.

About fifteen minutes later Chris Madsen, who'd been riding scout, loped into sight. As he came closer, he hollered: "Heck, cheep camp chust ahead, by Gott. Many cheeps and tree, maybe four mens."

Heck nodded and yanked his shotgun from under his knee. "Sheep camp ahead, we got time to lay in supplies before dark," he said. "Shuck your rifles, men, and follow me."

Johnny Blue sniffed the air. "I knew it! I been smellin' woolies for the past three, four miles." He wrinkled his nose. "Damn, that stink can sicken a man to his stomach."

You boys don't need me to tell you that sheep on the range are like a swarm of ravenous locusts. They crop the grass too short so that it burns up and dies, and they poison the waterholes. Even cows won't walk across range where sheep have trod unless you burn off the grass and let the land lie empty for a year.

The coming of sheep was a barefaced theft of the cattleman's grassland that was his divine right, and that's why woolies are such an abomination in the eyes of both man and God.

The sheep camp lay in a hollow between two gently rolling hills. It was nicely situated next to a stream shaded by a wide cottonwood. Four men drank coffee by a cheerful campfire.

Three of the four rose as we rode closer and Heck said: "Basques."

"What's Basques?" I asked.

"Oh, they're foreign sheepherders, come from Basqueland, I guess."

"Where's Basqueland?" Johnny Blue asked.

Heck shook his head. "I dunno for sure, but I think it's near Mexico."

When we rode into the camp, those sheepherders looked nervous and a mite scared, though one still sat by the fire, his face shaded by his hat. There was something familiar about that ranny and the way he wore his guns, and I kept a close eye on him as Heck threw up his hand and yelled: "We're officers of the law."

He turned in the saddle and said: "Murdo, you come up here with me with your rifle. The rest of you pick up their supplies, blankets, bacon, flour, coffee . . . whatever they have. Clean 'em out good, boys."

As me and Johnny Blue and the two Smiths began to load up the packhorse, the anguished Basques ran back and forth, wringing their hands as they jabbered at us in their heathen tongue. Sheepmen or not, I felt sorry for those rannies, so I looked up at Heck and said: "It seems to me this ain't exactly legal."

"Well, they got supplies and we need 'em," replied that lanky-back lawman. "It's all a question of supply and demand. Besides, I'll write them out a receipt afore we leave."

"Will Judge Parker honor it?" I asked.

"Nah," said Heck. "The Judge don't much hold with folks demanding money from him."

Just then the man by the fire uncoiled like a snake, rising to his feet in one graceful motion—and I looked into the cold, mother-of-pearl eyes of Shade Hannah.

"Well, well, well," whispered that ghastly gunman, "we meet again."

Shade's hands were very close to his guns and his lips were drawn back in a thin smile that held no warmth but only menace and pure hatred.

Heck, who'd seen plenty of dangerous gunmen in his day, recognized Shade for what he was and drew his own conclusions. "Friend of yours?" he asked me warily, never taking his eyes off Shade's hands.

"No friend of mine," I replied. "This here is Shade Hannah. He tried to rob an Army payroll back in Montana an' killed a civilian paymaster and a poor soldier boy before me and Johnny Blue stopped him."

Shade's smile didn't slip, it just grew thinner, meaner, and more dangerous.

"You're a damned liar," he said.

So there it was. In a land and a time where a man's word was his bond, to call him a liar was to take everything from him he owned or could ever expect to own. Like a saber cut, the wound of a man branded a liar would heal, but the scar would remain, stark and ugly for the rest of his life. And folks seeing the scar would give him no trust, and without the trust of others he could not live and prosper in the West.

Shade had called me square, and the only way to answer was with a gun. Like all riding men, I wore my Colt high on my right side, and I knew to draw, cock, and fire the piece would take me about twenty minutes, and by that time Shade would've filled me with lead.

Boys, I figgered I'd two chances—slim and none—and slim was already saddling up to leave town.

"What did you call me?" I asked, playing for time, knowing I was about to cash in my chips, and me in the prime of youth with a fine mustache and handsome as a hat model's picture in a Sears and Roebuck catalog.

"You heard me," Shade snarled, poised and ready, his hands hovering above the butts of his guns. "I called you a damned liar."

Figgering I was already coyote bait, I got ready to make my draw, but Heck's voice cut across the eight feet of space between me and Shade and stopped me cold.

"I'm the leader of this expedition, so if you got a quarrel, Shade, you got it with me," he said.

Never taking his eyes off me, Shade said: "I got no quarrel with you, Heck."

"You got a quarrel with him, you got it with me," Heck replied.

"Listen, Heck," I protested, "I can fight my own battles."

"You keep out of this," replied that martial marshal.

He pointed his shotgun right at Shade's belly button. "I got no warrant for you, mister, so you got two ways to go as I see it. You either ride out of here now or shuck your irons and get to your work."

Shade thought about it hard.

I could see his mind working behind those white eyes, figgering his chances against Heck, who was a known gun hand with the reputation of being tough as a trail-drive steak and hard to kill. Shade, his body quivering, kept his hands close to his guns. He could uncoil and draw with blinding speed—he knew it, I knew it, and Heck knew it—but he didn't like that Greener pointed at his brisket, not one little bit.

"You got the drop on me, Heck," he said finally.

"Drop?" Heck demanded. "What's this drop stuff? Shade, this ain't no Ned Buntline novel, so either yank them hog legs or back off."

I saw Heck's knuckles whiten on the Greener, and I reckoned he was about to cut loose with both barrels. Shade saw it too, and quickly moved his hands away from his guns.

"Not today," he said. "I don't want to fight today."

"Then fork your bronc and ride," Heck ordered, and there was no give in him. He kept his shotgun pointed at Shade as the gunman found his horse under the cottonwood and mounted.

"You!" Shade called out to me. "We're going to meet again real soon, you and me." He turned to Johnny Blue. "And that goes for you too. Hell is waiting for you, boys."

He swung his horse around and splashed across the

creek, putting spurs to the animal as it scrambled up the cutbank and on to the flat grassland.

Then he reined up and again did that strange thing he'd done after the fight over the payroll wagon. He sat his horse, his white eyes staring into mine, and pointed right at me. He sat there, his right arm extended, for maybe two minutes before he turned his horse around and was gone.

Heck shook his head at me. "I swear, boy, you make some powerful enemies. If the Judge hangs you when you get back to Fort Smith, it will be an act of mercy."

But Murdo, who was tightening up the ropes on the overloaded packhorse, turned to me and said: "You're probably doomed, laddie, but my best advice is to forget that Shade for a while. We've got things to do, and it's verra hard to fight an enemy who's camped out in your head."

We rode away from that sheep camp and left those Basques cursing their rotten luck and picking up and examining the few bits and pieces we'd left them.

In them olden days, the West was a harsh land filled with hard men, and the line between law and lawlessness was often blurred. We had taken all those sheepmen owned at gunpoint, using the authority of a tin star, but if anyone had suggested to Heck and the others that it was robbery, they'd have been mortally offended.

To Heck it was a simple matter: He needed supplies and the Basques had what he needed. So he took what he needed from them.

The same line of thinking had colored his dealings with Shade Hannah.

Shade was a dangerous gunman, so Heck would have cut him in half with his shotgun without warning because to do otherwise would have endangered his own life.

Heck Thomas was a fine officer, but he was nobody's fool and he was only as honest and as brave as he had to be in order to survive.

Later that night in camp, as Heck and the other marshals sat and talked and drank coffee by the fire, I felt a sense of foreboding I couldn't shake, like the angel of death was sitting on my shoulder and whispering in my ear.

Even when the conversation turned to cattle and ranching and how things were on the ranges since the big snows of '87, I didn't throw in my two cents' worth, the feeling that hard times were a-coming fast on me and Johnny Blue weighing me down and stilling my tongue.

When I glanced across the fire at Johnny Blue, that lanky rider was looking into the wind-dancing flames, holding Lo May's withered little flower and there seemed to be tears in his eyes. It was a trick of the light, of course, because Johnny Blue was a hard man not given to tears.

But later, when I rolled into my soogan and recollected what I'd seen, I felt cold, a gnawing chill that made me shiver.

Above me, the moon hid its face now and then behind scudding clouds and somewhere far off in the darkness a coyote howled its high lonesome to the night.

Across the guttering fire Johnny Blue rolled restlessly in his blanket and groaned, troubled in his sleep.

John Smith the Elder rousted me out of bed next morning with a none-too-gentle kick, and Chris Madsen was already by the fire cooking breakfast.

I put on my hat, nodded to Johnny Blue, who was grumpily building his first smoke of the morning, and poured myself some coffee.

Rain clouds were building, seeming to rise right out of the prairie grass, and I heard the distant rumble of approaching thunder.

"Ve eat ver' soon," Chris said. "Der weather iss not shaping up goot, and Heck must haff his bowel movement on time, by Gott."

As I watched, Chris shaved thin slices from a slab of salt pork and set them to parboil in hot water. When the water boiled, he poured it off and rolled the slices of meat in flour then fried them until they were crisp and brown.

He piled the pork on a tin plate and poured some of the fat off, using it to butter thick slices of sourdough bread.

Humming snatches of "Sweet Nelly from Fife" as he worked, he then browned some flour in the fat left in the frying pan, poured in some canned milk, and kept stirring until the gravy was just right. I handed him my plate and he dropped a couple of slices of pork onto it, smothered them in gravy, and handed me a wedge of bread.

Boys, let me tell you that was the best meal I ever et in my whole life. It beat my ma's chicken and dumplings to a frazzle, and it was better than the beans at the old DHS and even the fried beef and frijoles at the Yellow Rose in Dodge.

I guess it's no wonder that after eating that fine meal I began to feel better, finally shedding the melancholy of the night before. Even Johnny Blue was a mite more cheerful, roughhousing with John Smith the Younger over who was going to wash the greasy plates.

After he ate, Heck laid down his plate, tucked his elbows into his waist, turned his hands out to the side, and rubbed his fingers and thumbs together.

"Christopher," he said, "napkin?"

Chris rushed a blue-and-white-checkered cloth napkin over to Heck, who wiped his hands then his mouth and said, rising to his feet, "Now, Christopher, the Sears and Roebuck catalog, if you please."

Heck tucked the catalog under his arm and walked purposefully into a clump of mixed ash, elm, and oak trees beside the trail.

"Ol' Heck's about as dainty as a June bride, ain't he?" I said to Murdo after the big lawman had gone.

"Heck sets store by such things as good table manners," Murdo replied. "That and his bowel movement, of course."

"What's with the bowel movement?" Johnny Blue asked. "Everybody talks likes it's sacred or something."

"It iss, by Gott," said Chris. "It iss!"

"See," said Murdo, "one time Heck caught a bullet in the shoulder, and while it was being dug out, he and the doctor got to talking. Well, the doc was a graduate of Heidelberg University and had one of them pointy little beards, so Heck figgered that laddie knew what he was talking about. 'Heck,' said the doc, 'always remember that the basis of good health is a regular, unhurried bowel movement every day.'

"Heck cottoned to that idea right from the start and he's striven to live up to it ever since."

For the next ten minutes or so, Murdo kept his eyes on the trees. And when Heck reappeared, he rose and got his bagpipes.

With great ceremony, Heck handed the Sears catalog back to Chris, minus a few pages, then stretched out his hands. Chris poured water over his fellow lawman's hands, then gave him his napkin again.

"Thank you, Christopher," Heck said. He turned to Murdo: "Anytime you're ready, Marshal McKenzie."

The Scotsman nodded, placed one leg of them pipes into his mouth, and blew a short, wailing flourish.

Then he came smartly to attention, snapped off a palm-outward salute, and hollered: "The Thomas has had his bowel movement. The kings, queens, princes, and potentates of the world may now have theirs."

"Thank you, Murdo," said Heck solemnly, like this was the most natural thing in the world.

Now, boys, if'n you ever let good Christian folks read this account of me and Johnny Blue's adventures, they're bound to say, "Nah, that's too wild. It could never happen."

But what they don't take into account is that back in them olden days, we was all nuttier than squirrel shit. Cowboys ate trail dust for eighteen hours a day straight driving herds to the railheads, living with bad food, worse water, and the ever-present danger of stampede and the sudden death that came with it. Prairie wives, their beauty long gone as their skin turned to wrinkled boot leather, lived in miserable little sod huts in the middle of the wilderness, hearing the lonesome wind sigh all day, every day, until they just wanted to stand there and scream and scream. Soldiers were all cramped up together in dusty outposts deep in hostile Indian country where the bullet and the arrow provided moments of terror that served only to punctuate the weeks and months and years of mind-numbing boredom. Even townspeople were no better off, huddled in claustrophobic wooden shanties perched along the ragged edges of nowhere.

No wonder we was all loonies in them days, and what would get a man locked up in an insane asylum back East was considered normal, acceptable behavior on the frontier.

So when we mounted up and fell in line behind Heck, we didn't think him crazy, because we was all singing off the same song sheet. We was just glad he'd had a successful bowel movement and improved his health and we was proud to have been even a small part of it.

This time John Smith the Elder rode point and Chris faded behind us to cover our back trail. We'd been riding maybe three hours under a warm morning sun, the breeze bringing the scent of pine off the far mountain slopes, when Chris came loping back to the column.

As Heck called a halt, Chris said: "Two riders behind us, by Gott. Von looks like Frank Canton by the vay he sets dat big sorrel of his, der other is a vild Injun on a paint pony."

Heck shook his head at me. "Boy, you're in a heap o' trouble. I told you Frank Canton is a man best left alone and now he's after you and hunting trouble."

I sighed deeply and said: "So's the other one. He's a war chief named Red Horse. He was Buffalo Bill's Queen Victoria Injun an' he wants me too."

"Why, for God's sake?" Heck asked, alarm cracking his voice.

"He wants my hair," I replied, "an' maybe my mustache. But studyin' on it, I reckon it's mostly my hair."

"See, that Injun never took a red scalp afore," Johnny Blue offered helpfully.

Heck just sat his horse in stunned silence for a few moments. Then said to me: "Boy, it seems to me you're tied to the tracks and the train is on time. The Judge said to send you back with the settlers, but I can't do that with the whole territory gunning for you. Nobody would make it to Fort Smith alive."

He called over the two John Smiths. "You boys will take the settlers back if'n we find any. These two rannies"—he nodded toward me and Johnny Blue—"will ride with me."

John Smith the Elder shrugged and allowed as that was just fine by him, and Smith the Younger said he wanted no part of Frank Canton anyhow and that went double for Queen Victoria's wild Injun.

Heck shook his head again and said that being a marshal wasn't easy and that he should be paid twice what he was getting.

And Murdo added: "We're doomed. I tell ye, Heck, we're a' doomed."

Two hours later, as the sun climbed to its highest point in the sky, we rode past a low mesa crowned with stunted pine and beyond that a rocky saddleback, its sides littered with huge boulders and clumps of cedar brush on its lower slope. In the notch of the saddleback a thin plume of black smoke tied bows in the air, and Chris yelled: "Dat's Ned Barlow's ranch, by Gott!" Heck pulled his Greener from the boot under his right leg. "Let's go, boys!" he yelled, kicking his big roan into a gallop.

Following him, we set spurs to our horses . . . and thus rode into hell.

Twenty-one

The shallow valley was bordered by trees, and it had a good-sized spring and a pool of water. I saw no sign of cattle, the rutted trail leading into a hardscrabble ranch consisting of a pole corral, a lean-to barn, and beyond that a sod house with rock slabs built into the wall.

There was an open gate flanked by two tall pine posts and across these a crossbeam. Two men hung by their feet from the crossbeam, both of them covered in blood.

On the ground beneath them lay a dead dog, like the men, shot many times.

Heck and the others reined up their horses at the gate and Chris urged his skittish dun forward until he was right alongside the men.

"It's Barlow and hiss son, Jeb," Chris said. "Der troats ver cut den dey were hung up here and shot to pieces."

"Well, cut them down, for Chrissakes!" Heck roared. "Don't let them hang there."

As Chris and the others cut the dead men from the beam, gently laying the bloody bodies on the ground, Murdo's eyes strayed to the sod cabin.

"We have to look in the house, Heck," Murdo said quietly. "Mrs. Barlow and her daughters . . ."

"I know that!" Heck yelled angrily. "Don't you think I know that?"

He rubbed his hands over his face, and when he looked

at Murdo again, he seemed to have aged twenty years. "You don't have to remind me of my duty, Murdo," he said in a softer, almost apologetic voice.

"Maybe one of the others can do it, Heck," Murdo said. "Maybe one of the younger lads?"

By way of reply, Heck kicked his horse forward. "Let's go," he said.

When we opened the soddy's door and walked inside, there were three naked women there, Mrs. Barlow and her two teenaged daughters. All were lying on their own beds, and all had been raped and raped again because there were dozens of bite marks on their shoulders, wheals that stood out red and angry against the whiteness of their skins. Knives had been used on those women in unspeakable ways, and later each had been shot, a single bullet through the head.

Boys, those women had been a long time in the dying, and had suffered so much before the end that I can't bring myself to fully describe it here. Even now, so many years afterward, I close my eyes and still see them, their bruised white skin and the wide-open blue eyes and the scarlet splashes of blood.

That's a picture I don't want you boys to carry with you for the rest of your lives as I must, so I'm going to draw a curtain around it and tell you that I walked back outside into the sunlight and threw up my fine breakfast. Then John Smith the Younger threw up his and then Johnny Blue. Watching us, Heck said that no man should have to see something like that and he didn't blame us none, though we were marshals and should be hard men.

Later we buried the whole family on the hillside in unmarked graves now known only to God, and Heck said the words and we tried to sing a hymn but it wouldn't come easy, so we went back down the hillside again and Heck said we'd leave and camp far from this place.

As we mounted, a man hollered and waved and ran down the hillside toward us. He was small and thin and rat-faced and he carried a Henry rifle, along with a Remington revolver buckled around his waist.

When the man came up to us he said: "Name's Wild, Travis Wild. I was Barlow's hired hand. I watched you for a spell; then when I saw you doin' the burying, I figgered you was the law."

"Who done this?" Heck asked, his instant dislike for this man a palpable thing.

"It was Buck Starr and his boys for sure," Wild said. "I heard one of them call out the name 'Buck,' and there was twenty of them, maybe more. They hit us just after sunup and I took off for the hills."

"They killed Ned Barlow and his son," Heck said. "They raped and killed his women."

"I figgered that," Wild said. "It's a hard thing."

"Laddie, did you lie up there on the hillside and pick off a few?" Murdo asked, his face a stony mask.

Wild shook his head, his little eyes darting. "I didn't want to give my position away. Saw it all happen, though."

Heck's face was flushed. "Wild, you rode for the Barlow brand. If a man rides for a brand, he fights for it, and if he's called on to do it, he dies for it."

Wild hung his head. "It didn't seem so straightforward at the time."

"Well," said Heck, "it was."

We rode away from that place, and Wild stood there watching us go. He had no horse, but not a man among us would have offered to let him ride double.

Heck was right. A man who won't fight for his brand is less than a man and low down, and there's an end to it.

"I don't get it," Johnny Blue said as we rode, shaking his head. "How can a man like Buck Starr be so evil he'll do something like that? Why did he do it?"

"There's no why, boy," said Heck, who overheard him. "Evil is the absence of good, just as the dark is nothing but the absence of light. There's no good in Buck Starr. It's absent. Missing. He hates because he's raving mad. And he's raving mad because he hates."

Heck turned in his saddle. "We got to hunt him down and kill him."

During the next week we scouted clear to the Cimarron, daily making contact with farmers and ranchers. Bad news travels fast, and some who had heard about the massacre at the Barlow place elected to make the journey to Fort Smith. Others, tougher or just more stubborn, told us they'd stay right where they were.

We saw no sign of Dr. Chang, nor did anyone know of his whereabouts, and Johnny Blue became downright surly because he worried about Lo May so much.

In the end, about thirty people left with the Smith boys, and I was sorry to see them hardcases go. They'd rode on both sides of the law and had done their share of robbing and killing, but they were good men and braver than most.

As they rode out, me and Johnny Blue waved our hats and gave them a hearty Huzzah! and Murdo played a piece on his bagpipes that he said was "The MacDonald's Farewell to Glen Lomond."

It was a touching scene, except that Johnny Blue's horse had never heard the pipes before and he bucked and pitched, his eyes white and rolling. Johnny Blue grabbed for the horn and tried to hang on and got dumped anyhow.

Now by times Johnny Blue had a fuse shorter than an ant's eyebrow, and he got up and dusted himself off, and told Murdo that if he squeezed that damn animal again till it squealed, he was gonna draw his Colt's gun and shoot both him and it through the lungs.

But Murdo said if'n he tried that, he'd pull him through

a knothole so he could relive his birth, and for a spell things looked like they'd get plumb out of hand.

Then Heck stepped in and said there would be no fighting among ourselves because we had a common enemy to battle, and he allowed that he knowed we was all strung out because of what we'd seen back at the Barlow place but we'd all better shut up and act peaceful toward one another or he'd knock some heads together.

Johnny Blue, who never held a grudge for long, just smiled at Heck, then swept off his hat and did an elegant bow toward Murdo. "I'm sorry, Mr. McKenzie," he said. "No offense."

"None taken," replied that sporting Scotsman.

But as Johnny Blue went to mount his horse, Murdo let out with a squeal on them bagpipes and Johnny Blue was dumped on his butt again—and for a spell things were not real good between them.

Later that day we got word from a passing Cherokee Indian policeman that Buck Starr was reported to have been seen in the Tulsa area, so we headed north while Murdo covered our back trail.

That evening as we made camp in a shallow canyon bordered by pine trees, Murdo rode in and said there was no sign of Frank Canton, but that Buffalo Bill's Indian was still there, squatting over a hatful of fire about a mile back.

Boys, the thought of Red Horse following me, just a-waiting patiently to collect my hair, made me as nervous as a frog in a frying pan. But Johnny Blue said if'n I was dead, losing my scalp wouldn't make no never mind, and besides, red hair would be a handicap in hell anyhow.

"All a carrot head wouldn't do is attract the devil's attention, an' that's a natural fact," he said.

I studied on that for a spell and said: "You know, Johnny Blue, I never thought about that. Red hair like mine would attract Old Nick like a pig to slop, an' no mistake. I gotta admit it, you're right."

"Hell yeah, I know I'm right," said Johnny Blue. "The devil if I ain't."

Boys, I began to feel better about that scalp-hunting Indian and all, but as I rolled in my blanket that night, little did I know the tragedy that would befall us all the next morning—and I, all unknowing and innocent, was its cause.

After breakfast, Heck collected his Sears and Roebuck catalog and retired into the woods, warning us that he was not to be disturbed.

"You boys don't seem to pay much mind to being reg'lar," he said before he left. "You should, because a daily bowel movement is the foundation of good health." He slapped his chest. "And I'm living proof of that."

Me and Johnny Blue, Murdo and Chris sat around the fire drinking the last of the coffee as night shaded into dawn and the sky turned to lemon, washing out the stars one by one. A mist as tall as a man still clung to the bases of the trees and made their dark green tops look like they were floating in a ghostly gray sea.

"Murdo," Chris said, "I t'ink we come on Buck Starr pretty damn quick, by Gott."

The Scotsman, who was always surly in the morning, nodded. "There's only five of us against twenty at least, all of them gunslick." He glanced at me and Johnny Blue without enthusiasm. "We don't have much."

Chris shrugged. "Heck vill haff a plan. He always does."

"Plan or no, we're doomed," Murdo said mournfully. "I tell ye, Chris, we're a' doomed."

"You're jest nat'rally a cheerful feller, ain't you, Murdo?" Johnny Blue smiled, building a smoke. "I swear you're so down in the mouth you could eat oats out of a churn."

"I'm a realist, laddie," replied Murdo. "I call a spade a

spade, and I tell ye we're doomed. I can feel it coming. It's on its way like that mist in the trees over there, only it's like the one I remember as a boy. It came from the sea, creeping like a thief into the glen. Oh, that was a terrible mist, because dead things walked in it and wailed and gibbered and my mother, hearing them, would draw her shawl closer around her shoulders and shiver in the light of the fire."

Murdo cocked his head to one side. "Hark! I think I hear them now."

"Dammit!" Johnny Blue yelled, jumping to his feet. "That's not booger men. That's horses."

I stood and grabbed up my Winchester just as a dozen men galloped into the valley. In the gray dawn, light orange flame flared from rifle muzzles as the raiders fired as they came.

I cranked a round into my .44.40 and cut loose at the leading rider, but I missed him clean. Beside me Chris Madsen's rifle barked and the man I'd aimed at threw up his arms and toppled backward off his pony.

"They're trying to run off the horses!" Murdo yelled.

I cranked my rifle and fired, then fired again as the outlaws tried to circle around behind us and get at our horses. One of the raiders fired his Colt and the packhorse went down. He fired a second time and Chris's dun collapsed with a wild scream, its legs kicking.

"Buck!" Chris hollered. "Buck Starr, I see you, by Gott! You choot my horse, damn you!"

He fired at the outlaw leader, but Buck wheeled his mount around at the last moment, his Colt hammering, and Chris missed, his bullet plucking at Buck's sleeve. Now me and Johnny Blue and Murdo were all firing at the bandit and I guess he decided we were making things too hot for him because he waved a hand and hollered: "Back! Back!" and galloped toward his men.

As the outlaws fled, Chris fired at one man, knocked him off his horse, fired again, and another man fell. Murdo had also settled down and was using his rifle to good effect, shooting one feller's hat off his head and sending another fleeing with a bullet in his shoulder.

I guess the outlaws decided they'd done enough damage for now, and with four men down and a couple more wounded it was high time to get out of the valley away from those expert riflemen. Those boys had hoped to hit us when we least expected it, but they made a fundamental mistake—being hardcases, used to other, weaker and more timid men tippy-toeing around them, they'd grown to ignore the fact that there were rannies with hair on their bellies and gravel in their guts on both sides of the law—and in the end that's what done for them.

But they would learn from this mistake, and next time would be different. They wouldn't come at us in a rush again. They'd pick their spot and their time and they'd have all the advantage.

As Chris and Murdo went to examine the fallen outlaws, I glanced over at the bushes opposite our camp and saw a sudden movement. I figgered some of Buck's men had dismounted and were trying to sneak up on us using the trees as cover.

I upped my Winchester, and smoked the underbrush pretty good, firing six quick shots from left to right. Then I dusted a couple into the spot where I'd first seen the bushes rustle. I heard a yelp of pain, then silence.

A few slow moments passed; then Heck stumbled out of the underbrush, groaning. His long johns were down around his ankles and I saw a bright trail of red blood running down his right leg.

"Who shot me?" he yelled. "Who shot me up the ass?"

I was standing there with a smoking rifle in my hands, so I could hardly deny it.

"I took ye fer a bandit, Heck," I said. "Sorry."

I heard Murdo yell at me: "What did you do?"

Then Heck roared and raised his rifle to his shoulder and cut loose. A bullet split the air above my head, followed by another. I took off running and dived behind a fallen log, just as Heck's Winchester barked again and threw a handful of splinters into my face that stung like all hell.

"You shot me up the ass!" Heck hollered, firing again. "You shot me up the ass as my pants was down an' I was having my bowel movement."

"It was a accident!" I yelled, popping up my head like a gopher so I could see him over the top of the log. "We was pretty busy here y'know, Heck, when you wasn't around."

Heck didn't reply. He just fired again, showering more splinters off the log a couple of inches from my head. Because of his wound, that lethal lawman was a mite unsteady on his feet, so his aim was off, and that's what saved my life.

I heard a scuffle of feet and curses coming from Heck's direction, and lifted my head again in time to see Johnny Blue and Chris run to him and try to wrestle his rifle away.

"He can't help it, Heck," Johnny Blue yelled, yanking up the Winchester's muzzle as the raging, cursing Heck fired again and the bullet went skyward. "He's a poor loony," Johnny Blue hollered, "an' he don't know no better."

Johnny Blue got real close to Heck's purple face, holding the lawman's rifle down so he couldn't fire again. "Heck, he's a loony an' he takes mighty strange notions. One time he took it into his head to shoot everybody's hoss an' he left the whole Montana Territory afoot. Now he's done took another notion to shoot folks up the ass, an' he can't help it because he's plumb crazy."

"I'll kill him!" Heck roared. "So help me, I'll put that little runt under."

"Well," said Johnny Blue, "I wouldn't blame you none if you did. But you'd be shooting a poor loony, and that ain't right."

Heck, who was growing weak from loss of blood, slowly sank to his knees. He looked up at Chris Madsen and said in a pathetic whimper: "Christopher, how am I going to keep reg'lar now with my ass all shot to pieces?"

"Oh heck, Heck," replied Chris, wringing his hands. "I t'ink you be constipated for sure."

"Then I'm a dead man," Heck said sadly.

Boys, seeing Heck laid low like that was a sight that would have brought tears to your eyes, and all because of a innocent accident done in the heat of battle.

We did all we could for him, laying him out on the cold ground while Chris got his bowie knife and probed that striken hero's right butt cheek for the bullet.

Meanwhile Murdo reported that three of Buck's men were dead, and the other wouldn't last until noon. We brought the wounded man to our fire and he said he knew his time was short and he wanted to make his peace with God. He said he'd taken part in the Barlow massacre, but hadn't touched the women.

"That was all Buck's doing," he said. "Him and Shade Hannah and a couple of the others did the raping, and it was them who used knives on the women's . . . I mean, before they killed them. I told them I'd have no part in it."

The dying ranny was a young feller with a good-looking, open face. He'd been gut shot by Chris and he was in considerable pain and was dying hard.

"So Shade Hannah joined Buck," I said. "Well, they're birds of a feather."

"Yeah," the outlaw said, "it was Shade's idea to hit the Barlow ranch. He told Buck there were young women there and we all could have a little fun. But I didn't take no part in the raping. You got to believe that."

"You're time is short, lad," Murdo said. "Best you lie quiet and say your prayers."

"It hurts," the young outlaw groaned. "Oh God, it hurts so bad."

"You're gut shot," Murdo said. "A gut-shot man hurts. That's the natural order of things." As a kindness, he placed a thick piece of hard beef jerky against the boy's lips. "Bite on this. It will help with the pain."

The outlaw bit down hard, his breath hissing through his teeth in short, agonized gasps.

But after a few moments he spat out the jerky and said: "I shoulda never left Tennessee."

Then he died.

Chris looked up from the prostrate Heck. "I can't find der bullet," he said. "It's in too far, by Gott." Drop of sweat beaded Heck's forehead because Chris had probed deep with the point of his knife. "Then I got to go back to Fort Smith," he groaned. "Chris, you'll come with me because I'm in no shape to fight if we run into outlaws."

"Then we must all go back," Murdo protested.

"No," Heck snapped. "You and Johnny Blue and that damned little redheaded assassin will keep after Buck. Just keep pressing him. Give him no rest. If he's running and looking over his shoulder, he's not killing settlers."

"But, Heck, there's only three of us," Murdo wailed.

"It's enough," Heck said. "Don't let him bring you to a fight, just keep dogging his trail and let him know you're there. I'll send help just as soon as I reach Fort Smith. In fact I'll come myself if the constipation don't do for me."

"But . . . but—" Murdo began.

"That's an order, Murdo," Heck said sternly, leaning on one elbow, his eyes glittering hard in the firelight.

The Scotsman buried his face in his hands. "I've said it before, and I'll say it again—we're a' doomed."

Right then there was a halloo from the edge of the woods. I looked up and saw Red Horse sitting his paint pony, half concealed by the lower branches of the pines.

"Hello the camp!" the Indian yelled.

"Vot do you vant, by Gott?" Chris hollered, cupping his hand to his mouth.

"Is the stingy-sized waddie with the big, pointy mustache dead yet?" asked that relentless Redskin.

"No," Chris replied. "Not yet. Pretty soon though, I t'ink maybe."

"Damn!" Red Horse spat, thumping his thigh with his fist. Then he turned his mount and disappeared into the trees like a puff of smoke.

"God," I said to no one in particular, "I hate that Injun."

Later that morning we buried the dead outlaws shallow; then we had the sad and melancholy task of getting the injured Heck up on his horse.

The big lawman could only ride sidesaddle, with his wounded rump hanging over the side, and it was a heartbreaking sight to see.

Murdo walked up to Heck and took out his silver watch. "Give this to my wife. Give it to my Mary and tell her I'm doomed," he said, handing Heck the timepiece, dangling from its chain. "It's got my name engraved on it, so I know it will no go astray."

Next he took his wallet from his back pocket, opened it, and studied the contents carefully. After a while he shook his head and muttered: "No, I canna do it. I canna part with my siller." He shoved the wallet back in his pocket and sighed. "Tell my Mary she'll just have to make do with the watch."

Heck nodded. "I'll make sure she gets it." In turn, he handed Murdo the Sears and Roebuck catalog, and said:

"This is for your own personal use, Murdo. I greatly fear that I'll have no further need for it."

"We're a' doomed, Heck," Murdo said. "You know that, don't you?"

Heck winced as he moved in the saddle. "Just do your duty, Murdo, and stay reg'lar. I'll get help to you, never fear. Keep crowding Buck to the west and ride with the Canadian on your left and we'll find you. You have my word on that."

"Heck, it's a big country." Murdo laid his hand on his fellow lawman's saddle horn. "You could miss us real easy."

"I won't miss you," Heck assured the Scotsman. "I'll do the tracking my own self, and there ain't much I don't see on the trail."

The lawman looked over to where I was standing and beckoned me over with his crooked forefinger. "Now listen here to me, boy," he said. "You tried to kill me this morning; you tried to murder an officer of the law."

I made to protest, but Heck lifted his hand and shushed me into silence. "Now I don't know if I'll survive without my reg'lar bowel movement, but if I do, I'm coming after you. I would take you back to Fort Smith with me now, but that would leave Marshal McKenzie in even direr straits.

What I'm doing here is choosing the lesser of two evils. But be assured, I mean to arrest you, have you brought to trial, and see you hanged at Judge Parker's convenience."

Again I protested my innocence, but again Heck hushed me.

"Have I made myself clear, boy?" he asked.

"Heck," I said, ignoring his question, "you should shuffle and redeal them words. I was fighting them outlaws an' dodging bullets when you was squattin' in the woods enjoying a dump, and I take it right hard that you'd accuse me of trying to murder you."

"Well, boy, that's my opinion and nothing you say is going to change it," Heck said.

And so it was that me and Marshal Heck Thomas, a stubborn man who would not listen to reason, parted on less-than-perfect terms. But even so, as he rode away with Chris, who was mounted on a small bay pony that had belonged to one of the dead outlaws, I managed to get out a cheery Huzzah! and Johnny Blue yelled, "I hope your ass gets better," and all in all, I believe we gave him a real nice send-off.

But Murdo, standing there watching his fellow lawmen leave, groaned: "We're a' doomed." He shook his head. "The flowers of the forest are a' weed away."

The Scotsman sighed. "Well, laddies, let's mount up and do what Heck told us to do, keep Buck and his men on the move."

"How far and how long can we push him, do you reckon?" Johnny Blue asked.

Murdo smiled without humor. "Until he turns around and swats us like flies," he replied.

Twenty-two

Murdo McKenzie could read signs like an Indian. And it became pretty clear over the next few days that Buck and his boys were keeping the Cimarron to their north as they rode deeper into the Territory. To the south ran the Canadian, and between was a land thinly occupied by settlers, mostly farmers and one-loop ranchers with a sprinkling of small, jerkwater towns here and there. This was pretty country, flat grassland and gently rolling hills with thick stands of blackjack and post oak trees dotting the landscape, and knolls topped by low rocks and brush gave the eye additional relief from the endless prairie. Cottonwoods spread their branches over the shallow creeks where antelope and coyotes came to drink and the sky was full of birds: crows, doves, blue jays, and scarlet cardinals.

On our fourth day on the trail we found the body of the outlaw Murdo had shot in the shoulder lying at the base of a redbud tree. He'd been drilled through the head at close range and Murdo reckoned he'd been slowing Buck down and that the outlaw leader had taken care of that problem permanently.

"Poor feller looks like he'd lost enough blood to paint the back porch afore ol' Buck done for him," Johnny Blue observed, pointing the toe of his boot at the man's blood-stained shirt.

There were signs of Buck's depredations everywhere:

single travelers shot and robbed, farms burned and settlers killed, milk cows shot in their barns and even chickens stomped to death in the yards. And always women. Outraged women, some left alive at Buck's whim to weep bitter tears for their dead menfolk and the violation of their bodies.

Thankfully we dug no graves for children, for although Buck and Shade would have shot younkers with the same careless ease as they'd gun jackrabbits, there must have been some who rode with them who drew the line at child killing.

Now there was no question of returning settlers to Fort Smith, so we spent most of our time locating farms and ranches where there were strong and armed men who would hold their ground, especially if they had womenfolk who would take in and care for Buck's victims and understand their tears.

Boys, that was grim, heartbreaking work, and me and Johnny Blue, when we were out of earshot of Murdo, began to talk to each other about lighting a shuck for Texas and leaving this sorry mess behind us. One thing we both decided: We were not going back to Fort Smith to rot in that hellhole Judge Parker called a prison, so we'd best make our move soon.

Murdo began to suspect there was something in the wind, because he kept a close eye on us and he was never far from his rifle. I had no doubt he'd cut us both down any way he could if he suspected we were about to skip.

Then, along the way, we picked up a thin, careworn woman named Mrs. Flood. She was probably no more than thirty-five, but long exposure to the sun on a miserable, hardscrabble farm had long ago turned her skin to wrinkled leather so that she looked at least twenty years older.

She had a brood of seven towheaded younkers, four of

them girls, and she told us her man had died the year before.

"One day he came in from spring plowing with a pain in his chest and his left arm," she said, betraying no emotion. "That night he couldn't breathe and the fear of death was in his eyes and by first light of morning he was gone. I buried him later that day and put a marker over him. He wasn't a good man, or a bad one. He was just a man. He was forty years old and wore out."

Mrs. Flood said she didn't care about her own life, but feared for her children. So she packed up a wagon and hitched it to a swaybacked horse, tossed the solemn, unsmiling kids on top, and followed us, not even once looking back at her farm as we rode away.

I guess she saw some kind of question in my eyes, because she said: "That sixty acres took my man's life and now it's taking mine. I was sixteen and pretty and fresh as a field of bluebonnets when we moved onto the place. And now I'm old and wrinkled and stooped and I don't want that kind of life for my young 'uns."

Boys, twenty years of sodbusting can do that to a person. It's a hard life, and it's hell on women. Mrs. Flood replenished our supplies with a side of bacon and some fresh eggs, and she was a good cook as we learned at supper that night. She made a chicken stew on the fire, big pieces of dark and white meat sliding off the bones in a thick, yellow gravy, and a big dish of brown beans on the side topped with a fragrant and quivering slice of salt pork.

With the stew we had hot cornbread flavored with bacon fat and pickled beets and onions on the side.

It was a feast fit for a king, and me and Johnny Blue and Murdo set to with a will, though those skinny towheaded youngsters matched us bite for bite, and then some.

On the frontier in them olden days, feeding the family was a task that took most of everyone's time, and even for a farmer's kids, there was rarely enough food. In hard times, especially in winter, children knew real hunger, and Mrs. Flood's kids probably spent most of their childhood longing for enough to eat.

Now they were blissfully surrounded by chicken and beans and cornbread with plenty of hot coffee to drink and they were making the most of it.

Dinner was through, and we were sitting around with loosened belts in the glow of the firelight when a man's voice cut across the silence of the evening.

"Hello the camp!"

Murdo rose to his feet, shucking his Colt. "Come on in," he yelled.

"Smelled your coffee, an' I don't mind if'n I do."

A tall, impossibly thin man rode a donkey into the circle of the firelight, his feet trailing on the ground on either side of the little beast. He must have been six inches over six feet, but I don't reckon he went any more than one hundred fifty pounds. He had long black hair streaked with gray falling to his shoulders, and a beard of the same color stretched downward to his belt buckle. The dark, broadcloth suit he was wearing was four inches too short in the arms and legs, and a celluloid collar without a tie encircled his turkey neck. He wore a pair of old-fashioned, mule-eared boots on his huge feet, and his black eyes were sunk in his head, but they caught the gleam of the campfire and glowed like red hot coals.

He carried no gun that I could see, unless it was stashed in the blanket roll draped over his burro's rump.

"Who," asked Murdo, "the hell are you?"

The tall man made no attempt to get off his donkey.

"Better you ask me what I am," he replied.

"Okay, then what are you?" Murdo said. He was a short-tempered man at the best of times and, grim-faced, he was white-knuckling his drawn Colt as he studied the lanky stranger.

"I," quoth the man, "am the voice of one crying in the wilderness, prepare ye the way of the Lord."

"Well, laddie, as I'd tell Jesus Christ Hisself, get off that burro and make no fancy moves or I'll shoot you dead," Murdo said.

"You're a hard man," the stranger said. "And a profane one."

But he hopped off that donkey right quick as he saw Murdo's jaw set and his grip grow even tighter on his revolver.

"My name is Ishmael," the skinny man said hastily. "I am known as a prophet. I see tomorrow."

He shrugged. "And the next day."

"I'm a prophet myself," Murdo said, his face grim. "I prophesy that if you're a member of Buck Starr's gang, you've got about two seconds to live."

Ishmael threw up his hands in horror. "I am a peaceful man, doing the Lord's work. I have no truck with the likes of Buck Starr."

Mrs. Flood poured some coffee into her cup and sliced a wedge of cornbread and topped it with a slice of salt pork. These she handed to Ishmael. The tall man bowed, making a great display of fine manners, and Mrs. Flood smiled shyly. And between the soft light of the fire and that smile, she almost looked like the sixteen-year-old girl she once had been and still fondly remembered. His Adam's apple bobbing, Ishmael took a long swallow of the scalding coffee, then wiped his mouth with the back of his hand and said: "Buck Starr is about three, four miles ahead of you, camped on the Canadian. Behind you"—he jerked his thumb over his shoulder—"a man named Frank Canton rides with a dozen Texas hardcases and a Paiute scout." Ishmael sighed. "They all mean to do you harm."

"You also see an Indian in your crystal ball, preacher?" I asked.

"Ah, yes, the Indian," Ishmael said. "His name is Red Horse and he plans"—he pointed at my hair—"to take your scalp."

"Here, you," said Murdo suspiciously. "How do you know all this, if'n you're not in cahoots with Buck and the rest of them?"

"You heard him, Murdo," Johnny Blue drawled, smiling as he built a smoke. "He's a prophet. He sees things that ain't happened yet."

"Is that right?" Murdo asked. "Have you been seeing things?"

"Not seeing things," Ishmael smiled, "hearing things. It's no secret that you're Fort Smith marshals after Buck Starr. Buck knows it, though I'm told it hasn't been disturbing his sleep o' nights. As for Frank Canton, well, he offered me the hospitality of his camp a few nights back. He's a hard and determined man and hell-bent on revenge. It seems you"—Ishmael nodded in my direction, his hand wandering to his right ear—"wounded him in some desperate encounter and he means to kill you."

"He's tried that afore," I said, trying to look as tough as I could with the fear of God spiking at my belly. "He don't scare me none."

Ishmael smiled, as though at some private thought. "Perhaps. But this time he plans to succeed."

Murdo holstered his gun. "I guess you're on the up and up, preacher." He nodded in the direction of the horses. "Put your burro over there and spread your blanket by the fire if you've a mind to."

Ishmael nodded. "Thank you, marshal, that is indeed a kindness."

But the preacher didn't move. He just stood there for a

few moments looking at Johnny Blue. Then he did a strange thing.

He strolled over to that reckless rider and touched him lightly on the shoulder.

"Be brave, my friend," the preacher said. "And remember this: Do not count your tears of pain. Do not pore over your griefs. Let them pass through your mind, as birds fly through the sky."

I expected Johnny Blue, who did not like to be touched, to draw down on that preacher and tell him to back off. But Johnny Blue just sat there for a spell, his cigarette burning away between his fingers, looking into Ishmael's wild eyes.

"All grief begins with a loss," Ishmael said finally, "but if nothing is ever lost in the universe, what is there to grieve?"

Johnny Blue sat there for a few moments like a man in a trance. Then he shook his head, as though to clear his mind and said: "Much obliged, preacher. I appreciate it."

Something had happened between those two rannies that I didn't understand. I looked from Johnny Blue to Ishmael and back again, and saw nothing in their faces to explain what had just taken place.

Finally I shrugged and poured myself some coffee and said: "Johnny Blue Dupree, I swear, sometimes you're a strange one."

That lanky rider turned to me, but he was looking through me, into the darkness beyond the fire where the shadows lay, and I suddenly felt cold and shivery as if I had just lain down in the snow.

"Johnny Blue, quit that," I said. "You're spookin' the hell out of me."

Like a man waking from a trance, Johnny Blue smiled and dug into his shirt pocket for the makings of a smoke. "Sorry," he said. "I was miles away."

Ishmael nodded like he understood, then put up his burro and returned to the fire.

"How come you're in this neck of the woods, preacher?" Murdo asked.

"Spreading the word, brother, spreading the word."

"What word?"

"Why, that the Lord is coming. I mean, coming real soon."

"How soon?" Murdo asked, without much interest.

"Exactly?"

Murdo shrugged. "Whatever."

Ishmael looked around the fire at us, his eyes resting finally on Mrs. Flood, who was hugging her sleeping youngest to her breast.

"Look," he said. "And learn."

He picked up a piece of oak branch that had fallen out of the fire and in the soft earth wrote:

January 1 1900

"That," he said, "is the day of the Christ's birth. Nineteen hundred years after his birth in Bethleham."

Murdo shook his head. "Take care, laddie. The Lord is not mocked."

"There's no mockery here," Ishmael said. "When the time comes, I will gather the people and take them up to a high mountain so that we will be the first to be numbered among the blessed."

Boys, let me tell you, I'd already been spooked by Johnny Blue, and now that preacher was doing his best to scare me into salvation and a seat in Sunday school.

"How do you know this?" I asked, as icy fingers played up and down my spine.

Ishmael smiled. "Because the Lord Himself told me so."

"Here, that won't do," Murdo snapped, his long, Calvinist's face angry. "There's black superstition here, and I think I detect the stench of popery."

Shrugging, Ishmael spread his hands. "I know what I know."

"Then to hell with you," Murdo hollered, rising to his feet. "And let's hear no more of this nonsense. And damn ye for a rank papist."

Ishmael laughed. "I've been called many things, but this is the first time I've been called a follower of Rome."

Murdo, raised securely in his grim Scottish religion, was in a murderous rage at what he took to be the preacher's unholy cant. Knowing how quick-tempered he was, and how readily he could reach for his gun, I rose and stretched and yawned: "Well, nineteen hundred is a long time away, but now's the time to find the blankets."

Picking up on my signal, Ishmael allowed that it was high time he turned in as well.

For a while Murdo stomped around, muttering to himself about the pope and graven images and the world going to hell in a handbasket. But he finally settled down and sought his soogan beyond the firelight, leaving the rest of us to do the same.

"Ishmael," Mrs. Flood said, laying her youngest gently on a pile of blankets in her wagon. "When the Lord comes, I want to go up unto the mountain and be numbered among the blessed."

The prophet nodded. "You will come with me, Mrs. Flood, and when the time comes, I will take you and the children to the mountain and you will be of the chosen."

"Amen," said Mrs. Flood.

And just to be on the safe side with God an' all, I said Amen myself.

Come morning, Murdo was still in a foul mood, but he seemed prepared to let go what had happened last night.

When Ishmael tied his burro to the back of the wagon

and said he would ride with Mrs. Flood, Murdo said that was fine by him as long as there was no more talk of mountains and miracles, because man and boy, he'd had no truck with popery and he wasn't about to start now. And he warned Ishmael that the widder was now under the care and protection of Judge Parker's court until we could find a family that would take her in until Buck Starr was caught.

Ishmael allowed that as far as he was concerned, the matter was closed and people must decide for themselves what was truth and what wasn't and only time would tell who was right.

A hazy sun was already climbing into the pale blue of the morning sky as we hunched, unspeaking, over coffee by the gray embers of the fire. Somewhere a meadowlark sang an inquiry to the new day and out on the prairie the antelope were already moving warily, dark shapes against the horizon.

Johnny Blue, building his first smoke of the day, was watching Murdo intently. He touched his tongue to the cigarette paper then placed the finished smoke between his lips.

Johnny Blue thumbed a match into flame and touched it to his cigarette. "I don't think that ol' Buck is runnin' from us, Murdo," he said.

"I don't think so either," Murdo said. "Maybe he was when we were stronger, but he ain't now."

"Then don't you think you should head back to Fort Smith with Mrs. Flood and her younkers?"

"I've been studying on it."

Murdo fell silent, staring moodily into the ashes of the fire. Then he said stiffly: "You boys is thinking about lighting a shuck, ain't you?"

"No," I protested. "Why, the very idea never crossed our minds."

"I wouldn't blame you none," Murdo said. "Now you're

facing an attempted murder charge on top of everything else when you get back to Fort Smith." The Scotsman shook his head. "No, I wouldn't blame you none if you did."

He drained his coffee cup and rose to his feet.

"But I tell you this—if you try to skip, I'll come after you and kill you both," Murdo smiled. "No offense, lads."

"None taken," Johnny Blue said cheerfully, his mood improving with each drag of his cigarette.

"But you better come up with a plan right quick, Murdo, or we're a' doooomed."

Murdo laughed. It was the first time I'd ever heard him laugh and it came as a shock.

"You're right, laddie, we are a' doomed," he said. "But I do have a plan that will at least give us half a chance of surviving."

"Do tell," I said.

"We angle south toward the Canadian, taking Mrs. Flood and the preacher with us. As I recollect, there's a place called Cottonwood Creek where a fairly deep and wide stream comes straight off the river for about a hundred yards, then makes a sharp turn and runs parallel to it.

"If we set up a fortified camp at the creek," Murdo continued, talking like the old soldier he'd once been, "we can have the Canadian on our right and the stream behind us and to our left. If Buck and his lads come at us, they won't be able to try any outflanking maneuvers and will be forced to charge straight ahead. I think with us three riflemen and the preacher, maybe we can hold them off until Heck gets here."

"It's thin, Murdo," I protested. "It's almighty thin."

"You maybe have a better plan?"

"Yeah, we load them kids in the wagon and take off hell-for-leather toward Fort Smith an' meet ol' Heck on the trail."

"If Buck comes after us and catches us in the open, we won't have a prayer," Murdo said.

"Besides," he added slyly, "ain't you forgetting something?"

"Like what?"

"You got Frank Canton and a wild Injun lyin' for you back there."

"Oh," I said, a feeling of utter hopelessness clutching at my stomach, "I'd forgotten all about them."

"I hadn't," Johnny Blue said. He turned to Murdo. "Your plan sounds good to me, especially since it's the only one we got."

The Scotsman sighed. "Then let's mount up. The sooner we reach Cottonwood Creek, the better."

Twenty-three

Boys, there was one thing for sure, Buck Starr was no longer afraid of us, if he ever had been. As we rode across the open grassland, we saw riders in the distance keeping up with our gallant party but staying well out of rifle range. Every now and then the sun flashed on what I took to be a gun barrel, but Murdo shook his head.

"They've got a glass on us, trying to figure our strength. By now they've got a pretty good idea we're three marshals, a crazy preacher, and a woman with a passel o' kids."

The three of us rode close to the wagon, and Ishmael, hunched over, sat at the reins.

"You got a gun stashed somewheres?" I asked him. We were still two days from Cottonwood Creek, and the wagon was slowing us down considerable.

"No gun," Ishmael said. "I don't hold with violence."

"Preacher, I got a feelin' you'll change your mind soon," I said. "Before too long you're gonna need a gun and you're gonna need it almighty sudden."

Ishmael shook his head once. "There never was a time when, in my opinion, some way could not be found to prevent the drawing of a sword."

"Them's fine words right enough," I said, "but they don't count for a hill of beans out here."

"Do you know who said those words?" Ishmael asked.

I shrugged. "Some Bible banger, I guess."

"No, they were uttered by the greatest warrior of them all." Ishmael looked straight ahead. "Ulysses S. Grant."

"Well, Grant ain't here an'—"

A plume of dust kicked up about five feet to the right of my horse, followed by the sharp report of a rifle. A second fountain of dirt and grass spurted a couple of feet closer, and I heard the rifle bark again.

"They're testing us," Murdo hollered. "Testing our defenses." He yanked his rifle from the boot under his leg. "It's an old trick I seen the Zulus use in the Transvaal when I had the honor of wearing the Queen's uniform."

Murdo threw his rifle to his shoulder. "Well, let's not disappoint those laddies." He cranked off three fast rounds, but as far as I could see, they did no execution among the outlaws.

Me and Johnny Blue joined in, cutting loose at those distant riders, and I dusted the one in front pretty good—or so I thought.

But that ranny climbed off his pony nimble as you please, pulled down his pants, and mooned us while his companions jerked their middle fingers up and down and yelled that we couldn't hit an outhouse if we was holding on to the handle.

"They're out of range," Murdo said grimly. "But at least we showed them we're good an' ready." The ranny who mooned us pulled up his pants and remounted, and the bandits all gave us the finger again before galloping over the rise of a hill and vanishing from sight.

"From now on we ride with our rifles across our saddle horns," Murdo said. "Those outlaws know there's only three of us shooting, and they'll be back."

Murdo fed shells into his rifle and told me and Johnny Blue to stay with the wagon while he scouted ahead. "Any campsite we choose until we reach the creek has to be de-

fensible," he said, "and they're going to be few and far between in this open country."

Behind me in the wagon, a couple of Mrs. Flood's
younkers were crying, frightened by the shooting, and I
heard her try to soothe them, telling them that everything
was going to be all right. Ishmael took one of the littlest
girls in his long arms and held her close, crooning to her
softly, and gradually the child quieted down, snuffling as
she pressed her tearstained face against the preacher's chest.

"Bring on the wagon at your best speed, and stay on
the alert," Murdo said before he loped away.

"I fear we're closer to doom than ever before."

"Y'know," I said as me and Johnny Blue rode in front
of the wagon, our heads turning this way and that as we
nervously studied the country around us. "Thinkin' back
on it, I place the blame for this mess squarely on ol' Charlie."

"How come?" Johnny Blue asked, his interest quicken-
ing as he built a cigarette.

"Well, first of all, he sweet-talked us into going with
him into Blackfoot country and that's where we ran afoul
of them wolfers an' Shade Hannah. Then he made a right
poor showing with the Buffalo Bill Bear, forgettin' everything I learned him about grinnin' and tippin'. I mean, study
on it some, Blue Boy. Without the bear, the only job ol'
Bill would give us was shovelin' shit, and that right there
in the open where the law could see us plain as rabbit pills
in a sugar bowl.

"Yup, if you chew on it awhile like I've done lately,"
I added, "there's only one conclusion to be reached: It was
Charlie who done for us."

Johnny Blue nodded, scratching his jaw thoughtfully.
"Y'know, that's a true thing you just said. Now that I've
considered it some, I reckon this is ol' Charlie's fault right
enough."

"Damn that Charlie," I said.

"He's surely a man born to trouble," said Johnny Blue, lighting his smoke.

At midafternoon we came up on an old buffalo wallow. There was water in it collected from recent rains, so we let the horses drink, then turned them out to graze while me and Johnny Blue stood close by with our rifles in our hands.

Ishmael loaded his burro with wood he found in a nearby grove of scattered oak and chestnut trees and Mrs. Flood fried up some bacon and bread. After we and the young 'uns ate, we saddled up and took to the trail again.

Dusk was painting dark blue shadows across the grass when Murdo returned, coming toward us at a fast lope.

He reined up alongside me and Johnny Blue and pointed to the west. "Folks camped about a mile ahead." Murdo shook his head. "Damndest thing—they got a wagon covered with big round lanterns of some kind."

"What kind of wagon? What kind of folks?" Johnny Blue asked urgently.

"Dunno," Murdo replied. "I didn't get real close on account of how I didn't want to alarm them. But they're camped alongside a stand of redbud trees and near a stream, an' I could see womenfolk walking around."

"Johnny Blue, are you thinkin' what I'm thinkin'?" I asked.

"It's got to be them," Johnny Blue said, his eyes alight. "Lanterns, womenfolk, it couldn't be nobody else."

"Who?" asked Murdo, puzzled.

"An old friend of ours," I said. "A travelin' Chinaman feller called Dr. Chang and his three beautiful daughters."

Murdo studied on this for a spell, then said: "Well, let's do the mannerly thing and go a-calling."

He reached behind him and untied his bagpipes. "I don't

want to ride into that camp sudden like, the way folks are on edge right now. We'll let them know we're coming."

"What tune you gonna squeeze out of that poor animal?" asked Johnny Blue sourly.

With great dignity, Murdo replied, " 'The Campbells Are Coming.' " Then, staring hard at Johnny Blue, he added: "And damn ye for a heathen."

Having thus spoken, the surly Scotsman put one of the pipes in his mouth and began to play. It was a fine, rollicking tune, and as we rode toward what we hoped was Dr. Chang's camp, I picked up the melody—man and boy, I've always had a great gift for music—and added my own words:

> The Campbells are comin' haroo, haroo,
> The Campbells are comin' haroo, haroo . . .
> We're gonna be with you the noo, the noo,
> Me an' Murdo an' Johnny Bloo . . .

And pretty soon Johnny Blue was singing with me, and as we rode up on Dr. Chang's camp, our uplifted voices and the skirling pipes made enough noise to send the night-roosting birds a-fluttering out of the redbud trees and startled jackrabbits scattering from under our horses and the wheels of the creaking wagon.

Murdo ended his tune with a triumphant, high-pitched wail, then set his pipes aside and yelled: "Haloo the camp!"

A man stood by the fire, a rifle in his hands, and it was unmistakably the short, slight figure of Dr. Chang.

"Who goes there?" the Chinaman hollered. "And be aware, I'm armed and determined."

"We're officers of the law," replied Murdo, "and we have a woman and children here and a tetched preacher."

"I'll turn no honest man away from my fire," Dr. Chang said. "Come on in, and welcome."

Johnny Blue needed no other invitation. He set spurs to his horse and galloped into the camp, jumping out of the saddle while his mount was still sliding to a halt, scattering clods of dirt and grass into the air.

Lo May was standing just behind her father and she dodged around him and ran into Johnny Blue's arms. They kissed right then in the circle of the firelight, and I guess Dr. Chang was so taken back he made no move to stop them.

As the rest of us rode in, Lo May laid her head on Johnny Blue's chest and whispered: "Shonee Blue, I've waited so long."

That lanky rider made to reply, but the words seemed to stick in his throat, so he just hauled off and kissed Lo May again and they clung together like they was the only two people in the world and the rest of us didn't even exist.

But Dr. Chang had recovered from his shock and he said something right sharp to his daughter in Chinese. And that young lady, with a long, lingering look at Johnny Blue, slowly parted from him and walked back to her giggling sisters. Lo May stood there, never taking her eyes from Johnny Blue, and he in turn kept watching her and it was easy to see that little gal sure enough had her brand on his heart.

Murdo had watched what was going on with a dour expression on his face. I reckon he figgered he had enough troubles without getting in the middle between Johnny Blue and an angry father, so he said to that mooning waddie: "Go help Ishmael get the horses settled."

For a few moments Johnny Blue just stood there like he didn't know if he was getting up or going to bed, but finally Ishmael touched him on the arm and said gently, "Let's go unsaddle the horses and unhitch the wagon."

As Johnny Blue followed Ishmael, Lo May looked after him with mooncalf eyes, and Dr. Chang showed his displeasure at his daughter by glaring at her until that young lady dropped her gaze and blushed, her long, dark lashes lying on her cheekbones like fluttering butterflies.

"What brings you to this neck of the woods?" Murdo asked Dr. Chang. "This ain't no place for womenfolk."

The Chinaman shrugged. "I'm a peddler. I go where people need my goods and that's away from the settlements where there are stores and out on the prairie where there are none."

However, Dr. Chang told Murdo that he'd heard of the depredations committed by Buck Starr and his gang of desperadoes and was now heading for the safety of Fort Smith.

"With three daughters, well, a father can't be too careful," he said, and he looked hard at me as he said it.

Murdo nodded in agreement. "These are perilous times." He shook his head sadly. "Perilous times, and I very much fear we may all be doomed."

Dr. Chang's young ladies had found Mrs. Flood's children and they were fussing and fretting over them as womenfolk do, and I don't think those kids ever had so much attention in their lives. Mrs. Flood, freed from the responsibility of looking out for her kids, outdid herself by preparing a thick stew from jackrabbits Dr. Chang had shot, some antelope meat, and diced-up pieces of salt pork. And she served it up with cornbread and molasses and coffee that was strong enough to float a Colt's pistol.

By the time we'd finished eating, we all let out our belts a couple of notches, except for Murdo, who was standing guard out in the darkness beyond the firelight.

When he came in to eat, he touched Johnny Blue on the shoulder.

"Your watch," he said. He nodded into the night. "About fifty yards to the left there's a fair-sized willow growing by the stream. Hole up at its base. It will give you some protection should they come at us that way and you'll have easy targets because they'll be slowed by them steep cut-banks."

Murdo sighed. "If they come straight at us across the grass, just cut loose and give us as much warning as you can." He nodded toward the trees. "They won't come through the redbuds, not in the dark."

In this, as events would later prove, Murdo was dead wrong. They would come at us through the trees all right, though it would only be one man—a pale-eyed demon with hell riding on his shoulder.

Johnny Blue picked up his Winchester and rose to his feet. Lo May had given him one of them little cups of Chinese tea, and now he drained it, smiling at her across the firelight.

Dr. Chang scowled, then turned and whispered something to Lo May and the other girls. Giggling, all three ran toward their wagon as Johnny Blue, toting his rifle under his arm, disappeared into the darkness.

Boys, what happened next had to be seen to be believed.

Dr. Chang supervised his daughters as they set down one side of his wagon then used chains to pin it up and keep it level like a stage. Then he rose and beckoned to the rest of us. "Bring the children," he smiled. "They're going to see a magic show."

Dr. Chang disappeared inside the wagon as the girls lit colored lanterns on both sides of the makeshift stage.

Meanwhile we gathered up the kids and set them in front of the wagon, and Murdo, worried about them lanterns showing in the darkness, growled that this was no time for tomfoolery and magic shows with all of us in mortal peril, though he too took a seat on the grass with the rest of us, carefully laying his rifle alongside him.

Those kids never had much, hadn't seen much, and didn't expect much, but they were well behaved and obedient as all children had to be in them dangerous frontier days. They sat patiently with their legs drawn up, their little chins resting on their knees, eyes big and bright as new-minted pennies shining in the light of the rose-colored lanterns.

One of Lo May's sisters stood by the side of the stage, and she suddenly beat the gong in her hands as Dr. Chang appeared in a long red gown with a black, green-eyed dragon on the front and a funny little round hat on his head.

The kids let out a surprised "Ooh" as the gong clashed again and Dr. Chang produced a stick he said was a magic wand, and then his daughter handed him a stovepipe hat.

Boys, I know you're going to find this a passel to believe, but that Chinaman said some magic words, waved his wand over the hat—then pulled out a big, white rabbit!

He was a real, live rabbit, with pink eyes and ears and he kicked like crazy when Dr. Chang held him up and showed him to the kids.

Never in my born days had I ever seen anything like that, and I reckon I gasped and hollered and clapped my hands even louder than them younkers did.

Then Dr. Chang said some more words and pulled out a white dove!

The dove said coo! coo! and fluttered up onto the magician's shoulder and just sat there, and the kids and the rest of us hollered, "Ooh," and clapped our hands even louder than before, because this was great magic, no doubt about that. Boys, I'd never seen the like, and do you think anyone else, before or since, has done magic like that? I don't know.

Them kids of Mrs. Flood were up on their knees, and me right along with them, their eyes big as saucers as they Ooh'd and Ah'd, and it felt good to see them being allowed to act like children, even for a short while.

I wished Johnny Blue was around to see this, instead

of being out there in the dark on the singing shift, but I planned to tell him everything I saw, and then some.

Dr. Chang did one magic trick after another, and even took a silver dollar out of my ear. I asked him how to do it, because I figgered if he teached me, I'd never be poor again. But he said he couldn't give the secret away because magicians are sworn to never reveal such things.

Boys, then he took about a dozen little glass balls and juggled them all at once, moving them from one hand to another in a shining circle. Then he let them go one by one, and as they flew high into the air each one exploded with a loud POP! POP! POP! and bright-colored sparks in green and blue and red and yellow scattered in every direction.

Even Murdo's eyes were glued to the stage as Dr. Chang performed, and he seemed to have forgotten all his cares as he watched the magic unfold. Lo May was sitting close to me, and after the trick with the colored balls I turned to tell her that the little 'uns were really enjoying the show.

But she was gone!

Only the lingering memory of her perfume remained and the grass bent over where she'd sat. But of that little Chinese gal, there was no sign.

Twenty-four

I rose to my feet quietly. No one even glanced in my direction, because everybody's eyes were on Dr. Chang. Even Ishmael, who believed the world was about to end, sat beside Mrs. Flood holding her hand, entranced by what was happening.

"Hola!" Ishmael excitedly told the youngsters as Dr. Chang did yet another of his amazing tricks. "Here's wonderful magic indeed!"

I had a pretty good idea where Lo May had gone, and I figgered to head off trouble at the pass before it even got started.

Quietly I eased into the darkness, moving like an Injun toward the willow tree by the stream. And that's where I found them.

They were standing locked in each other's arms, both of them naked as the day they was born, and in the pale moonlight they looked like ebony and ivory grips set on the same gun handle. Slowly, Johnny Blue and Lo May sank to the ground, still holding each other close, their lips joined. And I, no longer wishing to intrude, snuck out of there and made my way back to the camp.

Boys, a lot of things was running through my mind that night. But most of all was the thought that me and Johnny Blue had ridden together for nigh on ten years, since we was both younkers of fifteen. Now it looked like those days was fast coming to an end. Johnny Blue had found a woman to share his life—and in that situation, three's definitely a crowd.

Don't get me wrong. I was glad for Johnny Blue. But I reckoned that ahead of me stretched only empty trails and the high lonesome—and that was a worrisome thing.

When I got back to the wagon, the show was over and Mrs. Flood and Ishmael were tucking the excited, babbling youngsters into their blankets by the fire.

I poured myself a cup of coffee and nodded to Murdo as he squatted by the fire.

"Enjoy the show?" I asked.

That dour Scotsman merely grunted in reply, then said: "I think Dr. Chang and his womenfolk better come with us. I'd surely hate to see them caught out in the open by Buck and them between here and Fort Smith."

"Sounds reasonable," I said. "An' it gives us one more rifle if things get bad."

Murdo lit his pipe with a branch from the fire, the star on his shirt glinting orange in the light.

"Things will get bad all right. I reckon we're going to need that rifle. Maybe sooner—"

BOOM!

The loud roar of a shotgun shattered the silence of the night, sending the kids bolt upright in their beds. A little one began to cry as Murdo rose, cursing, to his feet.

"We're under attack!" he yelled. "That came from the direction of the willow tree."

The marshal grabbed his rifle and pounded into the darkness, myself following close on his heels. Murdo turned his head. "Shoot fast, shoot low, and don't miss."

"Depend on it," I said.

"That," said the Scotsman as the tree hove into sight in the gloom, "don't fill me with confidence."

The first thing we saw as we reached the tree was Dr.

Chang. Still in his magician's robe, he held a smoking shotgun in his hands. On the ground, her eyes huge and terrified, Lo May tried to cover her nakedness with her dress, while Johnny Blue, cursing a blue streak, struggled into his pants.

"Here!" Murdo cried. "What's going on?"

"He," said Dr. Chang, pointing the muzzle of his gun at Johnny Blue, "has dishonored my daughter. That black devil has ruined her. My first shot was a warning, now I'll kill him."

"Hold up there, Chang," said Murdo, grabbing the barrels of the shotgun. "If there's any killing to be done around here, I'll do it." He glared at the Chinaman. "And let's have less heathen talk about devils. If you go thinking on the devil long enough, pretty soon his horns will appear on everyone you meet."

"But he is a devil," Dr. Chang wailed. "He's ruined my daughter. Who will want her as a wife now?"

"Perhaps," said a mild voice from behind me, "he will."

I turned. Ishmael was pointing at Johnny Blue, a wide smile on his face.

"Is that true, son?" Murdo asked that love-struck rider. "Will you take this woman to wife after you were fairly caught in fornication with her?"

"Damn right," said Johnny Blue, stamping into his boots.

"And you, young lady?"

"He's the husband I want," replied Lo May, her eyes downcast as she fluttered her lashes modestly. "Shonee Blue is the only man I'll ever marry."

"How about you, Chang?" asked Murdo. "It seems your daughter's honor is saved. A marriage between these two set okay with you?"

"No," snapped Dr. Chang, "it does not. I wish a Chinese husband for my daughter, even an unworthy and despoiled child such as this."

"Father," Lo May said, "I will marry no one but Shonee Blue. If you will not give us your consent, I will ride away with him. Now! Tonight!"

"How you have wounded me, child," Dr. Chang said miserably. "How you have hurt me."

"No," Ishmael cried angrily. "She hasn't hurt you, vain, selfish man. She's hurt your pride." The preacher strode up to Dr. Chang and snapped his fingers in his face. "And pride has no more value than that. It's a rooster crowing on a dung heap."

Boys, that Chinaman looked like he'd been slapped. He stood there staring at Ishmael for a few moments, his eyes wide with shock. He glanced at the faces surrounding him, including mine, and read the same message—that he was a pigheaded, unreasonable man whose stubborn pride was standing in the way of his daughter's future happiness.

Dr. Chang's thin fingers rose to his trembling lips and he looked at us from one to the other for several long minutes. Then he lowered his head and said: "My daughter has made her choice and it seems I must bow to the inevitable."

Dr. Chang stood quietly for a minute or two deep in thought. Then he shrugged. "You, Ishmael, are correct. If a man is selfish enough and proud enough to always seek his own advantage, what is the use of remaining among men? A selfish, proud man frustrates every chance to make all beings rejoice." He inclined his head slightly toward Johnny Blue. "I will take you as my son-in-law, though you are not Chinese and therefore unworthy."

"Then it's settled," Murdo sighed thankfully. "But Lo May, you must stay with your father until we can find a preacher. I will countenance no more godless fornication while I am in command of this expedition."

The Scotsman raised his eyes to heaven. "Oh, I'm glad my Mary isn't here, because what I've seen and heard tonight would make that virtuous woman blush to the roots of her hair." He wagged a finger at Johnny Blue and Lo May, who were standing, now fully clothed, in each other's arms. "For shame, you two. Caught in the vilest fornication. For shame!"

"Murdo, you've found a preacher," Ishmael said mildly. "I can marry them."

"You?" demanded the Scotsman. "What gives you that authority?"

"I'm an ordained minister, and therefore fully qualified in the sight of God to join a man and woman together in holy wedlock."

"Here, is there popery in this?" Murdo tilted his head suspiciously. "I swear I've been suffering the harlot scent of Rome about you since you first rode into our camp."

"No, not Rome," Ishmael replied.

"Where then?" asked Murdo. "What are ye, if you're not a damn papist?"

"Presbyterian, in fact," Ishmael said, shrugging. "And a Freemason to boot."

"Are ye sure?" Murdo asked suspiciously. "Beware now, laddie, make no mockery."

Ishmael smiled, grabbed the Scotsman by the arm and took him aside. The pair engaged in a short conversation and I saw Murdo's face light up. "I didn't have ye pegged as a traveling man," he said. He put his hand on Ishmael's shoulder. "Brother, my apologies. You have my official permission as a sworn officer of the law to wed this pair tomorrow."

I heard Dr. Chang let out with a long, shuddering sigh as I looked at Lo May and Johnny Blue. They were locked in each other's arms like they intended to spend the rest of their lives in that position, standing forever by the willow tree until the world came to an end.

Ishmael laid his hand on my shoulder. "Amazing, isn't it?" he asked.

"What's amazing?" I asked in turn.

"Amazing how easily the loving ones find love. It just comes to them, and they don't even have to reach for it."

I should have been glad for Johnny Blue, but all I felt inside was a strange, clammy coldness. I looked up at the moon, but it gave me no comfort. There was no warmth there. It was just a big, mother-of-pearl button holding together the edges of the dark, ragged sky.

Come morning, I felt better, and the unnamed fear I'd felt the night before was all but gone. We were up before first light, Johnny Blue so nervous his hands shook as he rolled his first cigarette of the day.

Murdo, a cup of steaming coffee in his hands, gestured toward Ishmael. "Preacher, keep the ceremony short, sweet, and to the point. I want to reach Cottonwood Creek by noon."

Ishmael nodded. "Johnny Blue is already married in all but name. I'll be brief."

"Aye, then see that you are," Murdo said.

He looked critically at Johnny Blue, set his coffee carefully beside him, and rose to his feet. He walked to where our pack lay near the horses and returned with a white shirt in one hand, his other hidden behind his back.

"Wear this," he said to Johnny Blue, holding out the shirt to him. "It looks a lot better than that blue rag you're wearing."

Johnny Blue nodded his thanks and took the shirt.

"Of course, I'll be wanting it back after the ceremony," Murdo said. "It was verra expensive, two dollars in Fort Smith, so be careful and see you don't spill anything on it."

Murdo brought his hand out from behind his back and it held a bottle of whiskey.

"This is Johnny Walker, scotch whiskey," Murdo said.

"It's verra precious and I was keeping it for a special occasion. This . . ." He waved a hand that took in Johnny Blue, the wagon where Lo May had spent the night, and the rest of us ". . . fits the bill, I believe." He uncorked the bottle and held it up to the firelight, gazing into its amber depths. Then he sighed, perhaps regretting his generosity, and said: "Hold out your cups, lads, and let me sweeten up your coffee."

I'd never drunk scotch whisky before, and found it had a fine, smoky flavor and its warmth instantly banished the morning chill. We were all drinking on an empty stomach, and pretty soon my head was swimming, but for the first time in weeks I felt relaxed and at ease.

As Murdo stood by with his rifle, Johnny Blue—who was fast becoming the West's cleanest cowpoke—bathed in the creek, then donned the white wedding shirt. He looked so fine, I gave him a hearty Huzzah! And Mrs. Flood, who had spent the morning in Dr. Chang's wagon helping get Lo May prepared, clapped her hands and gasped, "I do declare!" and she added that Johnny Blue was quite the handsomest groom in the whole world.

Dawn was pushing yellow-colored spires across the sky as we returned to the campfire where Ishmael stood, a Bible in his hands. Around him were arranged all the little Floods, their faces scrubbed and their hair wetted down and combed. Their mother immediately fussed around them, clucking like a chicken as she wiped grease off their chins, because each was chewing on a chunk of fried bread and bacon and none was making too neat a job of it.

"I swear," said Mrs. Flood as she wiped off yet another slick chin, "keeping these young 'uns clean for even a minute is impossible."

We all laughed, even Murdo, and that helped ease the tension we were feeling as we waited for Lo May to make her appearance.

As it happened, we didn't have to wait long. One of her sisters appeared and clashed the gong Dr. Chang had used in his magic show. Then a few moments crept by as all eyes were glued to the back of the wagon. Even the little Floods had stopped eating and stood there as though mesmerized, their bread and bacon growing cold in their hands.

Lo May stepped down out of the wagon—and she took my breath away.

She wore a dress of a lemon color that matched the morning sky, embroidered all over with little cornflower-blue blossoms. The dress rose high around her neck and fell to her toes, but it was split up one side so that when she walked I could see her slim legs and the yellow slippers she wore on her tiny feet.

Her black hair was piled up on top of her head in a bun circled by a gold band, and in her hands she carried a bouquet of pink and white wildflowers.

Boys, she was the prettiest woman I'd ever seen in my life, before or since, and the fragile, delicate vision of her as she appeared that morning will stay with me until I close my eyes for the last time and all memory is gone.

Johnny Blue stood there thunderstruck for a few moments. Then he walked to her and took her hand, gently, like he was afraid she'd break or fade away in the morning light like a fairy gift.

Lo May looked up into Johnny Blue's eyes and smiled shyly at him. "I've lived eighteen years," she said, "and this is the happiest day of all my life."

Johnny Blue tried to reply, but the words stuck in his throat, and he merely nodded and raised her hand to his lips.

"Ahem," said Murdo. He held his rifle in the crook of his arm and looked real uneasy. "We don't have much time." He turned to Ishmael. "Get on with it."

Dr. Chang stood at the wagon, watching the ceremony

from a distance. I don't think he could bear to be any closer, because he was a proud man, and when you get right down to it, this wedding was none of his doing.

"Dearly beloved . . ." Ishmael began, and Mrs. Flood lined up all the little Floods and made them stand to attention.

"We are gathered here today to join this man and this woman in holy matrimony . . ."

As Ishmael began the timeless words of the wedding ceremony, I looked toward the far horizon where the sun had already begun its climb into the sky. Under that sun lay the broad sweep of the grasslands that stretched all the way to the Canadian and then to the Washita, rolling westward until they met the pine- and aspen-covered foothills of the Wichita Mountains.

Closer, less than a day's ride, was Cottonwood Creek, where we would fort up and take refuge and wait until Heck fulfilled his promise and came to save us.

This was beautiful country, a place where a man and a woman could settle and build for the future. It had grass and water in abundance, a place to raise cows and kids. It was country where a man could grow old, full of sleep and wisdom, until his tall sons carried him to his rest and laid him snug and rooted deep under the soil of his own land.

Drowsy, and relaxed by the whisky, my attention wandered back to Ishmael, who was saying: "Is there anyone here who believes this couple should not be joined in holy matrimony?" He lowered his Bible and looked around. "Speak now or forever hold your peace."

All eyes went to Dr. Chang, but the cheerless Chinaman just stood there by his wagon, unmoving, his head bowed as though in prayer.

Ishmael nodded, as if agreeing with a question he'd heard only in his own mind, and turning to Johnny Blue, he said: "Do you, Johnny Blue Dupree, take this woman—"

Lo May's face was flushed with excitement, her eyes were on Johnny Blue, the adoring look of a woman in love with the kind of man she'd always dreamed of loving.

"—to be your lawful wedded wife, to have and to hold, in sickness—"

The pounding hoofbeats of a galloping pony cut suddenly across my consciousness.

I turned and saw a rider burst out of the redbud trees, scattering a flight of roosting doves, a revolver in his hands.

It was Shade Hannah, and he was coming fast.

"Jesus Christ!" Murdo yelled.

He unlimbered his rifle, fumbling for the lever. The shock of Shade's attack, coupled with the whiskey we'd drunk that morning, threw the Scotsman off balance. He dropped his rifle, and, cursing, bent to pick it up again.

My guns lay by the fire, both pistol and Winchester, and I turned and ran to them.

Shade didn't slow down. He rode past Johnny Blue and Lo May at a gallop, and the revolver in his hand barked once. "That's for the payroll!" he screamed as he thundered past.

I caught a glimpse of his flat, white eyes, as emotionless as the eyes of a timber rattler.

Johnny Blue cried out as Lo May, a sudden splash of bright scarlet blossoming on her chest, collapsed into his arms.

Murdo now had his rifle to his shoulder, but Shade was bent over his pony's neck as he galloped at breakneck speed toward the stream.

For a few fateful moments Murdo hesitated, unsure of his swift-moving target. He knew as I did that Shade would have to rein in his galloping horse to navigate the steep cutbank, making himself an easy target. So he waited . . .

He waited too long.

Shade didn't even slow for the cutbank. He crouched

low over his horse's neck and dug his spurs cruelly into its flanks. The mount tossed its head in pain and threw itself at the stream. It took off from the bank and soared over the rushing water like a demon, thumping onto the level grass of the other side a good eight feet beyond the sheer drop of the cutbank.

Shocked, Murdo yelled: "Damn you!"

He cranked off a shot, then another, but Shade was in the clear, riding fast, shooting his sixgun in the air, harooing and laughing like the madman he was.

"Damn your eyes!" Murdo screamed. He fired shot after shot at Shade until his rifle cranked empty, then he yanked it from his shoulder and threw it in the gunman's direction. For a few moments the Scotsman watched Shade fade into the distance, before sinking slowly to his knees, his face buried in his hands.

Johnny Blue was on the ground, Lo May's head in his lap.

Her wedding dress was no longer lemon, covered in them pretty blue flowers. It was crimson from her neck to her waist with blood that glistened like fresh paint.

She smiled at Johnny Blue and put her hand up to his cheek.

"Poor Shonee Blue," she whispered. "My husband."

Boys, one time when I was stringing wire on the old DHS northern range with Tube Wilson I picked up a little bird that had been hit by a hawk. I laid her in the palm of my gloved hand and held her for a spell as her little chest heaved up and down with every struggling breath. Then the little bird just closed her eyes, stopped breathing, and went away. There was no fuss and no fear, like she was apologizing for putting me to so much trouble.

Lo May died like that.

Her hand dropped from Johnny Blue's cheek and she just closed her eyes and went away.

Johnny Blue sat there for a long time, holding her close; then he looked up at me. "Help us?" he said. "Can you help us?"

I stood there, my mouth opening and closing because I couldn't find any of the right words. "Blue Boy," I said finally. "Damn it, Blue Boy. Oh, goddammit."

Mrs. Flood had ushered her crying kids away, but Lo May's sisters were screaming in grief, and Dr. Chang stood looking down at his dead daughter with a numbed, unbelieving expression on his face. Then he sank to his knees and bent over, rocking back and forth and moaning like a man who'd been gut shot.

Murdo came up to us then, glanced at Lo May's pale face, and squatted down beside Johnny Blue. "She's gone, boy," he said. "We got to get moving. They'll be back."

Murdo reached out his hands. "Let me take her."

"Get back," Johnny Blue said. "Touch her and I'll kill you."

The Scotsman threw me a despairing glance, and I said: "Johnny Blue."

Johnny Blue looked at me. "You're my friend. Can you help us?"

"Johnny Blue," I said, finding my tongue at last. "We came for a wedding, but now we got a buryin' to do."

For a few long moments Johnny Blue looked into my eyes. Then he bent and kissed Lo May on her pale lips, and now the front of his white wedding shirt was scarlet red.

Twenty-five

We laid Lo May deep in the earth. Me and Murdo dug the grave and we dug it well.

As we laid her to rest, still in her lemon wedding dress with the little embroidered flowers, Johnny Blue stood by the graveside, his head bowed, unspeaking, unseeing.

Murdo played his pipes, a haunting, echoing lament, each sad, wild note tearing at my soul like the claws of an animal.

Dr. Chang and his daughters stood, huddled close to each other, now beyond tears but not beyond their terrible grief.

Ishmael, who had been standing with his arm around Mrs. Flood, walked over to me and whispered: "Remember, God sends us nothing that is too hard or too hurtful to bear. He proportions all to our strength and abilities. Our trials are suited to our needs as the glove to the hand of the wearer."

Today, I can't recollect if his words helped me much, but they did make me forget my own sadness for a spell and think of Johnny Blue.

Johnny Blue was a black man, with a black man's quick pride, and he would not be handled. So I didn't move closer to him, only stretched out my arm and laid my fingertips on his shoulder, barely touching.

Even then, I expected him to pull away, but he did not. He just stood there, looking down at Lo May's blanket-wrapped body as she lay still and silent in her grave. He looked at her for such an endless time, my arm began to ache. But I didn't pull it away, hoping that perhaps I was bringing him a comfort.

Then he said something. I don't know where it came from. Maybe it was words he'd heard on a trail one time years before and never forgot. Maybe it was at the burial of some poor cowboy, because we'd laid to rest more than our share, and maybe he heard the preacher say it. Like I say, I don't know where it came from, and I don't know how he remembered it, but I do know that Johnny Blue slowly lifted his head until he was looking at the blue sky and whispered:

> Do not stand at my grave and weep. I am not there. I do not sleep.
> I am the thousand winds that blow. I am the diamond glints on snow.
> I am the sunlight on ripened grain. I am the gentle Autumn's rain.
> When you waken in the morning's hush,
> I am the swift, uplifting rush of quiet birds in circled light.
> I am the soft stars that shine at night. Do not stand at my grave and cry.
> I am not there. I did not die.

Then he turned on his heel and walked away.

Me and Murdo laid the earth on Lo May, and it seemed to me it settled on her very gently, maybe because for eighteen years she'd trod so lightly on it herself.

She lies there still, in her unmarked grave, in a place known only to God because that was how things were in those olden days when the West was still wild and violent death came to men and women in a hundred different ways from a hundred different directions.

Murdo, who had been a fighting soldier of the Queen and a longtime marshal and was well used to such things as death and dying, marched from Lo May's resting place and brusquely ordered the wagons hitched and told us to prepare to hit the trail.

He glanced at Johnny Blue, who stood off by himself, his face expressionless as he numbly watched the others work.

"Goddammit, get that shirt off of him!" he yelled at me angrily.

Johnny Blue still wore the white wedding shirt, its front covered in dried blood.

I unbuttoned the shirt and stripped it off him, while Johnny Blue just stood there letting it happen like one of Mrs. Flood's littlest ones come bedtime.

"What will I do with it, Murdo?" I asked.

"Throw the damn thing away," Murdo snapped. "Throw it far away."

The underwear Johnny Blue wore under the shirt was also soaked in blood and we had to strip him to get it off. Mrs. Flood, accustomed to the sight of a man's nakedness, sponged the blood off Johnny Blue's chest and hands and face; then we dressed him in Murdo's spare set of long johns and his own shirt and pants.

All this time Johnny Blue said not a word, his arms and legs flopping this way and that as we dressed him, like the rag doll one of Mrs. Flood's little girls carried with her all the time.

"Now get that poor lad on his horse," Murdo said when we finally had Johnny Blue dressed and on his feet. "It's time to ride."

"Murdo," I said, shaking my head at him, "I'm not goin' with you."

"Whaaat?" exclaimed the Scotsman. "This is treason! Black burning treason!"

"No treason," I said. "We've got Buck Starr and Shade

Hannah ahead of us and Frank Canton and a dozen Texas hardcases behind us, and I want them to learn something."

"Learn what?" Murdo asked warily.

"That I'm all through running. They want war, now I'm going to bring it right to their doorstep."

"You? Alone? Are you crazy, boy?"

"Not alone," I said. "I'll need Ishmael."

The Scotsman stood a step backward, a stricken look on his long, sad face. "Ishmael! He won't even use a gun." Murdo shook his head. "He's a Freemason and therefore my brother, but I have to say that the lad is sore tetched in the head and he'll be of no use to ye."

"I have a plan," I said. "An' it's brilliant, like all my best plans are."

"Let's hear it then, an' be quick about it."

In as few words as possible I outlined my plan to Murdo, and when I'd finished, the Scotsman scratched his jaw thoughtfully and said: "It might work. If nothing else, it will reduce their numbers and maybe slow them down some. But I fear both you and Ishmael are doomed."

"I'm willing to take my chances," I said.

"Aye," Murdo said, "but is Ishmael?"

When we braced him, the preacher said he wanted nothing to do with it.

"See, Mrs. Flood and me have reached a kind of understanding," he said. "She says she's willing to travel with me, spreading the word, until that day when we climb the mountain and meet the angels of the Lord." Ishmael spread his hands apologetically. "I'm not your man. I don't want her to be left on her own again with all those kids."

"Now the way I see it," I said, gesturing to the west, "is that if we don't stop Buck Starr now, there will be no Mrs. Flood and no kids." As cruelly as I could, I added the kicker: "They'll all be lying on the ground stone dead, Ishmael, and so will you."

I let the preacher stew on that for a spell, knowing there was no way he could tippy-toe around the logic of the thing, and I guess he saw the light because finally he said uncertainly: "I'm a prophet, but the Lord will not let me see what is just ahead of us." He shook his head. "I don't know the reason for that." He pointed a thin finger at me. "I'll do no shooting. No killing, mind."

"All I want you to do is talk," I said, adding grimly: "When it comes time for the killin' to be done, I'll do it."

Thus it was, boys, that me and Ishmael rode forth, me on my big American stud, he on his burro, to engage in mortal combat the deadliest gang of desperadoes who ever darkened the annals of the West, men who raped and killed and burned and robbed, just for the pleasure of it.

Murdo gave us the supplies he could spare and told us we'd meet up at Cottonwood Creek, but judging from the expression on his face, I knew he expected never to see us alive again.

Johnny Blue, unspeaking, like a man in a trance, sat beside Mrs. Flood on the seat of her wagon, while Dr. Chang and his daughters, still numbed with grief and a sense of terrible loss, brought up the rear.

As Johnny Blue passed, I took off my hat and waved it above my head and gave him a cheerful Huzzah! But he looked straight ahead, his eyes glazed, and didn't even seem to know I was there.

For a few minutes, me and Ishmael watched Murdo's brave little party depart; then we turned our faces toward Buck Starr and his gang.

My chin jutting manfully under the fine mustache I'd trimmed for Johnny Blue's wedding, you boys will know that I made a gallant and handsome figure as I headed due west toward the lair of the dreaded outlaws and my date with history.

Twenty-six

Me and Ishmael made no attempt to make ourselves hard to find, for I knew full well what I was getting into and I didn't care if Buck and his boys knew we was coming.

We scouted to the east, making good use of the telescope glass Murdo had loaned me, and late that morning, under a glowering sky filled with rain, we climbed the steep rise of a hill and spotted Frank Canton and his hardcases in the distance, strung out along the trail, the Paiute out in front. By this time Canton must have known the chase was almost over because the Paiute was smart and he'd know where the wagons were headed. Cottonwood Creek—flanked by the Cimarron and its winding tributary—was the logical place to fort up and make a stand.

As a result, them Texas gunfighters were in no hurry, letting their horses set the pace as they smoked and talked and idled on the trail.

But I'd no illusions. Once riled and alert, those hired gunmen would be as deadly and efficient as angry rattlers. And that fact fit in neatly with my plan.

"We got 'em, Ishmael," I said, snapping the telescope shut. "We got 'em right where we want 'em."

A fine rain had started and I shrugged into my slicker. Ishmael, owning no such luxury, sat hunched over on his burro, his long hair plastered against his face and neck.

"Now what?" he asked, without much enthusiasm.

"Now we find ol' Buck," I said.

We walked down the hill to our waiting mounts and headed due west.

The rain was coming down in earnest, a gray curtain that beat on my hat and the shoulders of my slicker and drove into my face. Beside me Ishmael sat hunched and miserable on his burro, his head bent against the driving rain.

The land we rode through was empty, stark, and desolate, offering nothing. It was mostly flat, but here and there rose shallow hills, perhaps only seventy or eighty feet above the plain, some of them covered in jumbled slabs of rock and brush and a few twisted cedars or elm trees. Now and then we forded small streams, swollen by the relentless rain.

We rode for the best part of an hour, at one point following in the tracks of Murdo's wagons in the wet grass until they angled to the south, and it was almost noon when I heard the first rumble of distant thunder.

I had no idea where Buck Starr was. I knew only that he was ahead of us somewhere in this wilderness. I huddled deeper into my slicker and watched my horse's ears, because they were the best guide to what was happening out there beyond the moving curtain of the rain.

When I glanced down at him, I saw that Ishmael was shivering from cold, so I swung my horse toward a shallow, tree-covered depression where there was the ruin of a cabin beside a small stream and dismounted.

The timber roof of the cabin had long since fallen in, but two of its log walls still stood, and I spread my slicker over the top of this corner, giving us some protection from the rain. There was plenty of wood lying around from the roof, most of it still dry, and I quickly built a fire and put

Arbuckle on to boil. I broiled some bacon on a skewer, and when the coffee was ready, we ate.

Thanks to the hot food and coffee, Ishmael began to warm up. Spreading his hands to the heat of the fire, he asked when I expected to come up on Buck and his gang.

I shrugged. "Hard to say. But they're close. I can feel it."

Ishmael nodded. "Me too." He tapped the two front teeth in his lower jaw with his finger. "See those teeth?"

I allowed that I did and that they was nice and white.

"Thankee," Ishmael said, "but what I was planning to say is that when danger is near, I get a funny, squiggly feeling in those two teeth."

"You feel it now? The squiggliness I mean."

"I sure do."

"Then ol' Buck's close," I said, "an' that's a natural fact. Teeth don't lie."

After we'd finished the dregs of the coffee, I retrieved my slicker and we mounted up and took to the trail again.

Another half hour's ride brought us to a bald hill taller than the rest, with a gradual slope to the east. Near the base of the hill was a solitary clump of brush and scrub pine, and within it a hollow that had been gouged out of the earth at some distant time.

We left our mounts in the hollow and clambered to the top of the hill to take a look-see around the surrounding country, covering the last few feet to the highest possible point on our bellies. I looked over and was only mildly surprised to see a camp below, because a nagging little voice inside my head had been telling me to expect it. The rain had stopped for now, but only one fire was burning, the rest reduced to smoking coals.

I put my glass on the camp, which was situated beside a thick stand of mature cottonwoods, and I thought I detected the gleam of water in a buffalo hollow a hundred yards beyond the trees.

A bearded man was tied to the trunk of one of the cottonwoods, and I saw his mouth open in what could have been a yell or a scream.

There were about twenty men gathered around the tree, and they were passing a slender, naked woman with some gray in her blond hair back and forth among them.

Those rannies were laughing, grabbing and pawing at the woman as they pushed her from man to man, yanking her to her feet with coarse jests every time she fell to the ground.

The man tied to the tree, no doubt her husband, suddenly burst his bonds and ran toward the woman, pulling her away from the outlaws. One of them, at the time I couldn't be sure who it was, even with the glass, shucked his revolver and shot the man down. Later I judged the killer to be Buck himself, recollecting his scowling mug on a wanted poster I'd seen in Fort Smith.

A huge, bearded outlaw wearing a black hat and a black-and-white cowskin vest dragged the woman closer to the fire and threw her down on her back. He quickly dropped his pants and then hurled himself on her. Some of the others, as they lined up to take their turn, laughed and pointed at the bearded man as he began to hump on top of the woman, and I snapped the telescope closed, not wanting to see any more.

"We have to go down there. We have to put a stop to this," Ishmael, who had no telescope but possessed eyes like an outhouse rat, whispered urgently.

I shook my head at him. "We wait."

"But—"

"Ishmael, if'n we go riding down there, we'll both end up dead and that woman will be no better off in the end, an' that's a natural fact." I put my hand on his shoulder. "We wait; then you'll do like I tole you to do."

Ishmael didn't like it one bit, but he sat quiet as the rain started again, the gray clouds so low I could have reached out and grabbed a handful of mist.

Thirty minutes passed; then I bellied up to the top of the ridge again and looked over. The outlaws were buttoned into their slickers, standing around the smoking campfire drinking coffee. The woman, still naked, crouched by her husband's body, her head on her knees, one hand on his chest. Her shoulders were shaking and she seemed in a bad way.

Bending low, I came back off the ridge and squatted on my heels beside Ishmael. "Okay, preacher," I said, "comb your fur and tune your purr, because it's time to cut loose the wolf."

Ishmael shook his head. "I ain't doing it and you can't make me. You just done told me those boys will kill me for sure."

I grabbed the front of his shirt and hauled him close, looking into his eyes. "Ishmael," I said, "do you want the same thing to happen to Mrs. Flood as happened to that poor woman down there?"

"No, I—"

"Then split ass into the outlaw camp, and don't let them stampede you. Believe me, they'll be so busy after you say your piece, they won't even notice you've slipped away."

Ishmael considered what I'd said for a spell; then his mouth set in a grim line. "Okay, I'll do it for Mrs. Flood. I guess I owe her that much."

"Damn right you do, what with her wanting to be with you when the world ends an' all. She's a good woman, too good to fall into the hands of Buck Starr and his outlaws."

Ishmael rose to his feet. "Let's go."

We walked down the hill to the hollow at its base and mounted up.

"Now," I said, "you know what you have to say?"

Ishmael nodded. "Uh-huh."

Now I wasn't sure that loco'd ol' boy had been paying attention, so I laid it out for him again.

"All you got to tell them is that there's a party of a dozen marshals led by a Paiute scout hot on their trail. Tell 'em they're just two whoops an' a holler away and that they're all determined men, well armed and well mounted." I studied Ishmael's face closely. "You got that?"

"I got it. I don't like it, but I got it."

Boys, when he had a mind to, that Ishmael could be one surly preacher.

"Good," I said, reaching down to slap him on the shoulder. "You just ride in there, say your piece, an' let me do the rest."

"It ain't gonna work," Ishmael said grouchily. "It ain't gonna work worth a damn."

"Nah, it will work good as a set of five-dollar store-bought teeth," I said. "Trust me."

I dismounted just before we rounded the base of the hill, then found a concealed vantage point among tall bluestem grasses where I could watch the gallant Ishmael ride into the bandit camp. The outlaws stood and studied the preacher as he rode toward them through the teeming rain, and when Ishmael got close, he raised his right hand in greeting.

"Hail and howdy, boys," he said.

That preacher had more guts than good sense, because the first thing he does when he rides into the outlaw camp is take his coat off and place it around the shoulders of the poor naked woman. Then he felt her husband's neck and said something to her, nodding and smiling as he said it. But that was as far as he got, because Shade Hannah—

I recognized those white eyes even at a distance—shoved his gun in Ishmael's face and thumbed back the hammer. Right about then that preacher did some fast and fancy talking, his Adam's apple bobbing like a frog trapped under a bucket, telling them outlaws about the federal marshals and all, just as I'd taught him. And Buck and his boys fell for it. They bit it all—hook, line, sinker, and bobber.

After Ishmael got through talking, the desperadoes became real agitated and did some quick cussin' and discussin'. Then they ran for their horses—and now was the time for me to act. I swung into the saddle, yanked my Winchester free of the boot, and rounded the base of the hill at a fast gallop.

Hollering, "Federal marshals! Surrender!" I cranked off a few shots in the general direction of the outlaws, then turned my horse and galloped back toward the hill. I glanced quickly over my shoulder and sure enough they were following me, rifle rounds already splitting the air above my head.

That American stud of mine was bred to run, and I've known him to gallop from sunup to sundown in about half an hour. Now he got the bit in his teeth, stretched out his neck, and flew. Behind me the outlaws were coming fast, shooting as they rode, but the back of a running bronc is no place for accurate rifle work and their shots went wild.

I rode straight toward the place where I'd last seen Frank Canton and his boys, gobs of mud from my horse's thundering hooves spattering my face and the front of my shirt.

Boys, let me tell you, that was some ride.

But even a horse as good as that big American can't run flat out for too long, so I eased him back into a smooth lope, and behind me the outlaws were in a mind to do the same thing, firing a testing shot at me now and then.

As I neared the ruined cabin where me and Ishmael had stopped to eat, the country grew hillier and for a spell I drove a small herd of antelope in front of me that had been grazing on the flat. But they suddenly veered north as we reached a crease in the hills that could have been a coulee or a draw, watching me warily over their shoulders as I rode past.

I loped around the pine- and brush-covered base of the second, higher hill—and almost rode right into Frank Canton and his hardcases.

Luckily, they all had their heads bent against the driving rain. All except the Paiute, who saw me coming and immediately yipped an alarm.

"Federal marshals!" I yelled, and cut loose with my rifle.

Canton's boys were taken by surprise and so were their horses. My rifle fire did no execution among them, but their startled mounts went into some gut-twisting bucks, and by the time them Texas boys had them all sorted out, I was hightailing it back down the trail again toward Buck and his gang.

"Marshals!" I hollered as Buck's party came in sight. "Surrender, you foul-hearted fiends!"

Frank Canton and his hired guns were right behind me, Buck in front of me, and boys, my plan was working perfectly.

As both parties opened up, each thinking the other was marshals, I swung my horse toward the coulee between the hills that the antelope had shied away from, figgering I was free and clear. I glanced over my shoulder as I reached the draw and saw half-a-dozen empty saddles as the outlaws shot it out, sitting their horses in plain sight of each other as they levered their rifles. After a few more minutes those outlaws would be so shot up they'd be no threat to Johnny Blue and Murdo and the others.

It was a crackerjack plan all right, and was working just like I'd figgered.

But I was building the coop before I'd bought the chickens.

Boys, I got this little devil who sets on my shoulder and whispers in my ear and he tells me to do things. And what he was telling me now was to make a good plan even better.

I should have stayed hidden in that coulee until the shooting was over, but I didn't. I decided to add to the confusion by riding right through Canton's boys at a fast gallop, firing as I went—but it didn't quite work out that way.

As I reached the Texans, a rider suddenly loomed broadside in front of me. I crashed into him, T-boning him with my big American horse, sending his screaming pony ass over tip.

But as he flew out of the saddle, the rider yelled, "You!" And he palmed his sixgun and fired. Not for nothing will Frank Canton go down in history as one of the West's deadliest gunfighters. That ranny was rattlesnake fast and poison mean.

Even before Canton slammed to the ground, I felt a blow low down on my side, like I'd been hit by a sledgehammer. The impact of the crash had thrown my mount to his haunches, so I yanked on the reins to keep his head up, and as he scrambled back to his feet, I set the spurs to him and lit a shuck out of there. Pain spiked into my side like a red-hot knife, and once the initial numbing shock of the bullet had worn off, I felt light-headed and dizzy.

I crouched low over the horse's neck, expecting at any moment to feel a bullet crash into my back. But it never came.

Canton had seen me and figgered I was up to no good. He'd smelled a rat and now he was trying to stop the battle before all his men were killed.

Behind me, I heard him yell: "Buck! Is that you, Buck?"

I couldn't hear what reply he got, but just before I galloped out of earshot, Canton hollered again: "It's me, Buck. It's good ol' Frank!"

Turning in the saddle I saw Canton waving his hat in the air, then Buck's men rode warily toward him. As the shooting slowed to a ragged halt, men began to mill around, talking to each other, slapping backs and shaking hands over the bodies of their own dead as they greeted friends and old acquaintances from many an owlhoot trail.

Me, I galloped fast away from there, a burning agony tearing at my side and the taste of fear in my mouth.

But inside me was an even greater pain.

And that was the terrible knowledge that I had failed . . . failed myself, failed my friends . . . and now that Buck and Frank had joined forces, I had guaranteed their deaths.

Twenty-seven

I'd been hit hard and was in no shape to fight.

My only thought now was to get away. To live. To exist. To somehow get back to my friends to die in their company.

I looked over my shoulder. Buck and Frank and their men were coming after me. Even after allowing for the desperadoes who'd been downed in the brief gun battle, there were still two dozen of them, all hardcases and determined men.

My horse was pretty much played out after my reckless flight from both gangs of outlaws, but I saw a hill shaped like a flat-topped mesa to my left, rising in a gradual slope maybe fifty feet above the level of the plain and I swung my tired mount toward it.

The hilltop was covered in jumbled sandstone rock and scrub pine with a few redbuds here and there. It was as good a place as any to stop and make my gallant last stand.

A jackrabbit bolted from my path as I neared the hill, and behind me I heard shots being fired and the angry buzz of bullets zinging past my ears.

My horse hit the bottom of the slope at a dead run, but then his front legs slipped out from under him and his nose dug a furrow in the wet grass. I hauled on the reins, pulling his head up, but he pecked again, this time stumbling forward. Weakened as I was by loss of blood, I couldn't stay in the saddle. I flew over his neck and hit the ground with a thud that sent a shock of agony through my wounded side.

The big horse recovered, but he jerked away from my outstretched hand and took off back down the slope, stirrups flying as he hit the plain and kept on going.

The outlaws were very close, and bullets kicked up fountains of dirt around me.

I stumbled to my feet and, bent low, scrambled up the hill.

By now I was becoming delirious and I reckoned I had a fever that was mounting fast. I stumbled and staggered up the hill, moving, falling onto the wet grass, rising and driving on.

I made it to the summit, then dropped on all fours. I crawled through a thick blackberry bush, its thorns tearing at my skin and clothes, and wriggled through a space between two flat sandstone rocks that had been pushed one against the other by glaciers in the olden days to form an inverted V.

Beyond the cleft between the rocks was a small, flat, grassy area open to the sky but for the branches of a wind-twisted aspen growing to one side of the clearing.

I crawled to the bole of the tree, and laid my back against it, closing my eyes against the pain and exhaustion sweeping over me in waves. I felt sick enough to puke and there was the taste of burning acid in my mouth.

I was scared, as scared as I'd ever been in my life and I heard the thump! thump! of my racing heart in my ears.

Then a voice came from beyond the tangled blackberry thicket. "There's blood everywhere, Frank. He's dead, or dying. You gut shot him. I seen it plain."

"That ranny is slippery," replied Frank Canton's voice. "He's a low person an' not to be trusted, and he's mighty slick with a gun."

"Well, I don't much cotton to going into those bushes after a man with a gun, dying or not."

That was Shade Hannah, and he added: "Let him lie in there an' bleed his guts out. He ain't goin' nowhere."

"What do you think, Buck?" Frank asked.

"That little piece of crap is more trouble than he's worth," Buck Starr said. I heard his voice fade, like he'd turned his head away and was talking over his shoulder. "You boys smoke them bushes good with your rifles. Let's see if we can flush him."

Almost immediately, half a dozen rifles crashed and bullets began to rip through the clearing, thudding into the trunk of the aspen, whining off the rocks.

Groaning in pain, I got on my belly and crawled between the cleft of the rocks and lay there, my face buried in the soft dirt as the bullets racketed around me.

I felt a bullet burn across my ankle; then another took away the heel of my left boot.

Then the guns fell silent.

"Do you think we got him?" a voice asked.

"Hell if I know," Buck Starr replied. He raised his voice in a shout: "You in there! Come out an' we'll set you in the shade and take care of your wounds. We're your friends."

I heard a muffled laugh, and then Frank Canton yelled: "Come on out of there now, and take your medicine like a man. Don't make us come in after you."

I lay perfectly still, my Colt in my hand. If they came in after me, I wasn't going to hell alone.

A few long minutes passed, and then Buck said: "Ah, the hell with him. You gut shot him anyhow, Frank. He's as good as dead, if'n he ain't a goner already."

"Well," Canton hesitated, "I dunno . . ."

"Besides," Buck said, "we got other fish to fry." Again his voice faded like he was turning and he said: "Hey,

Shade, did you say there was another Chinee woman at that camp when you done for the one in the yeller dress?"

"Two," Shade replied, "maybe three. And man, they looked ripe."

"Owned me a little Chinee gall oncet, an' she gave me the taste for that Oriental honey," Buck said. "She was working the Line when I bought her from a feller, but she was the tightest little gal I ever had, and willin' enough oncet you slapped her around some."

"What happened to her, Buck?" someone asked. "How come you don't own her no more?"

"Ah, I got tired of her an' traded her to some flatboat men up on the Big Muddy for a gallon o' Kentucky whiskey an' a bowie knife. I'd give her a big belly by then, so she was no damn use to me anyhow."

The outlaws laughed, and I heard Buck say: "Thinkin' back on it, though, I'd sure like to own another one."

The outlaws snorted again, and one yelled: "Hooraw for ol' Buck and the Chinee gal!"

"Then what are we waiting for?" Shade asked excitedly. "Let's go make an end of that marshal an' his uppity nigger and grab us some little Chinee gals. Hell, we can give 'em big bellies our own selves."

"Sounds good to me," Buck said. "Frank, are you in?"

"I guess so," Frank replied. "But I got to tell you, I don't trust that little runt with the big mustache. Gut shot or no, he's gunslick an' he can make fancy moves."

"The hell with him," Buck roared. "Let's go an' finish what we already started. The Paiute will find the trail of them wagons quick enough."

The outlaws cheered and I heard their voices fade into the distance, and then there was only silence.

I crawled out of the rocks and went back to the clearing and lay against the tree. Painfully, I stripped off my shirt to inspect my wound. The bullet had gone in low on my left side, just above the hipbone, and had exited out the small of my back.

I couldn't see the wound on my back, but the entry wound looked red and angry and swollen. I was hit hard, and I knew it, and if I didn't get help soon, I'd die for sure.

Leaning my head against the trunk of the tree I closed my eyes.

I don't know if I slept or passed out from pain and loss of blood, but I woke to pitch darkness and thunder and lightning forking across the sky.

The rain was lashing down, and the branches of the aspen were a scant roof, so I was soaked to the skin.

I thought about crawling to the shelter of the rocks, but I was burning up with fever and I knew I lacked the strength to make it even that far.

Thunder crashed right above my head and lightning plunged out of the black sky, long skeletal fingers of blinding light spiking again and again into the prairie.

Out of my mind with fever, I recollect turning my face toward the darkness of the sky and screaming: "Hell, I can sing better than that!"

Again the thunder roared, loud enough to jar pecans right off the tree, and lightning probed toward the hill where I lay.

Delirious, I began to sing, a song without words, just the soft crooning a cowboy uses to calm the restless night herd, something I'd learned when I was still a boy.

"Woo, woo, woo-woo-woo, woo-woo, woo, woo . . ."

The thunder crashed and a streak of lightning, wide as an outhouse door, flashed white and blinding into the clearing. I was thrown hard against the tree; then I rolled to my right, crying out in agony as pain lanced into my side.

There was a stench of burning sulfur in the air and the

odor of something long dead—and when I looked up, I beheld the terrible form of Amos Pinkney.

The bandit chief was on fire, his clothes and hair aflame. And his eyes glowed like white-hot coals.

Pinkney laughed, a sound as loud as the thunder itself.

"Welcome to hell, boy!" he roared.

"You're dead," I said. "I seen you dead with my own two eyes, 'cause I'm the ranny that done for you in the end."

Pinkney just stood there, his mad, fiery eyes glaring at me.

"I kilt you once afore." I pulled my Colt. "I can kill you again, you son of a bitch."

"All your friends are dead," Pinkney hollered. "The men dead, the women raped, their bellies ripped open." He threw back his head and laughed. "And it's all your fault. Your fault! Your fault!" I thumbed back the hammer of my iron and cut 'er loose, firing shot after shot into that fiery phantom.

But he just stood there, a pillar of fire burning red and orange and yellow in the darkness.

I tried to rise to get at him, but my knees wobbled and my legs wouldn't support me. I crashed to the ground, my head slamming into something hard and unyielding. And then I plunged into darkness, Amos Pinkney's mocking laughter echoing in my ears . . .

A finger prodding into my chest woke me.

"Are you dead yet?" a voice asked.

I opened my eyes, and beheld the face, not of Amos Pinkney as I had expected, but of Red Horse, the half-broke Injun who wanted my scalp.

"No, I ain't dead yet," I said weakly, "an' my scalp ain't ready to be took."

Red Horse made a little yelp deep in his throat that was half disappointment, half frustration.

"I was all primed," said that rascally Redskin. He brandished a blade in front of me. "See, I even got me a scalping knife."

"Then do it, damn you," I said. "Get it over with. I'm as good as dead anyhow."

Well, boys, right away that Sioux brandishes the knife over his head and goes to whoopin' and hollerin' the like you've never heard.

"What the hell are you doin'?" I asked him.

"Getting myself primed," Red Horse said. "Hell, you can't just scalp some ranny without getting yourself worked up about it first. Even a white man should know that."

My gun lay beside me and I picked it up and jammed the cold muzzle against the Indian's bare stomach.

"Well, I've changed my mind anyhoo." My head was spinning, but my gun was steady enough.

"Now drop that pig sticker or I'll drill you a new belly button."

Red Horse sighed and let the knife drop. "I wasn't gonna scalp you anyhow. Like I told you, I don't want to get into trouble with the white man's law"—he looked around—"even out here."

"Then help me," I said. "Help me get back to my friends."

"Why should I help you?" Red Horse asked.

"Two reasons," I said. "One, I want to get back to my friends and die with them, so you can be damn sure of gettin' my scalp when it's all over. An' two, if'n you don't, almighty sudden I might remember the Big Horn an' cut loose with this here hog leg."

"You make a powerful argument, cowboy," Red Horse said.

He sat there studying on things for a spell, his face creased in thought; then he nodded and said: "Okay, I'll help you. But don't you go leaving your scalp to some other ranny, mind."

"I wouldn't even think of it," I said. "Now help me patch up this wound."

Red Horse scouted around and returned after a few minutes with some dry wood. "You build a fire here last night?" he asked.

Weakly, I shook my head at him.

"Looks like there was a fire right here," he said. He placed the palm of his hand against a scorched area of grass. "It's still warm."

"Lightning maybe," I said.

"Maybe," said Red Horse, "but it don't look like any lightning strike I ever saw."

The Indian built a small fire, then sliced off some tree bark that he fashioned into a cup shape. He carried a canteen of water and he filled the cup. "The bark won't burn so long as the fire doesn't go over the water level," he said. "But I don't expect a white man to know that."

When the water was good and hot, Red Horse bathed my wounds, and that water felt soothing and good. He then packed the bullet holes with leaves and mosses he'd found, and plastered them down with mud, like a poultice.

"That will do you," he said. He placed his hand against my forehead. "Your fever's broke, and that's good."

"How did you know I had a fever?" I asked.

"Heard you. When a man's hollering at ghosts and singing crazy songs and shooting into the air during a thunderstorm, he's either loco or he has a fever. I know you ain't quite loco yet, so it had to be the fever."

Red Horse filled the bark cup again and shaved antelope jerky into the water, adding some herbs and other stuff I didn't recognize.

"Found your horse, by the way," he said. "He was out there on the flat, grazing with his saddle under his belly."

"I'm obliged to you," I said.

The Indian shrugged. "I thought you'd be dead, so I planned on snagging him for myself."

"That hoss don't take kindly to Injuns," I said.

"Neither do a lot of folks, come to that," shrugged the Redskin.

After a few minutes he took the soup off the fire and put the bark cup to my lips. "Drink this. It will give you strength."

I was suddenly hungry and I drank all of it down, and with the hot soup warming my insides, I felt a whole lot better.

"It's time for me to ride," I said, struggling to my feet.

The pain in my side where Frank Canton had ventilated me was a living thing, gnawing on me with fangs. My head spun and I leaned against the trunk of the aspen until the world steadied itself. I had to move. Get out of here. Reach Johnny Blue.

"You ain't fit to ride," Red Horse said.

"I'll ride," I said angrily. "Where are the horses?"

Red Horse, half pushing, half carrying me, led the way to the other side of the hill and down the slope to where our horses were grazing.

I saw with relief that my Winchester was still in the boot, and I grabbed the saddle horn, leaning my head against the horse until a wave of pain and exhaustion passed.

The rain had long since stopped and above us the morning sky was shading from gray to pale blue. A jay had found his way to the aspen on the hilltop and scolded us from its branches as we stood by the horses, and in the distance wary antelope moved on cat feet across the prairie grass.

Boys, I didn't know if Johnny Blue and the others were alive or dead. I'd failed them, failed all of them, and their deaths would weigh heavily on my conscience.

"Mount up, if you can," Red Horse said, reining up beside me. "We got a distance to travel."

"I know that," I said. "I want to reach the Canadian long before nightfall." I looked up at the sky where a lark was hovering, a dark shape against a brightening blue canopy. Shifting my gaze to Red Horse I said: "This is a good day to die."

The Indian shook his head. "You're crazy, cowboy," he said. "No day is a good day to die." He nodded toward my horse. "You need some help to get up on that bronc?"

"I can manage," I said.

When a man's sick, an American stud is a tall horse to mount. It took me three or four tries, once almost falling flat on my back, before I got up on him, and when I did, my side hurt like hell and the prairie looked like it was turning cartwheels.

Red Horse shook his head. "For such a runty little feller, I got to admit, you sure got a big pair of *cojones*."

"Let's ride," I said, my eyes popping out of my head as I tried to focus on the spinning flatlands. I still felt weak as a day-old kittlin', but whatever the Indian had put on my wounds had helped, as had the hot soup.

It also helped that in them olden days I wasn't even close to being civilized.

I'm sure you boys have noticed that when decent, God-fearing Eastern folks who go to church on Sundays get hit by a bullet, well, they take to their beds and pretty soon just up and die. But Western men, being all whang leather, bone, and bluster, can be shot to pieces one day and be bellied up to the bar—whiskey seeping out of every bullet hole—the next.

Don't get me wrong, it's a fine thing to be civilized, I just don't recommend it if you plan on getting shot anytime soon.

As I turned my horse toward the Canadian, that noble

savage Red Horse riding at my side, I was determined to join my friends or, if I was too late, go after the outlaws as had done for them. Either way, I knew with awful certainty that this was destined to be my last day on earth.

But when my time came, I was determined to take as many to hell with me as I could.

Twenty-eight

We rode steadily northwest, Red Horse scouting ahead most of the time.

Once we stopped because the mud poultices the Indian had put on my wounds had dried up and fallen off. Red Horse stuffed grass and some petals from prairie flowers he was a long time a-gathering into the bullet holes and we rode on.

We'd covered a lot of ground by the time the sun was hanging straight above us in the sky, but it surprised me considerably when the Indian came back from a scout and told me he'd picked up the tracks of the wagons.

"They drove across an old, muddy buffalo wallow about a couple of miles ahead. But I saw more than wheel tracks—there's a large party of riders following them wagons."

"That's Buck Starr and Frank Canton and their outlaw bands," I said. "How far ahead of us are they?"

Red Horse shrugged. "Hard to say. But them tracks in the wallow are cut sharp. I'd say they were made well after the rain stopped, sometime early this morning."

"Damn," I swore, "I figgered they'd be all the way to the Canadian by now."

"Seems like your friends holed up during the thunderstorm," Red Horse observed. "And so did the bandits."

Boys, although I knew Johnny Blue and the others were in deadly peril, the fresh tracks gave me hope that they were still alive, perhaps fighting for their lives at that very moment.

Before us the wide sweep of the prairie stretched all the way to the horizon, hemmed in by the Canadian to the south and the Cimarron to the north. This was wild and open country, hilly for the most part, but not a place for heavily loaded wagons to make a stand against mounted and determined desperadoes.

If Buck Starr and his men caught Johnny Blue and Murdo and the others out on the flat, they would be quickly surrounded and overwhelmed. It was a worrisome thing.

The pain in my side had settled down to a constant, dull throb and I was light-headed and giddy from loss of blood. Yet I urged my horse onward, determined to prevail against the bandits or die gallantly in the attempt.

I set a fast pace, alternatively loping and walking my mount as me and Red Horse rode through the heat of the afternoon. It was an unseasonably warm spring and even as far north as the Montana Territory the snows had melted early on the mountain peaks, blooming the grasslands and setting fruit on the blackberry bushes.

The sun was dropping lower in the sky, casting a long shadow of me and my mount on the grass, when Red Horse, who had once again scouted ahead, rode toward me at a fast gallop on his tough little paint mustang.

"Up ahead!" he yelled. "Wagons!"

Quickly my faithful Indian companion told me what he'd seen.

The wagons were pulled across a U-shaped spit of land that marked a sharp bend of a tributary of the Canadian. And at that moment they were under heavy fire from the outlaws, who were concealed in a stand of pine and aspen covering most of the northern slope of a shallow hill overlooking the bend in the river.

"How many men behind the wagons?" I asked Red Horse urgently. "How many shooting?"

The Indian shook his head. "I couldn't get close enough to see. But I heard firing from the wagons and a strange sound. It seemed to me like the wail of a great animal in pain, or the wind that howls around the tall lodges of the Sioux when the winter blizzards blow hard."

Murdo's pipes! Then they were still alive!

"Lookee here, Red Horse," I said, "this ain't your fight. I'm feelin' right poorly, I admit, but you can leave me now and I'll do what has to be done."

Truth to tell, I'd be sorry to see him go. Even though he'd helped massacree the gallant Custer and his band of heroes, Red Horse was a first-rate fighting man and shot as straight as a gut with a puppy pullin' on one end. He was a right good Indian, and he spoke American better than most Americans.

But that noble savage looked me straight in the eye and declared: "If you think I'm gonna miss this here fight, you're plumb loco. This could be the last chance I'll ever get to plug some white men and I'm not letting it pass me by.

"Besides," he added, "I'm not about to let your hair out of my sight. I reckon you'll get bumped off right quick, an' I'll be ready with my scalping knife."

Now, boys, this was such a touching speech from that faithful aborigine that I felt my eyes flood with tears, and the words caught in my throat as I thanked him most kindly and told him he was a first-class Injun chief and a credit to his race.

"Thankee, and think nothing of it," quoth that bashful brave. "I'm right happy to oblige."

"Well," I said, dashing a weak and trembling hand across my wet eyes, "let's go get it done."

"Not yet," said Red Horse. "We got time."

He had a buckskin possibles bag hanging across the withers of his pony and he rummaged around in this for a spell and came up with a small wooden box and a bone comb.

Settin' right there on his horse, he dipped his finger into the box and it came up bright blue. Red Horse used the paint to draw two blue streaks across his cheekbones and the bridge of his nose, then he put a dot of blue paint in the middle of his forehead.

After applying his war paint, the Injun proceeded to comb out his hair until it fell, long and black and glossy as a crow's wing, over his shoulders.

Well, boys, weak and hurting though I was, I couldn't see me being outdone by an Injun, so I reached into the bedroll behind my saddle and found the bottle of pomade Silas Bramwell had given me back to Fort Smith.

I rubbed the pomade into my hair and mustache and asked Red Horse: "Can I borry your comb?" Parting my hair in the middle, I laid it down on each side of my head flat and shiny, then curled the ends of my mustache into two fine points.

So it was on that memorable day in the spring of 1888, a day that will forever live in the annals of the West, that me and Red Horse—both splendid and handsome men in appearance—rode stalwartly forth to engage a ferocious enemy and save our friends from disaster.

Or die valorously in the attempt.

We had been riding for less than thirty minutes when the sound of firing made us quicken our pace.

As Red Horse had described it to me, a low hill hid the bend in the tributary stream from view where the wagons were forted up. The streambed, its meandering path marked here and there by huge cottonwoods and slender willows, curved around the base of the hill then angled away from us on our right, and the broad sweep of the Canadian River lay to our left.

The sun, fixing to set in another hour or two, hung above the top of the hill and cast its humped shadow on the grass like the spirit of a great buffalo. The air smelled sweet and clean, heavy with the scent of wildflowers, and the breeze on my cheek was warm with the promise of summer.

"Wait here," I told Red Horse. "I'll climb the hill and take a look-see with the glass."

When I climbed off my horse, my knees gave way and I fell heavily against his side. But I pulled myself together and stumbled away from the horse and walked slowly toward the hill. The stumble had opened up the wounds on my side and my shirt was wet with blood.

I walked, fell, got to my feet, stumbled, and somehow made it to the crest of the hill. Once there, I lay flat on the grass and swept the telescope glass over the dreadful scene below.

The wagons were forted up across part of the U-bend of the tributary, the other part blocked off by a huge old cottonwood that had toppled to the ground, its still-leafy branches hanging out over the bank. The stream itself was maybe twenty feet wide and over the centuries it had cut deep into the prairie, the banks maybe eight feet high at some points. Now that the melted snow runoff from the mountains was over, the stream itself looked to be only a couple of feet deep.

I scanned the area and saw Johnny Blue crouching near the rear wheel of Mrs. Flood's wagon, his rifle in his hands. He seemed to be alert and unwounded, and I whispered a prayer of thanks that he'd apparently recovered from the shock of Lo May's death.

Murdo sat with his back to the trunk of the cottonwood, his rifle beside him. He was playing his pipes, a wild, warlike tune that skirled into the quiet afternoon, but even at this distance I saw the whole front of his shirt was splashed scarlet with blood. Dr. Chang manned the space between the wagons, and Ishmael crouched near Johnny Blue, his long arms circling the widder woman and her kids.

The poor naked woman who had been so abused in Buck Starr's camp—now wearing Mrs. Flood's spare dress—was huddled behind Dr. Chang's wagon with his daughters, and I could make out the pale, terrified faces of all three as they looked toward the timber at the bottom of the hill where the outlaws were gathered.

The desperadoes stood beside their horses, and at a shouted command from Buck, they mounted.

I didn't wait to see any more. The outlaws, grown impatient now that nightfall was near, were preparing to charge the wagons and overwhelm the gallant little band that had kept them at bay for most of the day.

As I stumbled to my feet, I thought I saw the glint of a rifle barrel along the bank of the stream. If I was right, the bandits were also planning to attack the wagons through the streambed, circling behind the defenders.

There was no time to be lost.

I rose to my feet and ran down the hill, the pain in my side stabbing at me like a knife. I was halfway down when I lost my footing and rolled the rest of the way, gasps of agony forcing their way through my lips at every tumbling, leg-flailing turn.

Red Horse sat his pony watching me and shook his head slowly, making a tut-tut-tut sound as I picked myself up and staggered to my horse. I climbed slowly into the saddle and told the Injun what I'd seen.

We walked our horses around the base of the hill until the wagons came into view on our right. Buck and his men had not made their charge yet, and I yanked my rifle free and with a trembling hand tried to thumb shells from my gun belt into the loading gate.

Boys, between my weakness from loss of blood and my own clamoring fear, I was shaking so bad I couldn't get the rounds into the Winchester and even dropped a couple of them to the ground.

Watching me, Red Horse groaned then said testily: "Give me the damn thing!"

I handed him the rifle and the remaining shells and he loaded the piece for me. "You just ain't cut out for this line of work, are you?" he said.

Angrily I jerked my Winchester out of his hands. "Just you watch me!" And I set spurs to my horse.

I rounded the hill at a gallop, Red Horse close behind me, just as Buck and his men burst like a roaring whirlwind from the timber.

Throwing my rifle to my shoulder, I cranked off round after round at the charging bandits. Surprised, Buck Starr looked to his left and saw us coming. He wheeled his horse around and came right at me, the reins in his teeth, a blazing Colt in each hand.

I threw down on him and fired. Missing, I cranked the rifle again but Red Horse rode between me and the outlaw chief and I couldn't get a clean shot.

Meanwhile I heard a tremendous fusillade come from the direction of the stream bank, and at least eight bandits tumbled from their saddles.

But I'd no time to see what else was happening, because Buck was almost on top of me. Red Horse, yipping his war cry, rode right at him, his rifle in his right hand aimed like a pistol.

Then that crazy Redskin did something plumb loco. He tossed his rifle from his right hand to his left and slapped Buck on the shoulder as he swept past.

Instead of shooting the oncoming bandit, he counted coup!

Surprised as all get out, Buck's jaw dropped and reins

slipped out of his mouth. He turned in his saddle and fired one of his Colts at the Injun. But that wily warrior suddenly ducked behind the body of his pony and Buck missed.

Now the outlaw chief turned his attention to me again.

Cursing, he fired with both guns and my horse shuddered and went down. I flew out of the saddle and hit the ground with a thud, a scream of agony escaping my lips as pain lanced into my side.

My Winchester spun out of my hands, but I heard a roar as it went off, the hammer dropped by the impact of its fall.

Buck was still coming hard, but now his left eye and the whole left side of his skull was gone, blood and brains streaming behind him like a tattered gray-and-red banner.

I rolled out of the way of his horse. He galloped a few yards beyond me then hauled on the reins so hard that he forced his mount to its haunches, great clods of dirt hurling into the air.

Buck screamed, a terrible wailing screech of pain and anger as he wheeled toward me again. The bullet from my rifle had blown away most of his head, yet he was still in the saddle, a dead man driven by the urge to kill and destroy.

The outlaw chief was a fearsome sight as he slowed his horse to a walk and rode purposefully toward me, his Colts cocked and ready.

Around me the shooting intensified and I heard the screams and groans of dying men. But I saw only Buck Starr.

Above the din of the battle the steady clop, clop, clop of his horse as it walked slowly in my direction chilled me to the bone. My head was swimming and I felt weak and sick to my stomach. I glanced around for my rifle, but it was too far away from me. I yanked my Colt and steadied it with both hands, resting my wrists on my knees.

Buck Starr was a terrible sight to behold.

The bullet that had destroyed his left eye had blown the right one out of its socket, and it lay, staring and horrible, on his cheekbone. Blood and brains ran down his face and over his shirtfront, and his teeth when he opened his mouth were stained scarlet.

He was blind and couldn't see me.

But he began firing, working his Colts, the bullets kicking up dirt around me. I squeezed the trigger of my gun and Buck jerked in the saddle as the bullet slammed into his chest.

He screamed in inhuman fury and kept firing.

I shot again, and again I hit him in the chest.

This time Buck Starr, rapist, murderer, robber, leaned slowly over in the saddle and toppled to the ground, dead for a second time.

I rose to my feet, pain clawing at me, and picked up my rifle. I looked around—and saw a scene of carnage.

At least half the outlaws, including the big bearded man in the cowskin vest who'd first raped the poor naked woman, lay stretched out on the ground, unmoving. The rest, Shade Hannah among them, had their hands raised, frantically clawing for the sky.

Heck Thomas, Chris Madsen, and a dozen other marshals covered the surrendered bandits with rifles and shotguns. The lawmen were not mounted and must have snuck along the streambed then ambushed the desperadoes as they charged from the timber.

I'd seen the glint of a rifle barrel along the bank all right, but it had been a marshal's rifle, not a bandit's.

As I walked toward the wagons, worried about Johnny Blue and the others, I detected a rustle of movement among the trees at the bottom of the hill. Then a lone horseman burst from the timber and galloped along the slope, lighting a shuck out of there.

There was no mistaking the way that lanky rider sat a horse. It was Frank Canton!

I heard a yell from one of the startled lawmen as Canton rode down the slope, then hit the flat at a breakneck run. He was crouched low over his horse's neck, going hell-for-leather toward the open prairie and freedom.

Dropping to one knee, I sighted on the fleeting bandit and cut loose with my Winchester. I saw a puff of dust rise from Frank's britches and his hand shot back, grabbing at his suddenly bloody butt.

He kept on running and pretty soon was out of range of my fire, which was none too accurate at long distance anyhow on account of how weak and dizzy I was.

I rose to my feet and waved my hat in the air. "Huzzah!" I yelled to Heck Thomas and the other lawmen. "Another hoss's ass shot up the patoot!"

Boys, you'll recollect that Heck had vowed to kill me his own self for putting a bullet in his butt, but now, as he walked toward me, his face grim and a shotgun in his hands, I was too weak and too tired to care.

Chris Madsen walked at his side, but it was Chris who kept on coming after Heck turned back to answer a call from one of his men.

"I guess Heck is still mad at me for shooting him up the ass, huh?" I said to Chris.

"Oh, *nein*," said that grinning, mustachioed lawman. "Ever since he got chot, hiss bowel movements haff been better than effer before and right on time. He iss so happy is der Heck, by Gott."

"How come?" I asked, interested despite the fact that the world was turning cartwheels around me.

Chris shrugged and spread his hands. "Who knows? Heck, he tink maybe der bullet clear a blockage. But der happy, happy ting is, he iss more reg'lar dan clockwork, an dat iss goot, by Gott."

"So he doesn't want to shoot me no more?"

"No more," smiled Chris. "But you must go back now and face der Judge for attempted murder off an officer." Chris shrugged again. "That iss sad."

"You bet it is," I said.

Chris glanced down at my blood-stained shirt and exclaimed: "You are vounded!"

But I merely nodded, looking over his shoulder to where Johnny Blue stood outside the wagons, a gun in his hand.

I left the protesting Chris and hobbled painfully toward Johnny Blue. When he saw me coming, he walked in my direction. "Took you long enough," he said as he stopped in front of me.

"Well," I said, "I got shot, an' a bullet has a way of slowing a man."

"That's a natural fact," Johnny Blue said. He studied me closely. "You okay?"

"I'll live," I said. "You?"

Johnny Blue nodded. "I'm just fine. Murdo was hit hard when they first opened up on us early this morning and I think he's dying. He's asking to see you. For some strange reason, he's really took to you."

I was about to tell Johnny Blue right sharply that a whole lot of people took to me, despite what he thought, but when I looked into his eyes, I saw something there that disturbed me deeply.

"Are you sure you're okay?" I asked.

"Like I said, I'm fine," he replied. "But I got something to do." He reached out his hand. "Give me your Colt."

"Johnny Blue, I don't think—" I began.

But that reckless rider cut me off. "Give me your damn Colt."

Without another word I handed the gun over.

Johnny Blue opened the loaded gate and punched out

the spent shells. Then he reloaded the Colt from the loops on his own gun belt.

"I know what you're planning," I said. "Don't do it. They'll hang you for murder for sure."

"I got the right," said Johnny Blue.

Twenty-nine

Heck and the other marshals had disarmed the outlaws when me and Johnny Blue walked toward the prisoners. The marshals' horses had been brought up from the streambed where they'd been hidden with a wagon to transport the prisoners back to Fort Smith—including me and Johnny Blue, I thought grimly.

There was no sign of Red Horse. It seemed like he'd vanished off the face of the earth.

I was so tired and weak all I wanted to do was sleep, and the pain in my side had grown worse since Buck had killed my horse and I'd been thrown to the ground with such terrible force. I felt I already had one boot in the pine box, but I had to stay on my feet, especially now when I knew what Johnny Blue was planning.

Heck saw us coming, and suddenly he was wary.

"You boys lay down your guns and step careful," he said, the barrel of his shotgun coming up to waist height, covering us both.

The other marshals, sensing Heck's unease, trained their rifles on us.

"That one," said Johnny Blue, pointing at the smirking Shade Hannah, "is mine."

"I told you to drop them Colts, boy," Heck said, his finger growing white on the trigger. "I swear I'll cut you in half with this here Greener."

"He killed my wife, shot her down on our wedding day," Johnny Blue said doggedly. "I got the right."

"What's this?" Heck asked.

"He's telling you the truth, Heck," I said. Then in as few words as possible I told him what had happened to Lo May and how we'd buried her on the trail in her wedding dress.

"He's got the right," I turned and saw Dr. Chang standing at Johnny Blue's shoulder. "She was my daughter, but she was his wife. I say he's got the right."

A murmur of agreement went up from the marshals, and I heard more than one voice say: "He's got the right."

Heck was torn; I could see it in his face. He was torn between his sworn duty as an officer and his contempt for a man who would commit the worst of all crimes in the West, the murder of a woman.

But right now he was a far way from Fort Smith and out here with a tin star on his chest he was the only law—judge, jury, and executioner.

"Heck," Johnny Blue pleaded, "give me my right."

The big lawman stood there for a few long moments, deep in thought. Then he turned to the other marshals and said: "If I do this, then it's between us. It all ends here. It ends right here and it doesn't go any further."

"It ends here, by Gott," Chris Madsen said. "Ve all agree."

Again a murmur of approval went up from the marshals, hard men well used to the Common Law of the gun in a violent, lawless land.

"Heck! Heck come here!"

For the first time, beyond the assembled lawmen, I saw Murdo lying on the ground, his head on his saddle, his pipes by his side.

Heck walked over to the dying marshal and every man present heard the Scotsman say weakly: "It's his right,

Heck. I seen it, and I would do it. I would do it for my Mary."

Heck reached his decision. "Then it's done," he said.

He went over to Shade Hannah and jerked the little gunman to his feet.

"You heard this man. He says he has the right."

Shade smirked, his mother-of-pearl eyes offering nothing. "What's in it for me?" he asked.

Heck didn't hesitate. "Shade, you lose this fight, you die. You win, and you walk. You have my word."

Even a low-down skunk like Shade Hannah accepted that. At a time in the West when a man's word was his bond, it never crossed his mind for a split second to doubt Heck's integrity. Heck Thomas had given his word that he'd walk, and it would be so.

"Then, let's get to it," Shade smiled, a gunfighter supremely confident of revolver skills that had sent a dozen named men to the grave.

Heck returned Shade's guns and that poisonous little rattlesnake stood there and practiced his draw, twirling the revolvers around his trigger fingers before letting them slam, still spinning, back into the holsters.

The outlaws were cheering their hero as I walked over to Johnny Blue and whispered: "Are you sure about this, Blue Boy? You ain't good enough. You don't even come close to being good enough."

"I'm good enough today," Johnny Blue said. "An' I'll never be this good again in my life."

I grabbed his arm. "Don't do it," I pleaded. "Let the law take care of him."

Johnny Blue looked me in the eye. "You take your hand off me now, Sam'l," he said quietly. "I got the right."

The marshals cleared a space around the two men, carefully getting out of the line of fire. By the wagons Ishmael held a pale and frightened Mrs. Flood in his arms and Dr. Chang's daughters were ushering her kids to a place of safety.

"I've given you the right, Johnny Blue Dupree," Heck said solemnly. "What happens here today, ends here, no matter the outcome. It ends, you hear me?"

Johnny Blue nodded and walked toward Shade Hannah, arms at his sides, a Colt hanging from each hand.

Shade, smirking, watched him come.

The little gunfighter quickly dropped into his practiced gunman's crouch, his hands hovering above the butts of his revolvers, his flat white eyes glittering in the fading sunlight.

Then I saw a look of sheer horror cross his face.

Shade had killed men before, but always when he looked into a man's eyes he'd seen fear, hesitation, the dawning and terrible realization that this was real, that it was happening to him and his death was very close.

But he saw no fear in Johnny Blue's eyes.

What he saw was hate, determination, and a man's willingness to take the hits and keep on shooting as long as he could stand.

"Noooo!" Shade screamed. "Heck!"

Johnny Blue's guns were coming up fast. "You cheap little tinhorn," he said, "defend yourself." Shade drew both guns with flashing speed. A blur of movement and his revolvers were up and firing.

Johnny Blue staggered a step backward under the impact of the bullets, but now he was shooting, his Colts hammering at Shade, the big .44s jerking the gunman's frail body this way and that like a rag doll.

Shade dropped to his knees, trying to bring his guns up. But they seemed suddenly too heavy for him and he couldn't level them. Screaming defiance and hatred, he staggered to his feet, and Johnny Blue's bullets found him again and again, splashing the front of the gunman's shirt red with blood.

Shade staggered a few steps back, trying to get away from Johnny Blue's terrible fire, then spun around and fell.

Boys, Johnny Blue was all shot to pieces, but he was still on his feet, driven by the demons that had haunted him since Lo May was murdered.

He walked over to Shade Hannah, hooked the toe of his boot under the gunman's body, and turned him over on his back.

Shade was still alive. His strange eyes were open wide and his mouth was pulled back in a tight grimace of pain and fear. Shade raised a trembling hand toward Johnny Blue. "Mercy," he whispered. "Mercy for Shade."

Johnny Blue stood gazing down at the craven creature for a few long moments, his smoking guns hanging by his sides.

"Finish it, damn you!" Heck roared. "I gave you the right. You have the right."

Johnny Blue shook his head and turned away. "He ain't worth it," he said. He walked a few steps toward the wagons, then fell.

I ran to Johnny Blue and kneeled by his side. "Blue Boy," I whispered. "Blue Boy, talk to me."

He was still breathing, but his breath was coming in short, tortured gasps, and his whole body was covered in blood.

"Goddamn, it has to end here!" Heck cried. "It has to end here and go no further."

He walked over to Shade and the little gunman screamed. "Mercy!"

Heck put the barrels of his Greener against Shade's forehead and pulled both triggers.

A stunned, shocked silence followed the thunderous bellow of the shotgun.

Heck, his pants legs spattered with blood and brain, turned to the marshals, who seemed to be frozen into stone and said: "It had to end here. Don't all of you see that? It had to end."

A tall marshal with sky-blue eyes and a bloody bandage around his upper arm walked over to Heck and took the shotgun from him and jerked the Colt from his belt.

"It had to end, but only he had the right, Heck," he said. "The right was his alone."

Thirty

Well, boys, I've almost reached the end of my story, but I still got to cross every t and dot every i. Johnny Blue was carried to Dr. Chang's wagon and the Chinaman told me the Angel of Death was hovering over him.

"He may live; he may die," he said. "It's now up to my skill as a doctor and the will of God."

As for me, Dr. Chang pulled a silk scarf through my wounds, in one bullet hole and out the other, and that punished me something terrible.

"It will get rid of the poisons," he said. "And help you heal."

Then he put a salve on the wounds and bound me up tight with a clean white bandage, and right about then I started to feel a whole lot better.

The Chinaman was still digging bullets out of the unconscious Johnny Blue when a marshal came to the door of the wagon and told me Murdo wanted to see me.

"The old fellow is goin' fast," the lawman said. "You don't have much time."

Death's dark shadow was already painting the hollows and planes of Murdo's face when I kneeled by his side. He had his wallet in his hand and he gave it to me.

"You have an honest face," he said. "I always thought that." He pointed to the wallet with a weak hand. "That's my siller, give it to my Mary. I ken the exact count, it's forty-seven dollars, so I know ye'll no be tempted to short her."

"I'll see she gets it, Murdo," I said. "All of it."

"I know ye will. And one thing more, tell her . . . tell her I died with her name sweet as honey on my lips."

The Scotsman looked at the sky where the first stars were being lit and whispered: "Mary . . . my own Mary . . ."

Then he was gone, just as the sun set and the long, terrible day faded into the healing night.

"I'll take that wallet."

I looked up and saw Heck standing there, his hand outstretched.

"But he said I should give it to his Mary," I protested.

"There is no Mary, boy," Heck said. "Mary McKenzie died two years ago. Murdo could never accept the fact that she's gone." He took the wallet from my hand. "I believe he has a sister in Scotland. I'll see she gets this and whatever his horse and guns will bring."

I reached down and closed Murdo's eyes.

"And what about us, Heck?" I said. "I mean, me and Johnny Blue?"

Heck sighed. "I've talked it over with the other marshals, and we all agree that you and your compadre played the man's part today. From what we hear from the doctor, you and him have such grievous wounds, suffered at the hands of Buck Starr and his men, neither of you are expected to recover.

"That," Heck said, "is what we'll tell the Judge. It ain't a lie, it just ain't the whole truth."

"And you, Heck," I said, "what about you, bein' under arrest an' your guns and star took an' all?"

"That will depend on Judge Isaac C. Parker," Heck replied. "He will weigh what happened in the balance and then make a just decision. That is his right."

Boys, we buried Murdo with his pipes by the river, the dead outlaws at his feet.

Before Heck and the other marshals left with the prisoners, he said to me: "Boy, my advice to you is to get clear out of the Indian Territory and never set foot in it again." He shook his head. "You and Johnny Blue are surely born to trouble."

As the marshals rode away, I felt strong enough to give them brave lawmen a hearty Huzzah! and Heck waved his hat and I hollered: "I sure hope the Judge goes light on you!"

But he didn't answer and pretty soon that gallant party rode around the base of the hill and were lost from sight.

Ishmael and Mrs. Flood and her brood and the poor naked lady were the next to leave. They planned on raising a following to meet Jesus on the mountaintop when the end of the world came.

"Maybe come 1900, you might care to join us," Mrs. Flood said.

"Maybe so, if'n I'm still around then," I said.

"Bring Johnny Blue with you," said Ishmael, and the poor naked lady added: "Like me, he's had his heart broken and lost a precious one. Now he needs the love that only Jesus can bring."

I took off my hat and gave them ladies a bow. "I'll sure keep that in mind, an' I know Johnny Blue will set store by such advice so kindly given."

Over the next few days Johnny Blue hovered between life and death. But in the end, Dr. Chang's doctoring pulled him through and he began to grow strong again.

Two weeks after the great battle that made me and Johnny Blue's courage a legend throughout the West, we sat together at the base of a shady cottonwood by the stream, watching Dr. Chang and his daughters make preparations to leave.

"Lookee here," said Johnny Blue, pointing with his chin at a lone rider who was walking a paint pony around the base of the hill.

"It's that crazy Injun," I said. "Checking up on my scalp."

But when Red Horse came up to us and accepted a cup of coffee from one of Dr. Chang's daughters, he squatted and said: "I just came to tell you I'm not after your scalp no more."

"Well, that's right good to hear," I said, "but how come?"

"Because," said Red Horse, sipping his coffee, "I swear you got more lives than a cat and I'm plumb wore out chasing after you."

"So what will you do now?" I asked.

Red Horse drained his coffee and shrugged. "I'm off to join Buffalo Bill again. I hear them two big Paddies of his are still looking for me."

"Well," I said, "I wish you the best of luck, and say Hi to good Queen Vic for me."

As Red Horse rode away, me and Johnny Blue both gave him a loud Huzzah! because he was a good Injun and a right nice feller when he wasn't massacreeing decent folks.

"So, what about us?" I asked Johnny Blue as we sat in the warm morning sunshine.

"What do you mean, what about us?"

"I mean, where do we go from here?"

Johnny Blue shrugged. "I dunno. Cowboyin' I guess."

"Cowboyin'! An' us first-rate lawmen? You're crazy."

Johnny Blue fished in his pocket and brought out his tally book. At first I thought he was looking for that little flower Lo May had give him, but he carefully and tenderly set it aside and found a stub of pencil.

"I know what you're doin'," I said. "You're making a list of my faults again, ain't you?"

"Lemme see," Johnny Blue said. "Ah yes, stupidity. That's a good fault. An excellent fault."

"Well, if'n I'm so stupid, how come I've got our future all planned out?" I said.

"What plan?" he asked suspiciously.

"I ain't tellin'."

Johnny Blue shrugged again. "Suit yourself."

"Well, if'n you must know, me an' you is gonna join the Texas Rangers."

"No, we ain't," Johnny Blue said. "I've had enough of badges and lawmen to last me a lifetime."

"Listen," I said, "we sign up with the Rangers then head down to the border country an' find our little sister who was took by the cruel Apaches. We can do it all while gettin' paid. In other words"—I slapped my thigh—"at the taxpayer's expense."

"Well, I don't know about that," Johnny Blue said. "Rangerin' is a dangerous line of work."

"Hell, we can handle that," I said.

"I dunno—"

"And then there's the tea and cakes," I said, throwing in the kicker.

Johnny Blue turned to me, his eyes suddenly alight with interest. "What tea and cakes?"

"See, I never told you this afore, but one time I saw this Ranger recruiting poster down in El Paso," I said. "And right there on it, in big print, was wrote, 'We stop promptly for tea and fairy cakes every afternoon at four o'clock.'"

"You're feedin' me a load of corn," Johnny Blue said.

Shocked, I replied: "Would I lie to you? What I'm telling you is a natural fact, trust me."

"Then how come them Rangers, every one of them a hardcase, took to stoppin' for tea? Answer me that."

"Because," I said, "one of the very first Rangers was a Englishman, an' he stopped for tea and them fairy cakes every day at four, even if there was a big battle with the Comanche goin' on at the time. Well, pretty soon the rest of the Rangers took a liking to their afternoon tea an' cakes, an' it's been an honorable tradition ever since."

Johnny Blue was quiet for a moment; then he said: "You're sure that's a natural fact."

"As sure as I'm sitting right here," I said.

"Well, I still dunno . . ."

Boys, it was gonna take a powerful lot of convincing to get Johnny Blue into the Rangers and down to the Texas border country.

But I'd talk him into it. .

Hell, I always do.

Historical Note

When Charles M. Russell rode north to paint the Blackfoot in 1888, he was on the eve of great fame as a painter, though fortune always eluded him. He never tried very hard to make money out of art anyhow, and when he did, he generally gave it all away. In 1898, he was plumb ashamed when his wife asked—and got—$15,000 for one of his paintings. "It's too much, too much," the embarrassed Charlie muttered as he slunk away from the bargaining table, pulling his battered old cowboy hat down low on his head.

Today we know that it wasn't too much for a work that would keep alive the memories of the Old West for our own generation and those yet to be born.

For an account of cowboys roping grizzly bears, see the excellent reference work *Montana: A History of Two Centuries* (University of Washington Press) by Michael P. Malone, Richard B. Roeder, and William L. Lang.

Isaac Charles Parker, the Hanging Judge of the United States Court for the Indian Territory, fought the desperadoes of the Southwest for twenty-one years (1875–96). In those two decades he sent nearly eighty killers to the gallows, and lost almost that many marshals bringing them to justice.

The judge, a worn-out old man at fifty-eight, was still in harness when death took him by the ear. He was buried in Fort Smith near the court he served and close to the ordinary, honest people he loved.

Heck Thomas, one of Judge Parker's finest marshals, died from natural causes in his bed in Lawton, Oklahoma, on August 15, 1912. His death came five years after the territory he helped tame became a state.

The student of Western history will no doubt realize that the vicious outlaw Buck Starr is based on the true-life exploits of Rufus Buck, a two-bit criminal who decided in 1895 to make the big time. Rufus rounded up four other scoundrels and formed the Buck gang, which soon blazed a path of terror across the Indian Territory. Buck and the others were interested in just two things: loot and women.

During a two-week killing spree they robbed, murdered, and raped before they were cornered and captured by Heck Thomas and other marshals.

Convicted on a rape charge, all five were hanged together in Fort Smith on the same gallows. All that can be said in their favor is that they died game.